THE KABOOM BOYS

ELAINE HUME PEAKE

DON KEITH

Copyright © 2025 by Elaine Hume Peake and Don Keith.

All rights reserved.

No part of this book may be reproduced in any form or by any electronic or mechanical means, including information storage and retrieval systems, without written permission from the author, except for the use of brief quotations in a book review.

Severn River Publishing
www.SevernRiverBooks.com

This is a work of fiction. Names, characters, businesses, places, events and incidents are either the products of the author's imagination or used in a fictitious manner. Any resemblance to actual persons, living or dead, or actual events is purely coincidental.

ISBN: 978-1-64875-643-6 (Paperback)

ALSO BY THE AUTHORS

A Call to War Series

The Kaboom Boys

The Blacksmith of Dachau

Also by Don Keith

The Hunter Killer Series

The Tides of War Series

To find out more about the authors and their books, visit

severnriverbooks.com

From Elaine:
To my father, Col. Edward Thomas Hume, and in memory of those Bomb Disposal men who sacrificed their lives to save others.

From Don:
In memory of my dad, Private Clyde Euel Keith, who helped win WWII by cutting hair and making soup at the US Army induction center at Ft. Polk, Louisiana, as well as all those other men and women who did their part without recognition or reward.

During World War II, the Allies and Axis powers dropped millions of tons of bombs across Europe. An estimated ten percent failed to explode.

To this day, unexploded ordnance is still often discovered and must be defuzed or safely detonated, uprooting people and disrupting transportation and commerce in the process.

Even now, anyone injured or killed by these leftover remnants of combat is counted as a casualty of World War II.

PROLOGUE

Someone once told him that the explosives inside a German Luftwaffe bomb smelled like the breath of a rattlesnake. The captain has never been intimate enough with a rattlesnake to confirm it. And now, all he can smell is his own sweat and the fog of choking smoke and dust that hangs like swamp mist in the heavily damaged cellar.

Bracing himself against the cool rock wall, he leans in closer. He needs to try to gauge how physically stable this bomb might be where it has stubbornly wedged itself into the corner, so far refusing to explode. It has crashed through all five floors of the Hôpital de Cherbourg above him. There is blood and flesh on its metal skin. It is already a killer.

"A little more light over here, if you please," he whispers, as if too loud a voice might cause the thing to shift and tumble.

The corporal, crouching nearby, obliges, redirecting his flashlight beam. "What's she look like, Captain?"

"A four-thousand-pounder. SC-2000. Half the weight is the amatol warhead. Ammonium nitrate. Everyday fertilizer."

"I know all that, sir, but what I'm wondering is if she's okay to try to move or we gonna have to blow her up right here?"

"No offense, Corporal. Just thinking out loud..."

The bomb suddenly drops a terrifying six inches, splintering more timbers, sending up additional dust. Its pug nose is now inches from the stone floor. Both men instinctively scramble backward, crawling crablike over piles of rubble. Far enough away so it won't crush them, along with the roaches and rats likewise scurrying about. But they are all still a thousand feet short of where they need to be to avoid being blown asunder if the bomb suddenly decides to do what it was created to do.

"Guess that's your answer." The captain coughs as he dusts himself off and stiffly gets back to his feet. He checks himself for scrapes, nail holes, and other contusions. "We render her safe right damn here and right damn now. And by the way..."

"Yessir?"

"Let's hope she doesn't start ticking. That'd give us probably fourteen seconds to pray for forgiveness for our many sins." The captain glares hard at the bomb, as if daring it to go ahead and do something so crass.

"I remember that much from training," the corporal offers, his voice dry and tight. "You know, sir, there is one thing I never learned at APG," the corporal says with a sideways smile.

"What's that?"

"That kick-ass staring technique you're so famous for."

"Once we get through this job, I'll happily give you a lesson in advanced command procedure," the captain responds with a mock smirk. He gingerly runs a calloused finger along the rough outer casing of the bomb, thinking how innocent it looks. Like the propane gas tank hooked up to Mom's kitchen stove back home. It was a local scandal when she got that thing. Using propane in a coal-mining town was a sacrilege. "You remember the most important thing they taught us there, don't you?"

"I remember plenty, but what do you got in mind, sir?"

"Luck is a bomb disposal man's only true friend." The captain bends at the waist, overcome by another coughing fit from the billowing soot he has inhaled. It takes him a bit to catch his breath. He spits and stands upright. "Hand me my tool bag, and then go up top and tell somebody in charge to hurry up 'n' move as many more patients as they can."

"Yessir."

"And if you don't hear some kind of godawful explosion in the meantime, come *on back and help me pull the guts out of this son of a bitch before it shifts again and mashes us to death."*

By the time the officer finishes his sentence, the corporal is gone, wriggling through the wreckage of the two-hundred-year-old building toward a convenient hole blasted through the rock wall at the far side of the cellar.

The captain is suddenly overcome not so much by the difficulty of breathing but by a powerful sense of déjà vu. Not unlike a coal mine explosion back home. Collapsed timbers, scattered fallen rocks, the air thick and choking from pulverized concrete now reduced to powder, working with a frenzy because people's lives are in jeopardy.

He shakes his head to clear his thoughts. A hundred-plus patients, nurses, and doctors up there—many of them wounded American soldiers cut down during and just after D-Day—depend on his ability to render this steel monster harmless. He knows precisely how to do it if the massive device does not rise up and strike first.

He selects a screwdriver from his bag, gives its well-worn handle a quick, sincere kiss, turns, cuddles up next to the bomb, and gets to work.

1

———————

"You mind taking two steps to your left, Mr. Eddie?"

"What?" The young man, bundled in decade-old winter clothes, looked up. "Oh, sure, Cal. Sorry."

Edward Hume's mind had been someplace else, lost in a grainy photo. The one above the fold on the front page of the newspaper on the top row of Cal Stapleton's one-rack newsstand. Edward had been so deeply immersed in somewhere else that he had not even noticed his dog, Sarge, was growing impatient, nuzzling his hand, whimpering, suggesting they should move on. Hume had also failed to notice that Cal was trying to sweep the cracked-slate sidewalk where he stood. Edward grabbed the newspaper from the rack and granted Cal and his broom some room.

"World in Misery to Serve One Man's Senseless Ambition," read the headline above a photo of Adolf Hitler, the Führer, the Chancellor of Germany. And a sub-headline declaring, "Former Brit PM's Early Assessment Proves True."

"Malignant, narcissistic son of a bitch," Edward muttered.

Sarge growled threateningly, noticing his master's tone. A primitive sound of loathing from deep inside the dog's throat matched Edward's muted tone.

"What's that, Mr. Eddie?" Cal asked.

"Aw, nothing. Just the news some days is good for nothing more'n a sour stomach." Even so, Edward folded the newspaper, tucked it under his arm, and handed Cal three pennies.

"I reckon bad news sells papers, and that there is how I pay for groceries." Cal patted his sizable belly and chuckled. "And I love me some groceries."

It was, indeed, a fine day, especially for February in northeastern Pennsylvania. Cold, maybe, for a man like Cal who grew up down south, in Alabama. The sun was so brilliant in an azure sky that its rays even found their way through the constant smoke from the coal mine towers, standing like twin sentinels down at the far end of Mahanoy City's Centre Street. A light frost had long since evaporated, and the only remaining snow was in the deep, shaded areas. Nobody in these parts would complain about this weather. "Nothing could be done about it, anyway," the locals liked to say. Just as nothing could be done about the smoke and coal dust. Or a miner's perpetual cough. Or the occasional catastrophe over there in those dark and dank shafts. Truth was, smoke and coal dust equaled jobs. And with the country coming out of a dozen years of economic depression and now plunging face foremost into war, jobs meant life and self-worth and, hopefully, swift victory in Europe and Asia.

"Sarge is with you on that, Cal." The handsome boxer cocked his head when he heard his name. "No work, no pay, no food, no nothing. Right, boy?" Edward patted Sarge. "And that's another couple reasons I better get to work so Doc won't fire me."

"Not being nosey," Cal said, head down, still vigorously sweeping, about to be nosey. "But I was just wondering something..."

"Wondering what, Cal?"

"If you gonna sign up to go fight like most of the rest of the other boys 'round here?"

"I wish I could," Edward answered, without hesitation. Not the first time he had been asked the question. Probably not the last. "I sincerely wish I could."

"I know you do, Mr. Eddie. I'd just hate to lose another good customer to this damn war, excuse my French." Cal kept sweeping. "Okay, well, go have a good'un. Give my best to Doc."

The Kaboom Boys   7

Edward nodded and smiled to let Cal know he was not offended by the question. Or the language. He had been stopping by Cal's newsstand most mornings since he started to work part-time as a clerk for Doc Fenton. That was back in high school. Edward's three cents for the *Morning Call* out of Allentown hardly kept the gentle soul in business. Sacks of tobacco and rolling papers sold to the coal miners probably did that.

As Edward turned to walk off, it occurred to him that something else prompted the prying question. Edward stopped and turned back to look Cal squarely in the eyes. Sarge even stood at attention.

"Really, Cal, why you asking?"

"Mr. Eddie, I believe my boy Victor's gonna join up before they draft him," Cal blurted out. "He turns eighteen next week, but he was already wantin' me and his momma to sign for him to enlist. She's worried sick." So, obviously, was Cal. His eyes filled with tears.

"Your boy'll do fine, sir," was all Edward could think of saying. Then, "He's smart as a whip. I know he's been reading since he was three."

"Not sure how I feel 'bout it 'cause at home, we sure are patriotic flag wavers. But he's my only son," Cal told him. "Just ain't much choice for a colored boy in the service, you know. None a'tall if you're inducted. Well, guess there's nothing I can say or do. Victor's near a man now. His poor maw, though, she cries over it every day."

Conveniently, another customer stopped by just then.

"I betcha he'll be fine, Cal," Edward told him and snapped his fingers to get Sarge's attention. "Well, we best head on."

The newcomer grabbed a newspaper from the bottom row of the rack, uncovering something else that caught Edward's eye. It was a magazine with an especially colorful cover, swimming amid all the disturbing head-lines and dull black-and-white front pages arrayed there. He grabbed it as if it were the last cream-filled doughnut at Goll's Bakery down the street, fished deep into his pocket for a nickel, and handed it over to Cal.

"Jeez, that's beautiful," Edward stated to no one in particular, smiling broadly as he studied the picture on the cover.

"What's that you lookin' at, Mr. Eddie?" The magazine had been there for most of two weeks. Nobody had touched it that Cal had noticed. He was about to send it back to the distributor for credit.

"It's a place called Mont-Saint-Michel," Edward said as he read the caption beneath the photograph. "It's an abbey on top of a huge ancient rock island in a bay on the coast of Normandy, France." Edward showed the picture to Cal. "I did a report on it for tenth-grade world history class, and I've never been able to get that place out of my head. War or no war, I'm going there someday to see it for myself. If it doesn't get bombed into oblivion first."

"If anybody can, you will, Mr. Eddie."

Hume tucked the magazine under his arm along with the newspaper, then headed up the sidewalk beside Centre Street. Sarge, happy to be moving again, followed along with a tongue-out-the-side-of-his-mouth grin, angling as always for something new and different to sniff.

Moving ahead of Edward, the boxer's cropped ears abruptly stood straight. He stopped stark still, listening to something only a dog could hear. Edward almost tripped over him.

Seconds later, the calm, sunny morning was ripped apart by a painfully piercing siren, echoing shrilly off run-down storefronts, row houses, and hillsides. Sarge raised his nose and howled in harmony. Townspeople spilled out from their homes and shops, some still holding coffee cups or brooms or the morning paper with Adolf Hitler's picture above the fold on the front page. Women, their hair in pin curls and wearing housecoats, were out on porches in near panic. Several people instinctively began running, all in the same direction, toward the twin plumes of smoke from the coal mine spires down where Centre Street dead-ended.

"Tommy," Edward whispered. It was his first thought as he stuffed the newspaper and magazine into his jacket and dashed off that way, too. Sarge was at Edward's heels, trying to catch up. It was a half mile to the gate of the Hall and Pitt Coal Company, and by the time they got there, a frantic and angry crowd had already gathered.

"Eddie! Find your brother!"

It was his mother's voice, shrill with fright, a timbre he had heard before. Then, there she was, amid the escalating chaos, running his way, still in her flannel housecoat and fuzzy slippers. The ones he and his brother, Tommy, had pitched in together to give her the previous Christmas.

"I will, Mom. I will." Someone else awkwardly ran along behind Mom. She, too, was screaming Tommy's name. It was Velma, Tommy's wife, eight months pregnant with their first child. Edward shot the distraught woman a look, yelling to her the same promise: "I'll find him, Velma!"

He meant it. He had no idea what had happened inside the coal mine or what kind of rescue effort might already be underway, but he knew he needed to try to find his kid brother and get him out safely. Despite the chilly air, he stripped off his coat and handed it, along with the newspaper and magazine, to Mom. As he made his way to the gate, he rolled up his shirtsleeves, shoving aside the gawking people who blocked his way. But he also utilized his take-charge voice, yelling for them to follow him, to help him.

There was no sign yet of any rescue effort. As he watched, the eighty-year-old mine shaft belched and groaned again, and smoke poured out the side of the mountain. There were rocks and timbers and tangled wires piled up at the mine's entrance.

The gate in front of him was locked from the inside. There was nobody in there to unhitch it. The galvanized-steel chain link fence was ten feet tall and topped with barbed wire, deterring any thieves desperate enough to swipe coal to sell on the black market.

Just then, Edward heard a hacking cough from somewhere in the thickest smoke. A miner, bleeding and covered with soot and dust, stumbled out of the fog and clutter and collapsed five feet from the locked gate. Edward grabbed the fence with both hands, rattling it as hard as he could, shouting at the man on the ground. It was Cletus Washington, the outside foreman.

"Cletus, get up! Let us in!"

Slowly, the miner got to his hands and knees, coughing and retching, and crawled over to the gate on all fours. Somehow, he managed to get it unlatched before he again fell, spent.

"Did you see Tommy, Cletus?"

"I think...I think he's in there..." Washington coughed again, exhaling puffs of dust and smoke. "But they need air."

Edward motioned for someone to help Cletus and ran toward the mine entrance.

"Methane gas, Eddie...could blow..." Washington yelled as best he could.

The crowd that had been pushing and shoving at Edward's back while the gate was locked had pulled away once it was opened. It was as if that latched gate protected them from more collapsing debris, an explosion, fire, the bad news that might await them within. This was the same deadly beast they had encountered before. An ever-present reality of coal mining.

Edward waved for them—any one of them—to follow him, to come help. If Cletus Washington had made it out, they might save more miners.

No one joined him. Nobody but Sarge.

With the dog at his side, Edward raced ahead to the entrance and went to work, grunting as he frantically pushed, heaved, and dragged aside debris, wire, rocks, and slick, mossy timbers.

After several minutes, with Edward the only one attacking the jumble, three teenage boys ran in to assist him. Shoving aside one big boulder, they moved deeper into the shaft entrance—a place Edward had sworn he would never enter, at least as an employee of Hall and Pitt Coal—hoping to clear a way for clean air to rush in. The four of them could now hear mournful cries, gasping, and coughing coming from back down the main shaft.

The pleas for help blended eerily with the siren of an approaching fire truck. Moments later, an ambulance entered the gateway, joining the cacophony.

The next vehicle to show up was much quieter and in not nearly such a hurry. The crowd solemnly watched and then stood aside as the hearse from Fulghrum's Mortuary pulled to one side, out of the way, and parked there to patiently wait.

Edward worked on, calling his brother's name, as the firemen joined him and the boys. Sarge barked constantly, as if the dog, too, were pleading for Tommy to come out of that hellhole. Edward's fingers were bleeding, cold, and mangled, but he worked on. Finally, some of the other towns-people showed up to help, mostly off-duty miners. Bleary-eyed, graveyard-shift miners.

At long last, the soot-streaked, bloodied faces of more miners appeared, crawling through the rubble, hands ripped up from desperately scratching

The Kaboom Boys

and digging their way out. As Edward helped them climb to cleaner air, he asked each about Tommy. All they could tell him was that he was farther down the shaft when the walls and ceiling suddenly growled and collapsed.

Edward recognized one of the haggard survivors, a young miner, one of Tommy's friends from high school. The man waved, pulled Edward closer, and whispered, "I'm pretty sure he's right behind us, Eddie."

Another one of the miners emerged, hunched over, covered in grime. "Tommy went back deep to check on Fritz Schneider and Mullaney Murray. Air's mighty rank back there," he reported, mournfully shaking his head.

It was as if someone had punched Edward in the gut. Of course his younger brother would have gone back to try to save the others—men who were in worse shape or more danger than he was. And especially since they were two of his big brother's best friends. Buddies since before elementary school.

Edward closed his eyes, said a prayer, and went back to digging for all he was worth.

2

It was an answered prayer was what it was.

Edward spotted his kid brother coming his way through the blinding dust. Bloodied and bruised but with the familiar broad grin. His teeth were the only white visible on his face. It was Tommy-boy, spitting, hacking, but still offering Edward his hand. He pulled his younger brother to safety and breathable air, out of the maw of the piled-up debris, smothering coal dust, and volatile methane gas.

"I thought I was dead this time, brother," Tommy told him, his voice sandpaper raspy as he collapsed into Edward's arms. Sarge licked Tommy's face. "At least old Sarge is glad to see I ain't gone on."

"Don't say that, Tommy-boy," Edward admonished him as he eased him down to the ground. "Lookit, Velma and Mom and Pops are worried half-crazy about you. That's the thing. You're alive. We're gonna keep it that way. How many more coming out behind youse?"

"None." A mournful look passed over Tommy's face. "I tried to get 'em, Eddie. Just two more back there. They're gone. Mullaney." Tommy convulsed into a cough before he could share the rest of the bad news. "And sorry, Eddie, but Fritz, he's gone, too."

"Fritz?"

"They were helping some of the older guys get out. Gas must've got

The Kaboom Boys

'em." Tommy tried to stand. "Help me up, Eddie. I want the bosses to see me walk out of this godforsaken place."

Edward was numb as he helped his brother stand and walk, the joy over Tommy's rescue now eclipsed by the loss of a couple of his own best friends.

"Fritz is gone," he whispered. Edward's first true buddy. It felt as if he had lost a limb, a part of himself. Fritz Schneider had been a second brother since before first grade. "And Mully, too."

They had grown up together. Birthdays, weddings, baptisms, funerals. Football, soccer, wrestling, baseball, fistfights, and girlfriends. Bike races, playing war, and swimming at Bore Hole Quarry.

Fritz's story had been a compelling one. His family escaped Germany after the Great War. Only a week before this suddenly dark day, relaxing at Pops's Bar, Fritz had told Edward that he considered coal mining the same as being in the military.

"You work hard as a team, in tight quarters, and you could die together," Fritz explained, his words still carrying a trace of a German accent. He had decided to remain an "essential worker," a coal miner. He would not be drafted. Some had jokingly claimed he just didn't want to go shoot at his Kraut cousins. But Fritz was as American as any. "We need coal if we're going to beat the Japs and the Nazis. Lots of warships run on coal. I'll help whip their asses down there in the guts of that mountain."

Edward pulled himself together as Mom and Velma rushed over. His dad hovered behind Mom, worried how she would react to the sight of her youngest son lying there straining to breathe.

"He's okay," Pops kept telling her.

The moment he heard the mine siren, Pops had shut down the bar. Graveyard-shift miners often stopped by for a beer before going home.

Edward's boss—the town doctor and congressman from the district—Ivor "Doc" Fenton, was now on the scene. He had caught a ride with the ambulance. He convinced Tommy to lie down on a stretcher in the shade of a nearby hundred-year-old oak.

"Aw, I'm okay, Doc. Some of the older guys are worse off."

Fenton told him to cough as he probed Tommy's ribs. "I need to listen to those lungs." But once he started hacking, the young miner could not stop. Velma burst into tears.

"He's got to be okay, Doc," she wailed. "He's about to be a daddy."

"He'll miss a few days of work, dear, but I suspect he'll be around to chop down your next Christmas tree, all right?" Doc took the stethoscope from his ears and looked up at Edward. "Hey, Eddie, they tell me you did some special things here today. I'm proud of you."

"I couldn't help Fritz or Mully," Edward responded sadly.

"You can only do what you can do," the doctor reminded his young clerk. "And you did plenty, from what I'm hearing." Near exhaustion, Edward eased down on a boulder and silently watched Doc bandage a nasty cut on his brother's arm. "You got them enough good air to save most of them, and then you took charge and led the others out," Fenton was saying. "We'd have a dozen or more men asphyxiated had you not cleared that airway."

"I just wanted to help." Edward was suddenly very, very tired. "Nobody else was."

"Not everybody has your guts, Eddie," Doc said. "Not many would do what you did today."

Tommy grunted and squirmed as Doc poked at an ugly bruise on his thigh. He motioned for Eddie to come closer.

"Doc's right. You're a hero. It's like I've been telling you." Tommy tried to sit up but had to sink back down to find the breath to say what was on his mind. "You know this damn mine's the only way for some of us to make a living around here." He grimaced as he took a deep draw of air.

"Calm down, baby brother. We can talk about this later."

Tommy grabbed Edward's arm. "Look, there's only fifty or sixty of us full-time here now, and they're about to lay off a bunch of the third shift. They used to run three full shifts a day, close to seven hundred men out here," Tommy said. His dry throat made it hard to say what he wanted to. "We're only still here 'cause they need the coal for this damn war."

"I know. I know. Calm down..."

The Kaboom Boys 15

"The way the company's pushing us, cuttin' corners, it's gonna end up gettin' all of us killed down there. It was Fritz and Mully today. Who knows who next time?"

"Shuuush!" Mom ordered, now hovering over her boys. "Stop that kind of talk and breathe some of this sweet air. What if one of the bosses hears you?"

Edward closed his eyes, maybe listening to Tommy, maybe not.

"We couldn't have saved Fritz or Mully. Nobody could. They were in too deep," Tommy continued as two men lifted his stretcher and headed for the ambulance.

"Too deep, literally and figuratively," Edward muttered.

Tommy motioned for the men to wait a moment. He was not finished.

"It's like I been telling you and you ain't listening. They...and me...we made our choices. Knew the risks. It's time youse made your own, Eddie. Leave Mahanoy and don't look back. Youse got the smarts to make something of yourself." Tommy looked to Mom and Pops, clutching his ribs in pain. But he had one more thing to tell his older brother. "Book smart and street smart. Something most of us don't got, and that's why we work in the mines and you don't. You got a 4-F, too. So, get the hell out of here while you're still young and go do somethin' special!"

Doc patted Tommy's shoulder. "Settle down, son, and don't make those busted ribs even angrier than they already are." He motioned the men on to the ambulance.

Edward followed Doc over to help him examine another injured miner. As he wrapped the man's gruesomely broken arm, Doc spoke to Hume. "I hate to agree with that rascal, but he's right, you know. You got a lot more to offer. You're made for something special, Eddie. I think your only real fear is the fear of just being average." He turned to look Edward in the eye. "That paperwork of yours, it's still right there in my desk. I need to go ahead and sign it. A fellow like you should be—"

But before Doc could speak more to Edward's future, someone else did it for him.

"You two hush!" A woman's voice, strident, shrill, desperate. She stood next to Mom and Velma but was mostly blanked out by the powerful glare of the late-morning sun. Someone who had been eavesdropping on Tommy's rant and Doc's sober words.

It was Rachel Levine. Edward's girlfriend, kind of. Over the past couple of months, Edward had been having serious doubts about whether Rachel was "the one" and if Mahanoy City was "the one place" to live out his life. It had been Fritz Schneider who slyly set him up with Rachel shortly after luring Edward into a part-time job at her father's shirt factory just after their high school graduation. Then, after a rigged double-date, it was assumed to be a done deal, their future a foregone conclusion, a *fait accompli*, as Edward learned in the high school French class he shared with Rachel.

"Eddie and I have plans, Doc, so you and Tommy just keep your opinions to yourselves," Rachel commanded.

"Rachel, this is not the place or the time..." Edward told her. Kneeling, he whispered to Doc. "Sir, I wasn't going to say anything considering what just happened here, but maybe I should. If you could please reconsider your 4-F classification for me. You're the only one who can fix it."

"Days like this make people think about things in a different way," Doc responded. "But you better consider the ramifications. I'll look into it."

"I'd appreciate it."

With all the commotion around them, Rachel could not quite hear what they were saying. She heard the last part perfectly. She groaned and rolled her lovely, dark eyes. Edward stood, turned to her, and reached out for her hand.

"Fritz and Mully are both dead."

"I know. It's a shame. It really is," Rachel responded, almost coldly. But she did not take his hand. She was often jealous of his friends. His family, too. "It's a shame, Eddie, but we knew this could happen. But you'll never have to work in a mine because you'll work for my father."

He closed his eyes. "I don't know, Rachel."

She burst into tears, turned away, and ran, pushing through the thick crowd of townspeople. Edward watched, knowing he should probably chase after her, just as he had so many times before.

He turned back to Fenton. "Can I help you with anything else, Doc?"

"Nope. Looks like you got something of your own needs fixing. Go. We'll talk later. At the office."

"Yessir!"

He was slowed by all those wanting to pat him on the back and tell him what a hero he was. Even the fire chief, who told him if he ever wanted to be a fireman, he had a place for him on his squad.

Recruiting at a mine disaster, Edward thought as he hurried on.

He finally caught Rachel at the sharp turn-off from Centre Street that led straight up to Overlook Hill. It was only a mile from there to the spot where her father had built for his wife a grand Victorian-style house on the mountain. But she had died, claimed by the Spanish flu pandemic in 1920. They had intended to fill it with many happy children. But Rachel was the only child before her mother passed away.

Edward knew where Rachel was headed. A couple of hundred yards before the house was the young couple's favorite spot. An overlook, a place where they could park and make out after a movie date right up to her father's strict curfew. A place where her father could not see them. Where they could watch the sunset and see stars pop up one by one above their little town, offering the smallest of blessings. Where they would watch the moon cross the blue-black sky from mountaintop to mountaintop. Here was where they made plans. But it had always been Rachel who laid it out while Edward aimed for one more kiss, another intimate caress.

Now, when he caught up to her, he grabbed her arm, spun her around, and looked into her face. Even angry, agitated, and obstinate, Rachel Levine was beautiful. Beautiful enough to give him pause.

"Rachel, it's all just talk. We can figure out everything later. This is a bad day. I just need to consider, you know, all my options."

"Options? Is that what I am? An option." Big tears streaked her cheeks. "Look, I'm sorry about your friends. I truly am. But why doesn't Doc Fenton keep his nose out of our business? Just because you work for him doesn't mean he runs your life. And especially mine. 'My life is your life.' Remember when you told me that? In the back seat of my car right over there at the bluff, under a full moon."

"Doc's more than a boss to me, honey. You know that. He's important.

Here and all the way to Washington, DC. I need to take what he says seriously."

"We're not going to DC. We're not leaving Daddy. He'd be all alone."

"Doc could make things happen for me. For us," Edward pleaded. "We could see so much of the world and…"

Rachel jerked away from his grasp and angrily kicked a dirt clod, sending it skittering off the bluff. "And your brother, always spouting off about how you're too smart to stay here. If he loves you as much as I do—"

"Hey, Tommy loves me, all right. Leave him out of this. And about that 4-F thing. That's gonna be hard to undo, Rachel. Even if Doc tries." He was quickly running out of steam. And the right words to say. "Besides, even if I can enlist someday, I'll be back as soon as the war's over, and we'll get married. I can run the place like your dad wants me to. You've heard the talk. We'll have the Nazis and the Japs whipped in just a few more months and…"

She stomped away up the hill. Their hill. Then, with another thought, she stopped, spun around, and glared at him. Lord, she was beautiful! How could he even think about leaving her?

"As much as you talk about going places and seeing things, you know full well you won't ever come back to me once you go."

She put her hand to her mouth in frustration. Rachel was reading his mind.

"Rachel, I don't even know for certain what—"

"Look here, Mr. Edward Thomas Hume. Why don't you just go on back down there to that mine so everybody can pat you on the back and tell you what a hero you are. That's what you want. But heroes usually die. Go on and enlist in the Army or the Navy and go see that big world of yours you're always telling me about." She glared at him. "You go on over there and win the war all by yourself, Eddie!"

"That's not what I'm talking about at—"

"But you at least have a choice, Edward. You have a 4-F. But if you do go, and if you make it back home alive with a bunch of ribbons on your chest —and with both arms and both legs—I may be waiting for you. I may not. Daddy may still want you to come to work for us. Or he may not. Not after that fit you pitched when he mentioned you converting to Judaism. Think about what you're throwing away, Eddie!"

"Listen to me, Rachel. You know I don't want to be just ordinary. I want more for my life. For our life. I want to make a difference somehow."

Eyes wide with anger, she stomped her foot again for finality, turned, and double-timed on up the hill toward home, away from him. Edward took a step to go after her, then stopped.

"Rachel!" he called, but she was gone.

Rachel Levine wanted one thing. Edward another.

The town ambulance, red lights flashing, whizzed past below where he stood, on the way to the hospital in Pottsville. Doc Fenton waved to him from the passenger-side window, pointed back to where Tommy rode, and gave him a thumbs-up.

As Edward turned and started walking back down to the mine, another vehicle eased up the road toward him. It was going much slower, headlights on, even in the brilliant sunshine. The Fulghrum's Mortuary hearse. Carrying three bodies. Bodies of men who had long since made the decision to live out their lives right there in Mahanoy City, with no aspirations beyond these anthracite-veined mountains.

The hearse's driver did not bother to look Edward's way. He simply drove on with his sad cargo.

3

——————

"Next!"

The heavyset US Army master sergeant behind the desk looked over the top of his half-glasses at Edward Hume. As Edward hurried over and sat down, the recruiter continued to study paperwork in his hand, a puzzled frown on his ruddy face.

"Damn! New one on me," he finally said, shaking his head. "Hume, this is the third time you've tried to enlist. First in the infantry. Next in the Air Forces. Now in Artillery. And it says here you have a full deferment. You're flat-footed, you got a bad back, you're allergic to penicillin, you got some kind of hip problem, you can't swim...and hell, by the looks of you and what it says here, you're even too old."

"Sir, I'm only twenty-three."

"I'm not a 'sir,' Hume. I'm a sergeant." He looked for a particular spot on the form and stabbed it with his index finger. "Says here you'll be twenty-four next month. By God, son, it also says that you're sterile!" The last word was loud enough to be heard by every other potential enlistee in the room.

Edward blushed. He hoped nobody heard any of this. Some had. Several snickered. Most stared at him.

"Look, about not being able to swim," Edward responded, raising his left hand as if it would help in pleading his case. "I'm joining the Army, not

The Kaboom Boys   21

the Navy, so why would I need to swim?" Edward, collected and calm in most situations, knew he was likely blowing the interview. "I'm not sure about any of that. Especially that last one. I asked Doc Fenton not to—"

"Well, son, it's all right here," the sergeant interrupted. "Says you ain't physically fit to serve in the US Army, no matter how bad we may need your ass. Let's see. Fenton? That your doctor's name?"

"Dr. Ivor Fenton."

"That's it. Never could read a doctor's signature for the life of me. Also says here he's a congressman, too. From the great state of Pennsylvania. Important man." The sergeant peered hard at another bit of information on the paper. "And you work for him over there in..."

"Mahanoy City. I work in his medical office, but it's also his congressional office," Edward clarified. "I'm his legislative aide and medical assistant even though I have no formal medical training. I mostly answer letters, take complaints, clip newspaper articles, do research, write reports, deal with other politicians—"

The recruiting sergeant cut him off with a wave of his hand. "Yeah, yeah, yeah, I get it now. So, he's a medical doctor, a US congressman, and your boss, and you're telling me he's lying to the Selective Service and the United States of America about your physical state and fitness to serve, Hume?"

"Well, I didn't mean to insinuate..." He shifted uncomfortably in his chair. Edward did not want to get Doc in trouble. He knew the other men in the room wondered what kind of fool would throw away a free 4-F to try to enlist in the Army. "I think Doc was just trying to keep me alive, sir... Sergeant. I've bugged him for six months, but he felt like he needed me."

"You must've wore him down, Hume. I got the paperwork right here. He's now saying you're fit as a fiddle. I got to trust the judgment of such an important man." The sergeant appeared to have a sudden thought. "So, here's your chance to get in. You're unattached, no obligations? No kids? Since you apparently claim you're not sterile no more."

"Not married. No kids."

The sergeant studied Hume for a long moment. Then he pointed to a big photo on the wall behind him. An Army officer stood in a field with what appeared to be an enormous bomb—the weapon a good three feet taller than the man—propped up on its end next to him. The officer sported a wide, bright smile. Whatever kind of work the guy did or his relationship with the bomb, he was happy about it.

"I think I may have something that'll interest you, Hume. That there is Colonel Thomas Kane. He's been working on something new with the RAF in England. Specialized BD training. Trying to overcome a ten-week life expectancy for British BD guys working on UXBs. It'll be the first American unit. And that thing next to him, that's a German SC-1000 bomb. Weighs more'n a ton, filled with TNT and amatol. The Jerries got some bombs bigger than that one, too."

Confused about the acronyms and numbers the sergeant was citing, Edward had forgotten the others in the room. There was a quizzical look on his face. "You lost me. UXBs. BDs. Amatol?"

Edward sensed this might be one of those watershed moments, one that could define the rest of his life. He only needed the guy across the desk to guide him.

"Unexploded bombs. Bomb disposal squads. Amatol is basically fertilizer, like what farmers use, but this stuff blows up and breaks shit and kills people really, really good. Or bad, depending on whether you're above it or below it when it comes out the bomb bay. Just ask the Brits. And you'll get the opportunity to do just that if you play your cards right. Those sons of guns have been getting hit every which way by Hitler's boys for more than a year now." The sergeant examined Edward's face, expecting him to flinch. Most did by this point in the sales pitch. Edward had not. He only seemed more excitedly curious. "By the way, how'd you do in math and science, son?"

"All As." Edward leaned in closer.

"How about foreign languages? 'Youse' speak anything else besides East Pennsylvania English?"

"I took some French. And I learned quite a bit of German from a friend who..." Edward's voice trailed off. Fritz Schneider was now six feet under after the mine collapse. "Maybe enough to get by. A little bit. As Doc's aide, I used to help with the little old ladies who only spoke German. I'm not fluent, though, if that's what you mean."

"Good enough."

The Kaboom Boys   23

"But this BD. What's the deal?"

The recruiter tapped the desk with his pencil, as if keeping cadence for a marching platoon.

"Let me be clear, Hume. This is going to be big if Colonel Kane has anything to do with it. It puts you on a fast track to being an officer so long as you prove yourself. And a great way to serve the war effort and whip some Nazi asses." The recruiter continued trying to gauge Edward's attitude, a doctor taking a pulse. As far as he could tell, this Hume kid was as cool as they came. "Fact is, Colonel Kane is over there in England now, learning everything he can so he can teach it to his first BD squads."

"How about the pay?"

"Yup. Hazardous duty. That is, if you meet all the requirements and make it through the training, neither of which is a given. It's gonna be a tough haul." The sergeant chuckled. "But, if you make it through without your head in your hands, you'll come out a second lieutenant with a set of shiny silver bars, a 'shave-tail,' but an officer, and you'll go off and command your own BD unit. And you get combat pay even if you aren't in actual combat, because what you're doing is dangerous as hell. They figure by recruiting smart people who get the right training and who can send us firsthand reports of the different weapons they're seeing out there, maybe they'll increase that ten-week survival rate. Maybe to three or four months. And you can make a difference, save lives, and help win the war."

As the sergeant spoke, a grin appeared on Edward Hume's face, then grew bigger and bigger. Make a difference. Save lives. Win the war.

"I'll probably go to Europe? Maybe France?"

"Most likely. First squads will go where the UXBs are, and that's Europe."

"And I'd be saving lives, not killing people," Edward said, under his breath.

"What's that?"

"I'm in. When do I start?" Hume asked.

"You did hear that last part there? About the ten-week survival rate?"

"But you said it'll get better. With smart people and the proper training, it would help shorten the war. And save lives. I betcha I can beat those odds."

The recruiter looked at him hard. Then he abruptly stood up and shook Hume's hand.

"Sign here, here, and here. And I'll swear you in right now. Got that?"

"Got it."

After the new volunteer had fully committed, the recruiter explained that his basic training would take place two buildings over, right there at Fort Indiantown Gap, Pennsylvania. Then he would go to Officer Candidate School at Aberdeen Proving Ground in Maryland, with training overseen by the man in the photo on the wall, Colonel Kane himself. He would also get the beginnings of BD training there before moving on to get the full-blown course—on-the-job training—with the world's current experts on bomb demolition, the Royal Air Force in England. With the Luftwaffe bombing having gone on for more than a year already, the RAF had necessarily developed advanced bomb disposal methods and training. German scientists had now begun to create new bombs and detonation devices specifically designed to kill BD men. So far, there were no books, no manuals, nothing officially written down. This first group of American BD men would necessarily write the textbooks for those who would follow. From there, Edward would be assigned to command one of the first official US Army BD units.

Edward left the recruiting office fired up, ready to start boot camp. This was precisely what he had long been craving, what he had told his family, his friends, Doc, and Rachel about. He would get to see the world on someone else's dime. The American taxpayers' dime, to be exact. And yet be doing something good, valuable, even lifesaving. At the same time, he might even find a career in this mess of a war, something for the future. College had been out of the question because of the Great Depression.

One thing. If he washed out at any point in the training, he would be kicked out of the BD program and hustled off to the regular US Army. As a private. That likely meant toting a rifle in the infantry. No hiding behind a 4-F either. It would no longer exist in Edward's personnel records.

By the time the sergeant finished his pitch, Edward Hume would have immediately climbed aboard a bus to Maryland. But first, there was something far bigger for him to conquer. And he was far more worried about that chore than he was about learning how to neuter a two-thousand-pound Luftwaffe bomb.

He would have to say goodbye to his family—people he loved and had been with practically every day of his life—and somehow explain to Rachel Levine his decision to leave her behind for now. For the moment, that seemed much more challenging than defuzing ticking bombs.

♠

The morning after Edward Hume's twenty-fourth birthday, a cluster of folks—four of them—stood close to each other, shivering in the predawn mist in front of the Rexall on Centre Street. Pops had already emptied all the coffee from his big, black Thermos into their cups. It was the same container he took to work at the mines for twenty years before he had been hurt in an accident there. That was when he left that job and opened the bar. Many mornings as a kid, Edward had walked alongside his dad, carrying that Thermos for him all the way to the gate at the mine, just so he could listen to his father's tall tales. The boy had heard all his life how dangerous his dad's job was. Even as a kid, he was aware miners did not always come home from their shifts.

Now, standing there in the dampness of a chilly morning, neither man seemed to have any idea of what to say to the other.

For her part, Mom kept grabbing Edward and giving him painfully tight hugs.

"Mom, don't worry about me," he told her, over and over. "I'll be okay. This thing'll be over within a few months."

"You can't promise me that. It's a big war over there, and you say you'll be working on bombs and booby traps. I don't like none of that. I just want youse back home and safe," she told him and wiped her eyes with her hanky. He tried to ignore the clouds of guilt that were casting shadows on his excitement.

"You know me, Mom. I know how to take care of myself. Besides, you got a wee one coming soon, 'Grandma.' You'll be busy with that one."

"I'll still send you Epsom salts, Eddie. For your headaches. And to keep you regular," she promised.

"Aw, Mom." But he pulled her closer and whispered into her ear, "I'll be sure to send you that check every month."

She closed her eyes. "Oh, Eddie. You know we appreciate it. But we hate for you to do such a thing..."

"No, no! I don't mind. It'll ease my mind knowing you and Pops are doing okay." That guilt thing again. Edward knew the family needed any financial help he could offer, whether it came from working for Doc, moonlighting at the shirt factory, or from being a soldier in some far-flung corner of the world. "You've taught me and Tommy all the right things. You'll do the same for your grandchild. I love you, and I will come back."

They hugged and she kissed her boy gently on the cheek, just the way she had done so many times before.

In the still of the morning, they could hear the bus for Allentown wheezing up the hill from the west, grinding gears and huffing their way.

Tommy reached to shake his brother's hand but then grabbed him and pulled him into a full bear hug.

"You better be careful, or I'll whip your ass," Tommy told him with a brotherly chuckle. "And don't blame me if you get yourself shot or captured, okay?"

"All your fault, brother!" Edward told him, but with a laugh. "I do appreciate all the nudging that you did to get me away from here. Not that I needed it."

"Just get me the Führer's mustache for a souvenir, all right?" Tommy put a finger beneath his nose and opened his eyes wide in his best imitation of a rabid Fascist.

"You got it."

Pops was trying to do the manly thing, holding it together. But he suddenly grabbed his son, pulled him close, and hugged him tightly, something neither could remember ever happening before.

"I just want you to know I love you, Eddie." Edward hugged his dad even harder. Though he had never doubted his father's love for him, such a vocal admission of it had never happened before, either. "Here, son. I want you to have this."

Pops reached into his jacket pocket and pulled out his Swiss Army knife.

The Kaboom Boys 27

"Pops, no!" Edward responded. "You've had that since you were in the Great War. And I see you use it every day at the bar. They'll probably issue me one anyhow."

"Look, Eddie, I want you to have it," Pops said. "Then you'll think of me every time you open a bottle of beer. Sorta like a curse."

They embraced again. Said they loved each other again. It was the first time either had really considered it might be a while before they saw each other. This parting was for real.

The bus pulled to a squeaking stop and thoroughly fogged them with diesel smoke.

"Youse always know the right thing to do, Eddie," Pops told him, looking into his son's face. There were tears on the older man's cheeks. "Won't always be the easiest thing to do. But do the right thing and youse will always be okay."

"I will, Pops. I will."

Edward picked up his bag as the bus door accordioned open, then he tossed the last bite of his fried egg sandwich to Sarge, who gulped it down. The pup seemed happily unaware his master was leaving. Edward was just getting up onto the first step of the bus when he heard someone calling his name.

It was Rachel.

"Can you give me a second, boss?" Edward asked the driver.

"Make it snappy." The man pointedly took a big watch from his vest pocket and squinted at it.

Edward dropped his suitcase as she ran up to him. He grabbed Rachel up in a strong embrace. They kissed while his parents and brother pretended not to see.

"I was hoping you would come," he told her. "I didn't want to leave without us talking about—"

"Please come back to me," she said, interrupting him. "To all that big, bright future we planned for ourselves."

"I will, honey. I will." He wondered ever so briefly if she believed him. Or if he even meant what he was telling her.

"Let's go, pal!" the driver said impatiently, again checking his watch. "Or bring her with you. Ticket's a buck."

Rachel handed Edward a paper bag. He took a quick peek inside. It contained a box of stationery, a bundle of pencils, and stamps. He could see she had written in huge letters on the first page, *WRITE ME!* He caught a strong whiff of her favorite perfume from the bag.

"I will. I promise I will," he told her.

They kissed again. Then she looked up at him with a mock pout, turned, and went to stand with his family. With hands to mouth and eyes almost closed, she watched him pick up his suitcase and start to board the bus.

"Wait! Eddie, wait!" It was Mom. She had another small paper sack for him. The bus driver rolled his eyes. "I almost forgot. For the road."

"Jeez, you gals are loadin' me down!" He knew what was inside. He could smell it, a different fragrance than Rachel's bag. Ever since he was a kid, trudging off to school, she had made his favorite lunch, a sandwich with soft, buttered bread, ham, and sliced gherkin pickles made from cucumbers he had helped Mom grow in her little garden.

"Now you tell that driver to watch for deer!" he heard Mom say. It was his mother's favorite admonition whenever he or Tommy drove off in the family car. Deer in the area were plentiful and did pose a hazard to motorists. Even buses.

Edward looked back, nodded, threw them one more wave, and hustled up the steps.

Without even giving him time to find a seat, the driver shifted gears and pulled away, briskly heading off into the rising sun of a new and very different day.

4

Edward Hume was dizzyingly distracted by all the activity swirling around him. Soldiers marching or running. Long formations of other men doing calisthenics on large, grassy parade grounds. Still more troops scurrying about, mostly in uniform, headed somewhere in one big hurry. Then there were bunches of soldiers, training on mock bombs in deep trenches that trailed off in multiple directions like elongated graves. And as he passed a large house—very similar in size and style to Doc Fenton's fine double-sized row house back in Mahanoy City—the free-standing structure suddenly erupted with red lights flashing all around and a deafening buzzer sounding a pulsing, angry raspberry. Edward had picked up enough already to know that some BD trainees had just messed up a booby-trap drill and would most likely be sent packing.

Just be thankful that wasn't you that messed up, Eddie thought as he hurried on past all the raucous commotion.

In truth, though, he had left "Eddie" behind back in Mahanoy City when he stepped onto that bus for Fort Indiantown Gap. "Red Racer," too. That had been his nickname growing up. But both names had suffered the same fate as his civilian clothes, now stowed under his bunk in the barracks, and his longish, chestnut-colored hair littering the floor of the induction center, replaced with a boot camp buzz cut. The changes in his life had been just as startling as the drill house suddenly bursting forth with alarms and flashing lights. That suited Corporal Edward Hume just fine. He was confident and ready, still mightily craving new challenges and a worthy purpose.

All the bustle here at Aberdeen Proving Ground reminded him of the couple of times he, Tommy, and Pops had driven down to Philadelphia to watch the Phillies lose another one in the old Baker Bowl stadium. Even with the team's dismal record, the streets had been jammed with half-lit patrons before and after the games. There were more people milling about amid the traffic and streetcars than young Eddie and Tommy had ever seen before in one place. Until now. He would be sure to make the comparison in his next letters to his brother and Pops.

Then, as he hustled along toward the building where he was to attend his first class at the US Army's Aberdeen Proving Ground, he saw something he had certainly never observed in Philly. A silvery, four-engine B-17 bomber roared in low from out over the bay, angling in above distant dunes and hillocks, and released a fine necklace of test bombs. The ground beneath his feet reverberated as each blew up and the resulting blasts echoed off row after row of barracks and classroom buildings. None of the others around him seemed to take notice. Edward decided he would follow suit, be like the locals, and appear to be unfazed by those close-by detonations.

"Don't let 'em see youse staring at 'em," Pops had told his boys back at the Baker Bowl. "They'll peg ya for rubes."

The sheer number of people at APG had almost overwhelmed him. What was remarkable to Edward was that at any given time, about 25,000 soldiers were assigned to the base now that the US had entered the war. The conflict was chewing up and spitting out men. There were almost as many soldiers in his own barracks as people who lived in Mahanoy City. This was nothing like Fort Indiantown Gap, where there were far fewer trainees. That was where Edward had spent the previous month in boot camp, learning to march, dress, and when to salute. The physical training had been good for him. He dropped ten pounds and could run ten miles.

The Kaboom Boys 31

Edward assumed he and other trainees would mostly be in classrooms at APG, learning how to dispose of bombs. But they still spent lots of time on the parade grounds, marching and doing PT—physical training. There was much more going on outside the base, along the riverbanks where the Susquehanna opened up and emptied into the northern waters of Chesapeake Bay at Aberdeen, Maryland. A place where ducks flew in perfect, V-shaped formations, blue crabs seemed to willingly climb into nets, and large-mouth bass appeared to jump almost all the way up to the bellies of the B-17 bombers as if they were reachable dragonfly snacks. It was new territory. Edward Hume thirstily drank it all in.

I could live here, Edward thought. But he was aware this was only a stop on the way, an early milepost on an epic crusade to experience more of the world.

Watching the blooming dust clouds from the bombs blow away in the breeze, he realized that he had walked right past the building where his first bomb disposal class would be. He backtracked, stepped inside to a long hallway, then took a deep breath and opened the door labeled "BD-1 Classroom."

Almost every desk was taken, twenty-five or thirty officer candidates nervously waiting. The only open desk was in the front row, smack in the middle. Not his preferred spot. He would rather be farther back so he could get a feel for the room and those in it. Edward blinked, tried to ignore the stares of everyone else in the room, and hurried toward the seat, wedging himself in before anyone pointed out that he was two minutes late on his very first day. He assumed such lack of punctuality would not be tolerated.

"Hume, since you're coming into my class tardy, I got one for you."

Edward jumped, startled, then stood, snapping to attention. In his haste to become invisible, he had not noticed the man with the brush haircut and barrel chest standing behind a lectern at the front of the classroom. When he did, he recognized the officer immediately. It was the man in the big picture on the wall back at the recruiting office. The imposing man standing nonchalantly next to the German bomb. It was Colonel Thomas J. Kane. And somehow, Kane knew exactly who Edward Hume was.

"Colonel Kane, sir!" Hume responded, saluting. He was certain he was about to catch hell in front of the whole class. He figured he could withstand the inferno better if he remained on his feet and at attention.

"You heard the one about Hitler standing on top of the Brandenburg Gate in Berlin?"

"No, sir, I don't believe so, sir." Was the "American father of unexploded ordnance demolition" about to tell him a Hitler joke? The room was remarkably quiet. He could hear the boom of artillery on a distant test range. Or was it only his gut churning?

"Hitler turned to Hermann Göring and asked him, 'What can I do to cheer up the German people?' Göring told him, 'Mein Führer, you should jump!'"

Colonel Kane roared, as if it were the funniest joke ever shared. The other officer candidates dutifully laughed. So did Edward. Then the colonel stepped over and shook Edward's hand.

"At ease, Hume. Next time, be on time so you don't get singled out."

Edward nodded and shouted, "Yessir!"

"Have a seat. And welcome to BD. Now, we got lots to do..."

Kane headed back to the lectern, and Edward sat down while trying to tug his notebook from his leather bag, fumbling it in the process. The notebook landed on the floor, at the feet of a fellow corporal seated next to him. Edward would soon learn his name was Hedley Bennett.

Bennett leaned over, picked up the notebook, and handed it to Edward, flashing a broad smile.

"You may want to sit down, pardner," Bennett suggested, under his breath but with a pronounced drawl.

"Thanks," Edward said, his face red with embarrassment as he took the notebook and did as his classmate suggested. Edward was just as flustered by another fact. The guy who retrieved the notebook for him was so strikingly good-looking that Edward could not help but stare. Perfect hair, perfect face, and perfect physique—a true man's man. Edward's first thought was that this guy was a movie star doing his duty for his country. Certainly not a lowly BD candidate.

"Anytime," Hedley said with a quick wink, and then focused full attention once more on Colonel Kane.

The Kaboom Boys   33

Edward decided at that moment that this was one guy he needed to get to know. A certified leader.

Kane had made his way over to a blackboard that covered most of the room's front wall. "First, now that Corporal Hume has graced us with his presence, let me personally thank each of you for volunteering to serve your country in a time of war. Be assured you are special, the bravest of the brave. APG trains only the most elite officer candidates. And BD can only afford to take the best of the best for these top-secret assignments. You will receive rigorous training. You should know it's going to take everything you've got to do the job you'll be trained to do." Kane picked up a piece of chalk and scratched out the acronyms on the blackboard as he mentioned each. "At APG, you will learn to dismantle and render safe UXOs, or unexploded ordnance, unexploded bombs, or UXBs, land mines, and other kinds of nasty devices. If successful, you will go on to learn more in England with their bomb disposal experts and under the Royal Air Force."

The candidates looked at each other with an air of happy anticipation. An elite job. Becoming an officer. Going to England.

"Now, take a moment to look at the man to your left, then the man to your right." The trainees were puzzled. "Go ahead. Look at them. Of the three of you, only one will graduate from this program. That individual will go on to do the actual job. The rest of you will be issued a rifle and will go to the front lines. Harsh but true, as you'll see by graduation day. Got that?"

Kane looked intensely into the faces of the young men in front of him. They were all quiet. All but Edward Hume.

"I can promise you this, sir. That will not happen to me," the corporal said. The men to his left and right were frowning.

Kane snorted, then smiled.

"I like your moxie, Hume, but we'll see. You men are among the first to do this. Keep in mind we'll emphasize teamwork, but teams will be led by one smart captain in each BD squad. One thing you'll learn is you only make one mistake in this business. You're either an expert or you're dead." Kane let that settle in for a long moment. "One English war correspondent has already written that what we do is like 'playing checkers with death.' Got that?"

Most of the men shouted, "Yessir!" Edward Hume and Hedley Bennett were especially loud. But a good fourth of the trainees remained quiet, unsure.

"So, do any of you want to rethink your commitment to BD?" Kane asked. Nobody moved or spoke. "That was your first chance to bail out. There will be more. If you have doubts, I suggest you take one of those opportunities. We don't need people who are not dedicated to the task and accepting of the risks."

The room was quiet for half a minute, until the colonel used his chalk to write several words on the blackboard. The chalk screeched with every mark.

ASSESS + EVACUATE. Then Kane wrote, *NEUTRALIZE: CLEAR, DEFUZE, DETONATE.*

"Believe me when I tell you that UXOs can and will blow up at any moment. That's what they're designed to do. There is a Nazi scientist we know about who is right now designing a bomb with your name on it. Setting your death trap. You gotta be smarter than he is." Kane slowly scanned the room, looking at the expressions on each fresh face. "The fact that any UXB you're working on hasn't already exploded when you come upon it is either an anomaly, an accident, or it has a very clever delayed-action mechanism that was put there to lure you in and kill you as you work on it. Your job is to neutralize it before it kills you and everybody else nearby. The Luftwaffe has bombs that can level half a city block. That includes..." Kane walked over to stand directly in front of Edward. He pointed a finger straight at Hume's face and yelled, "...*you!*"

Edward jumped and nodded.

"We want to protect the local population. And our fighting men, of course." The colonel looked around the room for those who appeared to be queasy, uncertain, ready to pack it in already. "Don't tell their sobbing mothers this, but we can replace foot soldiers with more just like them. But it's damn hard to recruit and train men to do what we're asking you to do. Men who not only want to but are capable of doing the job. The US Army would prefer you don't get careless and blow your damn selves into little bitty pieces. Dead BD men can't disarm anything or save anybody. Got that?"

Edward sat up even straighter at his desk. There was a low rumble of chatter among the men in the room, acknowledging the point made. Clear-eyed, Edward merely looked up at the imposing figure of Colonel Kane and smiled. This was exactly what Edward needed to hear.

Kane tapped on Hume's desk with the chalk, quieting the murmurs.

"Now, for the next six weeks, you'll be learning the latest techniques developed by our allies and friends, the Royal Air Force and Royal Engineers, and perfected by some smart guys right here at APG. God knows, the poor Brits have had plenty of real-world training that we'll benefit from. They've lost lots of good men in the process, but we've learned from their experiences, so they did not die for nothing." He pointed the end of the chalk at several men in the classroom. "Got that?"

"Yessir!"

"Now get ready for the RAF boys to give you shit about the Americans' use of the word *fuse*. We teach that the cord—or the line—that gets lit to ignite a device is a *fuse*, with an *s* and not a 'zed.' A *fuze*, with a *z*, is the actual detonator inside the weapon that makes it blow up. Whether it's mechanical, electrical, chemical, or hydrostatic. The RAF insists on keeping it simple and only speaks or writes *fuze* for everything. But we'll do it the US Army way. Got that?"

"Yessir!"

"Once you're in the field, commanding your own BD unit," Kane continued, "you'll also be teaching the rest of us, including the next class and the one after that, based on what you're seeing out there. Intelligence is strategic to our effort. Your intel. You will make a difference and save lives by making and handing off detailed notes. You will have a photographer assigned as a key member of each unit. He'll take pictures of every UXB you work on, documenting every step you take to defuze every device you encounter. Your photos and reports will be reviewed back here in the States, and we'll try to keep up with any changes the Nazi sons of bitches make. If you do the job right, we'll have what we need to make the next BD bunch even better and more efficient. If you don't..."

Kane spun around and returned to the blackboard. This time he squeaked out the words, TEN-WEEK LIFE EXPECTANCY.

"You men heard that before?" Some, including Edward, nodded. Most had not been blessed with a recruiter as honest as the one he had. "Let me be clear. We want you to outlive these piss-poor odds of survival for BD men. Ten weeks. That's like Easter to Memorial Day. Baseball season is twenty-five weeks. Count 'em. Mark 'em off in a diary. On a calendar. Ten weeks is two months and ten days. Seventy days. We can do better than that. That's on average, mind you, but you will be one of our first trainees with some real instruction in the best way to do this job. We're counting on that improving your chances. You'll be counting on it, too. So will your mommas and sweethearts." Kane strode quickly down an aisle between the desks all the way to the classroom's back wall. He stopped next to a light switch and a film projector resting on a table. "But you will still need to trust your instincts."

He flipped the lights off. The room was dungeon dark. Coal-mine black.

"Trust your instincts."

The only sound was the distant grumble of another B-17 dropping more test bombs. It was a long half minute before Kane spoke again.

"Boys, nothing I'm about to show you can fully prepare you for what you're going to soon encounter in the field. You're going to see some shit. But this is the best I've got right now. If it chases you away or keeps you awake at night or makes you puke your guts out, then good. Nightmares are the least of your worries. Quit. I'm begging you to quit. Because if you do, it means you weren't meant for BD anyway. It's better to find that out now, not while you're all cozy with a thousand-pound UXB. Not out there in the basement of some bombed-out church or in an ordnance dump some-where. Nothing to be ashamed about. Few men are cut out for this job. Got that?"

"Yessir," was the response, but not nearly as exuberant as before.

The projector clicked to life and began casting harsh, disturbing images on a blank wall. Images of burned and dismembered human beings, soldiers from both sides ripped apart, bombed-out villages, blazing cathe-drals, charred vehicles, and flattened crops in fields pocked with bomb craters and strewn with carcasses of cattle, other farm animals, and soldiers.

Several men got up and hurriedly left the room. One was retching before he could get to the door. Nobody outside a war zone had ever seen images like these before.

The Kaboom Boys   37

Edward Hume felt a plum-sized lump in his throat, but he watched it all. He did not blink.

He realized now that he had a purpose. One bigger than him. Bigger than any one person. But to fulfill that purpose, he would have to learn all he could about being a BD man. And also learn to follow his instincts, just as he had been doing ever since he decided to overcome that blasted 4-F and enlist.

Learn it, learn it well, then go out there as one chosen to do what he could to stop some of this madness, mayhem, suffering, and death.

To make a difference.

Fourteen-year-old Eddie Hume. He and several of his friends have ridden their bikes down to Bore Hole Quarry, a swimming spot favored by all the local kids. Never mind the signs specifically saying: Off Limits! No Swimming or Diving Allowed! Danger! *The* No *on most of the signs long since shot away during .22-rifle target practice.*

Eddie is the only one not splashing around in the cold, clear water on this scorching summer day. Not swinging out and dropping from the Tarzan rope swing. That is because he has never learned to swim. He has always had something better to do. And the quarry water, very deep and fed by underground springs, is too cold, too taxing on less-skilled swimmers. Even Sarge, his pup, ignores the signs and hazards, paddling out with the others, swimming naturally, looking back at Eddie, grinning.

Besides, there is something about this place that deserves his time spent visiting it, looking at it. Such a chillingly dangerous place, yet so beautiful, too.

Eddie's friend, Fritz Schneider, pops up and shouts, "Hey, Hume! You're a coward if you don't come in!"

Eddie skips a rock in his direction, sending Fritz ducking under. When he comes back up for air, Eddie calls out, "Hey, Fritz. You know why squirrels always swim on their backs?"

"No, why?"

"To keep their nuts dry."

Fritz guffaws, as if it's the first time he's heard his friend's silly joke.

Eddie's buddies are having too much fun to notice a couple of other boys—

Edward does not recognize them, so they are likely from one of the other mining towns around—as they ride up to the edge of the sheer rock wall a hundred yards away, hop off their bikes, make their way over to a ledge overlooking the quarry, and appear to be ready to jump right in from twenty feet above an especially ominous black patch of water.

Jesus! No! Not there!

They do not know how treacherous that spot is. Just below the surface, hidden by the dark water, are old fallen trees, junk, and spiky scrap that has been shoved over the edge from above for years. Car thieves especially like to strip their booty of any valuable parts and roll what is left into that black hole.

Eddie stands, but before he can shout a warning, he hears the boys' good-natured cries as they jump in tandem. He sees two splashes. Then no sign of them. Neither comes to the surface. They have been swallowed up by Bore Hole.

"Hey! Hey! Fellas, did you see that? Two kids jumped in the water from the Last Ledge. They haven't come up yet."

Fritz is the only one to respond in his German-tinged English. "What are you talking about? Everybody knows you don't jump in there." It's true. If the cold water doesn't tie your muscles into knots, barbs of rusted junk just below the water will tear a body all to hell.

"No, they did. They're drowning, guys," Eddie shouts, pleading. "They went in over there, next to the old tree snag."

Curious now, Fritz and a couple of the others wade out of the water to look at where he is pointing. Eddie takes charge as he so often does. He grabs one of the younger boys and tells him to get on his bike and high tail it down to the fire station to get help. Then he tells Fritz and the others to come with him, that maybe they can assist the boys if they are in trouble.

"Hell, Eddie, you can't swim, and I sure ain't jumping off the Last Ledge!" Fritz says.

Some call the top rock shelf the "Last Ledge." Most call it the "suicide wall." Some coal miner with terminal black lung or a drunkard overcome by hard times jumps in there at least once a year, choosing death over the life he's compelled by circumstance to live.

Eddie keeps his eye on the spot where he saw the splashes. Still nothing. Not a ripple.

The boys make their way to the ledge. The two bicycles lay there, pitifully

The Kaboom Boys 39

abandoned. No sign of the boys. Only a few air bubbles on the surface. Then, abruptly, a big bass jumps three feet out of the water to snag his supper.

"We should at least go down to the sand and look for them," Eddie pleads.

"No way! I'm not going in that water, dumbass," Fritz tells him, now spooked. The other boys shake their heads, too.

Eddie ignores them and hastily climbs all the way down to the green water. There is a narrow strip of dirty sand there, what passes for a beach. He grabs a large tree limb lying nearby, propped up against the quarry wall.

"I'm going in," he shouts up to his friends. "Watch out for me if I get into trouble."

"Don't you dare go in there," Fritz commands, but Eddie is already splashing into what quickly becomes deep, deep water. "Dummkopf!"

The limb has just enough buoyancy to keep Eddie's head above the surface if he can somehow tuck it in the arch of his armpits. But it painfully rubs against the bare undersides of his arms as he paddles. His buddies climb down to the sand at the edge of the water, too, but nobody comes in. He aims the branch over to the dark spot in the water, to the place he knows is filled with tree limbs, rusted-out autos, water snakes, and more. Some of the mess is visible this close, defiantly jutting upward but still just beneath the oily surface.

The water is bitingly cold. His heart is pounding from exertion and dread. What if the boys suddenly appear and grab the limb in panic, dragging them all under? What if he slips off the limb? Or it soaks up too much water and sinks?

"Doggie-paddle, dumbass!" It's Fritz, yelling advice, his voice echoing hollowly off the vertical sides of the quarry. "Dog-paddle! Both hands, both feet, like a dog swims!"

Sarge splashes along nearby, demonstrating.

Then Eddie has the oddest of thoughts. The threat of dying is only making him more determined to do what he knows he must. Nobody else is helping to try to save those boys. Disheartening but not unexpected. Most of mankind would hold back before facing such danger. But for Edward, it is the danger—the reality of it, not the fear of it—that pushes him to do what he knows he must. He respects fear, but he is not afraid of being afraid. Amazingly, the closer he is to death, the more he feels alive.

He hears the fire truck's siren approaching and, as he makes slow progress, watches the firemen hastily climbing down toward the water's edge. Eddie spots something close by, just beneath the surface of the brackish water. At first, he thinks it is another bass, set to jump for a dragonfly.

No, it's a hand. The lifeless hand of a young boy. Eddie's stomach tangles up and flips over. Then, deeper down in the murky water, a young face, impossibly white, frozen in wide-eyed shock.

Before he can do anything about it, he vomits. And, in the process, almost loses his grip on the sodden limb.

He stops paddling. He hears voices. The firemen are yelling at him, asking if he needs help.

"No, but I found one of them. Right here. He's...gone."

Two of the firemen swim out to him. They confirm what he has seen and then help Eddie get back to the sand. Without urgency, they go back out and set about pulling the bodies of the two boys loose from where they are impaled on rusted-out junk.

After a flurry of questions from the firemen, Fritz fesses up that Eddie cannot swim, that he was the only one willing to go into the water. The fire chief turns and angrily unloads on Eddie.

"You are brave and noble and all that shit, but you are also an idiot! Even a good swimmer shouldn't try to save someone who's drowning. They panic and take you down with them."

"But sir," Fritz interrupts. "Eddie's the one who just has to do something. An instinct that he has to—"

"I don't care," the fire chief says. "Look, kid, we don't need another hero. You best control those impulses. Most heroes die and sometimes take one or two of us with 'em when they run back into a burning house or try to go in and pull miners out of a collapsed shaft. We almost had ourselves three fools to yank out of that quarry 'stead of two. Then we'd have to go tell another momma her baby boy ain't coming home for supper. Ever."

Eddie sits there, shivering, teeth chattering, still seeing that pale hand floating peacefully just beneath the surface of the water, that white face staring up at him. Even as the fire chief rails at him, he has no regrets about trying. Just about failing.

He has done the right thing. He knows that. His big sin—but still likely making no difference between life or death for those two boys—is never learning to swim.

The fire chief kneels down next to Eddie and speaks quietly.

"I know I was rough on you, son, in front of your friends," he says. "It was just for your own good. Look, that was still about the bravest thing I've ever seen anybody do. You ever want to be a firefighter and save people's lives and property the right way, you just let me know. Oh, and learn to swim, okay?"

Eddie looks sideways at the fireman. Recruiting at a double drowning?

"Tomorrow, sir. I'll start learning tomorrow."

5

The silvery metal object in the blast hole could have been an old metal milk barrel or a gasoline drum. But Edward knew very well what it was, even before he climbed down into the hole and touched it. A fifty-pound bomb. Inert, thank God. A click of a stopwatch caused him to look up to Colonel Thomas Kane, standing there, backlit by brilliant sunshine, with the timer in his hand. There were also a dozen or so BD trainees gathered around the hole, staring down at him, most of them thankful it was Hume down there being the brave one and not them, but also wondering if this kind of duty was really for them.

"What's first, then, Hume?" Kane asked, glancing at the watch to emphasize that the clock was literally ticking.

"Evacuate?" Edward asked, tentatively, raising a muddy hand to shield his eyes from the sun.

"Commanding voice, Hume! You're the captain and you're in charge, dammit!"

"Evacuate!" Hume imagined they could have heard him this time all the way back to Mahanoy City.

"Now say it like there are a hundred stupid people standing around, trying to see what you're doing," Kane told him. "Because that is exactly what you'll be dealing with out there in the real world."

Edward sucked in a lungful of air. "Everybody within two thousand feet get back and take cover! Now!" This time, the other officer candidates clapped.

Kane pursed his lips and nodded. "Now you're getting there, Corporal. You are the one in charge, and don't let any son of a bitch forget that!"

Kane made an entry in his notebook but nodded approvingly and with a slight smile on his face. "Okay, so tell me and your team here exactly what it is you got down there."

"It's a German chemical-based, delayed-action fifty-pounder. It has no anti-handling circuitry. Once armed, this type of device is set to detonate in thirty-six to forty-eight hours." Edward looked up with a proud grin.

"Good analysis," Kane said, turning to the other trainees. "I expect the same from all of you. Now, you also need to know that this one is timed to blow when some BD man is about to neuter it. Or an unsuspecting platoon of our Airborne boys are sitting here about to enjoy their scrumptious K rations. Since we already know the pretend Krauts dropped this device here two hours ago..."

Edward anticipated the question and, after some quick calculations, shouted out the answer. "You have thirty-four to forty-six hours to—"

The colonel interrupted him this time. "To defuze it. Or what? It'll instantly turn you into a fine mist of blood, bone, and guts." He paused to allow his vivid image to sink in, to be sure they would never forget it. "Now, we are also assuming we don't have means or opportunity to move it and detonate it somewhere else. And that the barracks right over there is a convent full of nuns and crippled children that cannot be evacuated. Got that?"

Edward nodded confidently, then kneeled back down in the mud next to the bomb and began to unscrew its delayed-action fuze. He felt all the eyes on him—especially the colonel's. Still, he appeared serene, almost at peace while he worked on the device. He had shifted the outside world to someplace else, away from his realm. He thought of nothing else, employing pure focus. He felt at ease and comfortable with the tools he was using even though this was something he had never imagined doing up until a few months ago. Those Saturday mornings helping his friends work on their cars were paying off now.

Edward Hume was now convinced he had been born to disarm bombs. He could not wait to work on the real thing, to rid the world of unneeded evil one device at a time, saving lives, not taking them. All he needed was to be prepared, to maintain a natural patience, and to accept that his quest was to do good.

Five minutes later, even with the ticking of the colonel's stopwatch often audible, he had rendered the practice bomb safe.

"Defuzed, ready to transport to that munitions pile over there, sir!" Edward again used his best command voice. Soldiers passing by stopped to stare.

"Men, that's the way we do it," Kane reported. "Hume there was confident in his assessment, knew how to address the problem, did not hesitate, and got the job done quickly, before a Junkers Ju 88 could come along and plant another one just like it on top of his head."

The men laughed. That seemed to annoy Colonel Kane.

"Men, I'm not joking. When you work on any device, you damn well better stay calm. When you lose your cool, you lose your ability to quickly and successfully deal with the task at hand. Imagine every scenario before you unscrew or clip anything, and do it the right way. But stay cool and do it quickly. A sniper could have easily put a damn hole in the side of Hume's head. But if you're worried about the sniper or whether your girlfriend missed her period two months in a row, you'll screw up or you'll take too long. Think clearly about the job you got to do. It's a hazardous one, but if your mind's right, you can do it. Got that?" The men all nodded vigorously as Kane motioned for Edward to climb out of the hole. "All right, tomorrow, those of you still with me will get a chance to examine some newly arrived examples of what you'll soon encounter in the field. From Deutschland by way of London. Hit the rack early. Then report back here at 0500 and before chow. We need to do some work in the dark and with you guys foggy headed from hunger, no coffee, and just getting your asses woke up, like it'll be in the field. Dismissed!"

Edward felt a hand on his shoulder as he walked away, now willingly allowing personal thoughts and concerns to flow back into his consciousness. He was intent on getting to the post exchange for necessities and the base post office to check for letters from home and mail Mom some money.

The Kaboom Boys   45

"Hume, you got more guts than you could hang on a fence." It was Hedley Bennett, the handsome guy sitting near Edward in the classroom, and, as Hume would soon learn, one of the few BD trainees who was, at twenty-four, about the same age as Edward. He was from Washington, DC, which was a surprise to Edward. Though his former boss visited there often as a member of the US House of Representatives, Hume was somehow convinced nobody was really "from" there. Bennett had an engagingly debonair and cosmopolitan air about him and spoke in a colorful way. Part of that came from having spent several years with the Civilian Conservation Corps and its construction workers, primarily in Texas. That was why he often used colorful cowboy expressions.

As Bennett fell in beside him, it hit Edward who the guy looked like.

"Anybody ever tell you that you look like that movie star guy. Clark Gable?"

"Every damn day."

Turned out that all the BD boys had been telling Hedley he looked like the *Gone with the Wind* actor. Just out of high school, Hedley had started working on sprouting and grooming his jet-black Rhett Butler mustache. He admitted it gave him a feeling of self-assurance and masculinity to be constantly compared to the "King of Hollywood." Didn't hurt with the ladies, either.

Shortly, the two were standing together in a long checkout line at the exchange. Bennett had his arms full of laundry soap, toiletries (including mustache wax), and a variety of candy bars. There was also a pack of rubber condoms. The essentials. Edward had fewer items, but as he passed a shelf, he spied and grabbed a small, leather-bound diary with dates preset, like a calendar, and added it to the things he put down next to the cash register.

"Gonna mark off the days 'til you get back to your filly, right?" Bennett asked, nodding at the calendar.

Edward started to reply, to tell him that was probably all over, but the young female cashier was giving him the "hurry-it-up" look. Just then, she spotted the condoms in Hedley's stack and looked wide-eyed and lustily at him. He winked at her.

"What time you get off work, Pumpkin?" he asked, ignoring her wedding band.

"Seven."

"Meet me out front..."

As the flirtation was going on, Edward noticed a copy of *Yank* magazine on the rack next to the register. He nudged Bennett, pointing to the color image of Mont-Saint-Michel on the cover.

"See that, Hed? Come hell or high water, I'm going there someday."

"Where the hell is that? Sure not anywhere near Rock Creek Park in DC."

Edward reached over and pulled the magazine off the rack for a closer look.

"You're not allowed to read it in line, soldier. Costs a nickel." The cashier was giving him a stony look, impatiently tapping her foot behind the counter.

Edward dug deep for a nickel in the pocket of his dirty coveralls but could not find one. He was about to put the magazine back in place when Hedley slapped a coin down next to Edward's other stuff.

"Buy me a beer at Al's Bar sometime," Hedley told him.

Outside, Hedley caught up with Edward and walked along with him, back toward the barracks. Edward ambled along slowly, quietly perusing the magazine cover.

"You got some kind of...what do you call it? You know. An obsession, or something like what I get when I'm crazy over some girl. Or car," Bennett said. "Where the hell is that place, anyway?"

"France. It's on the Normandy coast. I don't really know why, but I've had a fascination with the place for a long time, since I wrote a tenth-grade world history report about it. It's a symbol, I guess, for all the places I want to see. A Holy Grail kinda thing. If I make it to Mont-Saint-Michel, I'll have succeeded in breaking away, really living. I don't know why I'm telling ya all this, but I even dream sometimes of ending up there after the war with a beer, a mademoiselle, and a pizza pie about the size of a Buick hubcap."

"You are a romantic, Hume. Most men dream about naked women and fast cars. You got a sweetie back home, and I bet she has a problem with you having cockamamie dreams about..." Hedley glanced over at the magazine as they walked along. "What is it, anyway? A castle like King Arthur and the Knights of the Round Table with a moat and damsels in distress?"

Edward had slowed his gait even more, his attention still held captive by the color image.

"That was England. I'm talking France, here." Edward finally glanced over at Hedley. "It's just a place I hope to reach someday, a goal of mine."

"Looks like you're gonna need yourself a boat." Hedley reached for the magazine, but Edward ducked, stepped back, then stopped cold.

"Damn! I forgot to mail Mom's money." He put the magazine under his arm. "I'll catch up to you at Al's. I owe you a beer, you know."

"I won't make it to Al's tonight, but..." Hedley started, but Edward was already gone, out of earshot. Hume would be without a wingman for the evening.

A short while later, family obligations taken care of, Hume was back outside the post office and exchange, sitting on a bench, stowing his purchases—including the calendar and magazine—in his satchel. He had picked up some mail, too. A letter from Rachel and a package holding almost certainly another bottle of Epsom salts from Mom. She was convinced her boy suffered from headaches and constipation and that this stuff would help if he used it. He did not. But he kept the half dozen bottles of the remedy under his cot anyway.

He ignored the commotion of scurrying troops all around him as he sniffed the familiarly perfumed letter. That and another distinction alerted him that it was from Rachel Levine. As her usual final ritual, she heated red wax with the flame from a candle and stamped her envelope flaps with a large *RL*, using a gold seal with her family crest.

Inside it was a letter, written in Rachel's bold cursive script. She was a highly practiced calligrapher, a stickler for good penmanship. He could only imagine how she took his own hen-scratched letters to her. In addition, she had obviously used the ornate quill pen she preferred, dipping its tip into the inkwell on her desk. She told him she used the pen and ink because she wanted to carefully consider every word she would write to him for maximum emotional effect.

He imagined her sitting there at her grandmother's old rolltop desk in her upstairs bedroom. Pictured her yellow tabby, Ginger, jumping into her lap, purring.

Edward idly ran his fingers through his hair and read on. He could hear her voice, the inflection, the passion, in her words. His throat grew tight, and a coldness fell over him.

For that moment, he dearly missed Rachel.

The first words annoyed him, though. "Dear Eddie..." He had asked her to call him Edward now. "Eddie" was when he was a kid. Even so, he read on.

"It has been weeks since I last heard anything at all from you," she wrote in a stern tone, one quite familiar to Edward. "I know the Army keeps you busy, but I have absolutely no idea where you are, what you are doing, or if you are all right. Please write and *tell me something*. I promise I will not say a word to those nasty Nazis! I am not a spy!"

Edward grinned. Yeah, Mahanoy City was crawling with German spies. And Rachel seemed to be unaware of what Hitler and the Nazis had done to the Jewish people—her people—so far. He had tried to get her in the habit of reading the newspapers, but she only looked at the comics. He wanted his future mate to be worldly and aware. She had few interests beyond the picket fence that surrounded her house. And her father was fine with that, determined to shield his baby girl from such horrors.

Edward really had no good reason for not having recently written to Rachel. He typically sent a letter every three or four days to Mom and Pops.

"You might want to know that things at Pops's Bar have slowed down and it's no more cracking fun like it used to be before all you boys left to fight the war," she went on. Pops had hired Rachel to help out on Friday and Saturday nights, when the bar was busiest. That surprised Edward. It was likely his mother's idea. Rachel did not need the money, but she claimed it would help her keep in closer touch with Eddie and get the latest news about him. After all, they had left each other mostly on sour terms. "It is the coal miners and old people who come in anymore. By the way, Levi Loftus was in this week and told me to tell you hello and to go kick Mr. Hitler's...well...you know what."

Loftus was another coal miner, an older friend of Tommy's, who had taken advantage of the deferment for critical workers as well as a previous

The Kaboom Boys 49

mine-collapse injury to avoid the war. Rachel felt that to be a fine idea. Levi had lost his wife to pneumonia several years earlier, leaving him to raise three rambunctious boys. And it was not lost on Edward that Rachel was including Levi's name in her letter for a calculated reason, to make Edward jealous. It did not have its intended effect at all.

She ended the letter with her usual, "Love you *beaucoup*," with the French word wrapped up in whorls and curlicues like entangled vines.

Edward folded the letter and slid it back into the envelope, put it in his satchel, and tried unsuccessfully to ignore the lingering aroma of her perfume. He grinned. The fragrance was something she called "Danger." Or was it "Ciro"? It was French, he knew. All the rage since the early 1920s. He had for a long time assumed she was joking about the name, but he later learned there really was such an aroma. "Not for the timid," the magazine ads proclaimed. Like most things she did, the fragrance was her way of luring Edward into marriage, her goal since she was a cheerleader and he the quarterback for the Mahanoy City Maroons.

Maybe he was destined to be a lonely man when the war was over. On the other hand, he resented that she felt—with her perfume and attempted jealousy—that she had a hold on him. That *their* plans were really *her* plans. Most men would be thrilled with a girl like Rachel, with a rich father-in-law and a guaranteed job. One thing he knew for sure, though, and especially after that day's drill and Colonel Kane's words afterward: none of them could tolerate the distraction. Maybe the expression he had heard several times already was true: "BD men are better off alone."

He hurried on down to the barracks to drop off his purchases and change into clean coveralls before heading to Al's Bar. It was just outside the base's main gate and a favorite hangout for BD trainees, a typical soldiers' dive, like so many that ringed military bases around the world. Smoke-filled, cramped, dark, few choices of brands or types of brews but a seemingly unlimited supply of what few selections they did offer. Only the rowdiest got ejected. As an added benefit, there was a mere hundred feet of gravel road for the drunkest soldier to navigate back to base. The place was only half-full this weeknight.

Al's did have a Seeburg Audiophone jukebox. It was playing "I'll Never

Smile Again" by the Tommy Dorsey Orchestra with Frank Sinatra taking the lead with the Pied Pipers.

Perfect, Edward thought. But it decidedly was not, considering the mood in which Rachel's letter had left him. He found a stool near the end of the bar. He sat down, pulled from his satchel a sheet of stationery and pencil Rachel had given him, and began to compose a response.

"I am sorry I have not written more, but I can assure you that it gets very lonely here," he wrote. "We still have a lot to figure out. Right now, I am keeping busy learning how to stay alive once we ship out, but when we go to where the actual fighting is, it will be different. I need to keep my head clear." As he wrote these words, Edward realized he had some qualms he had not fully recognized until now. "It's difficult for me to admit, but I have had some second thoughts about this BD stuff. Maybe I'm just tired..."

Then he was stuck. He had no idea what else to tell her.

Edward was only half-aware that the bartender was now standing nearby. It was Al Stephens, an older African American man, missing his right arm, wearing a stained wool World War I Army overseas cap. Near an orange-and-white felt pennant honoring his beloved Baltimore Orioles, Al also kept several baseball bats to enable him to quickly put an end to any fracas that might erupt. Edward had not seen it yet, but he had been told Al was especially adept at using the weapon with his remaining arm to efficiently and quickly end any fight. He had also heard that Al's prosthetic limb was equally effective. But it was legally considered a lethal weapon if he ever used it. Al kept it under the cash register for that reason, but also because it was too cumbersome to wear. Still, it would be useful if a fight broke out. And its legendary status was usually a sufficient deterrent.

With surprising quickness, Al suddenly snatched up the letter Edward was writing, stepped back, rapped a beer pitcher several times with a spoon, and began to read it out loud for all to hear. Now all the other patrons could know the young soldier's innermost thoughts.

"*I can assure you that it gets very lonely here. We still have a lot to figure out. Right now, I am keeping busy learning how to stay alive once we ship out, but when we go to where the actual fighting is, it will be different,*" Al read, an exaggerated look of mournful sadness on his face. "*I need to keep my head clear.*"

The Kaboom Boys 51

Soldiers looked up from their lukewarm beers to stare and point at Edward, to laugh and jeer.

Mortified, Edward tried to take back the letter. "Hey, man. Give it back!"

Al only stepped farther away and kept reading, even louder. "*It's difficult for me to admit, but I have had some second thoughts about this BD stuff...*" Al snorted, wadded up the letter into a tight ball, and threw it down on the bar in front of Edward.

"Hey, soldier, I ain't going to allow you to send this shaggy-dogshit letter," he told Edward. "Not from my bar nohow."

Edward looked at him for a moment, then broke into a broad grin.

"I gotcha. Thanks. I'll know better next time."

The barkeep stuck out his hand. "I'm Al, the CO of this establishment. And it's a house rule that nobody writes love letters here at my bar. You sit. You drink. You write. You go. My rules." They shook hands. "Now, what you drinkin' tonight, soldier? You got two choices at Al's. Beer or whiskey."

"Beer. The coldest and wettest you got."

"Excellent choice." Al expertly operated the tap with his one hand and used his chin to pull the lever to get the right amount of foam at the top of the mug. Edward could not help but stare at the man's missing limb, gone all the way to the shoulder.

"Left it behind in France," Al told him. "The Great War. The War to End All Wars. I'd say there's a lesson in them names for all of us, son."

"My pops fought in the Great War, too, at Belleau Wood," Edward offered. "And he runs a bar just like this one back home in Pennsylvania."

Al's face clouded over. His deep brown eyes became distant and misty.

"I was at Belleau Wood. A part of me's still at the bottom of the Marne River," he said with a slight nod toward his right shoulder.

"You were? I didn't know there were any..." Edward stopped, took a big swallow of his beer. He was about to express his belief that no Black soldiers fought in the First World War. Obviously, that was not the case.

"Yeah, that's right. Guess your daddy didn't tell you," Al confirmed, reading his mind. "A few of us colored guys got to show we could bleed red and white and blue, just like your old man and the other white boys. Men like your dad and me, different as we might be, sure as hell had that experience in common. Two thousand killed on our side. Eight thousand wounded. Every damn one of them—white, Negro, whatever color skin—bled red. Makes a man wonder why they call it 'the Great War.' Not a damn thing great about it." Al Stephens nodded toward Edward's already almost-empty glass. "Let me know when that brew evaporates."

Edward, on his third beer and with no supper, was lost in thoughts of Pops and the experiences he mostly refused to talk about. Something else was nagging at him. Maybe his unresolved response to Rachel. Maybe some doubts about his choice of BD that he was now having.

Al lost an arm. If Edward botched a job, he would lose far more.

He failed to notice the three flashily dressed young women when they entered the bar with sexy swagger. The growing number of BD trainees, just off duty, certainly noticed, greeting them with catcalls and bold invitations. But one of the girls, tall and attractive in an openly alluring way, navigated right over to the empty stool next to Edward. She did not resemble in any way any woman he knew back home, certainly not in dress or manner. She sat down, her breasts brushing his arm, as she immediately began caressing with her long fingers the BD patch on his coveralls sleeve. Her nails were painted blood red, the same color as the patch. Something akin to electricity ran up and down Edward's spine.

He finished his beer in one gulp and then decided to smile at her.

"Al, another one, please," he called out. The woman looked him in the eyes and seductively licked her lips. The message was clear. Tipsy or not, Edward understood. "Uh, make that two."

Al gave Edward and his new friend a long look as he set two glasses of foamy brew in front of them.

"I'm Lois," she finally said, with an almost hypnotically low *Lo* and a viperlike hissing *is*. "Who are you?"

"Eddie. Edward. I'm going to be a bomb disposal captain. Maybe. If I can stay with it, that is." He was having trouble making his tongue and lips form words. And why in hell had he added that last bit of information? The beer. And Lois. Her perfume was even stronger—and in the moment more intoxicating—than that on Rachel Levine's letters. Danger. *Ciro*.

Al was still within earshot. He frowned and stepped closer.

"Sounds like you got doubts, young man," he growled. "You ain't about to go AWOL, are you?"

The Kaboom Boys 53

Lois was looking sideways at Edward, too, as she sipped her beer, also awaiting his answer.

"No. I'll make a great BD man. I'm just not so sure about the captain part." Edward was immediately surprised that he had said out loud a thought he had so far held close.

"Just remember, you become an officer, a CO of a bomb squad, your men's lives depend on how you train and lead," Al said. "The captain is the one that defuzes the weapon, too, you know. Every single one. Nobody else. APG follows RAF rules and regs. War's some damn serious business. BD is even more serious. A squad's only as strong as the weakest link in the chain. Don't let that be you, Private. Can't do nothing half-assed."

"I'm a corporal," Edward said with a slur.

"I know that. But you'll be a private again if you don't do your job out there. Protect yourself and your men first, then maybe you can clear bombs and save people's lives."

"I know that," Edward responded.

"No, you absolutely do not know. Least not yet. You and your pals..." He motioned toward the men who had by now filled every corner of the bar, raucous but friendly. The barkeep was becoming agitated. "You're sure as hell about to find out. But right now? You don't know nothin' about nothin'!"

Al angrily swept up the empty glasses in front of Edward and stepped away. Lois leaned in closer. Her perfume was even more stimulating. Edward tried to stay fully alert, aware.

"Don't mind old Al, there, honey. He gets grumpy sometimes."

Edward suddenly grabbed a cigarette from an open pack of Lucky Strikes lying on the bar nearby, picked up a match, lit it, and took a big puff. He coughed hard and long. He had never really smoked before. Just the occasional cigarette with the guys at Bore Hole Quarry, Camels they had swiped from their mothers. It was a nasty habit he had sworn he would never take up. Now, though, a culmination of things had brought him to this moment. Exhausting weeks of tense and intensive training. Worries about becoming an officer. The status of his relationship with Rachel. The pressures of war. He had suddenly wanted a smoke more than anything else in the world. Now he wondered if he would ever breathe again.

Lois boldly took the cigarette from Edward's lips as he tried to catch his breath. She sucked in a long draw, thoughtfully giving him time to recover.

"So, you think I'm an idiot, Miss...?"

"Lois. I'm Lois."

"I had a 4-F," Edward blurted out, completely unintentionally, the alcohol having its way with his judgment. "And I got it redone...retracted...reinstated...withdrawn. Whatever you call it. Like a do-over, you know. So I could go fight. Or actually go learn how to disarm bombs, which is, in a way, fighting. We do learn to shoot an M-1 carbine, take target practice with a pistol. You know, just in case."

She looked at him sideways again, through the thick smoke, eyes wider. "Yep, you're an idiot, all right."

"Hey, Lois, you want another beer?"

"I'm in a bar, ain't I?"

"Hey, Al. Two more!" he shouted. Mildred Bailey was singing "Lover Come Back to Me" on the jukebox.

"You keep looking around," she said. "You expecting a date?"

"No, my friend is supposed to join me," Edward answered. "Hedley Bennett."

She looked sharply at him. "Hed? You know Hed Bennett?"

"Yeah. Fellow trainee. Good guy. You know him?"

She smiled. "Damn right I do. He's out with one of my best friends tonight. I suspect she's doing more for him than buying him a few beers at Al's."

"Oh. I guess I got stood up." Edward felt even sadder than before.

"You got a girl back home, Ed?" Lois asked. "Bet you do. And you're being true to her until you get back and marry her, right?"

He winced at the question. "I did. I mean, I do. But I'm pretty sure I've blown that up once and for all. Right along with a career running a shirt factory. They just got a big order for military uniforms. Lots of pressure. Fifty workers per shift. Some of 'em grumpy old men who used to be coal miners and the rest frazzled women, most of 'em working two jobs. See why I enlisted in bomb disposal instead?"

She smiled, liking the answer, and put her hand over his. It was a surprisingly intimate move to Edward, but he made no effort to pull back.

The Kaboom Boys 55

"I work in a shirt factory myself," she said. "But we make parachutes now. Parachutes and uniforms and fatigues."

"Hey, I just told Mr. Levine he ought to go after some of those contracts..."

Lois sidled in even closer, her leg against his, her free hand scorching on his thigh. She whispered in his ear.

"You know why all you bomb boys don't have girlfriends?"

Edward actually gave the question some thought. "Uh, no. I don't."

"'Cause you all have little, short fuses."

Edward laughed, too much and too loud. Lois leaned in even closer, their noses and foreheads almost touching. Her fragrance was making him even more tipsy than the weak beer. The air in the room was suffocatingly hot.

"So, tell me, Ed," she said. "Why did you throw away a free pass out of the war and then sign up to do such dangerous work? You got a death wish or something?"

"It's 'Edward.' But I guess 'Ed' is okay among good friends," he told her. He thought about it for a moment, flustered by her closeness. "I don't know. I didn't want to do anything ordinary. I hate mediocrity. I guess I crave adventure or something. I just wanted to do something to help stop all this shit. The hurt and suffering and what the Nazis and Japs are doing. Yes, I want to help win the war someway. We've got to bring the world back to its senses. Disarming bombs. I can do that without being a killer. But really, it just seems like...I know it sounds strange...but the closer I am to death, the more alive I feel."

There, he had said it out loud. To a total, sweet-smelling stranger. Another deeply held thought he had never shared with anyone. It was the truth, though. This kind of work did make him feel more alive than anything he had ever experienced before.

"You're right. It does sound strange. But it also makes me feel funny inside, if you know what I mean." She suddenly kissed him, full on the mouth. It made his head swim even more. "You know what, Eddie? Turns out you're just my type. No past. No future. No entanglements. Looking for something besides the ordinary. My kind of guy for sure." She noticed the look in his eyes, bordering on fear. "Don't panic. Not for marryin'. Just for fun. We don't know what might be coming for either of us."

He eyed the beer glass, surprised it was already empty. He did not remember finishing it.

"No promises to keep on my part," he finally decided. "Not at the moment."

"Good. Me neither. I like living for the moment," she said, so quietly Edward could hardly hear her over the music and din of the bar patrons. "You wanna go somewhere else and do some livin' right now? If things go bad later on, for you or for me, we at least got us some fiery moments and great memories. Hell, there's a war going on. And you're playing with dynamite. What are we waiting for?"

Edward pulled his wallet from his satchel. "I don't know if I have enough to pay you for your...uh—"

She stopped him with a finger to his lips. "Don't worry about that, soldier. You have your way of surviving this war. I got mine."

She helped him slide off the stool and steady himself. Edward put a dollar on the bar. Al looked at him through squinted eyes.

"You be careful, son. Be sure you're doing what you want to do. Especially when it comes to commanding men. Not what somebody else expects you to do. *You* don't be the weakest link."

Edward threw Al a sharp salute, then allowed Lois to steer him out the door and into a dark, foggy night, bound for some place warm and welcoming.

The colonel stands at his office window, watching activity on the drill fields and training grounds. He is directly responsible for the futures—for the very lives—of most of these men, for them being adequately trained, and for determining if each is ready for a tough, lethal job. But, he reminds himself, at least he is training them to save lives, not to kill and maim. And to do a chore that might just help to shorten the carnage and destruction that chokes the entire planet.

There is a timid knock at the door.

"Come on in," he says, without bothering to turn around.

The young officer candidate steps into the office, hat in hand, nervous. "Good morning, sir."

"I've been expecting you. Have a seat."

"Sir? I don't understand...you know why I'm here?"

The colonel turns, motions for the trainee to sit, then settles down into the squeaky chair across the desk from the young man, pausing for a moment before answering his question. A long moment.

"You're having doubts about joining BD. You're not sure you made the right decision now that you've seen what's involved. How much there is to learn." The colonel cracks his knuckles and then taps the desk with an index finger as he watches the trainee's puzzled face.

"Not exactly, but—"

"Look, son, you're not the first since I started this program. And you won't be the last recruit to knock on my door with that look on your face and those doubts in your mind, either. That 'what the hell have I signed up for?' look. So far, about half of them have come to see me at one point or another. The other half want to, but they lack the guts. Congratulations at least for having the guts."

The trainee nods but remains quiet. It is obvious the colonel has a standard speech ready to deliver. The corporal allows him to do so.

"Like I said in class, I am not one to try to talk anybody into doing something they don't want to do. Our job's hard enough if you're one-hundred-percent willing. But if you push past it and get out there in the field and hesitate for even a second, that's when they'll have to ship what's left of you home in a pickle jar. Got that?"

The trainee chews his lip for a short moment. "Sir, I appreciate it, but you're not helping by saying what you're saying. See, I thought BD was exactly what I was looking for. The whole package. Now, I'm sorry to say I'm not so sure."

The colonel leans forward, stares intently at the trainee. "I've been watching you. You're smart. Instinctive. Fast. You got a remarkably steady hand. Patient. One of the best to come through here so far."

"Thank you, sir, but that's not it. I know I can do the BD job. It's tough, but I know I can learn about all the chemicals and the devices and all the types of UXOs. It's the captain part, leading men. Leading men where decisions and actions I take could mean they die. I'm not sure I have what it takes." The colonel's face has gone blank. This is a new one. "In high school, I ran for senior class presi-

dent, but I thought my opponent was better qualified. I voted for him. He won by one vote. I always try to do the right thing, regardless of the consequences. But when I was captain on the football and basketball teams, if I tried to get my guys to do something and it was the wrong thing, we just gave up a touchdown or lost the game. Nobody got blown the hell up."

The colonel settles back in his chair, his hands beneath his chin, fingers like a church steeple.

"You know what, son? When you knocked that weak-kneed, timid-assed knock on my door a few minutes ago, I was standing at that window right over there, thinking about pretty much the same thing. I'm sending you boys out there, and many of you won't come back. But I know I'm doing the best job I can to see that you do. I'm giving you the chance to make a difference. The dirty work you do over there will make it more likely that a lot more sons and daughters come back home breathing. And that Hitler and Hirohito don't spread their unholy evil and that we can do our part to stop the bastards."

"I understand, sir. It's just that I have no way of knowing if I—"

The colonel holds up a hand to quiet him, stands, then paces back and forth as he continues.

"I know what to look for in leaders. That's a big part of my job, and I'm damn good at it. That's why we pick the men we do, and even then we make mistakes and still have to run off some of them. You? I can see you savin' lives because you have a knack for keeping your wits about you. You'll lead by example. And you'll go back home after this hell is over and marry that sweet thing you left behind and raise up a litter of little ones."

"Don't know much about that anymore."

"The other thing. I see how quickly you pick up on all the samples in the warehouse. You get in the field, your men will have confidence you know what you're doing. They'll do what you ask because of that. And the notes you and your guys will send back will make us even more effective as we go. I think you already know something a lot of military leaders never quite grasp. Your men don't have to love you. They just have to respect you. You think we love General Patton? No, but by God, we respect him. We know he is going to do what it takes to win the skirmish and the war. And you can command the same respect, son. Your squad is your very own roving army. They depend on you, and you depend on them. I see raw leadership in you. It just needs a bit more molding. Down deep you believe *that, too. I see it in you clear as day, or you would already be packing your duffel and headed to the infantry."*

The trainee screws up his face. *"You really believe that, sir?"* It is the validation and affirmation he needs, and coming from the colonel, it is powerful. *"You see all that, just from watching me work?"*

"Absolutely. You think I'd say it if I didn't? If I thought you'd be a poor leader of BD men and get yourself and your men killed and waste all this time, money, and trouble training you? No! I'd be packing your bags for you and kissin' you bye on the cheek. I'd much rather make a rifle-toter out of you." The colonel walks over, leans on the desk, looks the trainee in the eye. *"But now's the time to follow through on those great instincts of yours. You think you're not cut out to be a BD man and to lead others into a hell of a tough situation, tell me right now. I'll sign the papers, and you'll be out of APG by sundown. But if your instincts tell you it's something you can do, that it's worth the risk to keep some soldier or a milkmaid or a farmer's kid riding past on his bike from getting blown to smithereens, then finish what you started. Take small bites at a time. You're building a foundation here. Having doubts is just part of the process of becoming a leader. Tell me you're willing to go do some good and save lives and win this war, and I'll forget we ever had this conversation."*

The trainee stands, thinking, then gives the colonel a smart salute.

"Thank you for your time, Colonel." The corporal turns and leaves.

The colonel, suddenly very tired, steps back over to the window. Outside, just down the way, a bright red light begins flashing next to the booby-trap-training residence, followed by harsh buzzing.

Another trainee team has screwed up a drill.

6

The buzzer was agonizingly loud, and the flashing red light put a blood-red tint on an otherwise nice day. Edward Hume gave Hedley Bennett a knowing wink. Another pair of their BD brothers had just messed up. Messed up big-time. Sure enough, the trainees stormed out of the booby-trap test house, sweat drenched and disgusted, arguing with each other like an old married couple over whose fault it had been.

"They'll make mighty fine infantrymen," Hedley said, vigorously chewing his gum. "If they manage not to shoot each other."

"Hell of a way to go," Hume agreed.

Colonel Kane stood behind them, shaking his head. Two more down. The washout rate was worse than even he had expected. "All right, Hume and Bennett. You're next. Please make an effort to cheer me up."

"Yessir," they responded in unison, trying to sound confident. They had watched as five other pairs of officer candidates had failed so far this day. And the only ones to get out "alive" had taken almost three hours to do so. Now, the "failures" stood idly by, not sure whether to cheer on their fellow BD trainees or not.

Kane motioned Hume and Bennett to follow him to the front porch entrance of another seemingly innocent, two-story white clapboard house, oddly positioned between barracks and trenches and behind the one that had stymied so many other candidates so far this day.

"New drill. Got to mix it up. You birds look like you're up for a real challenge. There are ten devices now, and you have to find and neutralize all ten. Quickly. Ready?"

Both men nodded as the colonel started his stopwatch. They ran for the doorstep as Kane settled into an easy chair someone had placed in the shade on the house's broad Victorian-style front porch. The others settled down to wait. Some made wagers.

The two trainees immediately went to work. Doorknob. Hinges. Latch. Frilly, feminine welcome mat. None showed signs of being booby-trapped. Bad form to get castrated before even getting inside.

Once through the front door, they found a large room, far too sparsely and shabbily furnished to fit such a nice house. A worn-out sofa, a chair gushing stuffing, a dusty, nicked end table, and a shabby lamp with a dim, flickering bulb. An old copy of *Yank* magazine on the table was opened to a page with a photo of Hitler standing at the Eiffel Tower, looking menacing but proud as he struck a pose with his entourage.

"Bastard," Edward growled.

"Son of a bitch," Hedley added as he raised his flashlight, searching.

"Remind you of an Easter egg hunt, Hed?"

"Yeah, but Easter eggs don't bite."

Edward was quickly on his knees peering and feeling with his fingers beneath the sofa as Bennett aimed his flashlight down a long hallway that veered off to the left. Edward felt a wire. He stopped.

"Device!" he yelled, loud enough for Colonel Kane—and the other trainees —to hear him outside. He took a long look before using his cutters to snip the wire, then carefully pulled out a small but evil-looking mock explosive. Had it been real, and had he not disabled it, it could have cut in half someone who might have casually settled down on the sofa for a moment's rest.

He found Hedley in the spacious adjacent dining room, methodically checking the frame of a door that led into the kitchen.

"Device two!" Hedley sang out, waving both arms over his head. Both men grinned and looked at the big red light mounted to the wall. "And we're not five minutes in. No lights or buzzers today, soon-to-be Captain Hume!"

"From your lips to God's ear," Hume responded. "But let's not jinx us just yet. Neuter that thing. Eight more to go." More cautious than his cocky friend, Edward remembered something he had once read. *Nothing causes a man's downfall as severely as arrogance.* "So, Hed, let's not get out in front of ourselves."

"Two down, eight to go. You're so damn good with math, soldier. You ever thought of a career in BD?"

In the kitchen, Edward promptly cleared the refrigerator, which was plugged in and running. Nice model, too. Mom had only gotten her first one five years before. The fact that this one was working was a telltale sign the testers really wanted a careless trainee to open its door. Edward was confident he had thoroughly cleared it, though.

He pulled the handle. No buzzer.

Inside, there was nothing but a single quart bottle of cold milk, its sides wet with condensation. No sign of a wire or switch. He grabbed the bottle, opened it, gave it a sniff, and took a big swig. Delicious.

Red herring for sure, but otherwise some fine cow juice for a thirsty BD trainee, he thought. The running appliance and the cold milk could easily be distractions from more tricky stuff to come.

Meanwhile, Hedley stopped still, studying a water-filled pitcher resting in the middle of a rustic farm table. Bits of ice floated in the water and condensation running down its sides confirmed it, like the milk, was temptingly cold. They had been outside in the sun most of the day, waiting their turn, with little to drink. Several glasses were lined up alongside the pitcher. No sign of any device attached to any of them. Hedley grabbed a glass.

"Thank you, US Army booby-trap riggers. This device clearing could make a guy mighty—"

Edward grabbed Bennett from behind just as he was reaching for the handle of the pitcher and jerked him backward.

"Device! Under the pitcher."

Sure enough, the tantalizing water container was resting on a small pressure switch. A wire led through a hole bored in the tabletop to a package of dummy dynamite taped underneath. Another wire led to what was surely a relay to energize the alarm lights and buzzer.

"I just saved your ass, Hedley Bennett."

"Sons of bitches," Hedley said in a raspy voice. "But that's three."

Almost two hours later, the duo had spotted and neutralized nine booby traps with no other close calls, no klaxon or red lights. The final one was still successfully hiding from them. And no place could be declared cleared and safe until every device had been found.

"Maybe the colonel's messing with us to see how we react," Hedley was saying as they made their way down a set of stairs to a small anteroom and the side exit from the house. "Maybe there's really only nine."

"Don't think so," Edward emphatically told him. "We just have to think like Nazi SS bomb experts."

"Hey, I sure would like to have a cold schnapps and a hot fräulein right about—"

"Device! Stop!" To make sure he obeyed his warning, Edward gave Hedley a hard shove, sending him tumbling into a sideboard next to the door. Preventing him from stepping on a floormat at the bottom of the steps with the warm sentiment, "May Your Every Step Take You Closer to Heaven" boldly embroidered across it.

The two grinned as they began taking care of the phony charge hidden beneath the rug.

"These APG drill guys are just as evil-minded as the Nazi bomb scientists we keep hearing about," Hedley said.

"We ought to thank them, though," Edward offered. "Gettin' us ready for some bad stuff. And with a sense of humor, too." Then Edward looked sternly at Hedley and said, "In case you're counting, Hed, that's twice I've saved you from the infantry."

Bennett nodded. Had he been with a different partner this day, odds are his BD days would have been done.

Colonel Kane looked surprised when Hume and Bennett strode around the side of the house and began emptying their satchels, counting out each of the ten devices they had located and neutralized.

"Boys, you finished in less than two hours," he told them, studying his stopwatch. "You're the first ones to do it that quick so far. No buzzers or lights. That earns you some stripes. A stick of butter for each of you second lieutenants!" Kane pulled a pair of gold bars from his pocket—they did look a lot like sticks of butter—and pinned them to the collar of each man's dusty, dirty, perspiration-drenched coveralls. "Keep it up and you'll be captains in a minute."

Bennett grinned broadly. Edward smiled, too. But when he stroked the bar with his fingertips, it felt rough. Sandpaper rough. The things were being manufactured by the thousands and at a breakneck pace. Though the significance was there, the workmanship was not.

For Edward, at least, the brass was hefty, when he considered the responsibility that simple officer's bar carried. The burden of leadership was already weighing heavy on his shoulders.

7

Edward Hume still did not feel as if he should be a leader of men. Sometimes, he thought, he had challenges enough just leading himself to do the right thing and justifying the confidence others insisted on placing in him. It bugged him for much of the trip across the Atlantic Ocean from New York Harbor to Southampton, England, often as he stood at the rail of the troopship, gazing out across gray water. Or as he lay on a cot belowdecks, listening to the snores and farts and bad-dream bleats of thousands of other men who were also steaming off to endure still more training and then, inevitably, war. The sleeplessness was made even worse by the ship's constant zigzagging through rough waters to avoid German U-boats.

Leadership. Seems he heard as much about those traits in those BD classes as he did about detonators and volatile chemicals. Mental and physical resilience, agility, adaptability, flexibility, competence, and, most importantly, character.

Colonel Kane would be lecturing about the fuze pocket of a German SC-50 bomb when he would suddenly stop and ask the class, "What makes a strong leader?" Then expect a cogent answer. Or be listing on the blackboard steps on how to properly render a UXO dump safe when he would abruptly spin around and say something like, "You know what, boys? Too many squad leaders feel entitled by rank and make decisions just because they can, not to protect their men or get the damn job done right. Good leaders supply subordinates with motivation, purpose, and direction. Moving forward with purpose makes a team. Figuring out what drives your squad will get the most from them. Maybe save their lives, too. Do what's best for your men and they'll make you look good."

Then the colonel went right back to whatever technical lecture he was delivering. Edward took meticulous notes, not wanting to miss a word or nuance. That applied to technical topics but also when Kane opined about true leadership. It all sounded good in the classroom, and even better later when he reviewed those notes.

Regardless, he was now in the real world, dressed in his crisp, starched uniform, his newly received twin silver captain's bars and fire-engine-red-and-yellow BD patch on his sleeve. His name—Captain Edward Hume—was etched on a small plaque on his assigned desk in a field office building on a Royal Air Force base in South Yorkshire, England. If he had doubts about the reality of the situation, all he had to do was count how many times he had already heard German buzz bombs passing overhead. Or when one exploded close enough he could feel the ground shake.

Ready or not, he thought. *Ready or not.*

Two things on the desk—the only other items so far besides the name-plate—brought it all home to him. One was the small pocket calendar he had bought months ago at the base exchange at Aberdeen Proving Ground. His first order of business as he settled into his office was to write the words *Week 1* and place a big check mark on the little box at the top left on the first page. It was Sunday, May 21st, 1944. He resisted the powerful urge to flip ahead ten weeks and see when that date fell.

Ten weeks, average life for a BD man.

Next to the calendar was a one-page dispatch with only a few sentences. All in capital letters. It was to inform personnel in the new bomb disposal units that one of their own, one of the first squads to be deployed and under the command of Captain Hedley Bennett, had failed to report in on time after a job somewhere on the English coast.

"Jesus, Hed," Edward muttered to himself. "You dead, alive, or injured?" Edward had rustled through other dispatches hoping to find an update. No luck. "Gotta be careful, man!"

The Kaboom Boys 67

Both totems were stark reminders—as if he needed them—that Edward was not in Pennsylvania anymore. Reality was that in a few short months, he was no longer dealing with some old lady calling Doc's office complaining about mice in the voting booth at Cherry Flats, ironing shirts on the night shift, choosing Rachel's birthday gift from the slim pickings in the few stores back home, or remembering to get Sarge dipped for fleas.

Then, as if he needed yet another prompt to confirm his new and considerable responsibilities, in walked six of them. Six soldiers, marching stiffly, then stopping, standing at attention, and snapping off smart salutes.

God, most of them were so young. It took Edward a long moment to realize they were saluting him. He stood and returned the gesture. "At ease, men. Gather 'round."

From his middle desk drawer, Edward retrieved six red-and-gold cloth BD patches and laid them out for all to see. He also took out a sign that read, in big, red letters: *BOMB MERCHANTS*. It was just like the one Edward had made for Hedley Bennett as a good-luck, going-to-war gift.

For the moment, he allowed the patches and sign to lie there on the desktop. Several of the men smiled when they saw the sign. A couple of the other soldiers had frowns on their faces.

Edward felt the palpable tension in the room. This was, after all, an arranged marriage. None of these men had a say about who else they would be working with in this perilous job. Or who their boss would be. It was luck of the draw, the results of which were just now being revealed to all. This was also the first time Edward was speaking to a unit that would be under his command. His mouth had gone dry, but he soldiered on.

"Men, I'm Captain Edward Hume, but you likely know that from your orders. I chose bomb demolition because I wanted to save lives and make a difference in this damned war. I hope you men share that goal. If you do, and if you do your jobs the way you've been trained, we'll get along with each other just fine. Now, since we're pretty much joined at the hip in this squad for the next little while, I figure we ought to get to know one another. I want each of you to tell me how you want to be called, where you grew up, and something about yourself you want everybody else to know before we start digging and defuzing and blowing up stuff together." Hume pulled a well-considered piece of paper from his pants pocket—he had spent most of the night studying the names on it—carefully unfolded it, placed it on his desk, and called out the first name: "Technical Sergeant Alistair Taft?"

A lanky, handsome man with dark, brooding eyes, black hair, and a shadow of stubble on his chin and cheeks stepped forward. He was maybe in his mid-twenties and appeared to be the oldest of the group. Edward checked Taft's birth date. He was twenty-four but presented as older. There was an air of sadness about the man. Edward felt it strongly. He made a mental note to dig deeper at a pints-in-a-pub meeting he planned to have with his two key assistants.

"Sir, you can call me Ace," he stated in a light brogue that would edge thicker and heavier with exhaustion or more pints of his favorite brew. "Scottish by heritage and proud of it. My dad still wears my grand-pap's kilt sometimes. I guess it'll get handed down to me, and I'll wear it when I want to impress the ladies. Like the bagpipes, not to everyone's liking, but that sound of a dying cow in a dust storm reminds me of the old country." Ace stuck out his chest. "I'm a fireman...or was one. From Camden, New Jersey."

"Ace it is. Gotcha." Hume wrote down *Ace* and *fireman* next to Taft's name. "And...Corporal Henry Anderson?"

"Call me Hank, sir, and I grew up in Denver," the young man next to Taft piped up. He had a Leica camera on a strap around his neck and wore wire-rimmed glasses. "Something about me? Geez. Well, I read a lot. I read the *Book of Knowledge* encyclopedia all the way through. Twice. I know a little bit about a lot of things."

Several of the men chuckled. Another couple of them nodded knowingly. Someone mumbled, "And ain't shy about sharing it." They had obviously gotten to know Anderson well enough already to confirm he was a know-it-all. Captain Hume made notes next to the twenty-year-old's name.

"Ace and Hank, I'll need you to stick around when we're finished here," Hume told them. "We got a few things to go over. Got that? Now, let's see. Corporal Eugene Wozinski?"

The tall, leggy man with the horn-rimmed glasses looked more like a very young math teacher than a soldier.

"Yessir. Call me Gene, sir. I was a high school science teacher when I

The Kaboom Boys 69

signed up." Wozinski started to step back but decided to add one more thing. "Oh, and I'm from Chicago, sir."

But there was something else that snagged Edward's attention. It was a very prominent gold medallion on a chain around Wozinski's neck. Hardly regulation. Hume leaned in for a closer look. He also noticed that the young soldier had a familiar smell about him. Not strong but not men's cologne. Ciro. The slender young corporal smelled of Rachel Levine's favored fragrance. Just a whiff, but enough to tell Edward that Gene Wozinski was his own man. Edward decided to save any comment for later and asked a different question instead.

"You know who that is on your chain there, Gene?"

"Yessir. That's Michael the Archangel. He protects people, especially warriors, from their enemies and from Satan."

Hume smiled. "Indeed, it is." A statue of Saint Michael also topped the abbey in all those pictures of Mont-Saint-Michel that Edward had collected. The captain decided to save that bit of information for later discussion, too.

"The nuns back home, they gave it to me when I signed up for the Army."

"Keep it tucked inside your shirt or coveralls, and I expect Saint Michael will do his job for you just fine. Don't let it dangle or get caught up in machinery or have some RAF stickler see it and get all military protocol on us. Got it?" Edward had decided to let this slide, already starting to make his own rules as the leader of the squad.

"Yessir."

"All right, next. Privates Morton Schwartz, Peter Ronzini, and...what's this? Calistos Kostas?"

"Close enough, sir." Kostas had the look of a Hollywood movie star, with blond hair and deep-blue eyes. "But make it easy on yourself and just call me Carl. I was born in Greece, lived in Alabama 'til I was twelve, then was mostly raised up in Los Angeles. I still got some of the South in my mouth sometimes, I reckon. Southern USA, not Southern California."

Hank Anderson gave Kostas a nudge with his elbow. "Maybe you can tell us if all those starlets out there will do about anything to get into the movies—"

"Later, Hank," Hume sternly interrupted. Kostas blushed a deep red as he took a step back. "Schwartz?"

The private who stepped forward also had a chain and pendant prominently displayed around his neck and a small pin of some kind clipped to his cap.

"I'm Morty. Lower East Side, New Yawk." It was a Star of David on the chain and a flag pin on his cap. Morty noticed his captain studying both. He pointed to the cap. "Flag of Poland. My folks came over from Krakow after the Great War. By the grace of God, I was born in the good old USA."

"All good, Morty, but same deal with your medallion as Wozinski and his Saint Michael. Keep it tucked. But the pin is not regulation, so it has to go."

Morty nodded, took the pin off his cap, and dropped it into his uniform shirt pocket.

"And the thing you need to know about me, sir, is I hate Nazis," the young soldier said with surprising vehemence. "Plus, I hate anybody else who don't hate 'em as bad as I do."

The look in Schwartz's eyes confirmed his loathing. All the men nodded their understanding. Hume quickly turned to the one remaining member of his unit.

"Right, so you must be Ronzini, then."

"Gang back home calls me Zini. Ma calls me Peter, 'specially when she's steamed at me for somethin'. I like Pete, though."

"Pete it is, then. Where you from, Pete?"

"Well, I'm a mutt, you might say. A little Italian. A little Swedish. Take your pick. Like a meatball, ya know. My ma made the Swedish ones for Easter, and my pa made the Italian ones for Christmas. And I'm from Bay Ridge, Brooklyn, New Yawk, not far from Schwartz over heah."

Pete gave an exaggerated stage bow toward Hume and a sideways wink to Morty.

"That's where Henny Youngman's from, you know," Hank chimed in, demonstrating once more that he knew a little bit about a lot.

"Yeah, we're all comedians in Bay Ridge," Pete said.

The men laughed easily. Everyone but Ace Taft. He began to cough. Gene offered him some water. Ace waved him off.

The Kaboom Boys

"I'm okay."

The others seemed comfortable with each other. Hume, a grin on his face, motioned for them to settle down.

"One thing, and this is important," Edward said. "Fear is going to be as big an enemy of yours as the Germans will be. But it's also your energy. Access it. Control it. Use it to your advantage. Ever been afraid and yawned? No! No, you haven't. Adrenaline flows through your body when you're afraid. Anybody here play sports?"

Everyone raised his hand.

"Okay, then, like any athlete, grab it and channel. Use it to your advantage."

Hank swung his camera around and clicked a quick picture of Edward motivating his men.

"Save your film, Hank," Hume told him. "We'll have much more important things to shoot in a little while."

As he swung the Leica once again behind his back, Hank asked, "You know where we're all from now, sir. But how about you?"

Edward hesitated as he studied the paper with his men's names and his just-added notes. Los Angeles. Denver. Chicago. New York. Kids from such cosmopolitan areas would hardly be impressed with a commander from the place where he grew up. He opted to deflect with humor.

"Little coal-mining town in Pennsylvania called Mahanoy City. The place is so small our Howard Johnson's only got one flavor of ice cream. The 'Welcome to Mahanoy City' sign and the 'Now leaving Mahanoy City' sign are on the same signpost. We only have one traffic light, and we only turn it on from noon to six on Saturdays."

It worked. More of the tension in the room began to evaporate with their easy laughter.

"See, even the captain's a comedian," Pete offered.

"Two hours northwest of Philly, right?" It was Hank Anderson again.

"Yeah, but how in hell..."

"I did a report in the sixth grade on coal mining. 'Mahanoy' is an Indian word, right?"

"That makes you a digger, Captain," Pete added.

"Plenty of diggers there, for sure," Hume said. "Place is full of damn diggers. And 'mahanoy' is an Indian word for 'let's not talk anymore about my hometown.'"

Pete nudged Morty and whispered, "That struck a nerve."

"Okay, now that we're all acquainted, let's get one thing straight." Edward looked from one face to another, confirming he had their attention. "You men have had plenty of apprenticeship with the Tommies and know pretty much what to do and how to do it. The RAF has passed along about all they know about UXBs and how to fix them, so we're gonna have to keep learning on our own as we go. That's the only real way to get expert at this kind of business. But remember this. BD rule number one. Only captains can render bombs safe. Got that?"

Everyone nodded and loudly shouted, "Yessir!"

"BD rule number two. Never touch a dead German or reach for a souvenir flag or helmet or gun. Booby traps. Lots of 'em are designed to catch BD men and make us dead. Got that?"

"Yessir!" they responded, even louder.

"Whoa! You boys are sure full of vinegar. I'm not a drill sergeant, you know. And for the most part, we'll leave our rank back at the base when we're working." Edward looked at Sergeant Ace Taft. "Ace, you'll be assisting me on every job we do, and you'll drive the jeep." Taft nodded solemnly. "Now, the first one with the correct answer to this question wins the grand prize." The men exchanged puzzled looks. "A platoon of soldiers stands in the blistering sun on the Fourth of July on a five-acre parade ground two blocks from a river. They are facing due west. Their captain shouts orders in quick succession." For effect, Edward shouted as loudly as he dared without disturbing others in the office area. "Right face! About face! Left face! Now, in what direction are they facing?"

"East, sir!" It was Corporal Gene Wozinski with an almost immediate answer.

"Correct, Gene. That means you get to drive the truck. And quite the truck it is, too. A Dodge three-quarter-ton weapons carrier pulling a trailer with our tent, tools, photo supplies, demolition kit with TNT, plastic explosive, reels of wire, and spools of safety fuse. In other words, everything that we need to do our job except our muscles and our brains. That makes you pretty damn important, Gene."

Everyone patted Gene on the back. He grinned broadly, proudly. Edward next turned to Hank Anderson.

"Hank, you'll photograph and document each job. This is key to keeping up with the German bastards building this stuff. All of us... including me...will be in the hole digging and running the pumps and timbering up the walls. If something happens to me, a new captain comes in from Aberdeen Proving Ground to take my place and you'll all be temporary duty...you know, TDY...with other squads until he gets here. Got that?"

Everyone nodded. Everyone but Hank, who had his hand raised.

"You got a question, Corporal?"

"Yes, sir, but wouldn't it make more sense that if something happens to you, your second-in-command would be promoted, him knowing the squad and all?"

"Not gonna happen. We adhere to Royal Air Force protocol in everything BD. And only officers trained by Colonel Kane at APG can head a unit. Not my decision. Colonel Kane's." Edward noted Hank did not seem to like the answer he heard. Hume made another mental note, then looked each man in the eye. "Besides, nothing's going to happen to me. Got that?"

Everybody nodded and sounded a little less enthusiastic chorus of, "Yes, sir!"

Then Edward began handing out the patches, asking if any of them had taken home ec in high school and could help their buddies sew them on their uniforms. Nobody admitted to such a skill, but he knew they would find a way. They were proud to have earned the patch. Then he noticed Hank, again frowning, studying the "Bomb Merchants" sign.

"I have to admit I don't much care for that name, either," Hume told him. "We sure as hell don't sell bombs, do we? Somebody else has that name already, anyway."

Hank looked up at him, now with a serious expression on his face. "Couple of us, once we knew we were going to be in the same squad, we kind of came up with another name on our own and were going to run it by you when the time was right."

"Right as it'll ever be now. Spit it out."

"Kaboom Boys. The Kaboom Boys. But, sir, if you think it's silly or..."

"Kaboom Boys, huh?"

"Yessir."

"You know, sort of like a gang," Pete chimed in.

"Hank, I think I like it." The smile on Anderson's face in response to his captain's thoughts showed how much the nickname meant to him and, presumably, the other squad members. And, Edward realized, though he really did like the name, he was team building at the same time. "In fact, I think I like it a lot."

"Then it's done?"

"Yeah, Hank. Suits me."

"Boys, listen up!" Hank shouted to the other squad members headed for the exit. "From this point on, we're the Kaboom Boys!"

A Thursday night at Al's Bar, just outside the gates of Aberdeen Proving Ground. Patronage is sparse and not really picking up. Captain Edward Hume and Captain Hedley Bennett sit across from each other at a tiny table behind an impressive collection of empty Pabst Blue Ribbon bottles. After a few silent sips, the two buddies ignore the rest of the half-drunk clientele. It is a two-man going-away party for Bennett. He will ship out the next day, a Saturday, bound for England and a month or so embedded with the Royal Air Force engineers. Edward desperately wants to sail on the same ship as his friend, but he will be among the next wave to make the seven-day crossing in a couple of weeks.

It is almost midnight. Now customers are beginning to wander out into the chilly, far less friendly darkness. Civilians bound for home and a bed. Soldiers back to rough, sagging cots arranged in rows in poorly lit barracks lined up like dominoes. Even Hedley, who never lacks for words or tall tales, has been quiet for a bit. Edward has avoided veering toward maudlin, but an urge overcomes him after a few bottles of the beer. Pabst Blue Ribbon is a local favorite. So much so, as the joke goes, some consider it dinner.

"Hed, you know I'm gonna miss youse," he says.

"Youse? What's a youse?" Bennett responds. "Been meaning to ask you that for a while. That like a gaggle of geese or a school of fish or a pod of whales?"

Edward ignores him. Hed is always picking on his northeastern Pennsylvania accent. Instead, Hume drains the remainder of his PBR, sets it down on the table with some finality, and proclaims, "So, I guess this is it, buddy."

"What you mean?" Bennett asks, head cocked sideways. There is now the slightest slur to his words when he speaks. He typically tolerates alcohol well. Not this night. "'It'? The last hurrah? Look, if the ship don't sink in the Atlantic, some bloke don't knife me in the ribs for sneakin' a kiss with his all-too-willin' gal, or a two-thousand-pounder don't decide to ignite underneath me, I fully expect to soon see your miserable ass somewhere over there."

Edward smiles. But then, from out of left field, he launches an odd question. "Hed, you ever wonder what you'd be willing to die for?"

"What kind of a question is that?"

"No, really. If you knew you were about to sacrifice your own life so a hundred people could live, would you do it?" Edward looks hard at Bennett, as if he fully expects an answer.

"If I knew some of them would be doctors or good fathers or preachers..." Hedley starts. Then stops. As if considering how many doctors, fathers, or preachers he'd be willing to volunteer to die for.

Edward presses on with, "How about ten? Or one? What about a kid on a bike or a girl picking up bread at a bakery? Would you give your life if you knew what you were doing would save one person?" Hedley now appears totally sober and truly pondering such weighty matters. Edward digs some more. "How about if you didn't know for sure if you were really going to die or not, but the outcome would be determined by what you did next, by your actions? That it was really risky, and the odds were against you, but you could possibly survive? What odds would make you back away?"

Bennett lifts his empty bottle to his lips. It does not matter. He goes through the entire pantomime of downing a big swallow, including wiping his lips with the sleeve of his jacket and unleashing a satisfied sigh.

"Different question, partner. 'Specially if I have some say-so in how long those odds are. By being prepared. Having the right tools. Being familiar with the device. Knowing my shit. Maybe having an alternative to defuzing." Bennett may be tipsy, but he sees the direction his friend's questioning is going. "Assuming, by the way, that we're doing all this hypothetical bullshit about BD."

Edward leans forward, halfway across the table. "So how do you ever know for sure? How do you know if that fuze you're about to touch is non-tamper, or if it's timed to detonate in the next second, or if it's standard issue and a breeze to fix? Did the guy who wired it have a bad day, or did he deliberately sabotage the device 'cause he's really on our side? You never know, and you will always consider the worst-case scenario." Edward takes a deep breath, ignoring the odd look on his friend's face. "And if you know which it is, how many people's lives or how many buildings that have been there for centuries have to be at risk before you decide to dive into that mud and try to defuze the son of a bitch?"

Hedley Bennett leans back in his chair, a slight smile on his Clark Gable face. His movie-star mustache has become quite impressive during his time at APG.

"Here's the thought process, Edward, old pal," he says. "Maybe I knew I could save a dozen people if I took a big risk on a touchy job. But if the odds are too high against me, how many other potential lives would I be saving if I decided instead to evacuate and blow the damned thing up in place and not risk the life of a BD captain...me...who might live to defuze a hundred more devices and save thousands of lives and plenty of other old buildings farther down the road?"

"All very good points," Edward admitted. "But what about luck?"

Bennett considers his answer before speaking. "There's no such thing as luck, I'm tellin' ya. I'd rather be lucky than good any day of the week. Still, you're a damn sight luckier if you are ready."

"How so?"

"Luck happens when you've been working your ass off learning everything you can and need to know about BD. Then something happens, and because you're ready, you know exactly what to do. That's my kind of luck." After lighting a cigarette, Hedley places the pack of matches squarely in front of Edward. "That should be your kind of luck, too."

"I get that. Some Roman philosopher called Seneca said something like that a couple of thousand years ago." Edward screws up his face as he tries to recall the exact words he once read. "Yeah, okay, I think it goes something like, 'Luck is what happens when preparation meets opportunity.'"

"Captain, you're smarter than you look," Hedley admitted. "What you're really saying is that lucky people create their own luck. They're confident in their skills. They listen to their gut. Good instincts will buy a bunch of luck. You've got quality instincts, Edward. Pretty sure that's why you're here and not digging coal out of the ground."

"How would you describe yourself, Captain Bennett?" Another out-of-the-smoke question, but clearly one Edward had been contemplating.

"A BD man. A damn good one. How would you describe me, Captain Hume?"

The Kaboom Boys 77

"A good friend," Edward said, without hesitation, and smiled. "You've helped me tremendously, and for that, I am forever grateful."

"Well, thank you. The same goes for you. And let's hope 'forever' is a long, long time. Not ten weeks in." Hedley sits back and thinks for a moment, his hands behind his head. He suddenly reaches over and flicks Edward's forehead with his thumb and index finger. "We're gettin' way too damn philosophical by now, don't you think? But do the job right, be prepared, be confident, and save yourself so you can save many others. That's my answer."

Edward slowly stands, his balance wavering just a bit, and allows himself a big smile.

"That is, of course, the correct answer, Captain, to my question about what you would be willing to die for. Now, as our RAF compadres like to say, I am totally pissed and would appreciate it if I could lean on you back to base."

"I'm pretty pissed myself, Captain Hume, but I'll do what I can for my fine friend," Bennett offers. He stands, wobbly as well, and puts his arm around Edward's waist. "But I won't kiss you good night. I have my standards, you know."

They are not the first buddies to lean on each other while leaving Al's this night. Not the first to say their goodbyes over cold bottles of Pabst Blue Ribbon. They won't be the last.

From behind the bar, Al snaps off a sharp salute in their direction as they depart. Then, when they are gone, he shakes his head and smiles wryly. Not the first or last ones to go off to win the war by themselves either.

"And Hed?" Edward asks as they make their way in tandem through the mist of the chilly night.

"Yes?"

"Promise me you'll consider the odds, every time."

"I damn sure will."

"And be careful. Be careful 'til I can get over there and give you the opportunity to lean on me. Got that?"

8

Theirs was a far from glamorous job. Though several of the men in Edward Hume's squad—the Kaboom Boys—claimed to have chosen bomb demolition because it seemed romantically dangerous, they soon learned it was mostly digging into peat and mud to find unexploded munitions, always aware it could be a tick away from erupting. Dealing with bombs or artillery shells that failed to go off when dropped from planes or hurled by big guns would soon become their lives. Or digging more holes in which to blow up the guts carefully removed from the bombs. Or preparing nasty ammunition dumps—a collection of dangerous, unstable explosive devices of various types from booby traps to mines to grenades to bombs—to make them safe to detonate on the squad's terms, not when the junk ordnance decided to go boom on its own with deadly, destructive results. Those jobs were easily the most frightening. At a munitions pile, a direct hit or an unstable device down deep inside a crevice could suddenly go off on a hot summer day, slinging out-of-control, sparking projectiles, fragments, and debris a shocking distance, leaving carnage and death in its wake.

German bombs or shells frequently bored into the ground more than fifteen feet deep without exploding. In the process, the lethal projectiles veered off at odd angles into the earth when dropped from high altitude. Some simply failed to detonate mechanically or chemically. They were

The Kaboom Boys

duds. Others had been deliberately sabotaged, built to fail by forced laborers who had plenty of reasons to go against the Nazis in the only way they could. Other bombs were specifically designed by scientists to have delayed detonation or anti-tamper devices to increase the chances of killing more people. And especially BD men, whose job it might be to neuter the device.

First task was to locate and uncover the hulk without causing it to suddenly detonate. They were almost always located in a populated area, a city, town, or village, or sometimes they were dropped in error near where a farmer lived with his family and his cows and goats. Everyone and every living thing had to be evacuated and that process completed before work could begin. The digging had to be done by hand, using shovels and picks, to avoid disturbing what was still likely a lethal combination of metal and TNT. Many detonators contained a condenser that could hold an electrical charge for days, weeks, months, years—remaining lethal even for centuries. Though some bombs had not exploded when dropped by an aircraft from thousands of feet, the devices could be so hair-triggered that they blew up if even slightly jostled. A clap of thunder or the scurrying of a mouse exposed even the most skilled BD men to a sudden and final fate.

The Allies knew that German scientists were inventing increasingly sophisticated methods to kill Allied bomb demolition technicians. That was the primary goal, but they also hoped such evil would at least cause BD techs to hesitate or make an error while digging the devices out or trying to neutralize them. Regardless of the size or inherent danger of a device, after Edward accomplished his job, he wrote a detailed report. It described the device down to the final screw or pin. Attached would be a series of photographs showing details of each device. For the Kaboom Boys, those photos were taken by Corporal Hank Anderson, using his US Army–issued thirty-five-millimeter Leica single-lens reflex camera that always hung from his neck when he was on duty. And most times when he was not.

There was usually no other way to get at UXBs but dig them out by hand. As they excavated, muddy water often filled the gulch they were carving out and pumps were used to try to stay ahead of it as they dug deeper. The hand-operated pumps the squad used were only good down to about thirty feet, and the hoses were often clogged by mud and rocks.

Wooden boards were required to shore up unstable walls and hold back potential cave-ins. There were soon tales of BD boys being buried alive when the timbers failed. Such conditions resonated with Edward, who could easily compare all this to life—and death—in the coal mines back home. Inhospitable and inherently dangerous places. The Kaboom Boys would hear harrowing stories from other soldiers who had witnessed those types of accidents.

Once the device was found, a stethoscope-like instrument was lowered to listen for any ticking sound. When the part of the bomb that contained the fuze was visible—usually they were located near the nose of the device and sometimes only viewable by using a mirror on a long pole—and once it was reasonably accessible, the squad captain cozied up to the device. "Made passionate love to it," some described it. His task was to determine what kind of nefarious mechanism was programmed to command it to blow up. That was the fuze. Once reasonably certain of that detail, he proceeded to try to neutralize it without waking the giant.

By the time Edward and members of his squad arrived in England, the Germans had begun to employ an anti-disturbance fuze that used a very sensitive mercury switch. If an armed bomb moved even three or four degrees, it was likely to detonate.

Sometimes defuzing the bomb involved pumping into the detonator's interior some "neutralizing fluid," a substance that prevented internal electrical circuits that would set off the bomb from allowing current to flow. The liquid was really little more than anti-freeze and salt, induced into the fuze under pressure from a typical bicycle tire pump. Only then could the bomb's guts be removed so the fat bastard—the weight sometimes more than two tons—was ready to be safely lifted from the sucking muck and hauled away.

Glamorous? Romantic? Hardly. Dirty, wet, cold, and constantly treacherous was most often the case, but that image would not have been fodder for the recruiting posters or pitches.

As they worked, the Kaboom Boys spelled each other as they used the implements of the trade, three or four shoveling while the others either climbed out of the hole to smoke or moved far enough away to avoid dirt clods or shovelfuls of heavy, sticky clay as they were being tossed upward to the rim of the hole. When they initially went to work, and depending on the complications of the job, they were often accompanied by Royal Air Force engineers, men who had been doing this type of nasty but necessary work since the summer of 1940, almost four years earlier. That was when the first Luftwaffe bombs began dropping on Great Britain. The RAF BD crews and the new US Army trainees who survived continued to do it. The ones who failed were missing a limb or two or did not live to learn from whatever mistake they made. The best survived, the careless did not, all in a very Darwinian example of survival of the fittest.

Even as their numbers increased and training improved, the BD boys did not get to all possible UXBs. It was still a common occurrence to have a farmer blasted to heaven or a centuries-old church or quaint house near a stretch of railroad to be abruptly blown from the face of the earth when an undiscovered dud decided to detonate weeks or months or years after first being deposited on British soil by a German Junkers Ju 88 or Heinkel He III bomber.

For the most part, the Brits and the BD boys got along just fine. Many, like Ace Taft (Scottish) and Hank Anderson (Welsh) were of British heritage, with considerable pride in their lineage. They now shared a potentially deadly duty, of course. Sometimes the "What took you Yanks so long to come join the party?" argument got out of hand, either in a mudhole or a tavern. More common was a bout of fisticuffs after several rounds of beers when some American soldier paid undue attention to a particular young English lady. Everyone was also aware the Americans made more money with their hazardous duty pay than the Brits did, and that was a source of friction. But when on the job, they all shared the chill, the dampness, the mud, the stress, and the peril. A common enemy, too.

As they worked, the talk among Hume's boys was usually of life back home, parents, cars, previous jobs, sports played and favorite teams followed, the reasons they signed up for such a glamorous, romantic job, and, of course, girls. Corporal Hank Anderson, son of a dentist, chose to work in a Denver service station, against the wishes of his father, who desperately wanted his boy to go to college and become a dentist, too. But when his parents divorced, Hank suddenly dropped out of high school and went to work pumping gas, wiping windshields, checking oil and tire pressure, and flirting with the older women who came in for a fill-up. He bragged, as he shoveled muck and manhandled pump hoses and those one-by-six timbers, that many of those women with whom he flirted still regularly wrote to him, including a few who filled their letters with romantic poems and sent him cigarette-and-candy-bar money. And they came in envelopes even more aromatic than the ones Captain Hume received from his gal back in coal country.

Private Carl Kostas had his own Hollywood story. He had worked at several film studios back home, usually as a stagehand or carpenter, and had fallen hard for and moved in with a young starlet named Noreen. But when the relationship ended badly, he found he could no longer land jobs on the notoriously gossipy film sets and had no place to go but home to his parents. They had moved back to Birmingham, Alabama, to open a Greek diner there. He did not want to wash dishes for them, so he joined the Army instead. And he picked BD for its air of danger and adventure, like that exemplified in the roles of his favorite movie heroes.

On one unusually nice day, the squad worked at an excavation site in a sheep pasture adjacent to a railroad spur. The job was to uncover what had been reported to be an unexploded five-hundred-pounder. The talk inevitably turned again to girlfriends.

Somebody asked Gene Wozinski why he never talked about his girl-friends back in Chicago. "Guess I just never was interested in girls," he told them, blushing deeply. "Too much trouble, too giggly, too expensive," he hastily clarified.

Woz quickly diverted the reaction to his reply by asking Ace Taft the question several of the men had openly pondered among themselves when the sergeant was not around.

"Sarge, how come you never talk about all those gals you must've romanced back in Jersey? Good-lookin' bloke like you?"

Ace had been taking a break, sitting on an empty ammo box at the top of the dig, smoking, soaking up rare English sunshine.

"I had a girl," he finally responded. "We had this big fire and explosion at the floor wax factory where she and I worked. She was a secretary in the front office. She didn't make it."

For a good three minutes, there was no sound but the slap of the mud

The Kaboom Boys

clods hitting the grassy ground at the top of the hole. It was Edward who finally broke the awkward silence.

"Nobody curious about my former life?" he asked. The mood needed modifying, and Edward knew it.

"Yeah, Captain," a grateful Ace urged. "Tell us about it."

"Well, by day I was a clerk for a US congressman. At night, though, I worked in a factory," he said as he gingerly probed with a non-magnetic brass rod into the sludge to try to determine the integrity of the casing of the bomb. "Shirt factory with a bunch of grumpy old men too old to go to war. And a flock of ugly-as-homemade-sin, tough-as-nails women running a bunch of antique sewing machines. We made expensive shirts for the swells in New York City to buy in those Fifth Avenue department stores. Nothing any of us would wear. Or could afford to buy." Edward now had his cold hands in mud and water up to his elbows, blindly feeling for the detonator access on the bomb. He would have to decide soon whether to try to defuze the bomb in place or just go ahead and blow it up where it had burrowed in. The pump was straining to stay ahead of the seeping water. "When I left, they had just gotten a big order for army fatigues. We may be wearing some of them now. But all that work just made the old men grumpier and the sewing machine women more man hungry. They wouldn't leave any of us young guys alone, but we knew their husbands would kill us and dump our carcasses in the quarry. Believe me, boys, I'd rather be in this mudhole with a squad of smelly men and a ticking German bomb than back there doing that shitty factory job with those old gals grabbing for our peckers every damn day."

The men laughed heartily, the solemn mood broken. His face devoid of emotion, Ace flipped his cigarette butt into the pile of clay, climbed back down the ladder, took the shovel from Pete Ronzini, and began digging.

Digging with what appeared to be a spirited vengeance.

♠

The next day before sunrise, Edward, Ace, and Hank were holding an impromptu powwow in the mess hall over day-old coffee and rubbery pancakes. The captain had just heard that Hedley Bennett and his squad had finally reported in. But they were down two men. The two had tangled with what was supposed to be a small, simple booby-trap device, left in an ammo storage facility, likely by a German saboteur. But Edward knew there were no "simple" devices. He was relieved to know Hedley was okay but unnerved that two men from his squad had died.

But Hume was pleased with how his own squad—and especially his two top assistants—had bonded and seemed to like each other. So far for the Kaboom Boys, it was no runs, no hits, no errors.

"Ace, what's your story?" Edward asked right out the chute, addressing the one man he was still not quite sure about. As a newly minted manager of men, Edward felt it vital that he knew everything he could about his crew members before they left the RAF base and crossed the Channel onto the Continent. No one would be safe there. They would be tested at every moment. Ace and Hank were the two he would depend on the most. The captain wanted all the cards on the table. Ace was up.

"My bag tells my story, sir," Taft answered, happily enough. He pulled his big and ever-present equipment satchel from beneath the bench and set it down heavily on the table.

There, sewed to the side of the canvas bag, was a patch from BD training at Aberdeen Proving Ground, another emblem depicting a silver wreath wrapped around a bomb from the Royal Air Force, and one that showed a fire truck, ladder, and hydrant, labeled in an arc across the top with the words *Camden Fire Department.*

"Basic training at Fort Jackson, then APG, then here for two months training with the RAF," Taft said, reciting his résumé. He proudly pointed to the fire department patch. "I was a fireman, too. You see, I was working at a floor wax factory there in Camden. We had an explosion and fire. Lots of people died." His voice tightening, Ace paused to clear his throat.

"That was a tough thing," Hank Anderson jumped in, giving Ace a sideways glance and a slight nudge with his shoulder. The two men had spent enough time together to become friends already. It was clear to Edward, too, that Hank knew this story well, and that he was afraid Ace was about to share too much too soon with their new squad commander. "Damn tough bit of business. But you found some good…"

"Yes. Yes, it was. That's when I decided I wanted to be a fireman, you

The Kaboom Boys

know. A way to help save people in trouble," Ace continued, his voice once again strong. "Same thing with BD. I thought I could maybe do my part to help end the war quicker and get back home, you know? I learned a lot with those fire guys and the department that I think will make me a good BD man. I could have stayed back as an essential worker, but I never could have lived with myself."

"I'm sure you will be, Ace," Hank added, nodding.

"And I want to be an officer, sir."

"Good. I like ambition. I'd like every man to want to become a leader. Why didn't you go OCS when you signed up, though?"

Ace took a long sip of the oily-black coffee and swallowed before answering.

"I did. I was a track-and-field guy and played soccer in high school. The recruiter said they craved athletes. Had good grades, especially in science. I was class president. Key Club president. Then, you know, a fireman. All the things the Army was looking for. But I didn't pass muster at APG. They said I lacked a command voice. It's funny, sir. I always had a strong voice until the explosion. My ma told me I changed after that." Ace looked down at his hands, folded in his lap. "Command voice? What the hell does that mean, anyway, Captain?"

Edward thought for a moment. "I guess somebody felt you weren't ready for command. Damn subjective reason to reject a guy who has all the other prerequisites for this kind of duty, though." Hume could see in Taft's face just how much this failure nagged him. "Look, you have a chance to prove yourself now. We'll work on that command voice of yours. And if you have what it takes, I'll sure as hell go to bat for you."

Taft smiled. Smiled with his lips but not his eyes. "All I can ask for, Captain. 'Preciate it."

Hank Anderson had a slight smile on his face as the conversation shifted to his backstory. Of enlisting after Pearl Harbor. His father reluctantly signing papers since Hank was only seventeen years old. Fixing trucks in the motor pool until a BD slot opened up.

"All right, guys," Edward said, wrapping up the meeting. "We probably got a hole to dig halfway to China. Let's go round up the boys and see how we can best kick Hitler's ass today."

9

So far, based at the Royal Air Force station in Doncaster, South Yorkshire, the Kaboom Boys had done nothing but scores of the same kinds of jobs over and over. There was still no word regarding when they might actually go to where the war was the hottest. There were rumblings, scuttlebutt. It was no secret that Eisenhower and the Allies were contemplating some kind of major move to try to turn the war. But scuttlebutt was all it was so far. They got up each day, did PT—physical training—ate breakfast, then went out on jobs that were exciting at first and then became mundane.

On this morning, the squad, except for Edward, was gathered around a table in the chow hall. None of them were eating.

"Damn cold biscuits again," Pete Ronzini groused. "I'd give my left nut for a bagel and cream cheese. Right, Morty?"

"Kosher," he replied. "Nothing's ever kosher here."

"This bacon's still squealing," Hank noted, holding up a limp piece of greasy meat. "How the hell does Eisenhower expect us to defeat the Hun on nothing but fat and gristle?"

The men looked up as Edward approached the table and stopped just long enough to say, "Eat up. We got night compass tonight after drills."

There were grumbles. Night compass exercises were the most confusing and maddening field ops a soldier would ever undergo. The objective was

The Kaboom Boys 87

for them to find—at night—specified geographic points, using only a compass, flashlight, and map. Most got lost, requiring them to be out all night on a drill that should only last a few hours.

The captain motioned for Hank to follow him, and they left. But not before Edward tossed out his usual, "Got that?"

"Got that?" Morty shouted after the two departed. He then turned to the rest of the men and, annoyed, asked, "What is it with the captain, anyway. Got that? Got that? Got that?"

Carl shoved his untouched grayish, cold, powdered eggs away. "Yeah, and why are we still training? Marching all over creation. I thought we graduated from that once we left basic."

Ace Taft jumped to the captain's defense. "Look, fellas, the captain is just doing what he's told and trying to keep us sharp and in shape is all."

Pete leaned close to Morty and stage-whispered, "How much the captain pay his tech sergeant to say that?"

"Ace is the captain's number two, which makes him a spy in my book," Morty shot back. "A real Mata Hari."

"Without the nice breasts," Pete noted, elbowing Morty, who finally allowed himself to grin.

"You turds know I'm correct, right?" Ace snapped back.

Gene set down his coffee cup. "Am I the only one who notices the captain don't like to talk about back home? 'Cept maybe for the other day in the pit with all that shirt factory stuff."

"Think about it," Pete offered. "The man wanted to leave that garden spot of a town and the coal mines and two good jobs so bad he signed up for BD and a chance to be boss of the likes of us. It was 'cause he wanted to get out of the clutches of that gal and her old man. Cap'n ain't stupid."

"Not sure he got away from the gal a'tall," Carl said. "You smell those letters he gets from her? That stink lingers like mustard gas."

"That smell don't bother me," Gene said. "Sure beats the smell of sulfur and cordite."

"Still got to wonder," Pete added. "Man with a future, working for a congressman who could pull some strings and keep him out. I think the man has a death wish or something. Just hope he don't take us with—"

"Hush," Morty interrupted. "Here comes Captain's number three."

Hank Anderson had entered the mess tent and was running their way.

"Let's go, boys. Captain needs us. It's an emergency!"

Just as they had drilled so many times, the squad raced to where the red-fendered jeep and the Dodge weapons carrier truck—also adorned with bright red fenders—sat waiting. Ace hopped into the jeep's driver's seat and cranked it, revving the engine. There was the neat "Kaboom Boys" sign in the corner of the passenger-side windshield. Gene quickly had the truck engine running as well while the others scrambled into the back of the vehicle and began inventorying the equipment, just as they had practiced so many times already.

Within seconds, Edward came running toward them from a nearby building.

"Ace, you and me, we're going to the runway." He turned and shouted to Wozinski, "Go find a place to dig behind the main hangar. Get busy on a hole at least a couple hundred yards from anything important. We'll need a big one. Big enough for the guts of ten nasty bastards!"

"Yessir!" Wozinski saluted smartly, ground the truck into gear, and raced off toward the big, flat area behind the air base's huge hangar. Typical assignment. Dig a deep hole in which to place UXB fuzes so they could be safely detonated. Gene was skeptical. He was already beginning to suspect that this was nothing more than another drill. He expressed that opinion to Hank Anderson, who sat next to him in the truck cab's passenger seat. Hank merely shrugged. The drill was busted already because their captain had told his squad photographer and documentarian to go to a field half a mile from the alleged incident, not close enough so he would be able to get decent photos. But they went on at near top speed to do their captain's bidding.

Drill or real. Mock-up or not.

Edward and Ace could see a column of thick, black smoke directly ahead of them. As they drew closer, there it was.

"This is going to be interesting," Edward observed, his eyes focused down the runway. "A plane on fire."

A B-26 Marauder two-engine medium bomber was resting in the middle of the runway, almost to its end. Pilots and crewmembers were sprinting away from their distressed aircraft. Smoke and flames gushed from its cockpit, but the rest of the plane appeared to be fine. This landing strip was different from most in eastern England. It was more than nine thousand feet long, running due east-west, and five times the standard width to allow distressed planes returning from missions a better chance of landing safely on something flat and solid. Aircraft that had been damaged and were coming in on a prayer. The runway was almost constantly under repair after crashes, fires, and various explosions had made a mess of things.

Now, Edward could see that other bombers lined up into the distant sky were aborting landings, optioning for some other nearby strip. Others were coming in short, making certain not to get close to the smoking bomber. With crashes, typical weather, and volume of traffic, it was common for warplanes of all types to have to find an alternate place to set down when returning from missions.

Ace veered the jeep to the right to flag down one of the fleeing flight crew and ask him a few questions. Edward did not like his breathless answers before the guy took one look back at his burning plane, turned, and ran on. Ace gunned the jeep and charged directly at the aircraft from which everybody else was fleeing.

"Sir, that is not good," Ace said, checking out the smoke. A former fireman was adept at assessing a situation immediately upon arrival. "Smoke that black means a volatile fire. It could be deadly to breathe."

"She's got ten five-hundred-pounders aboard," Edward yelled. He was already reaching for gas masks stowed beneath his seat. "Long as the fire doesn't reach the bombs, we got a chance. But we got to put out that fire before we can deal with them."

"Why in hell do they come back home with a full complement of bombs?" Taft asked. "And armed already!"

"Used to be not to waste any, but we got more than we can drop nowadays," Edward answered. "They're jeopardizing every landing strip in England doing it, though."

"Where's the damn firemen?" Ace asked.

"On another job."

"Bigger job than this?"

"Bad crash on the other side was what they told me at HQ. Several dead.

They probably don't want to have to deal with this fire, either, with that load of bombs and all the ammo she carries," Edward concluded. "All they told me is she's loaded, the bombs are armed, and the fire is hot. It's our baby, sink or swim!"

Ace gave him a worried glance, then turned his attention back to the windshield and the rapidly shrinking gap between them and the plane.

They parked the jeep a hundred feet behind the burning bird, ran to the small square hatch on its left rear fuselage, put on their masks, and climbed inside, into the smoky interior. At least the two Pratt & Whitney engines had wound down, but the wind off the sea was just enough to cause the smoke to swirl all around the aircraft.

First, using their field jackets and then a couple of blankets from a stack they spotted back near the dorsal gun turret, they began furiously beating out the flames. "When all else fails, improvise," Colonel Kane always said. No other choice here.

They finally found one fire extinguisher in the thick smoke, and Ace used that, too. The fire still seemed mostly contained to the cockpit instrument panel, the seats where the pilots rode, and the padded walls around the cockpit. But it had found enough kindling to gin up an amazing amount of thick, choking smoke. Gas fumes from the fuel tanks were the usual culprit in cockpit fires on the B-26, mostly on takeoff or landing. This one had been landing, back from a mission aborted most likely due to weather—or whatever glitch ultimately set off the fire in the cockpit—and still hauling its load of bombs and plenty of .30- and .50-caliber machine gun ammo.

As Edward and Ace knocked down the last of the flames, they noticed the conflagration would soon have begun cooking off ammunition in the front bubble below and in front of them had they not so quickly controlled it. That could have been very bad for the two of them.

Meanwhile, in the field behind the hangar, four of the Kaboom Boys had been busily digging a hole in the soft ground, using their picks and shovels. Hank stood on the roof of the truck, attaching a telephoto lens to his camera, which he had quickly mounted on a tripod. He was no longer miffed that he was not close-range, looking over the captain's shoulder with his camera. No, there was no Nazi ingenuity or ill intent to document here.

It was "one of ours." But when he saw Hume and Taft running bravely toward the burning plane, he realized he had plenty to shoot, even this far away. The first thing he saw through the long lens was the captain and Ace flailing away at the flames. They were just visible through the cockpit windows via the attached lens.

"Jesus! They're putting out the fire with their jackets," Anderson reported, loud enough for the men in the hole to hear him. "Now I see some fire extinguisher chemical."

Carl Kostas stopped digging and looked toward the smoke. "That thing's gonna blow," he pronounced loudly. "And we damn sure better duck, even way over here."

But soon it became apparent the two BD men were winning this phase of the battle. Even with primitive firefighting tools, the flames were soon extinguished. Now, there were other dangerous challenges for them. Ten of them.

As Hank watched, Ace and the captain dropped down from the hatch of the B-26, Ace carrying his heavy tool bag, and circled back beneath the bomb bay. There, as Anderson began doing a spirited play-by-play for the diggers, Edward dropped his own tool bag and began manually cranking open the doors of the forward bomb bay above him. The fleeing crewman had promised him there were no bombs in the aft bomb bay.

As Edward cranked, one of the bombs suddenly dropped through the opening, punching Edward hard in the shoulder. Instinctively, he managed to reach out and give Taft a hard shove from beneath the falling five-hundred-pound weapon or it would have certainly crushed him. But the combination of Edward's lifesaving push and a glancing blow from the bomb caused Ace to hit the cement runway face-first and hard, his helmet careening off into the tall weeds nearby.

"Jesus Christ! Looks like a five-hundred-pounder fell out and hit the ground hard," Anderson reported. "It did not detonate...obviously...but it may have hit the sarge. He's down." Hank peered harder through the lens. "Damn bomb's rolling over. It's gonna roll right on top of...no, it stopped. Looks like one of its tail fins stopped it."

Edward instinctively tried to grab the weapon when it began to roll toward Ace. He could never have stopped it. But thankfully it got snagged on one of its tail fins and halted on its own. And it had not exploded when it hit the cement runway. He first took a look at the bomb to confirm it was armed. The casing was painfully hot. He glanced at Ace, who was lying motionless on the ground. He would have to wait, though Edward did jerk away the sergeant's gas mask to give him more air.

"We're in a pickle, Ace," Hume calmly said, even if he was certain Taft couldn't hear him. Calm. A trait Edward did not remember working to develop. It just came naturally to him and had been valuable in other situations, even as a kid. Here was another opportunity to put it to good use.

If the bomb was armed and active, it could explode any second. So could any of the others still inside the plane.

"Ace, I gotta go in there and take a look," he shouted. Taft did not move. "If you can hear me, if you're there, help me when you're able."

The captain climbed up until he could begin quickly checking the other bombs inside the belly of the Marauder. Armed and activated five-hundred-pounders, chemical based, delayed action, with apparently no anti-handling devices. Their hulls were even hotter and had been jostled out of their cradles, subject to falling to the runway as well. Each would have to be defuzed before they could be moved. And it would have to be done quickly.

Edward looked out the bomb bay, down to the runway. "Ace! You okay? I really, really need your help!"

Taft suddenly sat up, shaking his head. Blood streamed down from a wicked gash at the hairline above his forehead.

"Just a scrape, Captain."

Edward climbed down and stepped over to where the sergeant sat.

"Blink for me, Ace." Try as he might, Taft could not blink his eyes. Definite sign of a concussion. Edward pulled a handkerchief from his coveralls pocket and wiped blood off the sergeant's face. Ace grunted with pain, grimaced, then began furiously blinking his eyes. Edward smiled. "Okay. Help me if you can. Then we'll get you seen about."

Edward dodged then as Ace violently vomited. Another sign of a concussion.

Ace wiped his mouth with a sleeve. "I'm better now. Let's get this done. You know you can count on me when you need me, Captain."

The Kaboom Boys   93

As quickly as they could, they began unscrewing the covers and ripping out the fuzes from each of the bombs. Meanwhile, Hank continued his description of what he was seeing through his camera lens as the rest of crew dug away.

"There's a bomb on the ground, right next to them. Ace's up and helping, so he ain't dead, but he's got a rag tied around his head, and it's bloody. Boy's been hurt. They're defuzing the bomb. The one on the ground. Now, they're climbing up into the bomb bay after the rest of 'em. Jesus."

The men had now stopped digging and were squinting at the plane, trying to see what Hank was seeing.

"We ought to go help those guys," Carl said.

"No, you know protocol," Hank told him. "We got our jobs to do. Besides, they're doing just fine without us."

"So far," Carl added.

"Yep, so far."

Sure enough, Ace—still unsteady—and Edward had removed the innards from the bomb that now lay inert and safe on the runway. He had shoved the remains of the fuze into a big burlap bag, and then they climbed back up into the bomb bay.

"Why in hell do they bring them back hot?" Ace asked Edward as they worked. "Why don't they just drop them somewhere out over the water?"

"Orders. That's the only reason. Maybe they think they'll spot a target on the way back and use what they got on something, anything they can claim for the mission. Something besides a big chunk of their airfield and a couple of brave BD boys."

It was delicate, dangerous work. Edward remained quiet as he fidgeted with a particularly difficult pin, got it, then moved on to the next bomb. A plane took off nearby, creating a welcome but dangerous gust of wind. A lone fly buzzed about Edward's face as the air grew even more stifling inside the bomber. He swatted at it, but the insect ignored the threat. Wires dangled. The plane's superstructure popped and groaned in the sunlight. Most of the smoke was gone, but there was still enough to sting their eyes and cause them to cough and sneeze.

Edward worked on. Ace, still dizzy, nauseous, and in pain, assisted as best he could. Several times he poured water into Edward's mouth from his canteen while the captain had both hands inside a bomb.

An hour went by. It seemed improbably longer, as if the clock were running backward. The tension, the gusting wind, and the heat of the sun on the tarmac did not help.

All the while, Edward tried to visualize the insides of each bomb. If one exploded, it would cause a massive blast, involving not only the bomb they were working on but all the rest of them, too. Including the ones he had already defuzed. They were still full of TNT.

"I'm going to make a note in our report," Edward finally said as he shifted to the next weapon, the final one. "The higher-ups in the Army Air Forces need to know there's gonna be more tragedies if this keeps happening. The pilots should drop their loads in the Channel or the North Sea before they try to land after a busted run. We got plenty of bombs these days and don't have to be so thrifty with them. Too risky to bring in a load of armed ones just to save a dollar."

Finally, after almost two hours of hard work, they had rendered each of the bombs safe to be removed by the RAF engineers, someone much better equipped. They gathered up tools and the now-heavy bag of bomb parts, climbed into the jeep, and raced over to the newly dug hole to dump the fuzes in. As the two of them climbed out, the other squad members stared at Ace Taft and the blood all over his coveralls and face.

"Purple Heart for sure," Carl stated.

"Just a scratch," Ace asserted.

"Not too sure about that, Carl," Hank said. "You gotta be wounded or killed as a result of enemy action. This was a bunch of our guys coming back hot. Yeah, our captain and sergeant sacrificed a lot today, but it was a friendly kind of situation?"

"Debatable," replied Carl.

The squad watched all the activity churning now around the B-26. Three fire trucks had just rolled up to make certain all the fire was out. Engineers were supervising a crane and a couple of flatbed trucks as they carefully removed the bomb casings to take them to be inspected. An aircraft tow truck was hitching up to the plane's front landing gear to pull it back to the hangar for repairs. It would likely be flying bombing runs in a few days, thanks to Hume and Taft.

"'Bout damn time those guys showed up," Hank said. "Fire's out. Bombs are about as safe as bombs can ever be. Just some heavy lifting after the captain did the real heavy lifting out there."

Suddenly dizzy, Ace eased down onto the ground, leaned back against a truck tire, and took in what his squad members were doing now. It was the final sacrament. Morty was bringing to Edward a long cord that led to and was attached to the pile of bomb remains in the hole. They were now laced with blasting caps and covered with dirt to tamp down the upcoming blast. The captain quickly hooked the cord up to a dynamite plunger.

"Captain, may I?" It was Gene. "It's my birthday today."

Hume looked at him sideways and with a wry grin. "You've had three birthdays in the last couple of weeks when it benefited you, Gene. But if you say so..."

"Fire in the hole!" Wozinski sang out and pressed down hard on the plunger handle. Everyone flinched even though they knew what to expect. The blast was loud and tossed dirt and mud high into the waning sky. Men working around the Marauder out there on the runway stopped, startled, and looked their way. A flock of starlings scattered, unsure which way to fly. The ground shook. Dirt flew. Dust and debris peppered the sky.

The Kaboom Boys cheered. They had just made an impossible job possible.

"And a happy Dyngus Day to you all, too," Woz shouted.

"Happy what?" Carl asked.

"Dyngus Day. It's a Polish thing, big back in Chicago, in da spring around Lent and Easter. Not really today, but 'dyngus' means 'Monday,' and today's Monday, so it's close."

"Then happy damn Dyngus Day!" Carl yelled.

Edward helped Ace into their jeep—Hank became the designated driver—and hurried away to get the sergeant to a medic for a good look at his head wound. The rest of the men were busily loading their tools and Hank's photo gear back into the truck.

"Guys, you know what I think?" Pete had paused to light a cigarette. With the tools all loaded, the others did the same.

"We probably don't care, but we're about to find out," Morty shot back.

"The captain has himself one big set of brass balls." Pete was the member of the squad who had given Hume the least credit. "Maybe we need to cut the guy some slack. You see the way he ran right out to that airplane, it on fire and full of bombs? Didn't hesitate for a second. I'm thinking we got him all wrong."

"Ace, too," Carl noted. "He hung in there and did his part. Even with his head half knocked off his shoulders."

The men all nodded in agreement as they tiredly took their places in the truck.

"Couple of brave sons of bitches, I say," Pete offered, then added loudly and in his best impression of a northeastern Pennsylvania accent, "Got that? Got that, Schwartz? Got that, Woz?"

As the truck drove away from the hasty dig, they all joined in on a random chorus of, "Got that?" It sounded most like a flock of happy, squawking geese aiming for a landing on a tranquil pond. The Kaboom Boys were headed for a shower in their quarters, shit on a shingle in the mess tent, and a night's sleep before an early call for still more calisthenics and marching in the morning.

Later, the group commanding officer submitted paperwork to have Hume and Taft be awarded the Soldier's Medal, a decoration for heroic action in a non-combat situation. The request was returned to the CO with a note saying the two men were only doing their assigned duty when they ran into that blazing airplane loaded with ten live bombs, put out the fire with their jackets and fire extinguisher, and then disarmed all those deadly devices before they could blow a crater in the RAF's nice runway. Not to mention Ace almost dying when the bomb fell from the bomb bay. Just another day at work, the brass ruled. It was a major disappointment for everyone in the squad, though neither Edward nor Ace would ever complain.

The Kaboom Boys had no way of knowing the details of the things that were at last coming together in a way that would sharply redirect their future. The long-anticipated Allied invasion of France would soon be underway. Then, depending on how that went, the march to Berlin to take out Hitler and his top aides would finally begin. After two and a half years of mostly being on the defensive, the Allies were about to become historically offensive.

Sure, they had heard the rumors. Added plenty of their own from barstools and barrack bunks. But two things they knew for certain.

One was that they would not be among the first to go ashore as part of any invasion force.

The other was that this next phase was coming soon. When they got there, there would be an ungodly amount of UXBs, booby traps, and dud ordnance that would test the BD boys to the limit.

Ernst Alwin is convinced of the righteousness of his mission. Now, squinting through thick solder smoke, he is completing the latest and—he is confident—the most effective of his efforts so far. A bomb fuze that defies its would-be defuzer, showing him wires that appear to go one way while actually going another. Ernst leans back from the workbench and takes a long draw from his Juno cigarette. He smiles. He is a loyal Nazi, even an enthusiastic and evangelistic one, and although his fellow German scientists have declared a link between tobacco and lung cancer, and despite the Führer's well-known hatred of cigarettes, they remain the one vice he refuses to forsake.

Still, the huge photo of Herr Hitler sometimes gives him a knot in his gut. It seems the chancellor is always watching him work from where his image hangs above the entryway to Alwin's personally designed secret laboratory in Dachau. But he does not allow any of the other fifty engineers and scientists he oversees to get a glimpse of such doubt. Grueling fourteen-hour days, seven days per week since before the war officially started, heads down, lined up at long workbenches, the labor necessary to conquer the world never stops.

They are toiling diligently on sophisticated delayed-action devices, smaller but more powerful and innocent-looking traps, most of them based on Alwin's designs.

Hopeful to one day get an audience with the Führer, Alwin's fervent wish—one he had only shared with his wife, Helga—is to one day be personally told by the leader of the German people how much he appreciates the ingenious inventions. Not only the special bomb fuzes designed specifically to kill the demolition men who might attempt to neuter them, making Alwin the nemesis of all BD men. Or the clever explosive devices—what the Allies call "booby traps"—that first attract the attention of curious, souvenir-craving soldiers and then quickly, surely, and inexpensively decapitate them with a small but lethal charge.

There is more, though. Those who oversee his work seem most impressed with Alwin's experiments that promise to deliver malaria via fleas airdropped over Britain. Or Project Dormouse, in which hordes of mice carrying bubonic plague germs would be released in countries who continue to oppose Germany and Italy. These were the sorts of things that could deplete the morale of the people—and especially the stubborn Russians—who would ultimately convince the military to lay down their rifles, remove and store away their tank treads, and become a part of the new European order.

Ernst Alwin feels no remorse about the work he is doing. Damn the 1925 Geneva Protocol that forbade such biological warfare. Damn the harsh tenets of the Versailles Treaty and the Allies who sought to enforce it! What had previous treaties and protocols done but decimate his country and its people? Destroy what had been one of the most vibrant economies on the planet? Chase his father from the coal mines and a career that had once provided a comfortable living for Ernst and his family? As he takes the final puff of his cigarette, he recalls watching people burn money to heat their homes because it was cheaper than burning now-scarce coal.

When Ernst heard Adolf Hitler in person for the first time delivering a powerful message of national pride and the rightful power of the German people, he decided to seek a higher education to land a crucial role in the Nazi Party and, ultimately, help Hitler achieve his dream. That first time as a member of Hitler's audience had been in Berlin. He and his final-year secondary school class had gone there for a physics camp field trip. That was also where he met the pretty, round-faced girl, Helga Graf, who would later become his wife and the mother of his two children. Two life-changing moments the same week! Ernst had boldly asked her to go skating with him at the Sportpalast on their last evening there, but it was closed. The new chancellor, Herr Hitler, was scheduled to speak there that night. Ernst and Helga stayed and listened, and both teens were changed, charged with hope for the advent of a new Germany, for the removal of the hardships of the past, and the reemergence of Deutschland über alles, Germany over all.

Ernst Alwin harbors big dreams beyond bugs and bubonic plague, bombs and booby traps. He wants to contribute to the effort to design ever more powerful rockets than the ones already causing havoc across the North Sea and English

Channel into Britain. He has also heard rumblings of a super-weapon, a bomb so potent that it requires only a single copy to eliminate an entire city from the map. His physics education means he fulfills perfectly the needs of such an earth-shakingly significant project. So do his loyalty and his fervor for the Nazi socialist cause.

But he vows to remain patient and disciplined for now, to put aside his personal ambitions, to continue performing this important work for the Reich. To strike his blows one enemy soldier, one Allied platoon, one town at a time. To cause the so-called bomb disposal heroes to hesitate, to develop doubts, to tremble ever so slightly while attempting to disarm one of his clever devices. That was his way for now to repay the Allies for the bitter misery and disrespect they have unleashed upon him, his family, and all of Germany back in 1919 with the harsh and heartless Treaty of Versailles.

Ernst grinds out the last embers of his Juno in a bucket of sand at his feet and carefully covers it over with more sand. He sometimes wonders what manner of man would volunteer to attempt to undo what he and his colleagues have so carefully prepared specifically for him. Courageous but also deranged at some deep level, for certain. Some are smart, but not nearly as smart as he. His only direct contact with those who are trained to defuze ordnance is with those pulled from the nearby work camp in Dachau—mostly the Jews, the homosexuals, the otherwise useless and disrupting intellectuals—who are forced to become "BD boys." Such conscription is often a death sentence. Involuntary. Unlike the British and Americans BD squads who willingly and foolishly take on such a task.

He knows if the Allies somehow survive and conquer one of his devices, they always document his work, study it, prepare better to defeat it when they see it again. Now, though, he and his comrades are moving to a point at which no two devices will be the same. What neuters one detonator tickles another hidden one with just enough current to ignite it. Though he never gets to view firsthand the results of his work, he hears about it from spies and others. He is confident he knows what it takes to strike a blow, to hasten an Allied surrender.

Ernst Alwin never considers himself a killer, though everything he touches is designed to end lives. Certainly not a psychopath, as the Allied propagandists stubbornly insist on labeling the Führer. Ernst—as is Herr Hitler—is only a soldier in a war against those who fired the first shot in Versailles in 1919. He is doing his duty, eliminating the enemy that threatens the Reich, assuring that his party and people and nation ultimately achieve their rightful place in the realm of global power that has been denied them. And, in the process, assuring that he earns his own well-deserved, lucrative, and powerful place in government and science. That the future will be bright for himself and his family. And for Germany. For the realm, the empire—the Third Reich.

The Thousand-Year Reich!

With two fingers, Alwin retrieves from his tongue a bit of spit and touches it to the tip of his soldering iron. It remains usefully hot, always on and ready. Then he prepares once again to melt solder to wires that are to be attached to the contacts of a tiny switch he has constructed from scrap metal.

But first he looks up and offers a grateful smile and a nod to the giant picture of Herr Hitler. Here Ernst is, the son of a humble coal miner who was given an education and a way forward. A conservative with a nationalist perspective who, like Hitler himself, is not from an aristocratic background at all.

He nods at the huge image keeping watch over him and his work, confident he and the Führer are of a like mind and will.

And for that reason, Ernst Alwin is proud to serve.

10

Tired, sweaty, and dirty—not from defuzing bombs or neutralizing explosive devices but from jumping jacks, pushups, marching in formation, jogging, and a spirited game of touch football—the squad finally collapsed in the middle of the parade ground. Despite their fatigue, they were in especially good spirits. Rumors were everywhere that they would be relocated at any moment to a staging area for a "big event." There, they would prepare for round-the-clock duty, getting ready for whatever was about to happen. The other shoe—M-42 combat boot, actually—was about to drop, and the Kaboom Boys would be on to their next phase.

Pete unscrewed his canteen cap and poured lukewarm water on Morty's head. Schwartz was too bushed to object.

"I baptize thee in the name of Ike, Hap, Winston, and FDR himself!" Ronzini crowed.

"And if I weren't so damn bushed, I'd baptize you in a Schwartz ass whipping," Morty replied, but without much conviction.

"Whoop ass. That's what they call it down south. But 'whoop' is really a British—" Hank started.

Catcalls and groans effectively silenced him.

"Men, I've been thinking," Edward interrupted, snuffing out any spark of dissension. "One of the other captains was telling me about a dance hall in some place called High Wycombe. They have a band and girls and plenty to drink. Seems like a good way to say goodbye to jolly old England. What say you to a mission over there Saturday night?"

Everyone whooped and hollered.

"Just hope we don't get sidetracked by a last-minute job or something," Ace said seriously.

His squad mates jeered until he grinned and held up his hands in surrender.

♠

The dance hall was huge, an older two-story building, set in the middle of an open area in the countryside market town, a part of Buckinghamshire. It was typically used as a gymnasium and for senior citizens to socialize over card games. There was plenty of parking, but Edward chose to put the jeep directly beneath the only streetlight, a dim bulb mounted on the side of a pole. Blackout rules prevailed. Although they could hear music and laughter from inside the hall, practically no light found a way out from around curtains over its many windows, and there was no illuminated sign. But based on the boisterousness, there was fun and joy awaiting them inside.

Wozinski stopped the truck directly behind the jeep, and all the men— except the captain—bailed out, ready to join the party. They looked sharp —and felt even sharper—in their rarely worn dress uniforms.

"Captain, you coming?" Ace asked. "There's a British lass in there with your name tattooed on her rump."

"No, guys. Go on. I'll be there in a minute. Save me the biggest mug of dark ale they got." Edward held up his ever-present leather bag. "I got a quick chore to finish up."

"If it's a behavior report, do it now before we get back," Ace said with a laugh.

Once they were gone, Edward pulled an unopened letter from the bag. He did not even have to hold it to his nose to catch its scent. Everything else in the bag now smelled of Rachel Levine's trademark perfume. He ripped open the letter and read it quickly in the weak light.

"Dearest Eddie," she had penned. "I write this with a painful heart. I am still not sure I will ever forgive you for leaving me. Things continue to change here. Especially for me. Your mother now works at the bar, too. She tells me your checks are a big help. You are a good son, even if not always a good fiancé. Or whatever you are to me now. We talk about you often. You should know that she believes you have done her wrong as well by leaving her and me, giving up a good life and promising future, to go off to fight someone else's war when you did not have to."

Edward gritted his teeth and stared into the darkness. It was a low blow by Rachel to bring his mother into the conversation. He took a deep breath and read on.

"By the way, your old friend Levi Loftus told me to say hello. He has been a gem. I hope you don't mind, but he has escorted me to several socials at the gym. At least I have someone to talk to and dance with who is nearer to my own age. And Daddy has offered him a position at the factory so he can leave the coal mine as soon as the war is over."

Edward again stopped reading and closed his eyes. He rubbed his chin. No reason to read between the lines. Her message was loud and clear. Oddly, though, he felt nothing. No jealousy. No sense of loss. In truth, he had left Rachel Levine behind long before now.

Besides, her words relieved some guilt he had been feeling for the way things had gone. In truth, Levi was probably a good match for Rachel. A widower with boys to raise. Someone who would be ecstatic about working for her father. Even converting to Judaism would likely not be as much a stretch for Levi as it would have been for Edward, a devout Lutheran.

"Oh, someone else says hello, too. Sarge! It is so funny that he still waits on your porch every morning for the walk to Doc's office. And it's pitiful the way he whines and carries on when you don't come out your front door."

Now she was even dragging his dog into her message. Still more odd, those last few sentences were far more disturbing to Edward than the obvious "Dear John" message in the previous ones. Sarge. God, he missed that critter!

He pulled out a sheet of paper and a pencil and began to write. He started telling her about their nickname, the Kaboom Boys, and how it served to instill confidence and build morale. How the squad was bonding, feeling like a "gang," as Pete liked to say. A special club, members only, and how much they had come to respect him as its leader, despite his inexperience and quick route to rank.

"Just what I have needed all along from you, too, Rachel. A little bit of faith in me and the decisions I make would have helped us both. Let's hold off on any future decisions about us until I return. Unless, of course, you want to end it now. I will get through this, and that is my number one priority every single day. Simply surviving and doing my job the best way I can."

He started to write more but stopped. Her words had prompted him to respond honestly. That was something he had resisted doing since the very beginning of their relationship.

The sound of the band and the laughter from inside the dance hall were calling to him. It would be good to finally let loose a bit. He put the paper and pencil back into his pouch, shoved it under the jeep seat, and headed off in search of happiness. In the happy light inside, locals, soldiers, sailors, and airmen could forget the war and get back to being themselves.

The band was playing a lively version of "First Jump." Out front on the stage, a nattily dressed and enthusiastic Black man led the group and played a cornet. The live music was sensational, a welcome diversion. The room felt warm and welcoming. It was all motion, filled with dancing American servicemen in their dress uniforms, soldiers, sailors, airmen, and an impossible number of beautiful English women of all ages. He saw few British military uniforms.

"Hey, Captain, you're missing all the fun!" Pete greeted Hume when he stepped into the bright room, then steered him over to join the others. They stood just outside all the merriment, scoping out the joint. A group of British nurses still dressed in their regulation navy-blue rain capes and white caps, walked by, headed to change in the ladies' room. Pete grabbed Carl in a mock bear hug to keep him from following them right on into the lav.

"I hear the English lassies fancy us Yanks," Carl offered, employing a very poor British accent. One of the passing nurses winked at him. "She could give me a sponge bath anytime."

The Kaboom Boys

"British soldiers despise us 'cause we make more money than they do. And the gals know that, too," Morty said.

As confirmation, a Royal Scots Guard soldier standing nearby grumbled loud enough for the BD boys to hear him over the music: "Overpaid, oversexed, 'n' over here!"

Gene did a double take as the soldier nodded at him.

Morty, Ace, and Carl quickly had dance partners and were feeling the throb of the music, bringing the girls up to date on the latest steps from America. Gene and Pete held back, idly tapping their feet to the beat.

"We may have to dance with each other," Gene told Pete, flashing a broad grin.

"I'm not much for dancing," Pete admitted with uncharacteristic shyness. "And especially with people who have peckers. Maybe we'll find somebody who just wants to talk. Or something."

"Yeah. Maybe so."

As the band leader kicked off the next song, Johnny Mercer's "G. I. Jive," dancers swayed with the captivating music, even shouting out the lyrics. Laughter and uninhibited fun diminished the uncertainty in all their futures. A youthful exuberance filled the smoky air. Dancers showed off their moves with abandon. When the song ended to thunderous applause, the band leader smiled and shouted into the microphone with a genuine Jamaican lilt. "Thank you. Thank you. I'm Leslie Thompson, and this is the Leslie Thompson Band. Thank you for making us feel at home. Welcome! There are so many Americans here tonight, we thought we'd play something to get you 'In the Mood.'"

Edward had wound his way through the crowd to the bar where Hank had a mug of beer waiting for him. The captain took a big swig, downing almost half the brew.

"Hank, that was exactly what I needed right about now," he said, wiping the foam from his lips with his uniform sleeve.

"You okay, sir?"

"Oh, I just got one of those letters. My girl. Her father. My family. Even my dog. They still don't get why I'm here and not there." Edward downed another big swallow of the ale.

Hank grinned. "My family has practically written me off. Everyone except my dad, who still bugs me to death in every letter about school 'n' shit. He has no clue what an education I'm getting here." Hank watched his squad mates out on the dance floor. "Sir, is it that 4-F thing, still?"

"That and you know that old saying about absence making the heart grow fonder?"

"It was, I think, a Roman poet that first said that, yeah."

"Well, it ain't necessarily so." Hume's next drink was a sip. He was already feeling warm and a tad dizzy. Really should have eaten those cold beans and hash back at the mess hall.

"Captain, you don't mind me asking, but do you really love that gal?"

Edward smiled. "Honestly, Hank, I really don't know anymore. She needs a white picket fence, a yard full of pink babies, and a nine-to-five husband. That's not me. I want something more. Not sure what, but something way more."

Hank smiled. "You know what they say. It's better to be alone than with the wrong one. Especially for us BD men. And I sure as shit have no idea who said that."

Up on the stage, the spiffily dressed Black cornet player kicked the band up a notch, really getting into the insanely popular "In the Mood." The crowd enthusiastically rode the wave.

"That guy is good," Edward noted with a nod toward the stage.

"That's Leslie Thompson. He's from Jamaica," Hank shouted to be heard over the music. "Used to play with Louis Armstrong. Couldn't get into the British Army band because he's colored."

"Damn, I've heard of him. They used to play some of his songs on KDKA, the Pittsburgh station that came in at night on the radio...," the captain was saying, but then noticed he had lost Hank's attention completely. A gorgeous redhead, probably about twenty, had cozied up to the corporal. She homed right in on the BD patch on his uniform sleeve.

"You're one of those new BD boys," she said in her alluring British accent. "I'm Charlotte. 'Sweet Charlotte,' they call me in these parts."

"And have I told you how much I like your parts, Sweet Charlotte?" Hank asked without missing a beat. She was already swaying against him in time with the Leslie Thompson Band. Edward was duly impressed with Anderson's clever pickup line.

The Kaboom Boys 107

Neither Charlotte, Hank, nor Edward noticed a couple of obviously drunk British soldiers who had entered the hall and were standing at the periphery of the undulating crowd. One average height, the other really tall. The frowns on their faces revealed their disapproval of what they were seeing.

Pete was now doing his best to dance with a lovely, petite young woman. He had admitted to his dark-haired partner that he did not know how to dance. He tried to get her to go out there with Woz instead. Woz declined.

"I told you, I don't know how to dance," Pete explained to her again.

"You will when I'm finished with you," she told him, eyes wide and smiling beautifully.

It was an awkward dance at best, but the young lady was more than happy to just be held tight and move about with him as she did her own unique version of instruction. Ronzini quickly decided it may not be dancing that they were doing out there, but whatever it was, it was not bad at all. More like lovers'-lane parking but on a packed dance floor.

Pete was just about to invite her to step outside for a smoke. Or something at which he was more adept than dancing. That was when he realized someone was casting a dark shadow over them. One of the British soldiers. The one who stood more than two meters tall—six feet, five inches in height, nine inches taller than Ronzini—and whose breath was enough to make Pete woozy.

"Eh, Yank, she's with me, you see," the Scotsman growled as he grabbed the girl's arm.

Pete stubbornly held onto his partner, looking his challenger up and down. He wore a kilt, the dark blue, black, and green tartan of the Black Watch, long known as fierce fighters. He turned to the girl. "What's your name, gorgeous?"

"Rose."

Pete turned to the soldier, bravery enhanced by several beers and the intoxicating proximity of Rose. "Well, mate, maybe you should oughta ask Rose who she's with."

With that, the soldier tried to pry the petite lass away from Ronzini. That brought the lady to life. This was likely not the first time she had been in the middle of two Allied troops fighting over her affections.

"Bloody hell no, Angus! Get your meat hooks off me!" she screeched, then jerked away and ran across the dance floor to join her girlfriends at the far end of the hall. Rose knew very well what came next. So did Ace, Gene, Morty, and Carl, who had now formed a line behind Pete. The show of unity did not phase Angus. He was angry or inebriated enough to believe he could take on the squad on his own.

"I'll gie ye a skelpit lug!" the tall Scot threatened.

"He's threatening to punch you in the ear," Ace translated. He had heard the phrase many times on the soccer fields back home.

With that, Angus launched a powerful roundhouse punch in the direction of Pete. Though he felt the wind from it, Pete easily ducked the swing, then gave the big man a sharp, breathtaking fist to the diaphragm. It was enough to make Angus go wide-eyed and wobbly, on the verge of toppling like a felled tree. But then there was another person joining the fray. The other kilt-wearing soldier, the shorter one, appeared to be twice as drunk and even angrier than Angus. He had pulled from somewhere a shiny and threatening blade.

"Knife!" several in the crowd shouted.

Only then, when light reflected off the steel and the crowd wisely moved away from the impending melee, did Leslie Thompson and his orchestra stop playing. The mood had been broken. Trouble was imminent.

"Bloody Yank bastard," the man with the knife yelled. Angus was still trying to find breath but managed to swing again, wildly, dangerously, but not close to anyone.

Ace looked up at him and asked in his best burr, "Angus? Yer Scottish, then?"

The big soldier looked puzzled. "Aye. I be from Glasgow. What of it?" Then he launched another fist, this one in Ace's direction. Taft also successfully dodged it.

"My family's from Loch Lomond," Ace calmly explained. "The bonnie, bonnie banks..." Then, as Angus squinted, pondering the point, Ace threw a powerful punch of his own that landed squarely on the Scotsman's snout, sending him reeling and big drops of blood flying all about. "Maybe ya will think twice before brawlin' with American BD boys!" Ace told him, his

Scottish accent becoming more South Jersey as Morty, Gene, and Carl looked on, impressed.

At the bar, Edward had been trying to ignore Hank and Charlotte, who were now about as close to intercourse as two clothed people at a busy bar in a crowded dance hall could be.

He could see that most of his guys had found a girl by now. Only Gene Wozinski appeared content to nip at a beer alone and observe the action from a shadowy corner.

Damn glad I issued condoms to the lot of 'em, Edward thought. It looked now like it could be one of those nights. He wanted to be sure his squad and the young ladies of England were all properly protected.

Now, Hume's back was to his squad and the dance floor. He was watching the bartender with professional interest, admiring his skill, when he heard the commotion on the dance floor.

"Captain! Trouble!" Gene came running up to inform him, then went back to help.

Sure enough, several of his squad members were tussling with a tall, lumbering Scottish soldier—now climbing back to his feet, bleeding liberally from the muzzle and patting down his pleats—and trying to get a huge knife away from another much shorter and equally drunk trooper before he did some real damage. Then, to add to the tempest and turmoil, the door suddenly burst open and a contingent of Royal Military Police, whistles shrieking, descended onto the dance floor. Edward was several hasty steps ahead of them, already on his way to help his men. He turned to see if Hank was still behind him, but he was nowhere to be seen. Nor was Sweet Charlotte.

"I'm fair puckled!" Angus said as he struggled to catch his breath. Even so, he ignored the RMPs and took another ill-advised swing, again at Pete. And again, he missed. This was not Ronzini's first bar brawl. He promptly retaliated with a hard blow to the guy's midsection. It seemed to have no effect.

Somewhere in the tussle, maybe from the knife blade, Carl had suffered an ugly cut on his arm. There was blood. But all the BD men were still battling with the two Scots as the RMPs finally made their way through the crowd and pulled everyone apart. Angus—blood streaming from his now off-center nose—continued to struggle, to try to break free of the policemen restraining him, to get another swing at the shorter but very elusive Pete Ronzini. Everyone skated awkwardly on the blood-smeared floor.

"Lemme go!" Angus was roaring. "Was the fockin' Yanks what started it! See, they's a fockin' mob of 'em against me and Danny here. Fockin' Yanks!"

Pete was moving back toward the big soldier, ready to duck and then punch him one more time for breaking up his rather enjoyable dance lesson. That was when his squad mates—including Hume—grabbed him and held him back.

"Pete, fight's over," Edward told him. "You don't want to get arrested. We need to get out of here."

But Pete was still incensed. He struggled to get loose.

"Cap'n, the damn guy jumped me!" Pete objected. "Rose and me was just havin' a fine time…" He glanced around, looking for his dance partner. She and her girlfriends were nowhere to be seen.

One of the RMPs noticed Edward's rank on his sleeve. "Captain, these boys belong to you?"

"Yes, I'm their captain, and I'll get them out of here straight away."

"Right, then. See you do or we'll be housin' 'em down at the glasshouse for a bit." The policeman noticed the patch on Edward's sleeve. "You bomb demolition?"

"Yes. Yes, we all are," Edward proudly said.

"You blokes are crazy as loons. Bloody barmy. But if you ever want to come over to the King's military, ring us up."

Recruiting in the middle of a dance hall fight?

Edward spotted a side door and promptly herded the squad in that direction. The cool air and spritzing drizzle helped Pete calm down some. Carl wrapped his arm in his handkerchief but nodded he would be okay. Ace had a worthy knot on the side of his head from a glancing blow somewhere in the scrum, but he assured everyone he was fine.

There were sirens then. More police rolling up. RMPs. A paddy wagon. An ambulance. But oddly all were without any flashing lights. The blackout thing again.

Back inside the hall, Leslie Thompson had the orchestra wound up again, playing "Boogie Woogie Bugle Boy." And the dance floor was filled once more, ignoring a drunk British soldier who had passed out in the middle of it and still lay there. Someone had expeditiously mopped up the blood. Apparently such gory fights were not out of the ordinary at this town-run establishment. They seemed well prepared to deal with such occurrences when people were together like this. People who had no idea what their immediate future might hold.

"Jesus, I can't take you boys anywhere!" Edward exclaimed. "What were you thinking, Pete?"

It was obvious now that Ronzini was beyond tipsy.

"Didn't start nothin', Cap'n," he replied, words slurred. "Just dancing with Rose, the future mother of my children, and that man of a mountain came after me, and it got ugly when I took exception."

"Pete, we can't afford this. Being stupid lucky worked this time, but next time you might get gored and killed," Edward warned. This must be how a parent felt. Protective of his children. Edward realized he was actually worried about the kid from Brooklyn.

"Didn't start nothin'," Ronzini muttered. Carl stood beside his squad mate, holding his bandaged arm and nodding his agreement.

"True, Captain," Carl chimed in. "Bastard was just pissed that an American was dancing with a British girl was all. No appreciation at all for us and what we're doing for them over here."

"And the other one came at Carl with the knife," Morty added. "Lucky the bastard was so drunk or he'd probably cut Carl's head off. And Carl's too pretty for such a thing to happen."

"He sure is," Gene Wozinski threw in, looking seriously at Kostas. No one seemed to notice.

"Okay, okay. Now, where's our boy Hank?" Edward said after quickly conducting a mental roll call in the dark. "I lost track of him when the battle broke out inside. Gene, see if you can find Hank before the RMPs change their minds and lock us all up for the night."

Gene first stepped to the open side door of the dance hall and looked inside. Only joy again in there. The orchestra, the troops, the girls all acted as if nothing had happened. The police had dragged the guy with the knife off the dance floor, and they were still struggling with Big Angus over near the main entrance, trying to tow him out to the police van. But no Hank anywhere inside the dance hall.

Woz made a quick circuit around the perimeter of the big structure, looking behind vehicles and in dark corners of nearby buildings, calling Anderson as loudly as he dared. Maybe Hank was hiding, afraid the skirmish had gotten worse. But that would not be like him. He was usually near whatever was happening. But he was the youngest of the squad after all and not familiar with bar fights. There were plenty of couples in the shadows doing what couples do, but no Hank.

Then, when Gene worked his way back to where they had parked the jeep and truck—someone had apparently knocked out the dim overhead streetlight—he finally spotted Anderson. And the girl from the bar that he was now getting to know much, much better. Woz headed that way without hesitation. He had his orders.

Hank was sitting in the jeep's passenger seat. Charlotte was on his lap, facing him, her legs straddling him, and her skirt pulled up to the tops of her thighs. Her bloomers were in the driver's seat. Hank had a hand on each of her exposed breasts. They were kissing. And just as she had been doing at the bar, she swayed rhythmically back and forth on his lap.

"Psst! Psst! Hank!" Gene whispered, hoping that would be enough to separate the two. They ignored him. Or couldn't hear him over their heavy breathing. "Hank, tell your friend it's time for her to bug off. Boss says we gotta!"

"I'm really, really busy, Gene," Anderson responded, breaking the kiss off just long enough to respond to him.

Wozinski turned his back so as not to see more of what was going on in the front seat of that BD jeep.

"Tell him to bugger off, Henry," Charlotte added. She, too, was breathing hard, perspiration dripping from her brow. "It ain't your fight in there, Henry."

She never broke rhythm as they once again locked lips.

"Look, Hank. There're RMPs and paddy wagons everywhere. We hang around, who knows? We gotta go!"

"Okay," Hank finally said, mostly as a groan, and Gene then trotted away, back to where the squad recuperated and waited for him and Hank to show up.

Charlotte continued her back-and-forth motion, perfectly in time to the music that once again spilled out into the night from inside the dance hall. "Sweet Charlotte, I guess...we'll just have to...finish this...after the war."

"We may not be alive after...the war," she said, now panting huskily. "We'll...finish it...now. Now. Now!"

"Yes. Yes. We will!"

When the squad members returned to the jeep a few minutes later, Hank was standing next to it, fastening his last buttons. Charlotte had gone back inside.

"Loverboy, you missed all the action," Morty told him.

"Henry, here, had his own kind of tussle, I suspect," Gene added. "Either one of you injured?"

Anderson ignored them. "You okay, Pete?"

"I didn't even want to dance," Ronzini explained. "That gal, she dragged me out on the floor. Next thing I know, a Neanderthal ape was punching at me."

"The Neanderthal man was not actually an ape. He was a—" Hank began but the squad, to a man, hooted him down.

"Guys, we owe the captain for keeping us out of the lockup while the RMPs sorted things out," Carl said, a bit of blood oozing through the gauze on his injured arm. Everyone agreed. "And way to go, everybody, backing our guys up."

"I don't think the locals like GIs dancing with their girls," Pete said.

Edward nodded. "Obviously. And they're still mad we didn't jump right into the war the instant Hitler started bombing them day and night."

"Timing's everything," Hank said with a satisfied smile. "Much as I would have liked to have been in there helping you boys, I wanted to do my part for international relations."

Across the lot, medics were loading the smaller of the two drunken soldiers into the ambulance while RMPs continued to struggle with Angus, trying to get him into a paddy wagon. The big soldier waved his fist in the general direction of the BD squad.

Pete Ronzini sighed. "Rose was one cute gal, though. I knew a girl looked a lot like her back in Bay Ridge."

"Worth gettin' your head cut off over?" Carl asked.

"Surprised you didn't get laid right there on the dance floor, 'Pretty Boy' Kostas," Pete shot back. "You were on track when the fighting broke out."

"I had my eye on a couple of them," Carl said.

"A whole bunch of them were eyeing you," Ace Taft noted. "I figured I was about to get caught in the stampede, not in a fistfight."

"So much for a nice, relaxing night out at a dance hall social for the BD boys," the captain told them. "But Carl's right. I'm proud of your teamwork in there, men. We all pulled together when we needed to."

"When we gonna have our next relaxing night out, Captain?" Ace asked. "This one got cut short, you know."

Hume did not offer an answer. He just motioned for Ace to crank up the jeep so they could be on their way. Sordid, unseemly, bloody, whatever had just happened, he knew, had brought his squad closer together.

That could only be a good thing.

11

"Up 'n' at 'em, boys!" the captain shouted as he roused his squad. "We're moving! C'mon, youse guys! Moving day!"

June 1st, 1944. Hume had gotten the orders late the previous evening. For some of the squad, it was old hat. The Army had moved them all about England, working with members of the RAF doing different kinds of BD jobs, soaking up and applying all they learned. But there had been some full-blown missions, each also rife with danger, in small towns, villages, and along beaches laced with heathland grasses. This next move, they knew, was going to be different. And certainly not long term. They were to relocate an hour south, to AAF-489, an Army Air Forces base in Lincolnshire, near Leeds and Sheffield and the North Sea. All leaves, passes, and days off were cancelled. US Army Military Police were to seal off the base and allow only official-business entry and exit. That confirmed for them that the next time they picked up and moved was going to be a big deal. Things had suddenly gotten even more serious.

Based on multiple intense briefings, Captain Edward Hume knew most of what was planned and the events that would likely take place, but he was the only one of the Kaboom Boys who did. He was forbidden from sharing any details, including the fact that the secret briefings had even taken place. At one point, he was asked to step into a room and give a short update on bomb disposal unit readiness. Among those in the group was General Dwight Eisenhower. It was easily the most top-secret wartime event in history. Diversionary tactics to convince the Axis powers that the invasion was still a long time away, or that it would occur at this place or the other and not the real location, had been both extensive and clever.

Those included inflatable war-machine decoys and a phantom army—part of a grand deception not-so-secretly known variously as Operations Fortitude, Quicksilver, and Bodyguard. Names allowed to be discovered on purpose by the enemy to try to fool clandestine listening ears and spies. Eventually General George Patton was placed in charge of the diversionary plan. He was someone considered by the Nazis as the "most aggressive panzer-general of the Allies." He was the one American general that the German high command feared more than any other. If Patton was in command, those operations were certainly real.

The plan eventually worked to the extent of diverting Axis attention away from Normandy, saving countless lives and finally providing the Allies with a foothold in Europe. But on the day Edward awakened his squad and prepared them to make the move—as part of the second wave, not the first —all those plans were merely a hopeful strategy, on paper and in the works, not yet applied.

Overall, the D-Day invasion force included 7,000 ships and landing craft manned by almost 200,000 naval personnel from eight countries, landing more than 160,000 Allied troops at Normandy, of which 73,000 were American. There were also just over 83,000 British and Canadian forces who landed on Gold, Juno, and Sword beaches. Many men arrived after D-Day to continue the fight. Allied casualties on June 6th have been estimated at 10,000 killed, wounded, and missing in action: 6,603 Americans, 2,700 British, and 946 Canadians. That was only the first day.

Other than watching how their captain was reacting, the Kaboom Boys relied on observation, telltale hints, scuttlebutt—as usual—and educated guesses by fellow soldiers. Then, with all the frenzied rushing about, it was obvious to them that Operation Overlord, the largest invasion of Europe by the United States and allies, was imminent. They also learned that their new temporary base would be one of the prime takeoff points for the highly trained paratroopers of the 101st Airborne Division, climbing aboard

The Kaboom Boys   117

C-47 Skytrains bound for the invasion zone. Wherever that might be. The Screaming Eagles, as the paratroopers referred to themselves, were especially tight-lipped about it all. They, of all people, wanted to keep the Germans guessing. But they were the primary reason for all the lock-down secrecy at Lincolnshire, not the presence of a bomb demolition squad or two. They would be dropped behind enemy lines—their first and only drop in battle—a moment for which they had trained for eighteen months. Half those men would be casualties on D-Day.

If the Germans knew what was going on at those key air bases, they would have launched brutal attacks. Precautions were extreme, just in case. Edward and his squad were even ordered to pile sandbags high around the jeep and truck in case bombs or rockets should begin falling.

Then, late on the night of June 5th, as Hume's BD squad sat on empty ammo boxes outside their barracks, smoking, talking, and watching C-47s take off one after another and roar overhead, they still could not tell exactly in which direction they were headed. It took the aircraft a while to get into formation. They only had their red navigation lights lit to avoid colliding during the process. It was also spitting rain and there was lightning in the distance, not a good night for flying in close formation. The planes were overloaded with paratroopers, many with their heads shaved except for a long patch of hair down the middle, Mohawk style, and their faces covered with black greasepaint. They were off for somewhere and to an event that would be mentioned in history books forever.

As the BD squad took bets on the destination of the aircraft and paratroopers, Edward sat in the darkness nearby, leaning against a flagpole. Despite the raindrops, he was perusing by penlight papers that were boldly stamped *TOP SECRET: EISENHOWER*. Though he was drinking his tenth cup of coffee of the day, he soon fell into a vertical nap, head against the steel pole.

He was dreaming a recurring dream, one that included Sarge, loping along beside him as he and the dog trotted up Overlook Hill in hopes of seeing Rachel. But the more he ran, the faster he jogged, the farther away her big house became.

"Come on! Hitler's not gonna wait for you, pal!" The voice was gruff, and the tap on Edward's head was painful. Neither were part of his dream.

Message delivered, the paratrooper ran on toward his Dakota ride. "Time to go!"

Edward checked his watch. 12:28 a.m., June 6th, 1944.

Those paratroopers were a part of an unprecedented middle-of-the-night invasion force and the largest use of airborne troops ever employed in warfare. Their primary job was to seize airfields and bridges ahead of the arrival of the primary beach-landing forces. Later, they would be joined by about 133,000 more men. And one woman. Foreign war correspondent Martha Gellhorn, wife of fellow war correspondent and writer Ernest Hemingway. She had, in defiance of her husband, found a way to cover the operation. She went aboard a hospital ship prior to the crossing, supposedly to interview nurses, then stowed away when the vessel left for Normandy. She then went ashore on an LST serving as a water ambulance, assisting medics in getting wounded soldiers back to the ship and filing reports as one of the few journalists on the beaches that day.

D-Day. Operation Overlord. The Kaboom Boys now knew it was underway. The Germans soon would.

As it turned out, the weather did hinder considerably the efforts of the paratroopers. Many drifted off course into the wrong locations and fell victim to German troops, especially snipers. In addition, five hundred powerless planes—gliders—were towed in and cut loose over enemy territory to soar down and deliver later in the day about 4,000 more reinforcements and communications personnel. They, too, encountered much resistance when things did not play out as planned. Despite setbacks and failures, the invasion did catch Germans off guard.

Once most of the paratroopers were gone and the growl of plane engines was no longer audible, Captain Hume stood, checked his watch, and ran off toward the tent that housed the Sixth Ordnance BD Squadron of the US Army Air Forces for the latest briefing. Along the way, he encountered still more paratroopers hurrying the other way.

Seems I'm always swimming against the tide, Edward thought.

Later that night, Edward learned he could finally share with the squad some of the details on which he had been briefed. The whole world would know it soon, anyway. The Dakotas were bound for the Cotentin Peninsula, a spike of land jutting out into the English Channel on France's northwest coast.

By the time he got back to their bivouac area, he found his squad soundly sleeping after a long day prepping gear, packing the truck, and getting the vehicles ready for a beach landing. He hated to interrupt all that snoring since sleep had become a precious commodity, but he had plenty to share with them. He banged his canteen with a spoon.

"Wake up, beautiful dreamers!"

Grumbling and grousing, the men groggily rose out of their cots. Flashlights flicked on.

"Cap'n, this better be good," Ronzini growled. "There's six of us and one of you, you know."

"Thought you'd want official confirmation, boys," Edward said, happily ignoring Pete's threat. "Operation Overlord is underway. We're invading German-occupied France right now."

"What? D-Day?" Hank questioned, now wide-eyed and awake. "Damn. D-Day!" They had known something big was happening. But some of them still thought it might just be a drill, preparing for the real thing when the weather was better.

"You know those paratroopers you've seen running around with their makeup on?" Edward asked. "They're dropping out of the sky on the Nazis right about now."

The squad hooted and hollered. D-Day, as far as they knew, meant the war would soon be ending with victorious Allied troops marching through the streets of Berlin. But Ike had gone ahead with this thing in such bad weather?

Edward quieted them down and handed Ace a sheet of paper, telling him to read it to the squad. Ace cleared his throat while looking at the top line.

"Geez. It's a message from General Dwight D. Eisenhower..."

"Louder!" Edward told him. "I want youse men to hear this."

"A message from General Dwight D. Eisenhower," Ace started again, louder, but with tears in his eyes. "Soldiers, sailors, and airmen of the Allied Expeditionary Force! You are about to embark upon the Great Crusade, toward which we have striven these many months. The eyes of the world are upon you. The hope and prayers of liberty-loving people everywhere march with you. In company with our brave allies and brothers-in-arms on other fronts, you will bring about the destruction of the German war machine, the elimination of Nazi tyranny over the oppressed peoples of Europe, and security for ourselves in a free world."

Ace Taft's voice cracked with emotion. He swallowed hard. He was the Scottish-born son of immigrant parents. European immigrants.

"Go on, Sergeant," Edward told him.

The paper shook in Ace's hand as he read on. "Your task will not be an easy one. Your enemy is well trained, well equipped, and battle-hardened. He will fight savagely. But this is the year 1944! Much has happened since the Nazi triumphs of 1940 through '41. The united nations have inflicted upon the Germans great defeats, in open battle, man-to-man. Our air offensive has seriously reduced their strength in the air and their capacity to wage war on the ground. Our home fronts have given us an overwhelming superiority in weapons and munitions of war, and placed at our disposal great reserves of trained fighting men. The tide has turned! The free men of the world are marching together to victory! I have full confidence in your courage, devotion to duty, and skill in battle. We will accept nothing less than full victory! Good luck! And let us beseech the blessing of Almighty God upon this great and noble undertaking."

Ace lowered the paper and looked at the faces of his squad mates. Then he added, "May all of us here make it through. And remember that while we're on this side of eternity, we must do what we must do!"

Except for the distant droning of a flock of C-47s headed for France, it was quiet around the cluster of tents as light rain fell. Then, in unison, they all yelped and cheered.

Edward finally waved to the men to regain their attention. But not to dampen their exuberance. "Okay, listen up. This base is now completely sealed off. I know you all know that, but I was ordered to say it again. No letters home. No information whatsoever shared with anybody. There are spies everywhere. Our orders ship us out day after tomorrow to AAF Station 519, High Wycombe. Buckinghamshire, headquarters of the Eighth Air Force. Not far from where we fought the battle the other night at that dance hall."

"Not Normandy yet, sir?" Hank asked.

"Not just yet. But starting tomorrow, we got two full days of getting ready." Edward checked his watch. "Well, starting today, as it turns out. Get some sleep if you can." He paused. "And if you are of such a mind, say a little prayer for our fellow BD boys among the first wave ashore and soon to be in occupied France. Guys like my buddy Hedley Bennett and his squad."

For the next few days, the BD boys could only sit and wait, listening to the radio when they could, knowing their day would come very soon. Not even Edward knew the precise day. And wouldn't until the night before they were to go. They did have strong evidence they would be going to France. They were issued so-called "funny money," fake French francs to use as necessary, and a small guidebook to help them navigate that country.

The night before they were set to depart, and as the squad members checked and rechecked all their gear for a water crossing and beach landing, they decided they needed to do something to symbolize their unity and determination. During a poker game, someone suggested they all get tattoos of the ace of spades from a deck of playing cards.

"Perfect," Morty Schwartz proclaimed as he laid down a flush and claimed a sizable pot. "We use a spade every day digging out UXBs, right?" Everybody groaned at the thought of having a shovel permanently tattooed on their bodies. Nobody worried about losing their "funny money" to Schwartz. They doubted they would have opportunity to spend it when they got to France, anyway.

"Geez! It's not that kind of spade, Morty," Hank Anderson chimed in as he tossed down his handful of useless cards. Carl covered his ears with both hands. Gene moaned as he rolled backward. "No, really. From medieval times, the spade on a card deck represents a leaf from the tree of life. It can stand for air and valor, but in the tarot deck it means darkness and death. I'd say we want no part of that."

Someone pointed out that one regiment of the Airborne troops had already adopted that for their symbol—a totem they claimed represented both valor and good luck—and they had the symbol stenciled all over their gear, including their helmets, as well as tattooed on their bodies.

As typical, Ace Taft had remained quiet during the discussion, but he finally had a suggestion. And a rare full-face smile. "I still like the spade.

Especially the ace of spades. And not just because my dad gave me 'Ace' for a nickname when I was four. My baby brother couldn't say 'Alistair' and called me 'Ass' instead. Dad figured Ace was a better choice."

Everyone laughed, including Taft. Another rare thing for him. But several of the squad members liked Ace's idea. Hank shot it down immediately. "Good nickname, Ace, and for damn good reason, but the ace of spades has also been associated with bad luck and death since the early 1800s. Wild Bill Hickok was holding one in his 'dead man's hand'—aces and eights—when he got shot in the back, murdered in that saloon in Deadwood, you know. We love you, but maybe we consider something else."

Ace looked disappointed, but even he—along with everyone else—agreed with Hank's logic. Plus, they decided, the symbol already belonged to the Screaming Eagles, so they should look for something else. Finally, they all agreed—including Captain Hume—to forego selecting any specific symbol for the time being. Instead, they borrowed something else from the paratroopers. They decided they would all cut off their hair. Not as permanent as a tattoo, but it made a statement just the same.

Pete Ronzini was something of an amateur barber, so he did the deed on everyone, then Morty Schwartz returned the favor for Pete. They were all pleased with their new appearance. They thought it made them look like Indian braves, ready for war. Everyone but Carl Kostas, that is. He instantly regretted leaving his curly locks—the ones that had grown out so nicely since basic training and invited lustful looks from every girl he met—lying there on the ground outside their tents.

"I'll never get in the middle of one of those French gals without my hair," he moaned, and would continue to gripe about it until it eventually grew back, thick, curly, and blond as ever.

As for Edward, the first thing he did when he found out for certain when their deployment was coming was sit down on the cot in his tent and write a letter to his mother. No way of knowing when he might have another opportunity.

"Dear Mom, by the time you receive this letter, you will undoubtedly know from the newspaper what's going on over here, so I won't bore you with all that. And, as you already know, I am not allowed to share any details, anyway. But what I can say is that me and my brave squad leave in the morning to begin the job of mopping up the mess left behind by our courageous frontline soldiers. It is our honor to follow them to the end of this awful war. Morale is good, and I want you to count on this. It WILL end soon, and I WILL come home." His eyes fell on his latest paycheck. It lay there on the cot next to him. "I am also forwarding what will probably be the last check…"

Edward thought about those final three words for a moment. He knew his mom. She would only see that part about "the last check" and burst into tears, assuming a completely wrong meaning to his words. He quickly erased and started the sentence again: "I am also sending you the enclosed check. It may be a while before I have a chance to get another one in the mail, but don't worry about me. We'll be busy and likely nowhere near a mail drop for a little while. But I promise I'll be okay and WILL see you soon."

He touched the tip of the pencil to his tongue, thought for a moment, and then finished the letter with, "I know you and a few others there think my joining the Army was a waste, but I'll prove to you it was not a mistake at all. We are making a difference and saving lives here, Mom. My love to Dad, Tommy, Velma, and that big boy of theirs. (Tell Tommy to wait and allow me to show my nephew the right way to throw a football before he messes up his arm.) Please tell Rachel hello for me, too."

Edward signed the letter with his usual signature, _EddiE_, underlined and with both _E_s capitalized. He tucked it into the envelope with his check, licked the flap, and sealed it tight, convinced he had written a letter that would make his mother happy. Then he held it next to his heart, eyes closed, and took a deep breath.

He only hoped he could keep that promise he had just made to her.

12

―――――――

"'Aven't seen the likes of you for donkey's years, old chap!"

Captain Duncan Smythe, RAF, was nursing a pint at The Horse and Cow, a pub a few blocks from the base, when he looked up and recognized his old friend, Captain Edward Hume, US Army, headed his way through the thick cigarette smoke. It had taken a last-minute assignment from the base commander himself to allow Edward to leave the locked-down facility at such a top-secret time, but Hume had readily accepted the job. After all, he knew the most likely spot where he could quickly accomplish his mission. The Horse and Cow Pub.

"We've been looking for you, sir. And I've been dispatched to find you. We need you back on base. Immediately." Edward was out of breath after jogging to the pub, but he saluted smartly. His orders were to go find Smythe, one of the RAF captains who had been instructing the US Army BD men since the day they began arriving in England. Now, there were questions about a couple of new German devices that pre-invasion scouts had sent back just that day. The Allies needed help from Captain Smythe to oversee the forensics.

Smythe returned the salute without standing, grinning broadly. Grinning, even though Edward had apparently caught him amid deep thoughts about home, family, the choices he had made, and impending, full-force war. The British officer's mood brightened considerably upon seeing Edward. But as Edward drew closer, he was taken by Smythe's disheveled appearance and gray face. He was thirty-five but looked much older.

"Have a set-down, my American friend. Thought I'd come in for a bit of brew, and by jeez I encounter somebody I can have meself a fine chin wag with!" Captain Duncan Smythe was only one of the many colorful Royal Air Force bomb demolition technicians Edward had accompanied on various jobs over the last months, learning and helping in about equal amounts. He was just another one who had taken a great liking to Edward. But Smythe was certainly the one from whom he had acquired the most practical knowledge. And had some of the most intriguing times. The two had shared some muddy, cold, and dangerous hours together. Quite a few pints of various textures of ale, too, once off duty. "Must admit I'm finding myself in a bit of a low mood, so I could use some cheery talk, young Mr. Hume."

"You know I can't talk with anybody about anything, Dunc," Edward told him. "Not even you. You understand? And time's tight."

"I know. I know," Smythe responded. "Finally, a chance for the likes of you Yanks to stop faffing about, leave our lasses to us to properly shag, and go do some real men's work, aye?" Smythe motioned to the full-figured female barkeep for another room-temperature Guinness. She and Duncan exchanged glances that hinted they knew each other well. Very well. Typical Dunc. The man was handsome and charming, much like Hedley Bennett, but in a more cunning way. Edward was intrigued by how a married man like Smythe could do so much philandering without any apparent guilt or worries. "So, we'll talk about beer and women and the weather in Wakefield, then. No complaints from the buggers about those subjects, I don't suspect, right? Krauts don't care. And, while we're jawboning, you might enlighten me on what the hell happened to all your hair!"

Smythe was staring at Hume's new and nearly bald pate. Edward smiled.

"The squad came up with the idea," Hume explained. "Team building before we...you know...do whatever we're doing next."

"Ah, esprit de corps!" Duncan laughed, then lifted his glass and swallowed all the beer that remained. "But you know that's what this fine brew is for."

"Sir, I'm here for a reason. We need you back at base." Edward checked his watch. "Look, High Command gave me only thirty minutes to find you and bring you back. They've happened upon some new German devices they need your expertise on." Edward was already worried about the time and how he might extract Duncan from his chair and walk him back to base. And if he was sober enough to be of any help on the devices. He had been there for a while and apparently consumed considerable Guinness.

Smythe ignored him. "All the same, you may want to put a couple pair of skivvies under your cap 'less you want your follicles to get sunburned this summer or ice over in the winter. Damn hot in Normandy this time o' year and brutally cold by December. So, fill me in on what's been going on, and don't yank me chain."

Edward winced at the out-loud mention of Normandy. He had also spotted something disturbing as Smythe turned up and drained his pint glass. "No time to chat, but maybe you want to tell me what happened there?" He pointed to Smythe's left hand. The pinkie and ring fingers were missing, and there was a bloody bandage around the hand. BD incident?

"Aw, that. Wifey caught me flogging a bar girl. Chopped 'em right off with a meat cleaver. Almost whacked off me bell end, too, had I not been so quick to jump and me cock too tiny to draw good aim." Duncan laughed uproariously. Edward knew his friend well enough to recognize a bit of fiction. The wound had to be painful. "Naw, can't fib to a fibber, I don't reckon. Clipped red when I should've clipped white on a booby trap circuit one of our spies brought back. By the book but the damned thing was wired different. Shows the bastard Nazis are gettin' bloody creative with even their basic circuits. Now, sit down and tell me what you been up to, Captain BD?"

"Not much to tell you, sir," Hume admitted. "Except they need your eyes and brain to help figure out some other new devices. But seeing you're not doing so well, maybe we'll let them figure them out on their own."

"Hey, this is my first medication-by-fermentation in weeks, 'cause of staying busy with all the Luftwaffe duds they're leaving behind," Smythe said, looking mournfully into his empty pint glass. "And this wee bit of a scratch on me hand cramps me style. Good thing I'm right-handed, anyway."

"Sir, I'll explain to the brass you're not in good condition to help tonight," Edward told him. He felt bad for his BD friend and his injury. And for how deep in the cups he was this night.

"Speakin' of new evil," Smythe said, impatiently motioning to the barmaid again for a refill. "The sons of bitches been developing some damn sneaky fuzes lately on their bombs, too. They appear to be like what we know, but they don't work at all the same. We got reports they have a whole lab full of scientists working on exploders designed to do nothing but take out us BD boys. A couple fingers here and a couple fingers there. Lucky if it's just that, right? They're after us, you and me and our squads, Eddie. Only thing we know is they don't have the usual serial number on the cover plate. Just the letter Y or some such cryptic symbol. Subject to change, of course."

"Good to know," Edward said, wishing he had his notebook. But that was not the kind of information a BD captain might forget. "Should we be flattered? We must be getting under Hitler's skin if they're so keen on taking us out."

"Perhaps. Kill us off and it'll be impossible to recruit anybody else to fill our boots. I hear the one running the shop is a wonky-ass egghead what's got a thistle in his drawers for anybody that ain't cheering on Adolf and the SS." Abruptly, another change of subject. "Say, Eddie, you still stringing along that dishy bird back home? She's a beaut from the pictures you showed me."

"Sore subject. But I'll tell you more later. I gotta get back to base or they'll sack me for sure." Edward glanced toward the door. "Besides, I'm not going to be so lucky as you, marrying a rich princess, a duchess, a queen, or whatever she is."

Smythe smiled. "Hardly royalty, but shall we say, aristocratic in a British sort of way. Lilly's the one with the money, though. Truth is, I'm skint as a pauper, Eddie. I had nothing. I deserved nothing. Then I got it all just by standing before the vicar and saying, 'I do.' You're the bloke that passed right on by Easy Street, way I recall. Future father-in-law about to make you head man at his dry goods emporium, give you the key to the place and it's on the same fob with the key to his daughter's chastity belt."

Edward checked his watch again. He had twelve minutes before he had to be back on base. But he knew he might never see Duncan Smythe again.

"Shirt factory," Edward corrected. "I only worked nights there, running presses and ironing. Then clerked, mainly, for a politician by day. Hell, Dunc, that's not the life I want. I'm looking to see the world. Do things that make me feel alive. Tackle shit head-on. Meet interesting blokes like you."

"Hear, hear!" Smythe shouted, slurring his words as he interrupted the hum of conversation in the pub with his loud toast with an empty glass. "To seeing the world, meeting interesting people, and staying alive! And encountering fascinating women, too. Don't forget that one!"

"And to ending the bloody war and bringing back Hitler's balls pickled in brine!" the fetching barkeep chimed in as she slid Duncan a freshly filled pint glass.

The two men looked at her and grinned. Edward clapped Duncan on the back. Others, all of them townspeople this night, happily joined in with a rousing cheer. Edward was having a difficult time pulling himself away from the magnetic personality of Captain Duncan Smythe.

"Captain, take care of yourself," Edward told him. "Then we'll catch up here at the Horse and Cow in a few months, once this damn war is history. So be careful and stay smart...and alive."

"You know my feelings on the subject, Eddie," Smythe said. "I have a craving for a bit of adventure me own self. But you can't fault a man for tempting fate. Even if it's just for the satisfaction of beating fate's ass another time or two."

"We're a lot alike on that sentiment, my friend. Well, I better get back to getting ready for...well, you know..." Edward stopped and winked. Duncan Smythe was an insider's insider and certainly knew far more about the upcoming assault plans than Hume did. Skirting the subject seemed silly. "Doing whatever General Eisenhower and the guys at Sunninghill Park HQ tell me to do."

"Aye, I know, my friend." Smythe was immediately serious. "I'll still be over here taking the oomph out of faulty German fireworks for a bit. Got another shit-pot full of Yanks inbound I'll be obligated to show a

The Kaboom Boys 129

trick or two, just like I did you. Hope this bungled-up hand don't scare them off. I'll just tell 'em I was in North Africa and a camel bit me fingers off. But you take caution. I hear even Eisenhower knows the assault will cost the lives of half the troops hitting the beaches and three-quarters the paratroopers. But they're sending them over anyway." He paused, an uncharacteristic weariness on his face. Then he brightened. "Maybe you'll have rinsed the Jerries soon, young Eddie, and we will enjoy another jar together, next time in peacetime. Or you can come up to the place for some pheasant hunting and meet the wife. And a dozen or so of me lady friends. I wager some of 'em could make you quit pining over that pixie back at the pants factory. One in particular I want you to meet. Dahlia Dahger...like the knife...all the way from India, she is. Pretty. Smart. Can talk politics with any man. She's nanny for our wee lads when wifey is sick, which is most of the time. Good companion for me, too."

"I'll take you up on that, Dunc," Edward said. Smythe seemed to be dealing with far more than a painful, disfiguring hand wound and the ever-present hazards of BD. "You be careful out there in the peat and clay, too. A blowup is a blowup. What is it you always told me? 'Try not to throw a spanner in the works.'"

"Remember one thing, me boy," Smythe told him. "This war is going to come to a conclusion someday. But considering the mess and all that's being left in its wake, our jobs may never end. Got that? Ain't that what you always say, old chap? 'Got that?'"

Smythe stood up, and the two BD men hugged unashamedly, then separated and sharply saluted each other. Smythe was having trouble standing.

"Sorry I'm too far gone to help tonight, Eddie," the RAF man said. "I'll stop by first thing in the morning and give a hand." He looked at the bloody bandage on his left hand. "Poor choice of words, huh, Eddie?"

They both laughed. As Edward turned away, Smythe was already grabbing and cuddling the female barkeep, maybe to keep from falling on his face, but certainly not in the same way he and Hume had just embraced.

Edward headed for the door and the next step in his quest to see the world and meet as many Duncan Smythes as he possibly could in whatever time God had allotted to him. Before he stepped out into the darkness, Smythe called out to him.

"Eddie! Live every moment, old chap! None of us is guaranteed the next one!"

Edward smiled and waved and walked on. Duncan Smythe seemed to always be walking a high wire on a windy day without the benefit of a safety net. Just another person who felt most alive when closest to dying. Hume now realized just how similar in nature the two of them were.

He made it back on base with two minutes to spare. That, he decided, was two minutes of wasted time.

13

The weather was dreadful. A stiff westerly wind seemed determined to push the landing ship right up onto the stretch of yellow-brown sand that had been designated by Allied commanders as Utah Beach. The vessel's crew kept the engine reversed and its twin screws throbbing. Cold waves crashed over the sides of the LST—landing ship, tank—dousing everyone aboard as they prepared to disembark and wade to the beach. It was dark, too. Clouds covered the moon shortly after 0100. When they looked ashore, they could see flashes of artillery in the night sky and even sometimes hear its thunder above the crash of waves against land. American or German firepower, there was no way to tell.

Under the veil of darkness, the members of the Sixth Ordnance Bomb Disposal Squad, Ninth US Army Air Forces, were finally about to join the party on the beaches and in the bocage country of Normandy, France. The guidebooks they had received described the terrain beyond the beachside bluffs as a mix of woodlands, centuries-old hedgerows, and pastures. None of that was visible this night. It was that same quaint landscape that was proving such a hindrance to the Allied forces. Hedgerows were often impenetrable without heavy equipment. The bocage offered a continual obstacle course for advancing troops and a big advantage for the German defenders.

Operation Overlord was still well underway. The going was rough and Allied progress pushing back the enemy agonizingly slow. Though no enemy guns were firing at them for the moment, the landing was still not easy for the waves of support personnel, fresh soldiers, ordnance, and equipment. Troops on the LSTs and other landing craft were weak from seasickness, cold, and miserable. In weather such as this, drowning in the waves was a risk. But the surge of men and equipment going ashore had not abated at all.

After bouncing around in the rough seas for most of the night, the Kaboom Boys and other troops on their LST Mk2 were sapped, sore, and beyond seasick. And it seemed they would never get the okay from the beach master to move in as close as they could get to land, drop the big gate and ramp on the front of the ship, and then make for shore the best they could, some walking and swimming, others trying to drive their truck, jeep, or trailer to dry sand. There were two Sherman tanks aboard, too, and they would have to go first because of how they were loaded. That prolonged the agony.

Only Hank Anderson remained relatively unfazed by the rigors of the crossing. While several members of the squad vomited overboard, he sat on a bench reading a book by flashlight. *The Sun Also Rises*. Ernest Hemingway. At the end of a chapter, he looked up to see a green-faced Ace Taft gripping the rail, hanging over the side, trying not to lose any more previously consumed nourishment into the murky waters of the English Channel. Waters in which the tops of stalled tanks and vehicles could be seen. And a skim of oil and occasional body parts added to the disgusting reality of the place.

"Wonder if this war will change men like it does in this book?" Anderson pondered aloud, but nobody could hear him. "Like Hemingway wrote, will we be a 'lost generation'?"

"What? What you..." But Ace could not finish his question before stretching back out over the top-deck railing, praying the cold sea spray would give him relief. At least he had learned to hang over the leeward side of the vessel so the wind would not blow his bile right back into his face.

"Hey, Ace," Hank called out. "You'd feel better if you read a book, you know. It'd take you to a different place."

The Kaboom Boys

"Hell, I'm in a different place already," croaked Taft. "And I don't love it here."

Meanwhile, Edward stood next to the LST skipper, doing his best to stay upright and not throw up in front of his squad or the ship's CO. He was surprised when the captain suddenly and loudly blew on a whistle and ordered into a microphone, "Prepare to disembark!"

Edward glanced toward the white-topped breakers way out there at the distant beach, at the expanse of water and waves between where they were and where they were going. He had already heard plenty of D-Day stories of soldiers in their heavy gear drowning when LSTs turned them out into the deep water and daunting waves. He faced the skipper, took a deep breath to try to settle his stomach, and made his concerns known.

"Look, there is no way we can make it to shore from here!" Wind whipped cold water into Edward's face. "The tide's too high. It'll drown our guys and stall our vehicles."

"I got my orders, Captain," the LST commander responded sharply, in no mood to argue. He had his perspective. He did not want to remain where he was any longer than required to deliver his cargo. Hulks of blown-apart LSTs were everywhere around them, testament to what the Germans could do from their remaining active gun emplacements, even if they were firing blindly. A few of them could still see their targets and take aim. At a top speed of only about eleven knots, the landing vessels were easy pickings. Stopped and with their bows wide open, disgorging troops and equipment, they invited shelling. Soldiers had already decided that "LST" stood for "large slow target."

"So do we," Edward shot back. "And the first one is to stay alive."

"Captain, you just make sure your men are ready to go as soon as those Shermans are down the ramp and before the damn Krauts get bearing and range on us. Hell, you'd think you didn't know how to swim!"

Edward gave the skipper a fiercely penetrating look. The big front gate of the LST was already being lowered into the surf to become a ramp for men and equipment to vacate the vessel.

"Look, we're loaded down. General Eisenhower didn't train us to defuze UXBs just so we could drown out here in the middle of the Channel," Edward shouted, punctuating his objection by leaning over the side and throwing up again. His men watched, catching fragments of the exchange above the bellowing of the wind and the din of the ship's two General Motors diesel engines. Wiping his mouth on his sleeve, Edward turned back, coughed, and defiantly stood his ground. "I will not sign the manifest until you get this vessel two hundred yards closer and into a hell of a lot shallower water. You got a flat keel and protected propellors and rudder, so I know that you can get us closer. Too many men before us have died this way, and that is not our plan of the day. Got that?"

The LST captain looked at Edward, at the sea in front of them, at the faces of the men preparing to go into the roiling surf. Then he touched a control on the panel next to him. The gate halted its drop, and the ship's engines, which were still revved and in reverse to prevent the wind and sea from shoving them closer to France, immediately slowed to an idle. The vessel then began to edge ahead toward the beach.

Hank sensed the change in the engine's speed. He looked up from his book, then at Ace.

"Captain just refused to disembark," Hank reported. "Whatever he told that chickenshit skipper must've worked. I think he may have just saved our lives, Ace."

Ace clenched his jaw. "For a few minutes, anyway."

Anderson had a point. The men wore over their drab, olive-colored battle fatigues heavy coveralls that had been specially treated to protect them against a chemical gas attack. It was either wear them or carry them. Not enough room in the vehicles to store all the cumbersome outerwear. Leaving them behind was not an option. Someone in procurement had told them it was the stupidest thing he had ever seen. The treatment on the garments had already sponged up lots of water before they ever left the LST. They also were burdened by their weapons and ammunition, steel helmets, and gas masks, plus each man carried equipment boxes covered with waterproofing material. It was almost a certainty, too, that the jeep and truck would be swamped if they emerged into too-deep water. Ace Taft and Gene Wozinski, the squad's designated drivers, would likely have to abandon their vehicles with all their equipment and swim for it.

The radio speaker at the LST captain's elbow crackled angrily. "LST 471

Oscar, why are you coming closer? You oughta be unloading by now and getting that tub outta here straight away."

The skipper lifted his microphone, his face without expression, and simply said, "Engine trouble."

"What kind of engine trouble, Captain?" The US Army beach master likely harbored doubts about the excuse.

"Not sure, sir. Working on it."

The men in the squad looked at each other and grinned.

After a pause, the exasperated voice came back on the radio. "Assess and advise! I got traffic backed up to hell and beyond."

The skipper gave Edward a nod. With the engines gently idling, the wind, tide, and current nudged his vessel close enough that the ramp was soon scraping sand and rocks on the bottom. Then he powered up enough to hold their position and try to keep from being elbowed sideways by the elements. Edward had his men get themselves and their vehicles off as soon as they could, just behind the two tanks.

Grim-faced, the LST skipper backed away the instant everyone was off his ship. Finally, soaked and still woozy, the Kaboom Boys were on reasonably solid ground, or at least something beneath them that did not buck and sway at the behest of salt water and zephyrs.

Only a few brutal days earlier, in the predawn hours and just beyond this three-mile stretch of sand designated Utah Beach, the 82nd and 101st Airborne divisions were dropped. Many did not land in their designated inland locations. Some drowned or were cut down by enemy fire. But the soldiers who did deploy successfully fought house-to-house in the towns, eventually forcing the Germans to retreat. Operation Overlord casualties at Utah, the westernmost beach, were not as grim as the other four landing zones strung out to the east like beads in a necklace: Omaha, Gold, Juno, and Sword. Statistics were not recorded at the time, which made it particularly difficult to confirm fully how many men were casualties. But among the Airborne landings, many of the paratroopers—some of whom Edward and his squad had witnessed racing around the base the night of their departures—did not survive. With over one hundred pounds of equipment on their backs, many landed in low-lying fields that the Germans had recently flooded. Quite a few drowned.

German losses remained mostly unknown.

The scene on Utah Beach was surreal. Spotlights swept back and forth across the sand and bluffs, all a hundred yards in front of Hume and his boys. Those steep headlands had been so much of a deathly challenge to the initial waves of invasion troops. To the squad's left was Pointe du Hoc, where Rangers had climbed ropes hundreds of feet to try to take out enemy guns they believed to be there and aimed down on both Utah and Omaha Beaches. They only found German troops firing rifles at them at point-blank range. The big guns had been moved inland already.

There had been plenty of shelling, though. Back where Edward and the squad came ashore, there were depressions everywhere in the sand from bombing and artillery shells. Most bodies and wounded men had been removed by now, either hauled back to ships on returning LSTs, or buried in temporary graves wherever space could be found. Teams would later identify as many as they could, mostly by dog tags, and find permanent burial spots, but for pragmatic, health, and morale reasons, it was important to get the dead out of sight.

There was still plenty other evidence of what had happened here on D-Day and since. Crushed helmets. Bits of bloody uniforms and fragments of weapons. Wrecks of blasted vehicles, some still smoldering.

Sea spray, foam, and an abundance of black smoke made the night even darker and more otherworldly as it curtained a weak but near-full moon. This was still an active battleground. There were pops of rifle fire and the staccato rattle of machine guns out there in the darkness and the boom and sheet lightning flashes of artillery farther inland. And shouting soldiers everywhere.

"Need a medic here! Now!"

"Bring that ammo! Pronto!"

"Get out of the damn way or get your ass run over!"

With more LSTs lined up, disgorging men and equipment, many of those impatient and often profane yells were being aimed at Edward and his squad as they struggled to get their vehicles out of the battering waves, clutching sand, and onto firm footing while being berated.

"Hey! Get the hell moving and the fuck off my beach," one muscular, no-nonsense beach master yelled.

The Kaboom Boys 137

Heavier than normal from all the webbing and waterproofing, the truck and jeep were mired in cloying, wet muck, their wheels spinning futilely. The men had to put shoulders to bumpers and push to try to get them out of the surf and find traction on dry sand, now only yards away.

"Hey, tanker!" Edward yelled to a sergeant atop the turret of a passing Sherman tank. "How 'bout a pull?"

The sergeant either did not hear or chose to ignore Edward.

A soldier who was working nearby stopped what he was doing and ran over to help. The man appeared to have been wrangling a set of cables tied to stakes in the ground. Those steel cables ascended into the black sky and were attached to big helium-filled balloons floating at staggered elevations above the beach.

With the help of the soldier and squad members, Edward ultimately pushed the truck onto ground that offered enough grip for it to move out of the surf. Breathing hard and sweating despite the cool breeze and chilly water, Hume stopped to catch his wind. He offered the other soldier a thankful slap on the shoulder and a handshake. It was a black hand that accepted Hume's gratitude. About the only Black people Hume had seen in the Army so far served in non-combat units, mostly dishing up meals in the mess tent or handling supplies, maintenance functions, or transportation far from where the fighting was going on. The look of surprise must have been obvious on Edward's face.

"Yep, Negro. I get that same look of surprise a lot around here," the man said. "I'm Corporal William Dabney, sir. Far as I know, the 320th Barrage Balloon Battalion is the only all-colored unit that's come ashore since D-Day. Proud to serve!"

Edward grasped the hand even harder. "And we sure as hell appreciate the help. That's a nice bunch of kites you got up there, Corporal."

Floating above the beach, oval-shaped, silver barrage balloons served as aerial defenses, designed to prevent enemy aircraft from flying close enough to effectively strafe or bomb targets. They were strong enough to actually rip off a wing or knock down a plane if one got tangled in the web of tethering cables or struck the balloon itself.

"Thank you, Captain. Just glad to be asked to do something useful," Dabney told him, smiling proudly, looking up at his balloons. "I'm hoping to catch myself a rogue Luftwaffe wing or propellor tonight. Got me two in our first couple of hours. Beautiful thing to behold. But I'm thinking we might have scared them all off." Dabney had been staring at the vehicles now that their protective covering had been peeled away. "Hey, what's with the red fenders?"

"Bomb demolition unit markings," Edward explained.

"Bomb demolition? Y'all crazy is all I gotta say," Dabney told him, flashing a broad smile. "But glad you're here. Welcome to the party." He started back toward his balloon tethers, then had another thought. "By the way, sir, I got a tip for you."

"We'll need all the help we can get."

"I'm hearing the Germans flipped a bunch of the road signs around to throw you off course. They're telling units to use their compasses."

Edward threw Dabney an energetic wave. "Thank you, Corporal. Now I owe you two cold ones when we get the chance."

Edward and the squad finished stripping off the waterproofing on their vehicles and stowing the equipment they had brought ashore in the truck. Then, as they settled into their assigned places in the vehicles, ready to ride, the same burly soldier acting as a beach master walked past, shouting first at Dabney, then at Edward.

"Get your lazy ass back to work minding them balloons, soldier! And Captain, get the hell off my goddam beach, right goddam now!"

Edward snorted. "Good luck, Dabney. Good meeting you, and thank you again for the push. Remember, I owe you a couple of cold beers next time I see you." Dabney winked. Then, as Hume jumped into the jeep's passenger seat, he shouted at the retreating beach master, "And thank you for that friendly welcome to France, you redneck son of a bitch! Floor it, Ace, before I decide to order you to run his ass over."

They could hear Dabney laughing. Taft obliged, gunning the engine, spinning the wheels, and tossing considerable sand and rocks all over the beach master.

Soon, they were working their way up the beach along a well-traveled but rough roadway where engineers had dropped iron grating to offer better traction in the sand, fine dirt, and mud. A few houses at the top of the bluff had lights blazing, already serving as impromptu medical units,

The Kaboom Boys   139

barracks, and headquarters for the Allies. Most had only recently been evacuated by the Germans, thankfully departing in such haste they had not had the opportunity to booby-trap them. It occurred to Edward that Hedley Bennett's squad had likely been the ones to check them out to be sure.

Edward motioned for Ace to pull to a stop just off the roadway. With his penlight held between his teeth, he studied a detailed map and referred to his compass.

"You're not superstitious, are you, Sergeant?" Hume asked Ace, talking out of the side of his mouth around the penlight.

"No, sir. Too much a realist for that sort of nonsense, I suppose."

"Good. We got a thirteen in our immediate future. We'll work our way south to Route Nationale 13. Then head east," Edward said.

From the jeep's back seat, Hank Anderson said, "Thirteen's unlucky because Judas Iscariot was the thirteenth man at the table at the Last Supper, so—"

Edward waved his free hand, signaling Hank to hush. "Lookit, in two days, we gotta be at Ninth Air Force advanced HQ at Grandcamp-les-Bains...or what's left of the place after the British navy shelled it to a pulp. It's not far, but they tell me the roads have taken some serious hits. And we may have a job or two on the way." Edward pulled his .45 Colt pistol from its belt scabbard. "Oh, and there's the possibility we may catch some static from folks who speak German and are not happy we're here."

Taft nodded. "I think we're all ready for business now, Captain. That full moon helps."

Driving without headlights to maintain blackout, Ace could just make out the road ahead and see across a broad field to his left by the light of the waning full moon. Soon the two BD vehicles were traveling on the narrow, paved-but-damaged road leading south toward the main east-west highway. They were making steady but very slow progress.

All in all, it was a mostly peaceful ride. Fortunately, there were no German bombers overhead. The Luftwaffe was a shadow of its former fearsome self. The cool night air was filled with the sounds of the ominously droning engines of Allied planes bound for targets farther inland in France and all the way to Germany.

Morty Schwartz sat in the weapons carrier's passenger seat, peering out at the mostly dark countryside, his rifle across his lap. "Well, we've been in France three hours now, and I ain't seen a can-can girl yet," he told Gene Wozinski. "All I can tell is we sure as hell ain't in Brooklyn no more."

Gene leaned forward over the steering wheel, nose near the windshield, mostly following the occasional red tip of a cigarette from the captain's jeep in front of them to keep him on course.

"Chicago neither. But I expect we'll get our chance to see plenty of French dirt and trees before it's all said and..." Wozinski started, but as they topped a hill, he could see Captain Hume standing up in the jeep, looking back at them, frantically waving, yelling for Gene to steer right.

"Other side! Other side! Right side! Get to the right!"

Then the jeep vanished.

Wozinski swerved hard right as commanded and simultaneously stood on the brake pedal. There was the sound of crunching metal. Gene smashed his mouth hard on the steering wheel.

"Damn jagoff!" Woz yelled. Behind him, from the truck bed, he could hear equipment shifting, men tumbling and grunting, then shouts of, "What the hell?" and, "Jesus, Gene! You trying to kill us before the Germans can?"

They had come to a muddy sideways halt just off the right side of the road, almost in a deep, flooded ditch. And right next to them, farther down in the trench, was the captain's jeep, which was canted at an odd angle, almost hidden by brush and smoke. Just before the abrupt swerve, Gene had seen the dark shapes of a truck and a convoy of more trucks behind it, stretched out into the moonlit distance, making its way in their direction. Traveling fast—at least fifty miles per hour—and in the BD boys' lane, their headlights also extinguished. That and the hill were why neither of the BD drivers had seen the convoy coming sooner.

As the oncoming vehicles roared on past, horns blaring, hardly slowing, the drivers of practically every one of the trucks had a comment to yell at Gene and Ace. "Assholes! What army taught you BD bastards to drive?" "What the hell you doin' on the wrong side of the damn road?" "Sons of bitches!"

None of them asked if they were okay, though. They just offered their shouted opinions of Hume and his BD squad, their intelligence and heritage, and allowed their middle fingers to finish their comments as they rumbled on toward whatever their destination might be.

Gene used his handkerchief to wipe blood from a busted lip, smashed nose, and the lenses of his eyeglasses after being thrown into the steering wheel and windshield. Hank frowned and rubbed his knee. It had slammed into the dashboard when the jeep came to the hasty halt. Ace appeared then, climbing out of the driver's-side door of the jeep. Edward came crawling out right behind him. They could hear the men in the back of the truck, cursing lustily, trying to get themselves upright, untangled, and out of their vehicle.

"Who's hurt here?" Hume asked.

"Everybody!" It was Pete Ronzini, walking around slowly from behind the truck.

"Anything serious?"

Pete was staring at Gene's bloody lip. "Woz here looks like he's gonna bleed to death. Otherwise, nothing serious, Captain, if scared shitless ain't fatal."

"Okay, pull the truck up a bit, and we'll try to push the jeep out of this ditch without turning it over," Edward told them. "We may have to use the truck to tow it out." Edward Hume looked around at his bedraggled troops, standing there in the moonlit roadway. He grinned. "And guys, my fault. Nobody else's. I had Ace driving in the wrong lane. We're in France now and not England, so we should probably drive on the right side of the road while we're here."

A good leader accepts blame when in error. Colonel Kane, again. If the leader is still alive after the screwup, that is. Several of the men had been giving Ace the evil eye, a couple of them blaming him under their breath for the near collision. Edward could not allow any of his men to be at each other's throat. Not this early in the game. They calmed down noticeably after the captain's words.

Hank threw up both arms in mock exasperation. "Man, all that training they gave us in England," he said. "And they somehow forgot to remind us which side of the road they drive on in France."

Ace had taken a quick survey. "Sir, it looks like everybody will survive. Just a few bumps and bruises and Gene's fat lip and bloody nose."

Hume shook his head. "We haven't even seen a Nazi yet and we probably got two or three of you characters putting in for a Purple Heart already."

"Hell, Captain," Hank Anderson chimed in. "We been in France for a few hours and we almost got ourselves killed twice already! During the landing and now on the road to Tipperary!"

Everyone laughed, including Gene Wozinski, whose lip and schnoz still hurt like hell.

"All right, let's see if we can get the jeep out of this ditch so we can be on the way to where we're supposed to be," Edward said. "Probably somebody's in need of a bomb squad by now, and we wouldn't want to keep 'em waiting too long."

Then he noticed several of the squad looking at him oddly.

"Captain, you may want to take a look at your helmet," Carl Kostas advised.

Edward pulled off his hard hat and inspected it using his pen light. There was a large crease from mid-crown to front rim. Sometime in the wreck something had hit him hard. Hard enough, he figured, that it numbed him. He had not felt or remembered the blow.

"Hmm. Guess these things are good for something besides washing socks and skivvies and lathering up for a shave." He put it back on his head, then glanced eastward, in the direction they were headed. The sun had just painted a peach-colored ribbon on the far horizon. "We're dumb driving around in the dark. We'll pull in and park first chance we get and wait for morning. Maybe get a little sack time."

It had been a long day already, just past 0400 now. No one had objections to the captain's plan.

14

They were only about a mile farther down the road—and it was still plenty dark—when Edward told Taft and motioned for Wozinski to pull off the pitted pavement and onto flat ground. From what they could see in the moonlight, they were at the edge of a field thick with bright sunflowers, just outside of what appeared to be a village and at the turn-off onto a cobble-stone street. There were plenty of signs of damage, likely from gunfire from Allied ships in the English Channel.

The men were quickly out of the vehicles with their sleeping bags, more than ready by then to bed down on soft grass beneath the truck. But a dab of breeze brought to them a horrible stench, so strong it made their eyes water.

"Jeez! What's that? Smells like something big died," Pete Ronzini said.

"Yeah, rotting flesh of some kind," Hank added.

"No, for once you're wrong, Hank," Ace Taft corrected. "I know that smell. That's burnt flesh."

Edward unrolled his bag beneath the jeep. "We may encounter worse up the way. Nazis like to use flame-throwers. We'll get used to the smell in a minute, like it isn't even there, and then we'll be on our way after a quick snooze, fellows. Morty, you take guard duty. Rest of you, find a protected spot. And sweet dreams."

"Captain, what's that under your seat there? Bottles of perfume, maybe?" Pete asked.

Edward shined his light in that direction. Three bottles, all right.

"Oh. No, not perfume," he said sheepishly. "My mother insists on sending me Epsom salts. She's convinced I got migraines, and that stuff is supposed to help. Those slipped out of my duffel bag back there, and I was going to stow them when I could."

"I've heard of the stuff. You suppose it would help that stink?" Pete persisted.

Edward just shook his head and crawled under the jeep.

"Smell something for a while and you stop smelling it," Hank was saying. "Like when I worked at the filling station and—"

"Hank, you don't shut up right now, I swear to God I'm gonna shoot your ass, okay?" It was Ace with the threat—and a laugh that immediately made the threat benign—from his spot in the grass beneath the jeep.

In the darkness, the sound of closing zippers on sleeping bags rivaled the sibilant songs of the crickets and tree frogs. Gene was sleeping sitting up, leaning against a truck tire. That made it easier for him to breathe through his busted nose. He also held onto his Saint Michael medallion for the comfort it brought. One blessing already: he had not smelled anything since his nose hit the steering wheel during the near collision with the convoy.

And for the rest, as both the captain and Hank noted, the smell seemed to fade, washed away by familiarity and fatigue.

Edward soon found sleep. It was Duncan Smythe who had advised that he learn to get rest any time, any way he could. He could not be much good to his men or at his job if he did not. Lack of sleep had claimed more than one BD captain.

No one seemed to notice when the last of the night's stars were erased by the coming light of dawn. Or that an all-enveloping fog had rolled in off the sea. Not even Morty, who fought sleep by pacing back and forth on the blacktop.

But a couple of hours later, they could not ignore the rumbling of not-so-far-away artillery. The innocent chirps of birds. Or the shouts of their captain, rousing them for the road.

The Kaboom Boys   145

"Drop your cocks and grab your socks, Kaboom Boys! We don't want the war to come to an end without our help, now, do we?"

"Yes. Yes, we do," a groggy Hank answered as he crawled from beneath the weapons carrier and stretched. "Jesus, that stink may be even worse this morning."

Ace was already standing at the front of the truck, taking a piss. "It's burnt flesh, all right. Once you get a whiff of that..."

"Guess we better get used to it," Carl said. "Smelling death."

"We're probably an hour, hour and a half from where we're going, if you guys want to eat some K rations," Edward advised. "I got no idea about the cuisine at the HQ, if any."

"Stuff tastes bad enough on its own," Morty noted. "Think I'll just smoke."

Stretching, Ace wandered across the roadway and climbed to the top of a small hill. A single poppy grew there. He picked it and put it in his uniform shirt pocket for a bit of luck. Just then, the sun tipped the horizon, a breeze moved some of the mist, and Ace could now see the vista in front of him.

"Holy hell!" he said, loud enough to get the attention of the rest of the squad.

Hank was the first to join Ace on the hillock. Just in front of them, beyond a rock wall, was a strip of ground covered with red dots. Poppies. Thousands of poppies.

"You know, the poppy is the symbol of eternal sleep," Hank said.

"Most appropriate, as it turns out," Ace told him, pointing beyond the stand of flowers. The fog had thinned enough now that they could see a bocage covered with the bloated carcasses of easily fifty cows. Some were hardly recognizable as cows. Others were on their backs with all four legs pointed skyward. Putrid gases escaped from the dead animals, making audible hissing sounds almost like the drone of bagpipes. Dogs, rats, crows, and buzzards busily pecked and pulled at the charred flesh of the bovine victims. Just beyond all that carnage, what had been a stand of trees was now only stubs and splintered timber, still burning and smoking.

Ace was startled by an ominous clicking sound behind him. First thought was it could be the bolt action of a German soldier's Mauser rifle. Then he saw it was only Hank, busily taking photos of the macabre scene.

"See that over there?" It was the captain, standing next to them, pointing to something in the midst of all those dead animals. Something familiar but even more out of place. It was a five-hundred-pound bomb, one of its fins shorn off and its nose buried in the black dirt of the field. "All right. Normandy, day one. Might as well get our hands dirty."

The rest of the men joined them and surveyed the scene, then they all got busy.

Ace ran to get his gear bag as Hank and Edward jogged off toward the bomb, stepping over, around, and into ropes of intestines, splintered bones, and other assorted piles of mutilated cow parts. Scavengers backed off, unaware of the danger of their banquet location.

The captain called back over his shoulder, "Gene, go find a place just beyond that tallest hedgerow over there and dig."

"Got it, Captain."

Edward soon had his stethoscope to the bomb's exterior, listening to a quick but pronounced rumbling going on inside the weapon, when Ace arrived with the tools.

"All right. It's one of ours, a delayed-action five-hundred-pounder, and it's singing to us." Edward leaned back and cocked his head sideways, and sang, "*There's a place in France where the ladies wear no pants...*"

Hank and Ace laughed. Tension broken, they went to work. At least there was no digging required to access the detonation system. Hank snapped away with his camera while Ace pulled out the appropriate tools. Edward took a piece of chalk from Ace's bag and wrote something on the bomb casing. The other two men looked at it, and then Hank took a photo.

The scribbling said, *TOMMY*.

"I promised my kid brother the first one we got on the continent would have his name on it," Edward explained. Then he grabbed a screwdriver and began carefully removing the cover protecting the detonator assembly.

An hour later, they had the innards of the bomb buried in the hole Gene and the others had dug, and a fuse line had been run to the detonation plunger set up a safe distance away. Other than being delayed reaction, the bomb's detonator had been standard, straightforward. Assuming it had been dropped the previous day, it would have blown up on its own in a few more hours. Edward left a note on the bomb carcass to let engineers know it was safe to move it.

With a shout of, "Fire in the hole!" Gene shoved the plunger down, and there was a substantial blast. The men all applauded and clapped like kids at a fireworks show.

First of many jobs in a real battle zone, and a success. That was worth a hearty cheer.

"Didn't even wake up the cows," Morty observed, nodding at the dead animals. Gene picked up a small clod of dirt and jokingly threw it at him, just missing. Everyone laughed. "Jesus, Woz, anybody ever tell you that you throw like a girl?"

Gene picked up another clod and was about to try again, a more serious look on his face this time, when the captain interrupted.

"All right, Kaboom Boys, let's hit the road," Edward ordered. "We don't want HQ to get nervous about us or for some of Hitler's SS to come out here to see what that explosion was all about."

Sure enough, as they walked back toward their vehicles, still jibing, the men heard the rumble of approaching traffic. The captain motioned for them to grab their weapons and lie flat until they could determine if what was coming was friendly.

They certainly were. Approaching them was a jeep and a three-quarter-ton truck, both with red fenders. Fellow BD boys.

The newcomers pulled in next to where Hume's squad was parked.

"You turds sure make a hell of a lot of noise!" the man in the jeep's passenger seat shouted as he climbed out and waved. "What, you trying to attract the Jerries?"

"Well, I'll be a son of a bitch," Edward said in disbelief as he stood and approached the newly arrived BD captain, who wore a sharp-looking Eisenhower field jacket and sported a thin, black mustache. They shook hands, then hugged warmly as both squads watched. Edward turned to his men. "Let me introduce you to Captain Hedley Bennett. We trained together at APG. I taught him everything he knows but not nearly all I know."

Bennett motioned for his own squad to get out of their vehicles and have a stretch and a smoke. "And men, it's my honor to introduce you to Captain Edward Hume. He's almost but not quite as good at BD as I am."

The men waved and then mingled, introducing themselves to each other. Both captains told their men to go ahead and eat breakfast.

"Let's step over here, Hed. I want to show you something." The two captains walked across the roadway and back to the hillock. Edward pointed toward the field of dead animals and leveled trees. "You got any idea what happened here?"

"The line got moved. We ended up on the wrong side of it yet again. Second time now. Getting to be a costly habit. I heard the Jerries were trying to hit a bunch of tanks passing through here, and all those cows paid the ultimate price. The bombers, ours and the RAF, tried to drop some bombs on what somebody decided were German tanks. Grand screwup is what it was. But that little village over there took the brunt of it." Sure enough, through the mostly denuded trees, the rubble of the small town was scattered all about. "A convoy coming past late yesterday spotted that UXB you just took care of, and we were on the way out here to do the job. You beat us to it, looks like."

"Glad to help," Edward offered. "Probably those guys we almost met head-on."

"Close call, huh?"

"Yeah, almost got run down by our own guys," Edward said with a nod. "Sounds like you've gotten way closer to the action than we have, Hedley."

"By sheer accident, my friend. And we got our asses handed to us as a result." There was a weariness now in Bennett's voice. "We lost a good man out of our squad already. They're telling me it'll be a good while before he's replaced." Bennett took a long draw on his cigarette. "I'm glad you're here, Eddie. You can't begin to imagine the mess we got to deal with around here. The Krauts are booby-trapping everything in sight, with special aim on us BD boys. And, of course, targeting anything that might be an HQ or has anything to do with the French Resistance. We could do nothing but UXBs around the clock and still never catch up. The ones we don't get to might be here and lethal for hundreds of years. And you can't imagine how many unstable ordnance dumps we're leaving behind after every battle. A lot of that dangerous junk is on top of what the Krauts

The Kaboom Boys   149

left." The two stood in silence for a moment. "So, where you going, buddy?"

"To begin with, Ninth Air Force advanced headquarters at Grandcamp-les-Bains," Edward told him. "You not headed that way, by any chance?"

"Naw. We got orders for Saint-Malo until we got sidetracked to come back over here for this job you stole from us."

"Saint-Malo?"

"You never heard of it. One of those places over next to the water."

"Oh, yes. I've heard of it. It's just west of Mont-Saint-Michel."

Bennett looked out over the devastated pasture as he took a bite of a hard, tasteless K-ration biscuit and tried to chew it. Then he spat it out.

"What they make this shit out of, Ed? Rubber? You still obsessing about that mount whatever-it-is, I see."

Edward smiled. "Mont-Saint-Michel is one of the most beautiful places on earth, the way things in France are supposed to look. Not like that." Hume pointed toward the bombed-out village in front of them. "It's a holy place, a fortress since medieval times. And I plan on visiting there, even if I have to wait 'til Hitler goes home in a bunch of pieces in a gunnysack."

"Yeah, in our briefing, they told us the Germans are still there. They really like it for R and R, and they've pretty much left the folks living there alone. At least so far and as long as they cook for them, the girls dance with them, and the locals keep pouring the wine."

"Well, I'm going to see it in person someday," Edward said, his tone resolute, then he chewed his own rubber biscuit for a moment. "Hed, you may not want to talk about it, but how did you lose your man?"

Hedley made certain his squad was well out of earshot. They were laughing along with Hume's squad about some joke somebody told. Only Ace was outside the circle, pacing, fidgeting with a cigarette.

"I probably need to talk about it. You know as well as I do how close you get to your squad. And how you take blame if something goes wrong. He was just a kid from Arkansas, and he died the stupidest way possible," Bennett said with clenched jaws and an angry face. "First thing Kane told us at APG. 'Don't try to retrieve any souvenirs,' he must've said a dozen times. Two guys were arguing over an SS helmet hanging on a fence post, but I got them away before they touched it. Then I heard a bang. The corporal had grabbed a Nazi flag off the fence. Boom! He had just turned twenty-one years old. I tell you, Ed, a hard letter to write to his folks."

"Damn shame. I preached about it all the time when we were on the other side of the Channel. If they didn't hear anything else...and clearly not your fault, Hed."

Edward had already noticed his friend was different from the last time he saw him. That night at Al's Bar. There was a somber air about him. Sadness edging out the usual mischievous glint in his eyes.

Bennett was now looking back to the vehicles, studying the two squads, watching them carefully. "Your guys? Good bunch?"

Edward did not hesitate. "Yeah. Yeah, they are. A couple of wise guys, a know-it-all. They blend in pretty well, though. Strong outfit." He chewed for a few seconds, then added, "My sergeant there, though. I can't quite put my finger on it, but he's..."

"Skittish, maybe. Yeah, I noticed him. Sure, I'd be concerned about him if I were you. Kinda quiet?"

"Yeah, but a good man for the most part," Edward answered. "He's very well trained, but there's something bothering him."

"We all get bothered, but the ones who hold it inside, those are the ones you need to pay extra attention to," Hedley advised. "But with all these damn bombs, who has the time?" Ace stood far enough away from the gathering of the squads to not be a part of it. He merely grinned when everyone else was hee-hawing. "Maybe you can get him to open up. You don't need a weak link."

"Hed, you know me. I'm concerned about everybody and everything. Taft's been fine so far. Better than fine. Damn brave. Hell, he even wants to go back and do officer training. He failed out when he tried before."

"Taft? He the one who helped you clear that bomber full of UXBs on the runway back in England? Sergeant Alistair Taft?"

Hume looked hard at Bennett. "You heard about that?"

"Damn right! Everybody in BD's heard about that one," Hedley said. "If it had been me, I might've told the blasted Air Forces to let 'em all blow and start building back after the smoke cleared."

"Yeah, it was Ace, and he did the job with his head cracked open. But the truth is, none of them's been really tested yet. Shit, even you and I..."

Edward hesitated. "Well, let's just say there's never enough training for the kind of work we do every day." The two captains turned and started walking back toward their mingled squads. "Right now, I just want to get to Grandcamp without getting run over, shot, or blown to hell and find out where they want us to go."

Bennett looked sideways at Edward. "Just know it's harder than you can imagine to lose any of your guys. I know. I had one who didn't even come close to that magical ten weeks. No matter what, it's on us."

"Yeah, we all want to improve those odds," Hume said. "I got that calendar I bought back at the post exchange at APG that day. I mark off the days and weeks like a damn lunatic. Hed, it's like a curse hanging over our heads. I wish they had never told us or our guys about that. But you know what? We're going to beat those odds and come out the other side of this damn war in one piece. You, me, our squads, too."

"Worthy goal, *mi compadre*," Bennett told him. "Sorry. *Mon ami.* We're in France now, right? I got to get my Romance languages straight."

"Couldn't tell it from the crazy weather. I thought it was supposed to be nice and cool at this latitude this time of the year," Edward said. "I heard we'd be in the nineties today and humid as hell."

"Seems like I noticed that, too. You don't suppose the Krauts got control of the sun somehow, do you?" Bennett grinned. "They've turned everything else sideways, so why not the weather?"

"Wouldn't put it past the sons of bitches," Edward responded. "I hear they got scientists working on everything from rockets to detonators to jet-engine airplanes. Weather finagling oughta be a snap for them."

Bennett nodded toward where the two squads sat talking, smoking, joking beneath the shade of a tree. "My sergeant is no peach. All he talks about is looking for Nazi buried loot. It's a dangerous distraction." Hedley laughed and pointed to the assemblage of BD boys. "Looks like you got a bona fide evangelist in your bunch, too, Eddie."

Sure enough, Hank Anderson was standing before the group, holding court, his back to Bennett and Hume, and was, as usual, sharing knowledge.

"Yeah, that's my know-it-all, Corporal Hank Anderson," Edward said as the two friends started walking that way. "He never got out of tenth grade, but he's smart. He's been a big help, but I got to say sometimes I'd like to throttle him. Boy loves to talk. He'd make a great lawyer. Or newspaper reporter. Or evangelist."

"No place in the world like this place, this Mont-Saint-Michel," Anderson was preaching, but for once, everybody was listening, apparently buying what he was selling. "It's surrounded by deep water at high tide. That's when the fishing fleet goes out and comes in. But when the tide's out, people can walk to the island on the mudflats, mostly Catholic pilgrims but plenty of tourists, too. Most want to visit the abbey up top. They just have to keep a watch because when the tides rush back in..."

"Who'd want to vacation at a church on a rock in the middle of a mudflat?" one of Bennett's men, the sergeant, asked.

"The Nazis, that's who," Hank told him. "I guess they like the good life."

Morty shouted, "But they don't believe in God, I tell you for damn sure!"

"I suspect some do, some don't," Hank said. "But they do like the finer things in life. Maybe that's why they invaded France. And why they haven't destroyed Paris."

"You're shittin' me now, man. Nazis don't go on vacation!" the sergeant said.

"Indeed, they do. And they love Mont-Saint-Michel. That's why they've left it alone while the bastards leveled just about everything else that's pretty or historic in this part of France," Anderson said.

"You boys gonna goldbrick all damn day?" Edward called out.

"Yeah, if telling tall tales was all it took to defuze UXBs, this war would be a breeze!" Bennett added with a sly grin. "Tell you what. I got an idea. Let's get a little wager going. First squad to get to Mont-Saint-Michel wins."

Edward scratched the stubble on his chin. "I like it. But what are the stakes?"

"First squad to get to the main gate of the place—can even be a single member of the squad, not necessarily the whole unit—wins a carton of Lucky Strikes from the other squad," Hedley announced. Edward grinned and nodded, and they shook on it. Both squads cheered.

"You're on, Captain Bennett," Edward told him. "But remember, the Kaboom Boys don't wait around for nobody."

"The who-the-hell-whats?"

The Kaboom Boys

"The Kaboom Boys," Edward told him, pointing to the sign in his jeep's windshield.

"I like it. I like it a lot. But our guys like being The Bomb Merchants, too," Bennett said. "Can't be outdone by this bunch of coffee boilers. And we can't let these flannel-mouthed grub-line riders beat us to...what you call it? Mount Saint Mitchell?...Now can we?"

"What'd he say?" Pete asked Morty.

"Hell if I know."

"He's Texas talking," one of Bennett's squad pointed out.

Hume watched as Bennett and his men climbed back into their vehicles, turned them around, brutally crushed a stand of poppies in the process, and then drove away, back toward the west, as previously ordered. As they pulled off, Hedley Bennett stood up in his jeep, cupped his hands, and shouted back to Edward.

"Keep your head down, Ed! I'm looking forward to those smokes!" Edward waved him off. "And next time you park your chuckwagon for the night, don't just give it a lick and a promise. Pick some place that don't stink like a three-day-old remuda pen!"

"What'd he say?" Gene asked no one in particular.

"Where'd you say he was from, Captain?" Ace asked.

"Washington, DC."

"Then why does he talk like a cowpoke?" asked Carl.

"To get your attention," Edward told them with a smile.

The men all looked at each other. "That explains it, then," Ace decided.

"No, really, he spent some time during the Great Depression with the CCC in Texas, and I guess the lingo stuck," Edward explained. "But it still gets him plenty of attention."

A curve in the road and a vine-covered stone fence soon had Bennett and his squad out of sight. But he could still hear the distant rumble of artillery. It was to their east, the direction they were headed. They had been lucky so far. Not a single German soldier or tank. Just considerable aftermath of the invasion so far. But common sense told them their improbable good luck was about to change.

Edward pointed to where the sun had so recently risen. "Let's go, Kaboom Boys. Our war's gonna be that way."

15

"We'll set up the new HQ in an abandoned château right here, one used as an HQ by the Nazis," someone was saying in a commanding voice from the other side of the tent flap. Captain was inadvertently eavesdropping, waiting to be admitted. "But first we got to get our BD boys to clear it. We know they left us some deadly welcoming gifts when they scrammed. We'll get it swept, but we have to be quick about it."

It was Army Air Forces General Henry "Hap" Arnold he heard through the tent flap as he stood there while the guard reviewed Edward's papers. He had seen the general at a distance several times back in England but was about to meet him face-to-face, by urgent order. Edward had already gotten word that Arnold had a dangerous job for Hume and his squad. Even more dicey than all the other ones they had taken on since landing in Normandy a few weeks before. Now, the captain was about to step into the temporary headquarters for the 358th Fighter Group, a large, heavily guarded tent—it reminded him of the traveling circus tents back home—to learn details of the mission.

The Kaboom Boys had been officially chosen to clear the new HQ for the Advance Landing Group, which was overseeing this entire sector of the European theater of operations.

Arnold, Chief of the Army Air Corps until 1941 and now commanding general of the Army Air Forces, stood at a large, round table, surrounded by other high-ranking Army officers and a couple of men dressed in black, mud-spattered clothes. They wore red berets and had rifles still slung across their shoulders. French Resistance. On D-Day, the Resistance fighters had come out of the darkness to fight alongside Allied troops.

His finger on a point on a map on the table, Arnold noticed Edward as he entered. The general walked around the table and offered a strong handshake.

"You my BD man, Captain? Hume, is it?" he asked.

"I am, General."

"Where you from, son?" Arnold asked, and it sounded as if he really wanted to know.

"Pennsylvania, Mahanoy City, up near Scranton."

"I'd recognize that accent anywhere," Arnold said with a laugh. "Me, too. Gladwyne, northwest of Philly, a couple of hours south of you." Edward knew Gladwyne was an upper-class suburb compared to working-class Mahanoy City. "You a Phillies man? A coal miner?"

"Phils, yessir. Coal miner, no, sir. My dad was, and my brother still is. Before I enlisted, I worked for Congressman Ivor Fenton." Edward had no idea why he added that last fact, but he was glad he had when Arnold grinned. The other high-ranking officers and the French Resistance men stood patiently by.

"I know Congressman Fenton," the general said. "Good man. Supports the military and the war effort. He probably needed your help and could have pulled some strings to keep you home. Why didn't you stay back and do something a hell of a lot less dangerous than bomb demolition?"

Loaded question. Edward decided not to ponder the answer but just be honest.

"Well, truth is, I could have, but I felt a need to serve." Edward wondered if his response sounded trite to a man who had suffered four recent heart attacks and could be helping run the war from Washington, DC, instead of from a tent in an active theater of war.

"Well, I'm proud of you, and I know your folks are, too. Not many would have the guts to volunteer to do the kind of work you do. Let me see your map." Eddie handed it to him. He felt good about the validation he had just been given in front of the other officers. "Hume, we've picked a busted-up château right here for HQ." He circled a small point on the map with a red pen. "But we need it cleared. Yesterday. We'll settle for 1900 hours tonight. Be aware it belonged to the Germans just a few days ago, and they had ample time to booby-trap it. Can you get it done?"

"That we can, sir. That's what we do."

"I know it is, Hume."

Edward was in awe of the general. Here he was, encountering one of those interesting people he felt the need to meet and get to know. Arnold was an Army air war pioneer. He had been taught to fly airplanes by the Wright brothers themselves. After each heart attack, he had received a special waiver from President Roosevelt allowing him to avoid the usual mandatory medical retirement. He had insisted on not staying back in safe, comfortable territory. Instead, he wanted to personally inspect Utah Beach after D-Day and was very much involved in running hands-on the Army Air Forces operations in Normandy. And doing it from Normandy.

"One more thing, Captain," Arnold said. "There's a noblewoman, a countess or something like that, who's asking to be allowed to move back into the château, her home. Be gentle with her if you see her. Tell her it's too dangerous. When we get things under control, we might allow her to resume living on the top floor. But not just yet."

"Will do, sir."

"Sad thing," the general added. "Her husband and a couple of sons are gone, so just reassure her we're going to protect her and her home as best we can."

Edward nodded as Arnold handed him back his map. Then the general turned and rejoined the men gathered around the table to get back to their planning.

Back outside, Edward waved his squad over and showed them where they were headed and shared with them what they had to do. In a hurry. By 1900 hours that night. As they piled back into the vehicles, he noticed somebody was missing.

"Hey, where the hell's Ace?" he called out. Everyone had been told to be there, ready to deploy.

It was Hank who answered. "He went off to inspect that ammo dump we passed on the way in. He had a fit about it, going on and on about how dangerous it looked." A pause as Anderson spotted someone hustling their way between two tents. "Here he comes now."

"Sorry, Captain," the out-of-breath sergeant said, scowling as he slid behind the wheel of the jeep, stepped on the clutch, cranked the engine, and ground it into gear. "That UXO pile over there, it's the worst I've ever seen, sir."

"Not doubting you, Sergeant. Nobody's had time to neutralize anything yet. But the general's got an urgent job for us. We'll check the dump the moment we get back."

"But sir! We need to take care of it now before it blows. There's enough land mines and Kraut grenades...if that dump goes up..."

Edward waved him on. "You heard me, Ace. The general has given us a mission, and we damn well do what the big boss says."

"But, sir, it'll be dark by then..." Ace's voice trailed off, defeated.

Hank looked hard at the captain. "Ace knows what he's talking about, Captain. Maybe if you told the general how volatile that pile is, we could postpone clearing the HQ until tomorrow. You stood up to that LST skipper, and that saved our lives. Why not now?"

The squad members stared at their captain, awaiting an answer, trusting he would do the right thing.

"Big difference, Corporal. We're talking a four-star general here. That skipper was a lieutenant. You hear me? The guy who's running a big part of this show needs a place to plan and sleep, ASAP. I'm bound to obey those orders. The general was very clear about the urgency of getting that château safe. We'll check the pile first thing when we get back. Got that?"

It was the first time his men seemed to be questioning his directives, his leadership. It was unnerving.

Hank said nothing. He turned and climbed into the back seat of the jeep. Ace looked as if he wanted to say more but decided against it. Instead, seething, he gripped the steering wheel so hard his knuckles turned white. He drove away, the truck following closely.

They had only gone a half mile when they happened upon another grisly sight. A peaceful field littered with the bodies of German soldiers. And likely a few Allied dead, too. Under the unusually hot sun, GIs were picking up bodies and body parts and trying to find identification. Shell and bomb craters still smoked. The banter among the Kaboom Boys quickly quieted. They slowed the vehicles to a crawl, as much out of respect as for caution.

There are worse jobs in this war than BD, Edward thought as he watched the troops do their gruesome work.

Behind the jeep, in the cab of the squad's truck, Morty asked Pete, "See the white flags?" Indeed, numerous small white markers fluttered in the cool breeze off the English Channel. "Land mines! Nazi bastards!" Morty said with sudden rage. He spat out the truck window. "And who knows if they put the mines there before they got killed," Morty went on, "or if they planted 'em later to get the good guys who would come along to try to give them a proper burial. They even booby-trap their own dead, hoping to get some Allied souvenir hunters. Or BD boys. Bastards! I hope whoever cleared that field did as good a job as the Kaboom Boys would have done or they'll have more pieces of people to pick up."

Just ahead of them in the jeep, Hank was expressing a similar opinion. "Sir, we really ought to take the time to neutralize all those mines before—"

"How many times do I have to say it?" Edward interrupted. "Jesus Christ, guys! A four-star general is trusting us to get that place cleared. He chose us to do the job. Keep moving!" Edward waved his hand high enough for the men in the truck to see, then twirled his finger in a "move 'em out" gesture.

Just then, Ace Taft abruptly hit the brake and pulled the jeep off the roadway. Edward gave him a questioning look.

"Sir, there's a Nazi flag on that dead soldier over there," the sergeant said, eyes wide, almost manic. It was the first time he had spoken since the ammo dump request was denied. "See, I promised my fiancée's daddy that I'd get him one for a souvenir. And I aim to keep at least one promise I made to the man." Before Edward could say anything, Taft had shut off the engine and was out and sprinting toward the SS soldier's body, taking a zigzag course between the land mine flags.

"Taft! Stop!"

Wozinski had pulled the truck to a smoky halt behind the jeep. He only shrugged his shoulders and frowned, as if to say, *"The sarge's a loon!"*

Edward was out and chasing Taft but could not catch him before the sergeant was already there, next to the dead German, bending down, reaching for the blood-specked flag. Without thinking, Edward did the only thing he knew to do. He gave the sergeant his best Mahanoy City High School Maroons football cross-body block, leaving both men sprawling in the mud beyond the flag-draped enemy soldier's body.

"You dumb-ass son of a bitch!" Edward hissed, catching his breath. Then he crawled over and quickly inspected the flag and the already decomposing, fly-covered body. "Device! I knew it! Damn device! What the hell were you thinking, man?"

Sure enough, the flag was wired, tied to an explosive package crammed into the bloody chest of the dead man. Anyone tugging at the flag, whether trying respectfully to remove the body or, like Ace Taft, attempting to claim a keepsake, would have been instantly decapitated.

"God, Captain. I'm sorry. I just wanted to get something for my girl's dad," Ace said, then sank back on his elbows in the mud, mortified by his own actions.

"No souvenirs. That's how soldiers die. I've told you guys this over and over. And this is not our job, dammit. We have a bigger assignment, but we'll fix this one as quickly as we can," the captain said, seething. "Fetch your toolbox...without touching anything but the earth under your feet... and get the boys digging a hole over there. Tell Hank to bring the camera. And the next time you pull a stunt like this, you're off BD and I'll make damn sure you spend the rest of the war cleaning latrines at Fort Polk. You got that, Taft?"

But the sarge was up already, jogging back toward the truck, head down, chin on his chest. Edward double-timed back to the truck. They were only three kilometers from the château.

What's gotten into Taft? Edward wondered. Ace was, at times, his most solid man, someone he could depend on. Sometimes, though, he was darkly moody or shockingly reckless, and he seemed to be getting more erratic and peculiar. Was the sergeant becoming a liability?

Part of the job, Hume knew. Just like defuzing bombs and neutering UXOs. But it was the part in which he was least confident. Somehow, when it came to his squad, he had to lead in a way so he could bring out the best. Suppress the rest.

And with Ace Taft, he already knew he had his work cut out for him.

♠

The château was only a couple of miles away, up a small lane atop a hill and within sight of the English Channel to the north, and a good view of the countryside in all directions. It was apparent now why first the Germans and then General Arnold desired this place for headquarters, as well as for bachelor officers' quarters and an officers' mess. There was a large outbuilding—likely stables—that the SS had used as a barracks. The Americans would likely do the same.

The impressive limestone château was mostly surrounded by tall beech trees. The six-hundred-year-old structure and surrounding grounds—once meticulously kept—had been shelled by both friend and foe. Clusters of apple and pear trees had been knocked down, and there were gaps blasted in the four-foot-high stone walls and once picturesque patchwork of bocage. Engineers had marked with white flags the land mines along the narrow roadway that led from the main road to the estate grounds and then along the lengthy crushed-stone driveway up to the château itself. Hank counted twenty-two such markers.

"You see all those flags?" Edward told Ace. "We start with clearing them, and handle any munitions and grenades on the grounds. Then the house."

"Wouldn't want General Hap to get his knickers singed," Ace whispered to no one in particular in his Scottish burr. Edward ignored him but was now keeping a running count of how many times Ace said or did something tantamount to being insubordinate.

The BD boys got to work. It took almost two hours before they were near the entrance to the château grounds.

Despite the war damage, there were still intermingling patches of woodland and heath, small fields, and tall hedgerows that enveloped the property. Once they passed through the stone gate, they could tell that the bullet-pocked but cathedral-like château looked to be in sound condition, its entrance massive and grand. Alongside the lane and around the courtyard, they saw plenty of junk left behind by German soldiers and officers. There were parts of discarded and ripped uniforms, helmets, empty beer bottles at what appeared to have been a makeshift guard shack, shaving kits, small arms ammunition, and hand grenades. There were also ammunition pouches, bayonets, entrenching tools, and even pistols still strapped in their holsters.

"Jeez, some of this stuff would be worth a fortune back home," Pete noted.

"And some of it'll kill you faster now than when it was in the hands of a Kraut soldier," Carl reminded him.

"Damn, Pete!" Morty Schwartz said, very disturbed. "Every time I think you've got some sense, you prove me wrong! Captain said don't touch nothin'. So don't touch nothin'! We're just here to dig a trench to put all this shit in."

A seemingly undamaged rose trellis along the front of the structure supported a massive blanket of bright pink petals that belied the awful things that had so recently happened here. On this cloudy day, the roses lent a splash of welcome hope to an otherwise gray scene. Though it was summer, the war and its damage seemed to have drained the countryside of much of its color.

Edward called to the men, "Okay now! Spread out! We gotta clear anything within two hundred feet of the buildings and roadway. The general's men will do the rest when they get here tomorrow morning."

Hank clicked his stopwatch to begin timing this phase of the mission for the captain's report later.

They soon found a number of objects fixed with explosive charges and detonators. It was as if the Germans knew the Allies would eventually show up and claim this location for an HQ and they wanted to make it as difficult as possible for the new occupants. Edward had been methodically defuzing and filling a sack with disarmed "potato mashers"—German stick hand grenades—at a quick clip.

Then he finally met his match and had to slow down. This one was trickier. It gave him a chill. It was a German helmet with a cleverly hidden detonator fuze attached to the primed grenade underneath. He carefully lifted the helmet's steel rim and gently touched the grenade with his left index finger. The wire leading to it was so thin he had trouble seeing it. He decided it was one of the new nylon surgery filaments that he had read about in a recent BD dispatch. Carefully, he snipped the string attached to the fuze to deactivate the grenade. Then he shielded his eyes with an elbow to prevent the sparks from the detonator reaching him as he pulled the string to trigger it. He dropped the once-hot potato into the sack. Only then did he exhale.

He called out to his men, "Don't forget to unscrew the fuze system first on these things. And do not pull the string to trigger it. Always shield your eyes, 'cause that blasting cap *will* go off and shoot enough sparks to do some damage to your handsome faces and baby blues. Got that?"

Everyone responded positively. It was a repeat of the instructions they had heard many times before. Edward went on. "Sparks only ignite an intact masher. But once the detonator is separated, it's inert and shouldn't explode. TNT or Comp B can't ignite if you don't yank that string. There's still a bit of ignition, though, so again, shield your eyes!"

After fixing the last trap, Edward stood, stretched, and looked around. He checked his watch. 1600 hours. Despite the distractions, they were still on schedule, but until he was inside the huge house, he had no idea how long it might take. Their deadline was 1900 hours.

Edward's instincts told him they were being watched. There could still be lingering Germans anywhere, even though he had been assured they were gone. Snipers, a single soldier or two, or even platoons separated from their units. So far, everything on this particular mission seemed to be a ploy by the Germans to slow down the Americans by carefully planting so many small but dangerous obstacles. Plus, plenty that appeared to be booby traps but were not.

They walked into the courtyard through a six-foot-high gate and past a stone fence, then drove the vehicles inside the main château grounds. Edward stood, braced himself against the windshield, and yelled like a football coach, "Men, let's huddle up before we clear that château!"

The squad gathered next to the jeep for a quick brief. Hank clicked his stopwatch to note the end time of the first phase. Carl nudged Morty and pointed to what appeared to be a carriage house in a grove of trees behind the main building. There was a burned-out German truck parked there.

The Kaboom Boys 163

Two dead Germans were visible, one hanging from each truck door, one snagged on his hobnail boot, as if they were in the middle of a too-late escape attempt from bullets or shelling.

Their attention, though, was snatched back to the stone château when the saltwater breeze startled them by catching and unfurling a big Nazi flag, billowing out from a pole extending off a second-floor balcony. The bold swastika caught a stray bit of sunlight, extending an evil welcome.

Nobody said a word until Ronzini piped up. "Got to admit it, guys. I'd like to have myself one of those. I'd be the cat's whiskers in Bay Ridge flyin' dat t'ing off the stoop on Seventy-Seventh Street."

Morty shook his head. "Dat's crazy, Pete. Them things, they're bad luck. And not just 'cause Ace here almost got his ass blown up by that one back there. Serious bad luck!"

"I could probably get a hundred bucks for it," Pete said.

"Bad luck, though. Really bad luck."

Meanwhile, Edward had walked closer to the château and its impressive set of rose trellises. Now, this close, he could see that only about half the flowers appeared healthy. The other half were brown, near dead, the vines distressed from ground level and up to the very top. He inspected the well-made structure carefully for explosive devices. Nothing. But when he grabbed the interlaced wooden strips with both hands and shook the trellis, gauging its sturdiness, dead petals flew everywhere, like a dirty snow flurry wafting along on the sea breeze. Then that whole section of trellis collapsed as Edward just managed to jump out of the way.

Undeterred, he gave the remaining trellis a vigorous shake. It hardly moved. He did prick his finger on a rose thorn in the process, reminding him why he never cared much for that particular flower. Sweet-smelling danger, he had described them to Rachel as an excuse for never buying her any. Carnations. Daisies. Flowers that did not bite. Never roses.

But they were Mom's favorites. Despite his distaste for their mean-spirited thorns, he had helped her grow beautiful roses in the only corner that saw enough sunlight in the tiny, dreary, slate-covered courtyard they shared with neighbors at their Centre Street row house. Sometimes she would just sit there smiling, staring at them. He would bring her a cup of hot tea. She was so proud of them. Always took a vase to church on Sunday mornings during the summer. Even kept some in a beer pitcher on the end of the bar despite Pops's claim that they only brought bugs into the place.

"*Morte. Morte.* Like so very many."

Edward jumped. At first, he was sure the person he saw standing at the gate behind him was his mother. But speaking French? In France?

It was an older woman. About Mom's size. From her dress, it was clear she was the noblewoman that General Arnold had told him about, the château's owner. From her face, it was equally obvious her life had not been so noble lately.

"No, *non*. Not dead. *Non mortes*. Just damaged," Edward told her, mixing English with his best high school French. "Is this your home? *Ta maison?*"

She walked closer. Close enough to confirm his uniform was not that of a German soldier. He could see the tears in her eyes. Now she spoke in English, preferring to talk in that language to show she was well educated.

"It was. The SS, they took it. So many bad things happened here, so much suffering, I do not know if I can ever live here again." She closed her eyes, expressing her doubts. "You are American, British, or Canadian?"

"American. Our commanders wish to use your beautiful home for their headquarters for a short while." He paused as she opened her eyes and looked up at him. They both knew she had no choice in the matter. "Then, the Army will either repair it or give you money so you can hire someone to do what must be done. The furnishings? The paintings? I do not know if they will pay. But soon, at least, you will be able to live here once more."

The noblewoman interrupted tearfully. "I have not been inside, but I know they took everything. I watched them. Some they burned. There is not much left."

Edward sighed and continued, "Well, when you move back in, you can tend to these beautiful roses." He looked back at the thriving half of her wall of flowers, then at those near death. "My mother, back home. She grows them, too."

The woman smiled for the first time. "That would be wonderful. My sons, two of them, they are with the Resistance. They cared for my roses. I do not know if they are dead or alive. If they do return, they can help. Can you help me find them?"

"I am sure they will return," Edward told her, but he was not sure of

The Kaboom Boys 165

anything. When Resistance fighters were captured, some were tortured, but most were lined up against a wall in their hometowns and, while their friends and families were forced to look on, they were executed. "Madame, I do believe I can save your roses."

She looked at him, frowning. He yelled for Pete to bring him the bottles of Epsom salts from the jeep, the ones he had shoved beneath the seat the previous night. Edward then told Pete to go to the hand pump at the edge of the wall and fill his helmet with water while he emptied onto the ground most of one of the bottle's crystals, scattering them amid the roots of the almost-dead roses. Then he dissolved them with the water from Pete's helmet.

"I will leave you the rest," he told her. "Use them each week, about this amount, and the roses will become beautiful once again, the same as your home soon will. And my men will tack the trellis back to the wall so they can climb, seeking the sunlight. You understand? *Vous comprenez?*"

She smiled and nodded that she knew precisely what he was saying.

"*Merci. Merci beaucoup.*"

"Now we must inspect your home for bombs." She cringed at the mention of the word. "We will be very cautious. I assume you have a place where you can continue to stay for a while longer." She nodded. Edward said, "Thank you."

He watched her walk slowly away, but then she turned and smiled back at him. "Thank you," she said, and walked on.

Satisfied now that the other trellis would hold his weight, Edward began to climb it like a ladder, toward the balcony and the flagpole, doing his best Errol Flynn impression. It was slow going as he tried to avoid the thorns that seemed to be reaching out for him with ill intent all the way up.

"Captain's lost his mind," Hank observed matter-of-factly as he leaned against the truck and smoked.

"He's got a reason, Hank," Ace countered, speaking for the first time since the incident with the other Nazi flag. "He always does for everything he decides to do."

When Hume was just below the balcony and while still clinging to the trellis with one hand, he carefully pulled the swirling Nazi flag away from the pole to see where it was bracketed to the portico. He almost lost his grip on the rose trellis when he saw what else was there.

Wires. And a device.

"Device!" he yelled. "A big son of a bitch, too!"

He had no idea why the Germans would have gone to this much trouble to place a device on a flagpole way up there. Or what caused him to suspect such a thing in the first place. But it was a big enough charge to do damage not only to a determined souvenir hunter willing to climb up there and get it but also to the entranceway to the château itself. And they certainly knew that the first move by any Allies occupying this house would be to remove that hated blood-red-and-black symbol of the Third Reich.

"Told you there was a reason," Ace reminded the squad.

"Who would have thought the bastards would have...," Gene started, then stopped, shaking his head.

But Edward was now furiously fighting with the swirling swastika flag. The thing was trying to engulf him in its billows, to wrap itself around him, pull him off his tenuous perch. He tried to reach his wire cutters in his tool belt but could not manage it one-handed while being buffeted by the clinging fabric. The trigger was likely set to go when someone tried to remove tension off the rope that held the flag to the pole. Still, there was always the chance all this jostling could set it off.

Legs trembling and his hand cramping where he kept a grip on the trellis, he decided the only way to disarm the device was to try to twist the wires until they broke, cutting off the electrical charge from the battery that would energize the exploder should someone try to give the flag's rope a yank. And he knew he had better not, in the process, tug on the flag or short-out the wires as he twisted them. Either would certainly set the device off in his face.

It took some painful twisting back and forth, but the wires finally snapped. Edward carefully pulled the remaining wire ends on the battery side far away from where the explosive charge had been taped to the pole. Then he unwrapped the tape and casually dropped the package to the ground.

"That's one!" he called to the squad. Gene and Morty had already pulled out tools, ready to go start digging a hole on the other side of a rock fence and near an apple orchard down the drive. No way yet to know how deep it would need to be. They had the potato mashers already, but this could be the lone booby trap at the château. Or there could be a hundred.

Hank was busy taking pictures of the explosives from the first device. Edward had managed to retrieve his wire cutters and decided to go ahead and cut the big Nazi swastika flag loose from the pole. It floated to the ground as Edward quickly scurried back down the trellis.

Pete galloped over and grabbed up the fabric and began folding it up into as small a bundle as he could manage.

"Sir?" he asked Edward as the captain stepped back down onto firm ground. "Okay if I keep it?" The captain thought for a moment, glanced toward Ace Taft and his sour expression, then nodded affirmatively.

Morty took a step back, hands up. "Bad luck. Don't say I didn't warn ya, ya asshole." He pulled the Star of David from the neck of his shirt and gripped it tightly. "One New Yawker to another, you are one stupid, crazy-ass son of a bitch!"

Gene was already gripping his Saint Michael pendant, too, pointing it toward the flag and mouthing a prayer, as if exorcising the banner of any evil spirits.

Ace did not say a word. His eyes were squinted almost shut, but his face held no emotion. He merely cinched his tool belt tighter, picked up his bag, and headed for the château's front door. Edward joined him in step.

"Pete, why in the hell don't you just grow up?" Morty asked Ronzini, who was finishing corralling the flag.

"Hey, pal, what's the rush?" quipped Pete as he hastily—and quite proudly—trotted over and placed the flag into the truck before Morty could give him any more grief about it. Or the captain changed his mind.

Hank went to the truck to wait for whatever Edward and Ace might find and bring back outside so he could get pictures. He might also get summoned to go into the château to photograph any unusual installation of a booby trap. Such images could help other BD squads avoid getting themselves blown up.

Pete, Gene, and Morty headed off to start on the hole in the ground so they could blow up whatever the Germans had left behind. They still animatedly argued about the wisdom of keeping the vile flag. Carl had drawn guard duty.

"Hey, you know we might find buried treasure out here," Pete offered. "And I bet your superstitious ass wouldn't be afraid to latch onto some of *that*."

"Buried treasure. Pirates? You're nuts, Ronzini," Morty said.

"No, one of Captain Bennett's squad, his sergeant, he was telling me," Pete continued. "He said the Jerries had buried money, jewels, gold bars, all kinds of valuables when they ran off so sudden on D-Day. They plan on coming and digging it up when they kick the Allies back into the English Channel."

"No kidding," Schwartz said, suddenly interested.

"Finders, keepers," Gene offered. "First one whose shovel hits it gets to keep it. Fair?"

"Better we split it three ways," Pete suggested.

"Four ways," Carl called out. He was leaning against the truck, casually holding his M1 rifle, close enough to hear the buried treasure talk. "One of us is always guarding our asses while we're burying UXOs. No fair he gets left out on the treasure."

"All right, Calistos. You keep us from gettin' shot, we can cut your Greek ass in on the fortune," Pete assured him.

"Mighty decent of you," Carl replied.

So far, the only enemy troops they had seen were dead in a field, already decomposing, and the two poor SS troopers hanging from the burned-out truck near the carriage house. Earlier, on the road to the château, there had been hundreds of them, trudging along in a lengthy line of prisoners being marched back toward a captured port, where they would be evacuated to Great Britain. Many more would eventually be shipped to camps in the United States and Canada. The POWs did not appear so tough, although several of them did scowl and even spit in their direction as the BD squad passed them by. One bitter officer had even broken into a goose-step march and raised his arm in a defiant Nazi salute while shouting, "Heil Hitler!" Then he spat at Hank, who was closer than the others, snapping photos. Still, Carl knew enough to be alert and ready, just in case. Heavy fighting continued and not that far away.

A flash of movement from an open window on the side of the big house startled Carl. Someone—a dark figure—jumped out of a château window, carrying a rifle, and ran at top speed toward the cover of one of the downed trees.

Carl aimed a few steps ahead of the fleeing person and unleashed a shot. The bullet kicked up a spray of dust and grass, causing the culprit to stop and drop the rifle.

Edward had been gathering his tools at the front door with Ace. Now, his pistol drawn, he threateningly shouted, "Halt!" and headed toward the subject. Carl, M1 pointed in the escapee's direction, began running that way, too.

But as they got closer, they could see that it was not a man in a German uniform after all. It was a young girl in regular street clothes, her long blond hair pulled up beneath her beret. And she could not have been any older than fifteen or sixteen. She had dropped her rifle but still held a Luger pistol at her side.

"Drop the pistol!" Carl ordered in English. She did, reluctantly.

"I am Resistance. Do not shoot," she told them in broken English, voice trembling.

In his limited French, Edward told her, "If so, then we are all on the same side. Do not be afraid. But you know you do not have to hide anymore. The Allies have captured much of Normandy and will soon liberate all of France. The Resistance is out of the shadows."

The girl stood there for a moment, eyes wide. Then, shrugging her shoulders, she said tiredly, in near perfect English, "*Oui*, but Hitler will not give up France so easily. The Allies have not yet achieved victory and might well retreat. And there are many Frenchmen, the Vichy French, who will remember what the Resistance did in the cause of liberation. They will not be the friends of those who carried out the campaign as we believed necessary."

As Edward considered her logic, the girl added, "That is why I must still run and hide." With that, she nodded, turned, and raced away, leaving her weapons behind on the ground.

Edward called for her to stop, to come back. "Your weapons. You should take them."

She paused, calling to them over her shoulder, "We have more."

Carl and Edward watched her go.

"Damn! She oughta be home somewhere clippin' movie star pictures out of magazines," Carl said. "Not out here carrying a rifle and trying to shoot Germans."

"True," Edward responded. "But here she is. And there she goes. I'm just glad she didn't locate one of our devices for us in there...the hard way. Now, we got a château to sweep before General Arnold shows up."

Carl watched the girl all the way until she disappeared like a ghost into the shadows at the distant tree line.

"That gal will have some stories to tell her grandkids someday," Carl said.

"Let's hope so, Corporal," Edward told him as he turned back toward the château. "And pray they'll care enough to listen."

16

Broken beer bottles and fallen plaster crunched beneath their boots as Edward and Ace walked across the parquet floor of the château's spacious foyer. They could only guess at what the splendor of this place had once been. And its age and history. There were discolored patches on the walls where paintings once hung. A few pieces of damaged fine furniture remained, but the rooms on the ground floor had been mostly cleared of furnishings, likely so they could be used for soldiers and their sleeping bags. Or a place for stretchers. Bloodstains were visible, dyeing the fine wood floors forever. This once ornate house had served as a field hospital. There were spatters of blood on the walls all around. And in a space off the foyer, an operating room, the floor still sticky with the fresh blood of German soldiers.

"What a shame that lady's expensive furniture is all gone," Ace noted. "You know she had some nice stuff." Most of her valuables had probably been carted off to Germany, but there were burn piles in the court-yard marked by gray, powdery ashes. Those were likely the remains of some of the noblewoman's priceless antiques, burned for cooking and warmth on chilly nights.

"Only thing worse than having no money or power is having plenty of both and suddenly losing it all," Edward said. Then he added, "I suppose."

A beautiful chandelier, draped with spider webs and covered with dust, dangled above the foyer from a few electrical wires. It now swayed gently back and forth like a pendulum in the cross-breeze from the half-open front door where Edward and Ace entered and the window where the girl had exited.

As they walked on, the chandelier suddenly crashed hard to the floor behind them. Both men fell prone amid the scattering priceless crystal, pistols drawn, ready to exchange fire with whoever had gotten the drop on them.

"Jesus Christ!" Edward shouted. "We don't get blown up, we get brained by a chandelier. Or die from this stifling heat." He looked at Ace Taft. The sergeant's face was pale, streaked already with sweat and grime, his eyes wide. Then he unexpectedly grinned.

"But it missed us, sir. You see? I knew it. We lead a charmed life after all."

"Hang onto that thought, Sergeant," was Edward's response. "Hope to hell you're right."

To their left, in a huge parlor, beer bottles—some shattered, some not—were lined up in a neat row in front of a massive stone fireplace. It appeared the previous occupants had used them for target practice.

"Good brands," Ace noted, looking closely at the labels as he also checked for wires or any other hint they might be booby-trapped. "Krauts know their beer."

Edward picked up one bottle and examined the label. "Löwenbräu. Pops had this sometimes at his bar. The owners of the brewery in Munich were Jewish. Pops said the Nazis called it 'Jew beer.' Guess that's why they were shooting at it."

"Bastards," Ace muttered.

"And they underestimate us BD boys," Edward said, pointing to a German helmet resting upright on a small table. Wires were visible beneath it. He and Ace quickly took care of it, dropping the explosive package into the sergeant's canvas bag and tossing the helmet into a far corner of the room.

"That's one," Taft sang out, beating Edward to it.

"Two, counting the one on the flagpole. Ace, you check the rest of this floor while I clear the upstairs." The captain was only halfway up the ornate staircase, his hand always on the butt of his pistol in its holster, checking each step on the way for devices, when Ace called him.

"Captain, you need to see this!"

Behind a sofa—the only other piece of furniture remaining in the room —and against the wall, there was a row of twenty helmets, resting upside-down on their tops, neatly arranged as if to entice any souvenir hunter. Most were filled with enough plaster off the shattered walls and ceiling to hide any explosives placed in them. Several had what appeared to be dried blood on them. Nazi blood would make them even more prized by scavengers seeking a profit.

There was no option for Hume and Taft. They would have to carefully inspect every one of them. They dropped to their knees and started.

An hour later, as the day's sunlight faded from the floor-to-ceiling windows at the front of the château, all twenty helmets had been checked and tossed into a corner of the big room. No devices.

"What a waste of time," Edward grumbled. Then the beam from his flashlight caught something glistening amid the debris in the corner. He stepped over for a look. It was an elegant crystal doorknob. Edward picked it up and shoved it into his utility trousers pocket. He figured he would find more like it on doorways throughout the house.

"Of all the souvenirs you could keep, Captain, a doorknob?" Taft asked.

"You never know when you'll need a good doorknob, Sergeant," Hume responded. He had a plan.

"Just think, like all that stuff along the roadway, they did this helmet setup just to waste our time and slow us down," Ace said.

"I suspect you are correct, Sergeant," Edward said, then had another thought. "Maybe they figured we'd get careless when we didn't find anything in these and the one on the table was so obvious. That tells me there are still gonna be some good traps set for us somewhere in this place. But look on the bright side. No soldier would have left his helmet behind when they bugged out. Each one of these probably represents a man who gave his life for the Reich and will spend eternity out there in a shallow grave."

"Bright side, yessir," Taft said quietly. "You know, all this is sure a hell of a lot more nerve-racking than the buzzers and flashing red lights back at Aberdeen. Even with Colonel Kane looking over your shoulder."

Edward grinned and started once more for the stairs. "And a hell of a lot more permanent if something goes wrong. Well, whatever happens, happens. At least you won't have to hear it from the colonel if you mess up."

Ace now stood at the foot of the stairs, watching Edward go up. "Sir, speaking of which, you probably ought to know, considering where we are, that I failed the booby-trap house at APG. Twice. I was going to try for a third time, but then I asked to become a squad member, not a squad leader. That's another reason I didn't make officer."

"You mentioned that before, just not the three-times-you're-out part. But I read the file on each of you coming into the squad, so I pretty much knew it already." Edward looked back down at the sergeant. Taft's face was hidden in the shadows.

"All that training was driving me insane, sir," Ace admitted. "I'd been a fireman, done real-world things. I knew I'd do whatever had to be done to save lives, but they were about to send me off to the infantry. They must've needed men for BD bad enough by then, so they let me go ahead."

"Look, Ace, we got a job to do. You and me. You know how to do it as well as anybody. Some people learn better on the job. Stay calm and trust your training. And your experience. Let's get this little bungalow safe and ready for General Arnold and his staff. Okay?"

A pause. Then a meek, "Yessir. Then we take care of the ammo dump back at Grandcamp?"

"Yes. Then the damned ammo dump," Edward said irritably. Then he turned, shaking his head, and started up the stairs once again. His sergeant was one obsessive son of a bitch.

"Sorry, sir. I just have to take care of that mess, or when it blows, it'll be something else I got on my conscience 'cause I didn't do all I could before—"

Just then, there was a crash at the top of the stairs. Before a wide-eyed, frozen Edward could even pull his pistol, something small and furry dashed down past him. Ace drew his pistol and was ready to fire, but the critter had already scurried past him and was out the open front door.

The sergeant stood there, stunned. Edward resumed breathing, then laughed.

"Hey, Ace, you know why squirrels always swim on their backs?"

A sudden ray of late-day sunlight allowed Edward to see the bewildered look on the sergeant's face.

"No, sir. Why?"

"To keep their nuts dry."

Hume did not wait to see if Taft laughed. He turned and climbed on up to learn what surprises the next level of the château might hold.

♠

"Captain, you know the biggest downside to being a BD man?" Sergeant Taft asked with a straight face.

"No, Taft. What is it?" Hume responded.

"It takes him six hours to open his presents on Christmas morning!"

Both men were just stepping out the front doorway of the château into the dimness of impending night. The sergeant lugged his now-heavy canvas bag over his shoulder. It was filled with neutralized devices. Twenty-six of them.

Intense stress effectively broken, Edward laughed and slapped Taft on the back. "Sergeant, that thing about becoming an officer?"

"Yessir?"

"You keep working on your command voice and doing what you did today, and I'll talk to somebody. Okay?" The two men stopped and shook hands. "Keep doing your job like this, and the recommendation will write itself. Hopefully we won't be too busy. The Army needs men like you to lead a BD squad."

They walked down to where the tired and dirty squad members waited. Melodious evening birds—blackbirds, nightingales, chiffchaffs, skylarks— had begun chirping as the men made a game of swatting at flies and waving off bothersome bees swarming from the rotten apples on the ground in the nearby orchard. An explosion of some kind sounded ominously from somewhere far off. Dusky shadows grew longer, signaling an end to what seemed an endless day. It was still not over.

176 ELAINE HUME PEAKE & DON KEITH

The squad waited in dusky darkness next to their vehicles, unwilling to risk a fire in the coming night. Or even a cigarette. Snipers. There could easily be snipers out there waiting for the slightest bit of light to target.

"Looks like they had fun in that ghost house," Morty said, nodding toward Edward and Ace, both of whom appeared jovial despite the long, tense task they had just completed.

Hank had clicked the stopwatch when he saw them exit. "Three hours, six minutes, forty-five seconds. And it ain't quite 1900 hours yet. We made the deadline."

Ace walked over and gingerly set the heavy canvas bag down next to a wheel of the truck.

"You guys ready to make a big boom?" Edward asked. "Counting the one we got off the flagpole, twenty-six devices in the house. That oughta wake up every chipmunk between here and Paris." Edward put his hand on Ace's shoulder. "And this guy found and neutralized more than half of 'em." Now it was Edward's turn to do a little validation. He turned to Wozinski. "Gene, get on the radio and let HQ know they have a nice château, all cleared and ready for their housewarming party. Full report coming first thing in the morning."

"Hell of a lot of paperwork in this war business," Hank said, scribbling entries in his notebook. "But you dictate it, and I'll write it up, sir."

Each man made a point of stepping over and shaking Ace Taft's hand before getting busy blowing up the bag of booby-trap explosives. The smile on the sergeant's face was the broadest any of them had yet seen.

The blast from the devices from the château was as spectacular as anticipated. Now, as soon as a guard detail arrived—they were on the way to make sure the cleared structure remained cleared during the night—the Kaboom Boys could go back and get settled into wherever they would be temporarily billeted at Grandcamp-les-Bains.

The squad was busily packing up their tools and preparing to head back to the tent farm when Edward noticed someone standing in the deep shadows beneath one of the trees alongside the roadway. A sniper? A rogue enemy soldier separated from his outfit, bent on revenge?

"Find cover!" the captain shouted, and his men hit the ground behind the vehicles. Then Edward realized who it was. "All clear. It's just the lady who owns the place. The noblewoman." He jogged over to where she stood watching them.

"Ma'am, I am pleased to tell you that we have successfully cleared your home without further damage," he told her. Her face remained impassive. "Understand, 'cleared'? We removed explosives. Small bombs. *Petit.*" She nodded her thanks but remained otherwise emotionless. Her home would only change hands from one army to another. She remained locked out. "And madame, I am glad you are here because I have something to give you." He reached into his pocket and pulled out the dusty but still lovely crystal doorknob he had retrieved from the château. "I assume this belongs to you." He blew dust off it and used his sleeve to shine it a bit.

The frail, elderly woman looked wide-eyed at what Edward held in his hands, then gently took the doorknob from him. She cupped it in both hands, as if it were very heavy, then brought it to her lips and began sobbing. She kissed it as tears rolled down her cheeks.

Edward did not know what else to say or do. He remained quiet and still.

She finally looked up at him and spoke. "This, all the doorknobs, they were a gift to me from my husband on our thirtieth wedding anniversary. He...he...died of a heart attack when the Germans arrived."

"My deepest condolences. I regret we found only this one," Edward said. "I assume the Germans stole the rest."

"But now, at least, I have this one," she told him through her tears. "I have so little anymore, but now, thanks to you, I have something of my dear Bernard. *Merci.*"

"Could we give you a ride? Take you someplace, madame? It's getting dark."

"No, but thank you, my American soldier friend. Thank you so very much." She kissed the crystal doorknob once more and held it tightly to her chest, her frail body and hands trembling. "I stay with the wife of the man who was once my gardener. Her quarters are simple but neat and clean, just the other side of the hedgerow. And she is now my friend." She looked up at Edward. "War changes the nature of so many relationships."

They said their goodbyes, then Edward and the rest of the squad watched her walk away through the orchard, into the deepening darkness.

Distracted by the tender scene, none of them noticed the sudden movement behind them, at the gate that passed through the stone wall, barely thirty yards away. Standing unsteadily, it was a bloodied Nazi soldier, helmet askew. As Edward turned, he spotted the trooper, who was already aiming his Luger directly at him.

There was a crack of gunfire. Three quick shots, the sound echoing off the walls of the château. Edward and the squad hit the ground and scrambled for cover. The noblewoman crouched behind the trunk of an apple tree.

Edward was surprised he felt no pain, saw no eruptions of dirt from bullets hitting around him. How could the German have missed him from such close range? But as he crawled beneath the jeep, he glanced up to see the enemy soldier drop his gun and pitch forward before any of the squad could even take a shot at him.

Then, from behind the wall, someone else stepped out, arms raised, rifle pointed toward the sky to show this person posed no threat to them.

"Well, I'll be damned," Edward said.

The girl. The Resistance fighter from earlier. She first kneeled to check the German soldier for any sign of life. Then, satisfied, she stood, blew them a comically exaggerated kiss, and disappeared again, this time into the warm darkness of the Normandy night.

As the squad rode back to their new base—a good hour trip—the men were unusually quiet. Exhaustion, tension, lack of food, and the final bit of deadly action had taken its toll. Edward could not help but reflect on a solid bit of truth. Life. Death. Everything in between. What had happened there at that château was a powerful confirmation for him of why he had chosen to enlist, to join BD. Why he wanted to serve in this way and do the hazardous work.

As they passed marching troops, lines of POWs, more refugees, and encountered convoys headed into battle, Edward felt especially good about this day. A fleeting feeling, perhaps. This was only one day. What would tomorrow bring?

Now, though, he was more certain than ever that he could make a difference in the war, as well as in the lives of people he might encounter along the way. People mired in warfare's brutal maw. He had renewed a proud noblewoman's faith in mankind and brought a small bit of crystal light back into her dark existence. And his life had just been saved by another, a brave French girl he would likely never know. A mere child who would certainly not have raised and fired a rifle at another human had this conflict not distorted her youth. So many more would suffer. Could a single BD captain do enough good to matter?

Yes, he decided. He could make a difference.

Unless some greater force got in his way, he *would* make a difference.

A hot day in July, 1944. At the entrance to the abbey at the top of the massive rock that forms the ancient island of Mont-Saint-Michel, nineteen-year-old Hélène LeRiche tries to avoid being noticed, mingling with a small group of elderly worshippers approaching the imposing crowning structure. She wears no makeup and covers her long, blond hair with a drab khaki scarf, even in the steamy heat. But of course, a German soldier notices the attractive girl amid a gaggle of seventy-year-olds. He stops her and her fifteen-year-old travel companion, Pierre Devereaux, who is slinking along behind her, trying to be invisible. The SS man gruffly demands to know if they are qualified to enter the forbidden coastal zone.

"Papiere!" he sternly orders.

Pierre promptly hands over his identification papers. His father has impressed upon him the value of being prepared to produce documentation. Hesitation creates suspicion. New to this zone, Hélène nervously fumbles for hers, although she knows the papers are in order, thanks to Pierre. But the Germans have been known to ignore such trivial things and still have their way with innocent detainees. Especially attractive young women.

The soldier openly leers at the pretty, blue-eyed young woman as she produces her documents. He even licks his lips like a wolf over its prey as he studies the papers. The same ones already perused and approved by a different leering, lip-licking wolf of a German soldier at the foot of the island, before she and Pierre began climbing the 350 steps up to the abbey. The latest soldier finally waves them past, still staring at her breasts, her backside.

Hélène and Pierre have ridden their bicycles more than six miles from the town of Pontorson to visit this place. An iconic spot that Pierre—a new friend she already considers her little brother—has told Hélène so much about. She has been here once before, but as a very young child. She remembers little of it. But she hopes it will offer the refuge from the war that she so badly needs.

Now, only weeks since she and her mother had come to Pontorson after twice fleeing their home due to the war—first from Cherbourg and then from Saint-Lô as the Allies pushed into Normandy—she is finally at the top of the monolithic rock, 256 feet above the shimmering bay that lies between Normandy and Brittany. Then she enters the quiet, cool abbey to pray. Originally a monastery and convent, it became a prison during the reign of Louis XI and the French Revolution, and then under Napoleon. Now, it is a place for German soldiers to recharge for battle. Before the start of the June Allied offensive, it also hosted German tourists. But even these blemishes on the history of the place do not diminish the peace Hélène already feels here, even if it still remains under German control.

Pierre Devereaux is a native of Pontorson, the son of a previously wealthy merchant who has suffered like so many others during the German occupation. He and his family live near what was until recently Nazi headquarters, at Hotel Montgomery. The boy amuses himself by playing tricks on the cruel occupiers, knowing it could be dangerous. Like letting air out of German military vehicle tires, cutting small power lines to occupied buildings, or sprinkling bits of rat poison into their morning baguettes just to make them sick. His hatred of the Germans is something he has in common with Hélène. Even so, it is odd to him that such a sweet girl harbors such negative feelings. The baggage of war, he decides. But that is only one thing they have in common. They share a love for laughter, for pranks, for joie de vivre. His boyish crush on Hélène has him dreaming of making her his wife one day, even if she is four years his senior.

Now, thanks to Pierre, Hélène has returned to this place of peace and hope, this icon of meditation and worship, beneath the golden statue of Archangel Michael. A tranquil place that seems so far from the gunfire and exploding bombs and loud, rude soldiers that have been the soundtrack of her life for the past four years. Since the Germans came to Cherbourg in June of 1940 and her father was taken away.

It was her father who had once carried baby Hélène on his shoulders across the sand flats, carefully skirting the quicksand, in that long-ago family pilgrimage —like ones made by so many other Catholics from France and far away—to Mont-Saint-Michel. It is now an episode she hardly remembers. Her father has been forced to work for the Nazis at the hospital in Cherbourg, sleeping there, *away from his family for weeks at a time. She and her mother have not seen him since the day before the Allied invasion. They do not know where he is or if it is safe to go back there looking for him. Her brother was a French sailor and is now a POW, performing slave labor for Herr Hitler somewhere in Europe. Hélène has reluctantly but necessarily put aside her baccalaureate studies—her long-time dream of studying law—while she and her mother seek peace and quiet and relative safety.*

She still has nightmares of the first days of the Germans coming to Cherbourg. Hélène had been fast asleep, exhausted from her studies, when the shelling started. She pulled a blanket over her head and shouted to her parents in the next room: "Tell them to stop! I'm sleeping!"

There were bad dreams of the sad journey from their home in the port city down to Saint-Lô with other evacuees, only to have that peaceful but vital crossroads soon become a brutal battleground as well. That sent the two of them off yet again, to Pontorson, almost to Brittany, to hopefully be out of harm's way.

Now, as they pray under the guidance of the solitary priest in the abbey high above the bay, they feel so close to heaven and God. Hélène finally feels peace wash over her as she kneels next to her new best friend, Pierre. The calmness follows them as they stand and leave the abbey and step out into the courtyard where so many nuns and monks had once reverently trodden. As they look back at the waning sun, not so subtly reminding them they have a long pedal back to Pontorson and must be inside their homes before the eight o'clock curfew.

Peace is fleeting. Hélène LeRiche knows this only too well. Some of her sadness returns as she and Pierre begin the descent along Mont-Saint-Michel's Grand Degré. But as she so often does, she employs her secret power to choose to be happy, even in the midst of ugliness. She jettisons her somber feelings, laughs, and tags Pierre, and a game of chase begins as they work their way down.

Down, down to the main street, to the entrance gate, to the sand flats and the quicksand and the mainland where the sheep still graze even as the war roars along with no easy end in sight.

17

It was just after 2300 hours when the squad got back to Grandcamp-les-Bains. The disposal of all the booby traps at the château had been quick, easy, and characteristically noisy. The *KABOOM* was especially satisfying for the men, like they were contributing something positive to all that was going on in this dirty war. Each explosion felt like an exclamation point at the end of a sentence.

Now, time for a late meal and some well-deserved rest. But there was some kind of roadblock or checkpoint at every intersection between the château and the base. There had been too many examples of German soldiers dressed in US Army uniforms, driving official Allied vehicles, speaking unaccented English, knowing perfectly well, when challenged, who won last year's World Series or who the pro football team was in Cleveland or how to whistle "Dixie." A new enemy tactic was recruiting German boys raised in America, giving them US Army uniforms, and having them pretend to be military police. They were getting past guard posts, entering sensitive areas, and shooting or blowing up soldiers. The squad felt they were roaming a no-man's-land crisscrossed by a depressing amalgam of destroyed bocages and crop fields in what was once bucolic countryside.

"Those guys up ahead, make sure they are who they say they are,"

The Kaboom Boys 183

Edward told Ace at the first checkpoint. He shouted loud enough for the guys in the truck to hear. "Weapons raised!" Edward drew his pistol as Hank lifted the snout of his MI rifle. Morty, Pete, and Carl did the same, ready for anything should they get the signal from Captain or see any sign they were being duped.

A guard shined a light in Edward's eyes and shouted, "Flash!"

The captain immediately yelled back, "Thunder!" That was the correct code word for the day. The guard waved them on through.

The mess tent was still open when they finally made it "home," but the kitchen had long since shut down. A couple of Black soldiers on KP—kitchen police—cleaned up what remained of the serving line, the tent, and its long rows of tables. There was no one else there.

The only food left was some cold shit-on-a-shingle, greasy fried potatoes, stale day-old biscuits, and a few crumbs of dry pound cake. Even the coffee was lukewarm and oily. Still, they sat down together to eat. All except Edward, who grabbed a biscuit and cup of coffee before trotting back to the command tent for an update. And Ace Taft, who had whispered something to Hank back at the truck and then headed off in the opposite direction from the captain.

The men found spots on benches at a reasonably clean table and tiredly reviewed their one day so far on the mainland of the European continent. They also made the most of what they had available for a late supper. Everyone agreed this slumgullion was better than the relatively new K rations that they had to resort to in the field.

"Jeez! Like I say, nothing's ever kosher," growled Morty, eyeing something on the end of his fork.

"Well, there is one thing this supper has going for it," Carl Kostas noted. "It's here and available for us to consume. I just wish we could wrap it in grape leaves. Us Greeks wrap everything in grape leaves."

"You know the K rats were first developed for paratroopers...," Hank Anderson started, but he was simply too tired to continue. And the squad too bushed to shout him down.

When Edward rejoined them, he sat down to a silent table. He clinked his spoon on his coffee cup, as if ringing a bell or proposing a toast.

"Guys, guys! I need your attention here. You know yesterday marked the end of our seventh week together," he announced. "From the day we defuzed our first bomb as a squad, it has been seven weeks to this very day, and we're all still kickin'! I say we give ourselves a round of applause!"

Everyone was awake now, reenergized. The men clapped, slapped each other on the back, banged the table, whooped, and whistled. The KP men looked at them oddly but kept working.

"And we're going to absolutely beat those damned BD-man odds, right?" the captain asked.

The men hooted and hollered even more. No wonder they were beginning to feel invincible. Three more weeks. A worthy goal. Beating the odds.

Edward was about to explain their bunking arrangement for the night when he realized someone was missing. "Okay, where's the sergeant this time?"

Hank answered, "He's out checking on that ammo dump again. That Scotsman's obsessed with it, you know."

"In the dark? I can't imagine how much he could see out there," Edward said. "And let's hope some trigger-happy sentry doesn't decide he's a spy."

The captain was interrupted by Taft, running into the tent, out of breath, agitated.

"Guys, they dumped a ton more bad stuff out there since this morning!" he loudly testified and then plopped down next to the captain, catching his breath, and stowing his gear bag beneath the bench. The sergeant appeared manic, eyes wide, visibly shaking, maybe from lack of sleep and food or the stress of the past few days. Or possibly from what he had seen out there at the munitions pile in the darkness behind the tents.

Ace pulled a bottle from his shirt pocket, shook out four or five aspirin tablets, and swallowed them without benefit of drink. Then he stared hard at Edward.

Everyone else was quiet, waiting for the captain's response. Edward chose to ignore Ace for the moment. Instead, he referred to a sheet of paper he held and spoke between sips of coffee.

"All right, guys, here's the deal. Headquarters has us a new truck." He looked at Gene Wozinski, then handed him a slip of paper. "Corporal, you'll be up early and down at the motor pool by 0630 to pick up the truck. And maybe a trailer, too. Bring it back here so we can get everything transferred over. We'll save you some breakfast. Got that?"

"New truck, yessir," and there was a broad grin on Gene's face. The old vehicle that had served them well in England had now been running rough since it was baptized in the English Channel during their landing. And larger was certainly a good thing. They would be adding new tools and equipment, and they carried lots of lumber for the supports to prevent cave-ins when they dug down deep to buried UXBs.

"Just don't forget to grab our sign for the windshield. We want everybody to know the Kaboom Boys are on the job," Edward reminded him. The captain then turned toward Anderson. "Hank, soon as I finish feeding my tapeworm here, we'll go over notes on today's job and get started on the report."

Anderson smiled. "Sir, I'll go ahead and write 'em up so you can get some shut-eye. I'm wide awake and would probably just read for an hour or so, anyway."

Edward considered the corporal's offer. "Okay, then. But be sure to have the report at the command tent by 0800. I don't need to review it this time. I lived it. Just make it short and sweet, and I'll sign it before you take it over. You got any questions, though, you wake me up. Got that?"

"Got that. Yes, sir," Anderson confirmed.

"There must be a hundred recovered land mines piled up," Ace blurted out, not caring if anyone was listening or not. His voice was high and tight. "I guess they're not blowing them up as they find them anymore. Unstable as hell, and with this heat—"

"We'll have two tents for you guys and one for me, on row Delta," the captain continued, still not acknowledging anything Ace was saying. "Usual split-up for the sleeping arrangements. This mess tent is on row Alpha. Look for numbers six, seven, and eight on the signs on the tent poles. Mine's number eight, so stay out of that one if you don't want to get shot. It'll also be our BD office, but not while I'm sleeping. Hank, be sure to announce yourself when you wake me up to sign the report. The Signal Corps has already installed a landline to the communications trailer and put in a phone for us. We'll have to use our sleeping bags tonight, but we'll have cots and blankets going forward."

"Another night in a fart sack?" Pete said with a laugh. "Really deluxe!" The others chuckled, including the captain.

"Only the best for America's fighting men. God only knows how long we'll be based here or how often we'll get to use those deluxe accommodations. But we're sure as shit about to find out. Got that?'

Everyone nodded and went back to eating. Everyone but Ace Taft, who appeared to be in a different world from his squad brothers.

"There are grenades strewed about everywhere, piles of 'em, in the open, and other devices that are leaking. Guys, I even saw some sticks of dynamite, just lying there," he continued, talking fast, agitated.

Hank Anderson, a frown on his face, appeared to be the only one listening to Ace. Then he glanced pointedly at the captain. Taft had shared with Hank his previous troubles, his history of untreated concussions, his sometimes-debilitating depression after the factory blast and loss of his fiancée. Had exhaustion and the day's tension brought all that to the forefront again?

"Reveille for the rest of you guys is 0700," Edward went on. "Shit and a shave and mess tent by 0745. Gas up at 0830. We got a new job, and I'll brief at the jeep at 0845. We leave out at 0900. Got that?"

More nods. Rise and shine at 0700 sounded good for a change. Even if they would be sleeping in a bag on the hard ground.

Ace Taft was still trying to talk, growing even more frantic. "Sir! Sir! When the sun hits that dump, and with it being as damn hot as it's been lately and it s-starts all that...that...unstable ordnance cook-cooking, it'll... it'll b-blow, sir," he pushed on, stammering in his effort to make the captain understand the urgency. Then, out of breath, dissipated physically and emotionally, he finally put both elbows on the table and his chin in his hands. "I've seen it before. I warned them about the heat and the chemicals that time, too. Just not often and loud enough. I can't let it happen again. I won't! Somebody's gotta listen this time. This thing's gonna blow."

Edward nodded slightly but kept chewing. Hank again looked hard at the captain, frustrated that he was ignoring Ace and his desperate message.

Hume finally turned toward his sergeant and took in the exasperated expression on his face. "Okay. Okay. Ace, meet me at the pile at 0630. We'll

The Kaboom Boys

187

take a look and come up with a good plan, if it'll help you sleep better. That's what we all need now. Some sleep."

Ace brightened up. "Good plan! Right, Captain! Six thirty. Good plan."

"But you know there may not be a damn thing we can do about it for a few days, right, Sergeant? We may have other priorities. Like we did today with General Arnold's orders. But if we don't clear it, another BD squad will. I already sent word. HQ knows the situation."

"If you give up, all could be lost," Ace responded, eyes wide. "Long as you're fighting, you still got a chance. It's a dance, sir. I'll do whatever I have to do to save lives this time. We have to make the right decision every time, sir."

"Good advice, Ace," Hank Anderson added, backing the sergeant. "We won't give up. The Kaboom Boys don't give up." Tired as they were, the others had noticed how peculiar Ace was acting.

"I'll do whatever I have to do to save lives, Captain," Taft repeated, an odd look on his face. Maybe determination. Locked-jaw determination that bordered on obsession. Edward ignored it. It was late. Everybody was bushed. Including Ace Taft.

Edward shook his head to clear it. "Now, you guys eat before they close down completely and kick us out. Hank, you ready for the notes?"

"Yes, Captain." Anderson had already pulled a notebook from his jacket pocket. "But you know if Ace says—"

Hume interrupted, handing Anderson his scribbled, real-time notes on specifics of each of the devices they had located and removed from the château. "Damn helmets. Lined up, inspected, not a single device there. Just a huge waste of time."

As if he had just remembered something, Ace abruptly reached down beneath the bench and pulled an object out of his gear bag. He set it in the middle of the table. A German officer's helmet. One of the plaster-filled ones they had so tediously checked. And one of the ones spattered with what was certainly human blood. Painted on its right side were SS runes on a silver shield and on the left, a swastika on a red shield.

The men stared at it for a moment before Pete Ronzini asked, "Ace, you wanna sell that? There's guys back in Brooklyn would pay lots of money for that thing. 'Specially with Nazi blood all over it."

Morty Schwartz had a different opinion. "Look, some damn Nazi got wounded and probably died with that piss bucket on his head. It's bad luck. Get rid of that thing, Ace, before it taints everything!"

"I'll take it off your hands," Pete told Ace. "Fifty bucks?"

"I got an uncle back in LA would probably give you a hundred bucks for it," Carl said. "Runs a Greek restaurant in Santa Monica, and he's got a wall full of souvenirs from—"

"You bidding against me?" Pete asked, scowling. "If you are, then show us your damn money!"

Edward shook his head and held up a cautionary hand. Sometimes, commanding a squad was like being the father of six rambunctious boys.

Ace grabbed the helmet, raked it off the table, and shoved it back into his bag. Then he stood and went to draw a cup of coffee from the pot and get a cold biscuit just as the KP were removing the pot and trays for cleanup. He paced back and forth between the tables, sipping, taking bites, still shaken by the UXO dump so near their new bivouac area.

"Only one device on the first floor," Edward was saying. "The rest were all upstairs. I found that one crystal doorknob in a dark corner. You superstitious fellows don't object, I gave it to the noblewoman who owns the place. It was hers, anyway. I doubt it brings her more bad luck than what she's been through already. Maybe you guys want to check your Ouija boards or tarot cards or ask a witch or something to make sure we're not cursed."

Hank looked up from his notetaking, a frown on his face. "No codes or maps or top-secret messages, sir?"

"I said, nothing else. You writin' a book, Corporal?" Hume shot back irritably, though penning a book was not out of the realm of possibilities for Hank. Only when Edward realized how sharp his retort had been did the captain grasp just how fatigued he was. "Write 'All Clear' so the CO knows it's safe for him to occupy his new HQ. Keep it simple. Got that?"

Anderson grunted. He continued writing furiously in his notebook.

"Okay, men, get some sleep. We got a long ride to the job in the morning through territory we believe to be under our control. But you never know. And I suspect we'll continue to find other messes to clean up along the way, too." Hume stood, stretched, then headed toward the vehicles to retrieve his sleeping bag and gear and go find his tent. He stopped and looked hard at Ace Taft. "Sergeant, you best quit pounding out a trench in the mess tent and get some rest, too. We'll evaluate that dump first thing, and then we'll do the right thing about it as quickly as we possibly can. Got that?"

"Uh, yessir," Taft acknowledged halfheartedly. Then he followed his captain out the tent opening and into the night. "See, it's just that I warned people at the factory, and they didn't take me seriously."

The captain had hurried on, though, and was already well out of earshot.

♠

Tired as he was, Edward had considerable trouble finding sleep. It was too hot for the sleeping bag. Mosquitoes and biting flies zoomed in on him when he tried to doze in his skivvies on top of the bag. He crawled out the tent opening to sit in the slightly cooler night air. He was soon counting stars, as he had done when, as a boy, he went camping up the side of the mountain with Fritz and other buddies. Tonight, however, instead of telling ghost stories, he was thinking about how those same celestial bodies several hours later would be dropping pinpoints of light on Mahanoy City. The time difference only made him feel more distant from home. The stars had him thinking about Mom and Pops, Tommy and his wife, the new nephew he looked forward to getting to know one day. And Sarge, too. Oh, to be as happy-go-lucky as that pup!

He was not homesick, he told himself. Nor did he have regrets. He was doing exactly what he had set out to do. See the world. Do demanding work. Find a life balance on the edge of a sharp blade. Make a difference. Do it with gusto. Not think too much because he had done too much thinking over the years already. Now, he just wanted to *do*. But whether it was thinking of home, the immense fatigue he felt, or the blinking flashes and deep grumbles of not-so-distant artillery fire that sullied the peace and quiet of the night, his attention returned to the here and now.

He stood and walked past the open flaps of the nearby tents where his squad members—his boys—slept. He pulled his penlight from his tool belt and used it to check on each of his men, like a nervous father making sure his children were safe and still breathing in their cribs. They did seem like his own kids, though he was practically the same age as they were. Rank meant he was responsible for them, though. For making the right decisions that could affect them in good or bad ways. For trying to keep them positive, toeing the line, doing the right thing. Responsibility he had sought and, finally, willingly accepted. But it was never easy.

Still, he had to admit, he sometimes wondered if he was up to the challenge. But he told himself he had to be. No choice in the matter now. And he would get better at it.

In the first tent, Hank had a copy of *A Farewell to Arms* open across his chest, his own flashlight still lit. But now, he was asleep, snoring slightly. Edward stepped close enough to switch off the light and save the batteries for future fiction.

Ace slept fitfully nearby. Edward turned off his own penlight as the sergeant rolled over and groaned pitifully, as if in the throes of a nightmare. But before his light went out, the captain had spotted the pilfered bloody helmet. It was lying there on the ground next to Taft's sleeping bag, within an arm's length. The sergeant's pistol was there next to it.

Edward shook his head. Ace Taft was one deep and moody character. The captain had hopes he might be able to figure him out. The guy had a keen mind, a fine work ethic, motivation to do the job without fretting about the consequences, the potential to not only be a key member of the squad but to maybe command his own squad someday. The former fireman was a nut Edward might one day crack. Then he would be a fine BD man. But at the moment, that potential positive was tossing, turning, and talking in his sleep, tormented by demons. His number two, his sergeant, should be an asset, not a liability. His fervent hope was that Ace Taft would continue to rise to the occasion and prove Edward right about his value.

Like Hank, Gene Wozinski seemed undisturbed by the noises of Ace's bad dreams. Woz was in the far corner of the tent, his back to the entrance and the other two men, sleeping soundly. Even in the semi-darkness, Edward saw something dangling from a nearby tent support. The Saint Michael medal on its gold chain. He flipped his light on just long enough to admire it.

In the other tent, Morty, Pete, and Carl were sleeping peacefully. Satisfied all was well, Edward again settled down in the matted grass in front of his own tent. Only then did he pull from his jacket a folded and worn envelope. He had received the letter the day before they left England, and it had been in his breast pocket since. He had postponed opening and reading it. The handwriting on the envelope was his dad's. They were usually addressed by his mom. And up to now, the three previous times Pops wrote him a letter, it was bad news, as if Mom had insisted on him doing the dirty jobs.

In the first such letter, Edward learned that his uncle Claude had fallen down a shaft at the Luzerne County mine where he worked. Every miner at his funeral wore a hard hat throughout the service with its carbide light burning. In the next letter, his dad informed Edward that his second cousin, Henry Stoves, had been confirmed as killed in action on Guadalcanal in the Pacific, trying to quell a Japanese machine gun nest. The Marines doubted they would ever recover his body from those dismal swamps. And in the last one, Pops informed him that Victor Stapleton, the son of Cal, the newsstand owner, had indeed enlisted in the Army and was now missing in action. MIA, even though his job was to win the war by cooking and serving meals to white foot soldiers.

Now was as good a time as any to see what the latest bit of bad news was, Edward decided. He tore open the envelope with his thumb. When he unfolded the single sheet of note paper, something fell out into his lap. The note paper was blank. The item was a creased newspaper clipping.

Before he unfolded and read the article, Edward looked up at the star-flecked sky. What could be so awful that his father had not even been able to scribble a note about it? So bad he would allow a newspaper article to tell the story? Or maybe it was something good this time, a positive bit of news. Something interesting enough that Pops thought it might cheer up Edward. Maybe the days of dread before opening the envelope had all been needless worry.

A sudden shooting star crossed the entire width of the sky above him. It was so bright it illuminated the rows of tents lined up in all directions in the hastily built bivouac area. It even momentarily erased the artillery flares that blossomed in the skies farther inland. He took a deep breath, deciding the shooting star was an omen urging him to go ahead and see what the article was all about.

As he read the headline from his home county newspaper and then scanned the first paragraph of the article, tears welled up in his eyes. He found it difficult to draw in a breath of air. By the second paragraph, he was no longer able to see the words through tears.

Carefully, hands trembling, he folded the article back up, placed it inside the blank sheet of paper, put both back inside the envelope, and returned it to his breast pocket. Then he switched off his penlight, crawled back inside the tent, lay down on top of his sleeping bag, and stared at the canvas above him, stretched tight like a fatigue-green, starless sky, until exhaustion and overwhelming grief forced him to shut his eyes and lose himself in labored slumber.

Already hot. Brutally hot. Looking at another day above 100 degrees, the radio threatens. Record-breaking temperatures for the Philadelphia area. Especially for Camden, south of the Delaware River in New Jersey, where it seems the breezes are weaker and far more helpless against heat and humidity, trapped by multi-story buildings and reflected off sticky asphalt.

But Alistair Taft is as happy as he has ever been, and that's saying plenty. His 1935 high school yearbook named him "Mr. Optimist." His tuneful whistling and big smile are evidence of it as he walks toward work with an energetic bounce. Many of the people that the handsome young man meets are infected by his mood and return his grin. At age twenty, he already has a good job at the Whiz Floor Wax Company, one that pays a decent wage. Especially good from the perspective of those who have come of age during the Great Depression. His fiancée, Susan Ferguson, who is also the child of a Scottish immigrant, like Alistair, works there, too. Second shift, just like him, 1:30 p.m. until 10 p.m. with a half-hour meal break. They share dinner each evening in the company cafeteria or, when it is not hellish hot or the clouds are not spitting bits of sleet or snow, they eat on a bench outside the main office. They often plan for their future together as they munch on scones or teacakes she bakes for them.

Susan always uses the nickname "Ace," the one his father gave him. That is because, as she tells him—and anybody else willing to listen—that she was lucky

The Kaboom Boys

to draw him since he is "the most valuable card in the deck." He is fine with her using the name, as well as her logic, even if his mother does not care for it. "As long as it's ace of hearts, clubs, or diamonds," he tells her, then asks, "The ace of spades is unlucky, right?" Susan admits she doesn't know. She thought it was the other way around, that the card was lucky.

Ace's mother, Iona MacGregor Taft, and her late husband, Cameron Hugh Taft, migrated with baby Alistair to the US from the banks of Scotland's Loch Lomond. Iona likes Susan, though she does not generally care for most people, and especially those by the last name of Ferguson. That is due to a bitter, centuries-old feud between the MacGregors and the Fergusons—not at all unlike the Hatfields and McCoys, but Scottish style, bad blood from back in the old country since the early 1600s. But Iona is willing to make a rare exception so long as the girl does not break her boy's heart.

That is Iona's primary purpose in life, her son's happiness, now that her husband is gone to his reward. She, of all people, is aware of how happy Susan makes her son.

But one thing does bother Ace as he approaches the Penn Street entrance to the factory. It silences his happy whistle, cancels the smile, and brings a furrow to his sweating brow. He has repeatedly tried to explain to his foreman that there could be problems with the way the company stores naphtha—basically lighter fluid— in big rusty barrels against a wall of windows on the west side of one of the buildings. A spot where the sun is hottest in the afternoon. It is something he remembers from chemistry class at Haddon Heights High School. Now, even more concerned during the heat wave, he has visited the library and read more. Heat— especially this year's record summer heat—could make the fluid dangerously unstable.

But Floyd Buttram, the mixing room foreman, disagreeably ignores Ace's warnings. He has forty years on the job, working at Whiz, and nothing's ever blown up on his shift.

"Shut up yer gripin', Taft, or go see if RCA or somebody else is hirin', which I doubt," he says. "They pay less, anyhow. Or join up with the Army. You want an explosion so damn bad, you might find yourself one if a war comes along, like they sayin' in the papers."

In the summer of 1940, few in the US want war, but the chatter about such distasteful things flows nonstop in the huddle on the football field, on the sidelines of a soccer pitch, in the bars, at the dance halls, and at church socials.

A worrisome prospect some discuss and others try to ignore. It has been only ten months since Hitler's army marched into Poland, but President Roosevelt declares America will remain neutral.

Ace Taft has decided to be quiet and try not to worry about the volatile chemical, just as he has about the possibility of war. He will do his job in the mixing room and not antagonize Buttram. Save money for a ring. Eat dinner with Susan. Wait on a job promotion to the lab in the air-conditioned room in the building adjacent to where she works. Take her to the movies or for a ride on the river in the little boat his father built. Then, when the time is right, when that promotion comes through with the spike in pay, he will pop the question. No need to risk losing his job for complaining, postponing their plans.

As he joins all the other second-shift workers marching toward the Penn Street entrance, lunch pails in hand, Ace again whistles happily. The pavement is dappled from shimmering heat. But Susan is bringing haggis for supper. They plan on catching the late-night showing of My Favorite Wife at the air-conditioned Cherry Hill Movie House after work. Susan is a fan of Irene Dunne and even wears her hair like the star. She also tells Ace he is a dead ringer for Randolph Scott. He is not at all sure about that.

None of it will happen.

Ace Taft's idyllic world ends at 1:04 p.m. on Tuesday, July 30, 1940.

The unbelievable force of the blast knocks Ace and many others to the ground as they approach the entrance. That likely saves their lives. A blast wave and mass of solid flame and shrapnel pass just over their prone bodies, slamming into and igniting storefronts and row houses across the street from the factory. Deafening explosions sound from throughout the complex, one after the other, as flammable mixtures erupt into bright, hot blazes and turn several city blocks into roaring hellfire.

Ace shakes his head to try to comprehend what is happening. He is dizzy, disoriented. He can hardly hear. But he can feel the heat. He bleeds badly from a cut on his forehead. He wipes blood from his eyes. He has hit his head hard on the pavement. The pain makes it impossible to focus. He must have been knocked unconscious. How long was he out? He senses more explosions from inside the factory. When he tries to stand, he falls back down and vomits.

The Kaboom Boys 195

Workers run past Ace, some injured. He sees a badly burned woman staggering and stumbling his way. He recognizes her. The head of the secretarial pool where Susan works. Adrenaline kicks in. He jumps up, grabs her, instinctively puts her over his shoulder, and, though wobbly, moves her farther away from the hell that so recently was a thriving factory. When he eases her to the ground, he knows she is gone. He does not have the opportunity to ask her about Susan.

Then, even with skeins of the woman's flesh still on his hands and arms, he has the presence of mind to limp down to the corner of Ninth and Penn and pull the fire alarm on a pole there. For some reason, he yells, "Fire! Fire!" Anyone in the area can see that the entire world has been ignited. His shouts are muffled by the roar of the flames and popping of breaking windows.

Even after the fire trucks have rolled up, screeched to a halt, and unfurled hoses, Ace continues to help as best he can to get the badly injured people away from the blistering flames. As if he is driven to do so. Even as he suffers from his own painful burns and throbbing head and blurred vision, he risks his own life to help those who are in danger.

He tries to work his way to Susan, but flames and smoke drive him back, and he cannot see where he needs to go. He knows she likes to start her shift early so she can have donuts and Bible study with her coworkers.

As long as he keeps fighting, he has a chance. She has a chance.

It is a fire captain who finally orders Ace to get out of their way, to find medical help for himself. "But if you ever want to be a firefighter, kid, you come see me, okay?" the captain tells him.

Recruiting at the outskirts of hell.

Ten people die that day, mostly women. Susan Ferguson is one of them. So is Floyd Buttram. More than a hundred are badly hurt, including several firemen, and many of them will die later. Fifty buildings have been destroyed. Sixty families are left homeless. The next day's newspaper reveals, "Police believe the first explosion may have been caused by heat igniting a drum of naphtha."

At Susan's memorial service, the same fire captain approaches a numb Ace Taft and again offers him a job. Recruiting at a funeral.

Despite his world having come to an end, Ace knows he needs employment. The factory and his paycheck are both gone. He has to help his mother get by. He does not have to think about it. Being a firefighter seems like a way to remember the woman he loved but could not save. His only request, if he accepts, is that he be assigned the toughest jobs a fireman might have. No number of challenging rescues could ever make up for not being able to get to Susan. But at least he would do whatever it took to try.

He gets his wish. One of those tough assignments is a five-alarm fire at a seven-story office building down Ninth Street, not far from the ruins of the floor wax factory. It is also home to a US Army recruiting office. The recruiter notices the strong, daring, take-charge, and hardworking young firefighter and, as soon as the blazes are out and the hoses depressurized and rolled up, he approaches Alistair Taft. The recruiter tells Ace he has special jobs in the Army for guys like him. Guys who want to make a difference. Who seem fearless. Who thrive on staring down danger. Jobs that save lives instead of claiming them and lead quickly to earning an officer's commission and pay.

Recruiting at a five-alarm fire.

Iona Taft mourns the change in her handsome boy after the tragedy. He has always been happy-go-lucky, and more so than ever since meeting Susan. An athlete, especially good at soccer. A science buff with a good grasp of chemistry. Perpetually happy.

"Och, he's not the same, ever since that fire and losing his lassie," she tells anyone who will listen, her Scottish burr even thicker when she talks about her son. "Aye, that playful wee bairn of mine, he's gone as surely as if he got blown up over there at that factory, too."

She sees a sadness in his dark eyes that was never there before. He is haunted. He spars with bouts of deep depression and experiences blinding headaches from the hit he took from the blast. Then several more concussions suffered as a firefighter.

But once he is signed up for the Army and BD and as he prepares to go off to Maryland for training, she sees another change in him.

"Why are you so stubborn to do this? This dangerous thing?"

"A chance to help save people, Mam. If you give up, it's lost. Long as you're fighting, they still got a chance," he tells her. "BD gives me a chance to make a difference."

His mother is pleased to note that as young Alistair packs his duffel bag, he is once again whistling a happy tune.

18

"Shit! Batteries are used up," Hank Anderson muttered irritably. Damn things would be hard to come by here, too. But then he realized the flashlight switch was in the off position, though the book he had been reading was still open on his chest. He flipped it on. The light was bright and lively. "Must have turned it off in my sleep," he muttered. And since he had been so dead-to-the-world tired, he had not rolled off his back all night. "Sometimes I do my best work in my sleep," he told himself as he sat up and stretched. A sliver of sunlight parting the tent flap had awakened him.

His wristwatch showed six o'clock exactly. He could doze for another hour, but that was not Hank's style. Once awake, it was up and at 'em. He was always the first to the service station each morning, the first to crawl beneath a car. "If you're five minutes early, you're ten minutes late," his dad always told him.

At the back of the tent, Gene Wozinski had already shaved and was dressed, about to leave to pick up their new truck.

"Mornin', Woz. Sunrise woke you up, too, huh?"

"Nope. All that racket. You'd think there was an Allied invasion going on out there."

Then Anderson noticed all the nearby commotion for the first time. Sounds of machinery. Men yelling at each other. Vehicle engines revving.

Officers shouting orders at throngs of soldiers. They would later learn the aviation engineers started early each day, cutting down apple trees—the bivouac area was in the middle of a huge orchard—stacking them, and burning them. Then newly arrived bulldozers and steamrollers were clearing and grading for a short runway, room for more tents, and a few solid structures, including a hospital. They also put down metal mesh to cover landing strips and roadways as they were constructed out of soggy farmland.

Last thing Wozinski did before stepping out of the tent was reach for his Saint Michael, give the archangel a quick kiss, and drape the medallion around his neck.

Hank nodded approval for the ritual and smiled. "We'll take good luck and protection from anybody offering it, right?"

"Right!" Gene said and trotted away.

Ace Taft's sleeping bag was empty, his tool kit and canvas bag gone. His appointment with the captain at the UXO dump was half an hour away yet. Hank grinned. Ace was a go-getter, too. Five minutes early was ten minutes late. Angling for an officer's commission, for sure. But sometimes he was more like a man possessed.

A passing soldier noticed Hank stirring and stopped.

"Hey there, we heard you BD guys had finally shown up."

"Finally?" Hank shot back.

"Well, just so you know, we dug you fellas a latrine right behind your tents, in the holly bushes, so be careful where and how you squat," the soldier told him and promptly moved on.

"And a good morning to you, too," Hank growled as he stood up and began digging in his duffel bag for his dopp kit. Then he pulled on his trousers, put on his helmet, and, barefoot and shirtless, stepped out into the French morning to christen the new latrine and find a place to shave and brush his teeth. Hopefully a spot with a hint of a breeze. It was suffocating hot already.

Carl Kostas was just emerging from the other three-man tent. He was sweating as he swatted at something buzzing around his head.

"Mornin', Carl," Hank offered. "You up early, too, I see."

"Who could sleep with all this noise and heat and these damn bees?"

The Kaboom Boys 199

Kostas responded.

It was true. The dawning sun was just winking through the few remaining apple trees. British warships on D-Day had pummeled the area with big shells aiming to take out German artillery batteries. They annihilated plenty of apple trees. The engineers had since gone to work downing the rest of the orchards, obliterating tons of ripe apples and eliminating any chance of finding natural shade. It was already stifling even before the sunshine had a chance to heat up the still air even more. And there were bees everywhere. From all the apples sacrificed to make a temporary home for soldiers, Rangers, airmen, and support personnel streaming in along the invasion beaches on both sides of Grandcamp-les-Bains. Most of those troops would only stop briefly before pushing on south and east.

"Don't know if the bees belong to the Luftwaffe or not," Hank said as he looked for a convenient limb on which to hang his shaving mirror. He was especially careful with it as he unwrapped it from pages of the front section of the *Denver Post*, dated six months earlier. It was another of several going-away gifts from his mother. They were her way of making up for his dad, who was still devastated his boy dropped out of high school to join the military. "I suspect there's a secret lab in Berlin where Nazi scientists train zillions of bees to come torture us."

"If the bombs and the bees don't kill us, this damn heat certainly will," Carl continued to grouse.

"You know, this is historic ground here where we stand," Anderson went on, whether Carl was paying attention or not. Hank found a holly bush for the mirror and was pouring some water from his canteen into his helmet to mix with chips from a bar of Ivory soap and conjure up some shaving lather. "General Charles de Gaulle, the leader of the French provisional government, was here, right about at this spot, a few days ago and spoke to the townspeople who have survived all the..."

But Carl was gone, off to the mess tent, clearly uninterested.

Hank shrugged and grinned. Kids. And Carl was a kid, even if he was a couple of years older than Anderson. A Californian by way of Alabama to boot. Spoiled by fine weather and sweet baklava and easy blondes.

Anderson began to scrape soap and whiskers from his chin. Then he noticed something odd. The birds had ceased their cheerful singing. There was no buzzing from the bees that had been humming a discordant symphony only seconds before.

Then, a blinding flash of light as if from a million colliding suns. An instant after, a powerful, swift-moving shock wave. Hank was thrown backward. Something powerful sucked the air from his lungs. Then an eruption of ground-rippling rumbles, one after another, louder and louder. Each more intense than anything Hank could have ever imagined.

Hank lay on his back on the ground. Stunned. Deaf. Breathless. Something hot and sticky filled his eyes. As he wiped at the blood and tried to stand, he pulled a shard of glass—a piece of his shaving mirror—from just above the bridge of his nose. Then he felt the impact of two additional explosions. He sensed the rush of hot wind surging past him after each.

"...the fuck?" he yelled, but he could not even hear his own voice asking the question.

He pressed a thumb on the cut from the glass to try to stop the bleeding. He realized his eyeglasses were gone. For some reason, he believed if he could just locate them and get them back on, he could better understand what had just happened. But when he found them on the ground, bent but unbroken, and put them on, he was still swimmy headed, confused. It was difficult to stand.

Then, as the intense chiming sound in his ears began to subside and as he started to feel a bit steadier on his feet—and decided he was alive and not seriously injured but others were likely not so lucky—Hank first assumed the damn Germans must have dropped a two-ton bomb nearby. Hitler. Hitler or Satan. Maybe both, working in tandem. But he had heard no bomber engines droning overhead just before the explosions.

Artillery? Usually, one could hear several shells hit the ground as the attackers walked the blasts in to find range on their intended target. There had been nothing at all but songbirds and humming bees before that leg-buckling blast.

Hank stepped unsteadily back into his partially collapsed tent. He most wanted to lie down. Lie down and think. Think and rest until his head stopped spinning and throbbing with each heartbeat. Instead, he eased down onto his sleeping bag and began using the rest of the water from his

The Kaboom Boys

canteen to wash the blood and soap from his face and bare chest and check himself for more wounds.

"You okay, Hank?" It was Morty Schwartz, hesitantly crawling out of his own tent nearby, as if he were wary of what he might find out there. There was no response from Anderson. "What the hell was that? Hank?"

Then Hank noticed Morty, coming his way on all fours. "I'm fine, I think. I just can't hear so well. What the hell happened?"

"Shit, Hank. You're bleeding."

"I'll be okay." Hank had both fingers in his ears, moved his jaw about, trying to get his hearing back.

"Look, let me help you to the medical tent," Morty offered as he pulled another piece of glass from Hank's cheek.

The air was rank with the smell of cordite and smoke and dust. Bits of metal and paper fell from the sky. Some were on fire and burned holes in the tents where they settled.

"Just go find out what happened," Hank said loudly. "See if we can help."

"Holy shit! That pile!" Morty suddenly exclaimed. "Ace was right. That damned ammo dump went up!"

Hank could now hear enough to get the gist of what Morty was saying. Still with bloody soap all over him, eyes wide behind his crooked and dirty spectacles, Hank jerked his head up to look directly at Morty. "Jesus. Ace. Ace and the captain. They were going over there to..."

The awful realization was almost as mind-numbing as the sudden stunning blasts had been.

"Just go check," Hank shouted, though Morty was right next to him. "See if you can find them." Morty ran off in the direction of the dump.

Hank knew they needed to do something. He pulled another piece of glass from his chest, just above his left nipple. His body in shock, he felt no pain as he placed the heel of his hand on the wound to stop the bleeding, as if he were doing a hand-over-heart salute to something or somebody.

Gene Wozinski suddenly appeared, disheveled, confused, half-dressed, covered with dirt.

"I gotta go get that truck," he said, but only stood there.

"First, I guess, we better check the dump and make sure there's not more stuff ready to blow," Hank told him as he dug for a shirt from his bag.

"Hank, I gotta go get that new truck," Woz told him, words slurred. "Captain's gonna be royally pissed if I don't have it back for the..."

The two men looked at each other. The truck probably did not matter now. Still, it was an order. They decided Woz would get the truck and head for the ammo dump. Or what was left of it.

Dressing hastily, Hank pulled on and tied his boots, then stepped out to retrieve his dopp kit and pieces of the shaving mirror.

That was when he saw something he would never forget. On the ground near where he had been standing when the detonation cut him down and altered his consciousness.

It was a man's charred and mangled forearm, the hand still attached. On it, the tattooed letters: *CFD*. Camden Fire Department.

Hank fell to all fours, retching violently, sobbing.

♠

The envelope from Pops still burned a hole in the breast pocket of Edward Hume's fresh fatigues. He had slept fitfully most of the night and finally gave up trying just after 0500. He used his penlight and reread the newspaper clipping, just to be sure the whole thing had not been a stress-induced nightmare.

No, it was for real.

With there being no point trying to sleep, he got dressed, shaved in the dark, and walked over to the mess tent for a cup of hot black coffee. Somewhere along the way, he decided he would go get their new truck himself. Then he would get back before Wozinski was even awake. Let the kid rest.

With that chore taken care of, they could get right to work transferring all their tools over to the new Dodge truck with its freshly painted red fenders. Then they could head out more quickly to their job.

Back to work. No time to think. But he did remember to get the "Kaboom Boys" sign from the old truck.

There was the usual bureaucratic delay at the motor pool. Even at that hour, it was busy there as wave after wave of invasion troops and vehicles continued to come ashore. But Edward was finally able to lay claim to the new three-quarter-ton vehicle. That was only after he had to guarantee he would personally bring their trade-in back to the motor pool by 0900 or have truck theft become a part of his permanent service record. Every vehicle was valuable.

Once out of the bedlam there, he had to drive slowly, avoiding all the soldiers stirring about in the predawn darkness. There had been plenty of activity during the night, but now the place was a beehive. He was hurrying because he wanted to get back to the tents before Wozinski headed out.

He was still a good quarter mile away when the loudest sound imaginable caused him to instinctively hit the brakes hard. Dust billowed, fogging the inside of the truck cab, as if kicked up by a sudden windstorm. Then, straight ahead, he could see the eruption of smoke and dirt rising high like a thunderhead in the morning sky.

Edward knew immediately what it was. He checked his watch. 0610. He figured Ace would not be at the UXO pile yet. Thank God. But the tents of his squad and hundreds more men were close enough to be in trouble if the blast was as potent as it appeared to be.

Blowing the truck horn and yelling, he drove as fast as he dared. But most people were distracted by the blast, standing in awe in the narrow pathways between the rows of tents, looking at the smoke, speculating.

He decided he would go straight to the explosion site to check for any more possible detonations. As he approached the smoking crater in the field where the dump had been, he spotted Hank Anderson running that way.

Three other men stood a hundred feet away, looking at the mess, shielding their faces from the heat of a hefty fire. Ash fell around them like rogue snow. Only BD men would have been this close this soon after the blast. He quickly realized these were his guys. Some of them, at least.

As he jumped from the truck, Edward mentally took roll as Hank joined the other three. Pete Ronzini. Morty Schwartz. Carl Kostas. All there, apparently okay, though Anderson had dried blood in a path down his face from an ugly cut on the bridge of his nose.

"Where's Wozinski and Taft?" the captain asked as he ran up to them.

"Woz is okay," Hank answered. "He went to the motor pool for the truck." He glanced toward the vehicle in which the captain had arrived.

"Ace? Anybody see Ace?"

The men looked at each other but said nothing. Pete made the sign of the cross. Hank walked away, even closer to the fire and smoke, toward something lying half-buried in the ashes on the scorched ground. It was dangerously near the edge of the pit.

Edward also stepped closer to the pile, which still sizzled, hissed, and spat, a reminder—if he needed one—that it remained perilous. There could be more unexploded stuff in there, ready to blow.

"You guys get back!" he yelled and waved to the others. The men stepped quickly to a spot on the other side of the truck. But not Hank. He seemed transfixed, head down, studying the object on the ground. "Corporal, that's an order, and it includes you! Move it!"

Anderson still did not step away. Instead, he leaned down and picked up the item, shaking off the dirt and ashes. Ace's canvas bag, scorched and ripped. He turned it upside down. The German officer's helmet fell out.

"Hank, for God's sake, get back!" Edward ordered once more, but this time more as a plea.

With that, Anderson kicked the helmet as hard as he could, sending it spinning into the flames. Only then did he turn, head still down, and walk mournfully over to where the rest of the squad waited in the shelter provided by the new vehicle.

Edward had taped the "Kaboom Boys" sign in the passenger's side windshield. But somewhere, somehow, it had suffered a noticeable rip, right down the middle.

19

Plans changed. The job they were rushing to—a couple of German bombs next to a landing strip near Caen—was assigned to another squad. Hedley Bennett's unit, they would later learn. Hume's squad was to spend the rest of the day checking the safety of the remainder of the ammo dump, getting squared away with the new vehicle, getting Hank Anderson some stitches for his cuts, and gathering up Ace Taft's belongings. Edward had a heart-wrenching letter to write to Ace's parents, and another one to write to Mom and Pops.

They were ordered to leave the next day for an important crossroads town called Saint-Lô, twenty miles inland from the coast. Germans still held the area, but a massive Allied bombing was planned for after dark that night. Then there would be plenty of work for the BD boys once that ended, assuming the Germans had sense enough to withdraw.

Back at the still smoking ammo pit, several of the men watched as gloved workers recovered a few other body parts as well as the hand and forearm near their tents. The detail respectfully dropped them into a large cloth recovery bag, in which they would soon be buried in a temporary local military cemetery at Sainte-Mère-Église. One that was already near capacity.

"Jesus Christ!" Pete exclaimed as he watched the men perform their ghoulish task. "They puttin' Ace in a damn pillowcase!"

Edward counseled the engineers on ways to make the pit safer if they planned to continue dumping ordnance there. Despite the furor of the explosions, no one else suffered more than minor injuries. They would later learn that Ace had commandeered a nearby bulldozer and shoved much of the junk munitions more to the center of the pit, where it was deeper, and piled up dirt between the UXOs and the closest tents. That helped to funnel the blast skyward, upward instead of outward. Ace had apparently been off the bulldozer, likely standing at the edge of the pit when it blew. The machine was damaged but not destroyed. The dozer's seat was still intact.

One thing was clear. Had Ace not moved the pile and pushed up the dirt, the men sleeping in nearby tents and so many others in the area would have been killed or hurt. Ace had certainly saved the lives of his squad mates.

There was no time to mourn. Back at the tents, Carl, the former Hollywood movie set carpenter, supervised as several of the squad rounded up wood from artillery-shell shipping crates. Then, as they had seen RAF men do back in England, they cobbled together a two-hole seat and cover to place over the latrine trench. It made "going" much more comfortable, so long as they watched out for splinters.

The BD men then changed to clean uniforms from the dirty, dusty, sweaty ones they had worn for the morning's hot and nasty evaluation job at the pit. Heads down and sad, they headed off to the mess tent for some nourishment. That was when Edward noticed Hank was not with them. Gene told the captain where he would likely be found.

Sure enough, the corporal was back at the still-smoldering pit. Edward walked up and waited silently next to Hank. Both men stared into the fading fire for a few minutes. Tears ran down Hank's face as he stood there, hands in his pockets. He pulled out Ace Taft's Camden Fire Department patch and looked at it as he began to talk.

"Sir, you can court-martial me or bust me back to buck private or do whatever you want, but I need to say something before I blow up bigger than this damn dump. Can I speak man-to-man?"

The Kaboom Boys 207

"Get it off your chest, Hank."

"I knew. You knew."

"Knew what, Hank?"

"And more importantly, Ace knew, and told you. Emphatically so, but you ignored him!" Hank's voice was trembling with anger. "You knew this was going to happen, but you went on and cleared that château for the general instead of addressing the real problem when you had the chance. Sir, you put your men in jeopardy. Especially Ace."

"Wait a minute, now." Edward kept his voice calm, steady. "We had orders, and we were bound to follow them. And Ace was fine with that."

"No, Captain, all you wanted to do was impress the big brass. The legendary Hap Arnold. The second that general spoke, you snapped to attention like a puppet, and then dragged us off to sweep that damn fancy-ass château. Why didn't you tell the general about this death trap over here? They could've slept in their tents here one more night 'til we cleared the château." Anderson abruptly bent over and picked up something from the ashes. It was a bullet for an M1 rifle. He tossed it into the fire. It promptly popped. Neither man flinched. "But I guess there's no glory in cleaning up a junk pile." Jaw clenched, Hank was now seething. "Not when you can get the general a nice, safe château to sleep in. You've bucked authority before when you knew it wasn't right. Why not this time? And you knew Ace was a long way from being 'fine,' too."

Edward had finally heard all he could take. He reached for his command voice and responded firmly. "Check yourself, Corporal! There is nothing I could or would have done differently."

"Is that so?" Hank had to know he was teetering on insubordination.

"A life without risk is not a life worth living," Edward shot back. "I know that. All BD men know that. Ace knew it, even better than most because of his experiences before BD. We would have examined the dump early this morning and done what we had to do. Now the engineers have investigated and figured out what happened so—"

"With respect, sir, that's a song and a dance. You always had the option to send him back. You're in charge. You could have quit humoring him and sent him home when you saw how anxious and tentative he was. He was all torn up about this and plenty of other things, too. The whole squad saw it from day one. Or you could have at least sent him back to England." A telling pause then, "Sir."

Edward shook his head. "You are aware that we're in the thick of it now. Everybody's nervous and on edge. And nobody who can help the cause is going to get sent back if they're still able to do the job. It's just the way war works. Yeah, severe cases get sent back. Sure. But Ace Taft was not severe. Got that?"

Hank threw up his hands in exasperation. "No, sir, I don't 'got that'! He was skittish, Ace was. That made it dangerous for him and for all of us."

The captain lowered his voice, searching for calm, suppressing his rising anger. "Ace was a complicated character, all right, but a top-notch BD man. He knew his stuff. And he was regaining his confidence after what happened back in the States, working on his grit. I saw it in that bomber fire on the runway. And at the château yesterday. And he truly did neutralize half the devices. Under that stress, he was the most alive I've ever seen him. He was even cracking jokes."

"Sir, at the end of the day, all your jokes didn't change a thing. He was still wound up. Tell me you didn't notice."

"Listen, Corporal, you don't know this, but I was confident enough in Taft that I was about to put in orders to send him back to APG for another chance to qualify as a BD officer. He knew that."

"What? Ace as an officer. He would've gone nuts." Hank blinked disbelievingly. "Pretty darn sure he already was. We all knew that. I think he wanted it to end..."

"What are you saying?"

"That son of a gun had convinced himself something bad was gonna happen. He dealt with it the best damn way he could, despite you and the consequences."

"Are you saying you don't think this was an accident?"

Hank ignored the question. "Then the minute we passed that UXO dump on the way back from the château, he was all nerves again over us being camped so close. Not for himself. He was worried about us if the thing blew. How could you not notice that? You wouldn't listen to him. You had to be the hero, I guess. Get that promotion."

Edward looked sharply at the corporal but checked his temper. "Hank, you're not answering my question. My first priority is always to protect the squad. I made a decision based on the facts at the moment. Yes, Ace told me about that munitions pile. But who knew it would be so much worse by the time we got back? It was pitch dark. We couldn't have done anything until the morning." Edward took a deep breath. "I need to know. Are you saying Ace died by accident or on purpose?"

"Hell, I don't know anything for sure, sir. But I figure Ace fixed the problem the only way he could."

"It's killing me that we've lost Ace—"

"Poor choice of words, Captain."

"The engineers say it was the heat. We have to go with that."

Hank kicked a chunk of charred metal into the fire. "Believe what you want, sir."

Edward went on, ignoring Anderson's comments. "I know Ace aspired to be a BD officer. It was what he wanted. Wanted more than anything in the world. The thing is, that dump blew because of the heat. We both knew it was similar to the disaster he went through back in Camden. It brought back too many bad memories for Ace sometimes. Things like that cut a man deep. But that was what made him become a fireman, then volunteer for BD. He had a purpose. That's why he wanted to go on, earn a commission, and do what I do."

Anderson was quiet for a moment, still fingering the fire department patch, carefully considering what he was about to say.

"So, you really believe Ace could do what you do? Defuze live thousand-pounders? Sir, he was nuts. He was one of my closest friends in the US Army, but I know he was nuts. A desperate kind of nuts. Ace wanted to die while saving lives. He knew this dump was too close to our tents. This was his way out. What happened here is proof of it!"

Hume snapped his head around toward Anderson. He could see the look of resolve on the corporal's face.

"So, you're saying this explosion was not an accident? That the heat didn't trigger it?"

"Maybe not," Hank answered. "Maybe this was Ace's way of taking care of the problem you chose to postpone while we showed off for the generals. Or maybe he decided he could fix this mess all by himself, save our lives and those of a bunch of soldiers, and rejoin his sweetheart in heaven at the same time. I don't know. But I think he did this on purpose."

Edward shook his head. "I don't think so. I've gotten to know Ace pretty well lately. He had plans. He wanted to make captain. At the château, he talked about marriage and kids and a career in the Army. He would not have set this thing off, knowing how much damage and hurt it could cause. It was the damn heat. It was an accident. I hope we're square on this, Corporal Anderson."

"Yeah. Maybe so. The heat. At 0600 in the damn morning." Hank slipped the patch back into his pocket and sarcastically added, "We probably have work to do."

"Yeah, and I got some letters to write," Edward said. "Hard letters to write."

"Anyways, thanks for letting me vent, sir," Hank said, walking away from the steamy pit.

"Sometimes you have to take the pressure off the detonator or she'll be a hell of a lot more likely to blow," Edward offered. "Just believe me when I tell you. Ace was a good man, and he would have made a good BD captain, too."

"Thanks for that, sir. But I guess we'll never know."

Edward thought for a moment about a response but decided to let it be. Both men silently walked back toward the BD tent two hundred yards away.

Back to repairing gear, packing up supplies, getting ready to pull out for Saint-Lô.

As Edward struggled to find sleep that night, he heard the bark of a dog somewhere out there in the still distance. Sarge! It sounded forevermore like Sarge. So much so that he abruptly sat upright in his cot and bumped his head on a tent stay. Was he dreaming? He could not be sure.

He smiled as he lay back down. Probably just some farmer's dog, lost, disturbed, disoriented amid the upheaval of battle. But somehow, the staccato barking reminded him so much of home. Of his previously known universe, before every damn thing went and changed on him.

Two deaths so close together. One he may have had some control over. The other, not at all. Life was momentary. He had to do whatever he could to hang onto it while he had it. He needed to look at dying and danger in a different way, though. Every moment spent near death and ultimately surviving its sting was just another bit of compounding, elusive success.

And for some reason, that thought was what it took to calm his roiling brain.

As that distant canine's chant helped him finally find peaceful rest, Edward realized what he now had to do.

♠

"Corporal, wake up. You and me, we got a job to do."

Hank Anderson shook his head to clear the fog. He had remained awake most of the night, unable to avoid the presence of Ace Taft's empty cot and duffel bag there next to him in the tent. Now, someone who strongly resembled Captain Hume was shaking him awake in the still-early darkness.

"What? What we got to do?"

"Just come on, Corporal. I got Ace's remains in the jeep. We got permission to take him and bury him. But we got to be back in time for the morning brief." Edward was out of the tent, Anderson following as he pulled on his uniform and grabbed his helmet and boots to finish dressing on the way. The two men spoke little as they rode. The bag that held what was left of Ace Taft was on the jeep's back floorboard, a morbid presence on the short journey.

The signs confirmed the place was called Sainte-Mère-Église, the first French town liberated by the Allies after the initial landings on D-Day. A large field there was now being used as an Army cemetery. By the time Edward and Hank rolled up, even before the sun had appeared over the horizon behind them, the place was busy. Most of those being buried were men from the 90th Infantry Division—the Tough 'Ombres division—and a few paratroopers from the 101st Airborne, easily identified by the spade emblem on the helmets that were strapped to each man's chest. As the Germans realized the invasion by the Allies was happening early on the morning of June 6th, they set fire to buildings in the town. The descending paratroopers, illuminated by the flames, made easy targets. Many more were sucked into blazing buildings as they descended. With the stifling weather and large number of casualties, the temporary cemetery was a necessity for the Airborne troops and others killed in action. There was no time to ship them elsewhere for a proper burial.

The two BD men could see that truckloads of dead soldiers were waiting in line, stacked five and six high in vehicle beds. Edward and Hank sat in the jeep and watched while the dead were unloaded, placed on stretchers, their dog tags checked and noted in journals, and then carried on to rows of graves hastily dug in the sandy ground in sight of the English Channel.

Edward flagged down someone who seemed to know what was going on and explained their situation. The man, a member of the Graves Registration team, first asked for the dog tags of the deceased man. Of course, the bomb disposal men did not have them or have any idea where they might have landed. But they were able to personally attest to the circumstances of death as well as the name, rank, and serial number of the soldier whose remains were in the "pillowcase" on the rear floorboard.

They also got permission—the Graves Registration soldier was too busy and of too low a rank to be able to stop a captain, so he shrugged, gave them a grave number and a corresponding number on a white wooden cross, and waved them on—so they could personally escort Sergeant Alistair "Ace" Taft over and gently lower him into one of the narrow graves. Chaplains of various denominations walked up and down among the maze of open holes in the ground in the eerie, early-morning light, saying prayers, offering last rites, or saying a Hebrew prayer in lieu of conducting the traditional Taharah, a cleansing ceremony as part of the special Jewish ritual.

It was while they were standing there over Ace Taft's resting place that Hank noticed something that greatly disturbed him. The men unloading the stacked-up bodies from the trucks and carrying them to the graves were German POWs. So were the men furiously digging the holes in the ground, trying to stay ahead of the constant stream of cold, dead bodies of American soldiers. For some reason, that realization angered Anderson immensely.

The final indignity, murderous German soldiers dispatching American boys to the very ground they had come to these shores to liberate. Sons, brothers, and fathers who had died trying to do so. He grabbed the next chaplain that passed by—a Catholic priest—to let him know how he felt.

The chaplain appeared disoriented already by this ugly, most unholy experience swirling all about him. He was clearly drained, tired, maybe even spiritually challenged. But as the sun's first rays of the new day broke, and as he allowed Hank to speak, the priest smiled and nodded that he understood the corporal's distress.

Hank pointed to the German POWs. "Why are these men digging graves for our soldiers? They are not fit to touch our men."

"I know. But this is the only way," he responded softly. "It would be far less respectful to allow the earthly bodies of these heroes to rot away out there on the battlefield. And every POW with a shovel means there is one more soldier with a rifle we can send to battle to end this war. Believe me when I tell you, I have seen the faces of the Germans doing this work, then spoken with some of them and confirmed my impressions. There is no greater punishment they could endure than seeing so vividly the carnage they have caused in the name of their Führer and the Third Reich."

Hank closed his eyes as Edward looked on. The corporal finally relaxed and nodded. "Thank you," he told the chaplain, mostly in a whisper.

"God bless you," the priest replied. "I pray you'll find at least some of the peace you seek."

As she and Pierre Devereaux finish up their playful game of tag down the steps from the abbey of Mont-Saint-Michel, Hélène LeRiche comes to a realization. Here, at this most unique and peaceful place, and in only a few hours of prayer and meditation, she is once again her true self. The person she was before the war. She is once more a girl who enjoys life, a person who can, at least for the moment, forget the nastiness of war and what it has done to tear apart her family, her life, her future. For this fleeting feeling alone, she is enormously grateful to Pierre Devereaux for insisting she come here with him this day.

"I don't understand war, Pierre. I try to, but I really can't," she tells him. "Promise me that you will never join the military like my brother did. That you will run away before the Nazis make you join."

"Very well. I promise," Pierre says with a smile, but he stares at her with the expression of a teenaged boy with a deep crush on a lovely but probably unattainable older girl. Only another reason he is willing to make her a promise he doubts he will be able to keep.

A flight of Luftwaffe Stukas passes low in the distance, bound for England and some unfortunate target. God, how much more can those poor people take? The two teens pause at a spot that overlooks the island's tiny cemetery. Pierre merely shrugs. To him, the war is just a concept, something he will need to deal with firsthand should he be drafted. But nobody knows how much more anyone can take. Hitler. Mussolini. Hirohito. Stalin. Churchill. De Gaulle. Roosevelt. They have no idea, either.

Hélène is distracted by the raucous cackle of a woman from somewhere down below them. Then there is the laughter of several tipsy men. Pierre leans over a wall and looks straight down, as if gazing into hell.

"Otto! Could we have a more wonderful place to be away from the fighting?" It is an obese German officer in full SS uniform, sitting at a metal table in a courtyard outside a street bar, sipping from a huge stein of beer and wiping his lips with the back of his hand.

"Ja! Ja, Willem! We have beer and food and beautiful women like our friend here. It is a good night to be alive." Otto sits across the table from his fellow officer, behind a huge platter of sausages, scalloped potatoes, and asparagus. A woman in a seductive scarlet off-the-shoulder dress sits between them. She has one leg draped across Otto's lap, and he toys with her bare knee and thigh with a hand disgustingly greasy from the sausages. "For a few days, at least, we can allow our brothers to conquer the world while we celebrate the victories of the Reich, ja?"

Willem reaches over and grabs a stick of asparagus from his friend's plate. "I could remain here forever if the Allies will only have the good sense to stay away."

"Nobody knows we're here, Willem," Otto crows with a burp and a laugh.

"The war, she has forgotten us! 'Rommel's asparagus' has made all the difference after all," remarked Willem, raising up the purloined stalk as a sacrament.

The soldier refers to the millions of twelve-to-sixteen-foot-tall wooden poles German Field Marshal Erwin Rommel has ordered to be placed vertically, sprouting from open fields and pastures throughout Normandy and the Netherlands. The intent is to damage Allied gliders and other small aircraft in the event of an invasion. Many rise from the tidal flats right up to the ramparts of Mont-

Saint-Michel, but here, they are only a threat to the fishermen, their boats, and nets.

As Pierre—and now Hélène—eavesdrop from above, a phonograph at the streetside bar begins playing a scratchy recording of Austin Egen's "Blutrote Rosen," "Blood Red Roses." It is supposedly Hitler's favorite love song. The inebriated German soldiers dutifully begin to sing along in surprisingly sweet harmony.

Hélène whispers in Pierre's ear. "Not only has the war forgotten them. They have forgotten the war."

"Drunk as they are, yes. They are disgusting pigs," Pierre growls. "And with so many going hungry all around, how do they eat all our food without indigestion?"

As they watch, several more women and SS officers dance in the courtyard. Otto and Willem stand and begin to dance comically with each other before the woman at the table joins them in a three-way two-step.

How could they be so happy amid so much suffering brought on by their brutal occupation? Hélène cannot fathom such a thing.

"Boche!" she suddenly shouts, much too loudly. Boche, the derisive term the French have used for German troops since the Great War, a word that translates to "cabbage head."

"Hélène, not so loud!" Pierre whispers. "The Allies have not yet come. They may never come."

"I only hope these pigs will be slaughtered right here when they do!"

"Shhh," Pierre hisses, a finger to his pursed lips.

"Did I not tell you, Pierre, I hate war? They have killed so many innocent people. I saw it in Saint-Lô. Before that in Cherbourg."

"Please, Hélène, they'll hear you."

As she stews silently, he leans further over the wall. The recorded song has ended. So has the dancing. The officers are still raucously greeting each other, drinking their beers and wine, laughing at jokes, freely fondling the women, who seem only too happy for the attention, regardless of the source.

Pierre's elbow accidentally dislodges a small rock from the ledge. It tumbles down and almost strikes one of the SS troops. He looks up, but Pierre has pulled back.

"We better go," Pierre quietly tells her. "And by the back route so we do not have to pass that courtyard. It's getting late. The curfew, you know."

"If only the Americans would get here soon," Hélène tells him as she grabs Pierre's arm and they hurry down.

"They will come. The British, the Canadians, too..." Now he feels the need to reassure her, if only to calm and quiet her.

"All we can count on is the setting sun," Hélène says sadly as she looks to the west, to the soon disappearing orb, now huge and crimson colored.

She glances up and stops. A German aircraft flies very low and directly above them, aimed for the battlefront. The gold Archangel Michael statue carries a blood-red tinge as well. And he seems, at least to the young girl, to be pointing in anger at the plane that dares trespass the sky above this holy rock.

"Cast them out, Michael," she says, as if in prayer. "Cast them out just as you banished Satan from heaven."

Pierre looks into her face and is shocked by the loathing in those beautiful eyes. "Come, Hélène. We should hurry. The tide will rush in soon. And the curfew."

"Cast them out," she says, one more time, quietly, allowing her friend to lead her down the steep pathway, toward the gate that will take them outside, back into the real world.

20

"We're going to a place called Saint-Lô," Hank announced, finally breaking the dense, awkward silence around the mess tent table. "Interesting place. Lots of history."

They were a sad-looking lot. Hank Anderson was the worst. His face was bruised and bandaged, and his eyeglasses were still bent where they rested on a big patch of bloody gauze and tape on the bridge of his nose. Everyone else—even Pete, the usual one to find dark humor in any situation, no matter how distasteful or morbid—remained quiet. The melancholy was palpable.

Not even ten weeks yet, and they had already lost a squad mate. Inevitable, perhaps. But, in the minds of some of the men, preventable.

"Saint who?" It was Carl, his mouth full of powdered scrambled eggs.

"Don't remember the nuns ever mentioning a Saint Lo back in Sunday school," Gene mumbled.

"Saint-Lô. Not much there, but because the place has been invaded by about every tribe and empire since the first century..." Hank paused to take a sip of coffee, waiting for one of the guys to stop him. Nobody did. He went on, reciting information recently gleaned from his guidebook. Stuff none of the others had bothered to read yet, or likely ever would. "It was built as a Gallic fortress, then came the Romans, followed by the Saxons. Even pirates laid claim to it for a while. It sits on low ground, near a loop of the Vire River, surrounded by hills that give it a strategic advantage. They're like the hub of a wagon wheel where the spokes are main arteries for troops to march in or out from every direction. It's thirty miles south of here."

"Didn't we invade it already? Like a month ago?" Morty Schwartz asked.

"Nope. Jerries still hold it, but not for long, way I hear it. It's their central communications hub for the whole region, and they'll not surrender it easily. It's on the main route for German reinforcements from Brittany, too. They want us standing by to go in as soon as the Brits bomb the hell out of it tonight," Anderson said. "Guess there'll be enough UXBs to last us a lifetime..."

Hank's voice trailed off as he noticed Captain Hume entering the tent, coming their way, a slip of paper in his hand.

"Detour, boys!" the captain called out. "New orders to Cherbourg. They've got a Nazi four-thousand-pounder and it's stuck in the basement of a hospital full of patients. Locals and our boys, too. Down that coffee. Let's go!" Edward looked back over his shoulder and added, "You can piss over the side and water the sunflowers on the way."

Outside, the jeep and new truck were parked in the shade beneath one of the few remaining apple trees. It was hot and humid, even this early in the day. Wozinski trotted toward the jeep, stood on the step, and picked an apple from a branch before sliding behind the steering wheel. Carl climbed up to the driver's seat of the truck. The squad had already discussed it among themselves. Unless the captain overruled them, Woz was a corporal and the natural one to drive the captain's jeep now, with Ace gone. Morty, Pete, and Carl flipped coins. Odd man became the truck driver.

"Belay that, Woz," Edward called out. "You're still the truck driver. Hank, you drive the jeep. You're my second now."

Hank Anderson frowned, hesitated a moment, then took Gene Wozinski's place behind the wheel of the jeep. Ace Taft's place.

"Yessir," was all he could manage to say. He had driven various military vehicles all over various US military installations and most of the British Isles. He certainly knew how. And he had been closely involved with, completed, and photographed scores of bomb neuterings and UXO fixes under the tutelage of the RAF. He knew what he was doing there, too.

Certainly, it made sense to put him in the spot directly next to the captain. Had the situation been different—were Ace still alive—Anderson would have been elated, honored. Such a move meant a possible field promotion to lieutenant or even, eventually, to captain, and maybe command of his own squad.

But Ace's seat in the jeep? Not just now. Not after what had led to this move by the captain. Not for the reason why the jeep driver's seat was so hauntingly empty. But the captain was ready to go.

"You remember the way back to Route N-13, Hank?" Hume asked as he examined his map. He had his calendar, the weeks marked off, wedged between his knees. "We're headed northwest, toward the coast. Cherbourg is twenty miles, not far from Utah Beach, but there may be some bad guys along the way. So, let's haul ass."

"Yes, sir," was all the corporal said as he shifted into first gear, released the clutch, and pulled away.

♠

Now awkwardly alone in the jeep with the captain, Hank hardly spoke on the ride up to Cherbourg. Not even when Hume gave him all the usual cues.

"You know, Napoleon was the one that made this place a major military port," Edward noted, employing his best Hank impression as they passed twisted ruins of burned-out port structures. Hank grunted. "Hard to believe, but the Germans had nearly forty thousand troops here just a few weeks ago. More than thirty-five thousand surrendered to Seventh Corps." Another grunt. "They said in the briefing this morning that this will be the busiest port in the world by the end of July, once the engineers get all the wharves and warehouses back in shape."

Hume looked hard at Anderson, forcing a response.

"Eh...could be...sir." The corporal drove on, shifting gears frequently, dodging shell-cratered sections of roadway ahead of them. Or slowed to try to figure out signs for directions. Some had been flipped the wrong way by fleeing German troops. He mostly peered through the windshield as the captain looked out upon once beautiful countryside now marred by war.

They saw no enemy activity, but there was evidence of plenty all around. Smoke in the distance. Artillery noise. They were constantly encountering Army roadblocks and checkpoints. Or waiting for convoys or big formations of marching troops to cross or pass them by. And groups of prisoners, marching solemnly along toward their fate in camps in England, Canada, New Zealand, and the United States. It seemed half of them were nonchalant, maybe even relieved to be done with war or thankful not to be among the million or so captured by the Russians and sent to work farms and death camps. But the other half appeared belligerent, sneering and scowling at Hume and his two-vehicle convoy, or even cursing or spitting at them if they passed close enough. Edward had begun returning their disdain with a broad smile and a casual salute. Hank simply ignored them, eyes focused on the rough road ahead of them.

It was well after noon before they reached the hospital, located near what was left of the former German-built naval facilities in the harbor. There was activity all about. New buildings and docks were under construction or getting repurposed by the Allies for landing craft, supply ships, and other vessels. There was a rush of medics transporting the injured to the hospital, procurement teams moving supplies for the hundreds of thousands of newly arrived troops, and a general buzz of nonstop activity. Men manned anti-aircraft guns all around. Cherbourg was about to enter yet another phase in its long history, becoming a crucial port of entry for the continued Allied invasion of France.

The hospital was in pitiful shape but, out of necessity, remained as functional as they could make it. It was on the outskirts of the most heavily bombed military installations in the city and had suffered much damage. Allied soldiers wounded in door-to-door street fighting filled all the rooms, sometimes five or six to a room. The Army had kept the facility in service because of three functioning operating rooms and a hundred well-equipped beds, abandoned by the Germans in their haste to bug out. They had not had the opportunity to destroy it before they were overrun by the Allies. With only a few more hours' notice, they would have strapped explosives to support beams and brought the hospital down. But the night before Hume and his squad were called in, the Luftwaffe had targeted the hospital squarely in an air attack. Despite a huge red cross painted on its

The Kaboom Boys 221

roof declaring this building to be a hospital, they pounded the structure with several bombs.

One of those bombs had failed to explode. Edward had to assume it was time-delayed, set to take out wounded troops from the Battle of Cherbourg. There were also doctors, nurses, and medics helping those warriors recuperate. It was becoming obvious that the German scientists were developing increasingly sophisticated bombs. A growing number of bomb demolition men were being blown up, an apparent goal of the psychopathic bomb designers. Hume and his squad were furious yet somewhat flattered that these monstrous Germans were aware of their work and had gone to such great lengths to do them in. The fewer BD men there were to neutralize those devices meant there would be more deaths.

The device that brought the Kaboom Boys to this place was in the building's basement. It had plunged through five levels of the hospital on its way down, killing four patients, three medics, a nurse, and a surgeon on the way. Now it was precariously lodged in the corner of a supply room. Dust and smoke made it difficult to breathe. And even harder to see. Hank and Edward pulled on field scarves and goggles and began to climb down cautiously into the partially collapsed basement.

"A little more light over here, if you please," Edward whispered as he wedged himself into the narrow space between the bomb and the cold, damp rock wall. He deliberately spoke quietly, as the coal miners usually did in such tight situations below ground. Any loud noise could cause the walls to implode or the bomb to dislodge. And now they were facing something different, one of the newer anti-tamper German devices.

The captain suspected right away that this beast he was hugging was different from any of the other German SC-2000s he had seen so far. He could not yet tell exactly how it was unique. It was more intuition than observable data. Hume knew intuition was important in this game. Sometimes he had to bet his life on it. And today, Hank's life, too, along with those still in the hospital above. He knew the only way to hedge that bet was to get inside this critter. But trying to do so could be abruptly fatal, too, if his gut was telling him the truth. It was like solving a new but very lethal puzzle.

"What's she look like, Captain?" Hank Anderson whispered, now willing to talk since they had a monstrous forged-steel rattlesnake hemmed up in a tight corner.

"A four-thousand-pounder. SC-2000. Half the weight is the amatol warhead. Ammonium nitrate. Everyday fertilizer." The bomb was about the same diameter as a submarine torpedo but a third the length.

"I know all that, sir, but what I'm wondering is if she's okay to try to move or we gonna have to blow her up right here." Hank looked up at the low basement ceiling hovering above their heads. "We'll need to evacuate a shit-ton of seriously wounded people upstairs if that's the case."

"No offense, Corporal. Just thinking out loud..." Hank was still mighty damned prickly when speaking with his captain. "It's probably delayed action, so..."

Edward's leg was cramping, so he shifted his position ever so slightly. The bomb suddenly dropped a half foot, fracturing several timbers and sending up billows of dust and bits of stone and splintered wood. Hume and Anderson, without thinking, scrambled backward, trying to avoid being crushed if the thing toppled over.

"Shit. Shit. Shit. Shit," Hank hollered, eyes wide, waiting for the roar.

It never came.

"I guess that's your answer," Edward quietly said, coughing, spitting out dust. "We render her safe right damn here and right damn now. And by the way..."

"Yessir?"

"Let's hope she doesn't start ticking. That'd give us probably fourteen seconds to pray for forgiveness for our many sins."

"I remember that much from training," the corporal said. "You know, sir, there is one thing I never learned at APG."

"What's that?"

"That kick-ass staring technique you're so famous for."

"Once we get through this job, I'll happily give you a lesson in advanced command procedure. You remember the most important thing they taught us there, don't you?"

"I remember plenty, but what do you got in mind, sir?"

"Luck is a bomb disposal man's only true friend." Hume coughed hard again, then finally stood up straight. "Hand me my tool bag, and then go up

The Kaboom Boys 223

top and tell somebody in charge to hurry up and move as many more patients as they can." "Yessir."

"And if you don't hear some kind of godawful explosion in the meantime, come on back and help me pull the guts out of this son of a bitch before it shifts again and mashes us to death."

Anderson wriggled out through the wreckage of the historic old building, making use of a convenient hole punched through the cellar's solid rock wall by previous blasts.

It was still difficult finding a decent breath of air, and once he was alone in the hospital cellar, it was a vivid, powerful memory that made Edward suddenly dizzy and disoriented. The whole scene, the collapsed timbers, the scattered, fallen chunks of rock, a collapsed wall, the air full of dust and smoke, the imminent danger of more blasts. That put him once again amid the coal mine collapse back home. The one that claimed the life of Fritz Schneider, his boyhood friend. Pulling away rocks and timbers and praying that he did not bring the whole mine—and now this hospital—down on top of him. Trying to find Tommy and Fritz in all that chaos and destruction.

And just the gut-punch thought of his brother and best friend made his vertigo worse.

He knew he should not allow such memories to distract him from the touchy job at hand. Not unless he used those experiences to help him now.

Then another memory flashed. Not nearly as powerful but now far more important. RAF Captain Duncan Smythe had been the first to mention that the German scientists—or at least one especially evil-minded SOB whose specialty was the SC-2000—had created a fuze assembly especially for the newly arrived American BD squads. One that would immediately explode if the usual neutralizing fluid was employed to make the detonating assembly benign. "One wonky-ass egghead what's got a thistle in his drawers," Duncan had told him. Could this bomb be an example of the bastard's handiwork?

Edward had read a classified dispatch on the new developments since that conversation, but he had not really considered until this moment that this particular UXB might be one of those vengeful innovations. It would be a lot of trouble for the Germans to go to in order to take out the few BD boys who had made it to France thus far. Seemed they would have far more important strategies with which to concern themselves besides guys castrating rascally bombs and sweeping structures for booby traps. Especially guys who already averaged a mere ten weeks of service before meeting their maker. However, the scientists were clearly motivated, meticulous, and competitive, and they were proudly scheming at Hitler's behest.

"Phew!" Edward shook his head to try to clear it. Now, what clue had Smythe mentioned that was the distinguishing feature of the new fuze? What other warning besides his instincts could Edward rely on?

Then he remembered. A *Y* in the place of the serial number. That was it. Now, he really needed to confirm it. The lives of more than a couple hundred people depended on him.

He picked a particular flat-head screwdriver from his bag, gave the thick yellow handle a quick good-luck kiss, then began working his way again around behind the big mother so he could hopefully see the fuze cover.

He took ten seconds to use the blade of the screwdriver to scratch out a name on the bomb's casing. *TOMMY.* The kid deserved a second go-round.

"They're getting everybody out who can be safely moved." It was Hank, crawling back through the hole in the cellar wall. "A couple of brave souls are staying with the rest, standing watch. They wished us luck."

"I hope they get their reward here on earth and have to wait awhile for heaven," Edward told him as he finished unscrewing the fuze cover. "I think we may have one of Germany's special BD-man-killer fuzes on this one, Hank."

"Yessir." The corporal's voice had gone high and tight.

Edward worked silently for another two minutes, then paused and said, "This time and this time only, I'll give you the option of staying, helping, and photographing or getting the hell out of here while I work on this thing. I make no guarantees, though, if you decide to stay."

Hank did not hesitate. "No, sir. If this is something new, we need good photos so everybody else sees what we're dealing with. That's my job. Yours, on the other hand, is to make sure our moms don't become Gold Star mothers."

Edward nodded. This weapon could shift again with him working on it. It was difficult to believe it was still standing upright, just the way it had come out the bomb bay of the Luftwaffe warplane. Should it topple, its weight would crush him. Or it could explode. Unlike with Ace Taft, that outcome would not leave enough of either of them to scrape together, put into a sack, and be buried by German POWs.

Edward eased his body farther around the steel behemoth, making himself as skinny as he could, avoiding touching anything that appeared to be helping to support it. Finally, he was in a position to see the cover plate over the access door to the device's innards. These bombs appeared to be clever but basic, using a propeller to turn a shaft as the bomb fell earthward. That caused an arming stem to rotate, soon cutting through a seal and releasing a corrosive chemical, which eventually ate away a series of celluloid delay disks. That was what made the ticking sound, not an actual timer. When the disks were mostly dissolved, a very strong spring they had been holding back expanded, pushing the firing pin against the detonator, causing the bomb to explode. The thickness of those disks determined the delay time. Some were known to take more than a week after being dropped before they detonated.

"Hank, can you get your camera up here?" Edward asked. "I need a picture of something important. Or hand it to me and tell me how to focus and shoot."

"I've crawled around enough under hoods to get at the motors of cars. I think I can get in there without tipping it over."

"I need a shot of this *Y* label here first," Hume said. "HQ needs to see it ASAP."

Somehow, Anderson did manage to fit himself into an impossible position adjacent to the bomb and take a photo of the area where the captain pointed. The area that featured no usual serial number. Only a single letter *Y* stamped onto the metal label.

"Please tell me you know how to take care of this cute little innovation," Anderson told him.

"I know how we were taught to handle them three weeks ago while we were still getting drunk in pubs and chasing English gals," said Edward as he studied the disks and wires. "But this model is less than a week old, most likely. Pray the Krauts have been too busy dodging our ordnance to have gotten too creative with this bastard."

"I'm praying, sir. As hard as I have ever prayed." Anderson was not in any way religious, never went to church, and due to the trauma of his parents' divorce, he had not ever been baptized. But his lips were moving now as he said a silent prayer.

Meanwhile, in an open area about three hundred yards behind the hospital, the rest of the squad had just finished digging a deep trench and were taking a smoke break.

"Have I mentioned how much I hate this part of the job, the waiting?" Gene said with a long sigh.

"Yeah, couple a hundred times, but I am glad I'm a digger and not shacked up with that bomb in there," Pete responded.

"Maybe Captain and Hank'll get to keep their brass balls for souvenirs when this is all over," joked Morty. They all laughed nervously.

Constantly wiping sweat from his eyes and pausing the operation for dust-induced fits of coughing and sneezing, Edward's focus never left the fuze compartment. It took almost an hour of surgeon-like effort before he finally had access to the portion of the fuze he needed to get to: the delay disks and the spring the disks were supposed to eventually allow to uncoil, detonating the bomb.

"Damn!" Edward suddenly exclaimed.

Hank looked up quickly. He had been handing Edward the tools he requested and squeezing into tight spots to take photos of each step along the way.

"Your 'damn' requires further elaboration, if you don't mind, sir."

"I don't know how quickly this corrosive, the acetone, works, but I'd say we got between a few minutes and maybe less than an hour to plug this thing. The disks, they're almost gone. We shoot neutralizing fluid in there right now, it would only flush out what little bit's left of the celluloid disks, the spring would get sprung, and the firing pin would hit the detonator. Then we would very suddenly get to meet all our ancestors—" Edward stopped. The newspaper article about Tommy, the pillowcase holding the remains of Ace Taft, both flashed through his mind.

Hank swallowed hard. His face had gone pale. "So, how do we keep that from happening?"

"There's a package of hard rubber shims in my bag. Hand me those,

Hank. And my ball-peen hammer. The time for being delicate has officially passed."

"Hammer?"

"Yep. I've got to insert a shim here to make sure it stays where it is and doesn't get sprung. We've got a bet with Captain Bennett, remember. We gotta get out of here clean and beat him to Mont-Saint-Michel."

"Whatever motivates you to do your best work, Captain." And, for the first time in the last thirty hours, Hank Anderson laughed. A nervous giggle but it qualified as a laugh, nonetheless.

Less than an hour later, Edward and Hank delivered the key elements of the fuze to the impatiently waiting squad members. They stood before the hole, ready to safely blow up the detonator remains and other internal parts of the bomb. They could hear the loud diesel motor of a crane maneuvering into place to extract the inert bomb from the hospital cellar.

Then, that job accomplished, the Kaboom Boys were southbound, headed for the strategically important town of Saint-Lô. And for what would turn out to be a sleepless night of truly impressive fireworks.

♠

The once peaceful town of Saint-Lô had fallen to German Field Marshal Erwin Rommel and his 7th Panzer Division way back in what now felt to its citizens like a lifetime ago. But it had actually only been four years prior, in June of 1940. The action was part of Germany's takeover of Cherbourg and its strategically important deepwater harbor, located an hour to the northeast. The invaders quickly built an underground hospital in Saint-Lô to care for wounded German troops but refused to treat locals injured in the German assault on their peaceful town. The unusual structure was built almost entirely by French slave labor. Even so, the conscripted workers considered themselves lucky because they could go home each night after laboring twelve or fourteen hours daily. Many other conscripts had been shipped east, as far as Russia, to help construct buildings, airdromes, artillery emplacements, and cement bunkers. And to shovel up, stack, and inter the remains of the dead.

Not only was the town a key communications crossroads for the SS, but it was also an important entry point into the Normandy region for reinforcement troops coming in from Brittany to challenge the Allied invasion. Its railway station was humming around the clock with soldiers on the move.

The going for the Kaboom Boys slowed soon after leaving Cherbourg. There was plenty of action going on around them, and their orders were to stay at least a mile away from any fighting. Twice they had to stop and wait while a skirmish wound down. Twice Edward had to remind his squad that they were not to grab their weapons and gallop off to try to help. That was not their job. Not unless they came under attack themselves. Should another member of the squad become a casualty, it would be much more difficult to replace him and do what they were assigned to do. Who knew when replacements would be available? Back in Maryland, APG was doing what they could. However, recruiting volunteers for such duty and the dismal wash-out rate for trainees was a considerable hindrance. Demand exceeded supply when it came to BD boys.

An unspeakable tragedy had struck Saint-Lô well before Edward and his squad arrived. There was a story circulating that days before the devastating D-Day bombardments in the region, there had been an attempt to warn residents that the Americans would bomb the town on a particular night and that they should move away from several particular targets. However, leaflets that contained the information were dropped from aircraft and were blown astray by a brisk wind. Few knew ahead of time of the coming destruction.

This story would later be disputed, with claims there was no warning attempted. Many suffered and died because of what some termed excessive force, an American "bombs away" attitude. That and the lack of any alert for the town's twelve thousand residents. Thousands lost their lives that night, including more than two hundred men imprisoned by the Germans in the local jail.

Five miles from Saint-Lô, with the falling sun already eclipsed by the horizon, and with the squad finally making better progress, the jeep topped a rise to find the road blocked ahead of them. Hank had to slam on the brakes so hard they skidded to a stop, finding themselves yet again in a shallow ditch. Instantly, a half dozen rifles were pointed at them. It took only a few anxious seconds for Hank and Edward to determine that, thankfully, the guns and the men who were staring down their barrels at them were American infantry.

"Americans!" the captain was shouting as he crawled out of the jeep's floorboard. "American bomb squad! Red fenders!"

"You bastards almost ran down a crew sweeping for land mines over here!" one of the soldiers angrily shouted back. "We oughta shoot your asses just on general principle, speedin' along like you own the damn road!"

With purpose, Edward aggressively stepped over to the soldier—despite the young man still aiming a rifle in the captain's direction—and pointedly told him, "You forget yourself, Private. You do not talk that way to an officer." Edward looked around, his lower jaw still jutting out. "Who's in charge here?"

"I am, sir. Sergeant Lennox," came a shout from a nearby field where a squad of men appeared to be searching for buried devices.

"Sergeant, I suggest you have a talk with this private. Do you understand?"

"Yessir, I will. But it's a little tense out here, you know."

"Of course I know that! But we have to maintain command structure, or we lose discipline and order. And if we lose that, we lose the war. Got that?"

"Yessir."

Edward nodded. The short speech had not been just for the sergeant or the private. Hume had made sure his own squad was able to hear him.

He quickly made certain they could easily get the jeep out of the ditch without a tow—the truck had not skidded into quite as much trouble—and then walked over to talk with his men.

While reorganizing his gear, Hank glanced down and noticed Edward's leather bag had slipped from beneath the captain's seat. Some papers had fallen out and ended up lodged against the gearshift. He managed to gather it all up to put it back into the satchel so they could quickly be on their way.

Hank could not avoid noticing that the top item was not a document at all. It was a well-worn newspaper clipping. He read the bold headline at the top: MAHANOY CITY MAN KILLED IN TRUCK ACCIDENT. And that naturally drew his eyes to the story below.

"The victim was delivering a truckload of spirits to Pops's Bar, owned and managed by the driver's father. A deer leapt from nearby woods into the truck's path. The driver apparently swerved to miss it, slamming the driver's side of the truck into a big tree on Overlook Road. The passenger, Levi Loftus, was not seriously injured. The driver, local coal miner Thomas McAdam Hume, died in the accident. Tommy Hume is survived by wife, infant son, his parents, and a brother, Edward, who currently serves his country with US Army Bomb Disposal in Europe."

When Hank glanced up, Edward stood there, looking at him. There was no expression on the captain's face.

"Sorry, sir. It spilled out when we..." Anderson handed it all to the captain. "I'm sorry about your brother."

Edward took the papers, carefully returned them to the satchel, and climbed back into the jeep.

"Pull straight ahead, and you're out of the ditch," the captain said. "Follow the sergeant there. The one waving at us. He'll walk the route and guide us through the minefield."

"Yessir."

Neither man said anything else as they eased along in low gear. Then, just as they were exiting the danger area, they passed a sign indicating they were on the road to Saint-Lô. Edward looked up from the map he was studying and spoke.

"Hank, I'd appreciate it if you didn't mention the thing about my brother to the squad. No reason to distract them. Not with my personal problems. Nothing anybody can do to bring him back. We're about to be really busy, you know. We got to stay focused." The captain swallowed hard. "We got too much bad luck lately, anyway."

"Of course not, sir."

"There should be a roadway not far...yeah, there to the left," Edward said, examining the map. "Take that to the top of the hill. Just take your time and follow the ruts."

They stopped beneath a copse of weeping beech trees and next to a rock wall that ran along the spine of the ridge. It offered a protected view of the countryside well into the distance. Spiking just above a line of trees several miles to the west, there was a church steeple that looked like a finger pointed toward heaven. Through their binoculars, they could see against a star-studded black sky the tall spire, ever-present in French towns and villages. Their destination. Saint-Lô.

"Impressive view," Hank offered. "I bet this was a pretty little place once upon a time." But the captain was already out of the jeep and headed back to talk to the squad. Hank followed.

"We'll camp here, fellows. No fires, lights, or cigarettes. That town over there is still in enemy hands, and there are plenty of SS there. But the Air Force is going to give them a rough night tonight, and our troops fight their way in at first light. That's when they'll need us."

The squad worked quietly, unloading sleeping bags and rearranging tools in the back of the truck. Hank tapped Carl on the shoulder.

"CK, you got a spare pair of red-handled pliers? I lost mine back at the Cherbourg hospital job. I can use hemostats I swiped from the hospital for some of the work, but they can't do all of it."

"Not too sure if I do, but I'll look."

Hank looked over Carl's shoulder as he rummaged through his equipment bag.

"There's a pair right there," Hank said. Edward had just walked up.

"Where?"

"See the red handles?" Hank asked, pointing.

"No. Sorry. I'm color blind," Carl said matter-of-factly.

"Are you kidding me, Corporal? How'd you get in the Army?" asked Edward, a quizzical look on his face.

"They didn't ask," Carl answered, shrugging his shoulders, pulling out the pliers, and handing them to Hank.

"Uncle Sam must have been mighty desperate the day you signed up!" Hank said with a laugh.

"You should've been a 4-F," the captain added.

"Yeah, maybe so. But I'm here now, so what can anybody do about it?"

Edward grinned. "Good to know, though, 'cause when I'm snipping red, blue, and yellow wires, I won't ask your opinion."

"Damn, Carl! How the heck do you tell the difference between a blonde, brunette, or redhead?" asked Hank.

"By the way they kiss, of course," Carl answered as he tossed his sleeping bag beneath the truck.

Gene Wozinski drew first watch while the rest tiredly unrolled their sleeping bags beneath the shelter of the two vehicles and the ancient, towering trees. However, they had hardly settled in when they heard the first murmur of approaching aircraft. The planes were soon roaring directly overhead. The initial bombs fell just after 2100 hours, unleashing an Armageddon of smoke, fire, and grumbling, earthquaking thunder, shaking the ground beneath them, even this far from the epicenter.

Bombers and their escorts continued coming in wave after wave until a couple of hours before sunrise. There was no rest for the Kaboom Boys, even if they were a good distance from the bombings. It was like watching distant fireworks, but a show seemingly with no end. And one without joy.

The squad would later learn that the devastation unleashed that night would seal the fate of the martyr city, Saint-Lô. It would be dubbed "The Capital of Ruins" after ninety-five percent of the town's structures were destroyed during the previous weeks' bombing and then that July night's grand finale. Three American infantry divisions were poised to move in at first light that morning to take on what was left of a German infantry division and a parachute corps. In all, more than three thousand American soldiers and thousands of French would die here in the two-week assault on Saint-Lô, with most of those coming in the few days following that long night of infernal bombing.

One thing was obvious to the squad, though, as they watched the onslaught from beneath their vehicles that night. There would be plenty of BD business for them. Munition dumps, booby-trapped buildings, grenades on the belts of dead soldiers, UXBs galore after all the ones the Army Air Forces were dumping like a nighttime hailstorm on the town.

Sure enough, it would start the next morning with a brief radio call giving them specific instructions even as the sun painted a scarlet canvas in the eastern sky. But gloomy, black smoke climbed high above the town itself, putting much of the beautiful bocage country beneath an ominous, man-made storm cloud.

The Kaboom Boys

233

"I'd sure like to know whose idea it was to drop perfectly good bombs in the ocean instead of bringing them back home!" No one answers because Captain Jacob Morris is talking only to himself as he guides his single-crewmember P-47 Thunderbolt fighter/bomber back toward his new home base at Pontorson, Normandy, France. Behind him, five other Thunderbolts follow in formation. Morris is the "Old Man," the twenty-two-year-old squad leader. Each of the planes still carries two "perfectly good" five-hundred-pound bombs, armed and ready. However, high-topped thunderstorms churning about over their mission's intended target— a railroad yard in Tours—has prevented them from dropping their loads this day.

Morris knows the answer to his own rhetorical query. Several bombers, including a B-26 Marauder on a runway in England, had either crashed or caught fire with live bombs still aboard. Some bomb demolition bastard had written up a report, too, and the guy's conclusions made perfect sense to the brass. The Allies no longer seriously lack bombs, so it is okay to waste them on codfish and seaweed. The new policy, in effect for a month, requires any unused bombs to be dropped before returning to base, armed or not. The ocean is the preferred dumping area. Only sea critters are harmed if one of the things explodes. Rural areas are an alternative, regardless of how bad they might scare cows, sheep, and already frazzled townspeople.

Now, Morris aims westward, toward the nearest open water. There are occasionally Luftwaffe fighters in the area. He does not want to meet one with a thousand pounds of bombs strapped to what is already the heaviest fighter/bomber in the Allied arsenal.

He spots the towering structure of the abbey on the island in the distance, surrounded by the waters of the bay. Morris has flown a time or two within sight of the odd-looking rock with the religious house on top. Mont-Saint-Michel, it says on his map. It reminds him of one of the spires of Saint Louis Cathedral on Jackson Square in his hometown, New Orleans. But he has never been as close to this place as he is today. Oddly, the island now looks different to him. The pilot does not recall the water in the bay surrounding the island being this dark and deep. From an altitude of a thousand feet, the rock previously had been surrounded by mudflats. But now, as he leads the others over the former German airdrome at Avranches and toward the bay, he realizes the sea comes well up to the walls that surround the cluster of buildings that seem to claim every inch of ground.

Morris checks his fuel gauge. Circling the city of Tours, hoping for a break in the weather, he and his buddies have exhausted most of their gas. They need to ditch their bombs quickly and turn back home.

"We'll shit 'em out right over there in the deep water," Morris says into his microphone and banks hard to the left. His wingman dutifully follows. "Won't bother any-damn-body out there."

Morris is unaware that the blue-black water they are now targeting may, indeed, be fifty feet deep. But that condition will be short-lived. Soon, the bottom will be completely exposed to air and sunlight. The tide has already begun to rush out toward the English Channel.

The pilots line up and drop the bombs in a single-stitch pattern. All twelve devices, with their M-112 detonators, turn midair and head nose-first toward the water's surface. Seagulls scatter as the first ones hit and immediately disappear, plunging toward the muck on the floor of Mont-Saint-Michel Bay.

But the bombs do not tunnel nose-first into the sand as designed, burying themselves as much as fifteen or twenty feet deep into the bottom. Instead, the swift tide pulls them sideways as they go deeper into the water. Most of the twelve bombs settle instead on their sides, exposed, laid out in near-perfect symmetry, like beached whales.

Unbeknownst to Captain Jacob Morris and his P-47 squadron, they have just dealt the mayor, townspeople, and especially the fishermen of Mont-Saint-Michel a very bad hand indeed. The pilots fly on, certain the weapons they jettisoned will never again be seen by humans.

Curious, Morris swings his nose around to lead the squad near the spire that tops the medieval abbey-fortress. He has already noticed the bright, gold object at the very top. Now he is awed by the close-up view of the statue of Archangel Michael, the Protector of all Warriors. A good Catholic boy, the pilot recognizes him at once. Sunlight glints beautifully off the sword held high by the winged angel, like a holy beacon.

How the hell did they get that statue way up there? is the young pilot's primary thought. Then he is over land again, the fields below populated by eddying herds of sheep and cattle, spooked by the low-flying warplanes' engines.

They are only six miles from their base at Pontorson. They have survived another mission. But Morris has no idea of the magnitude of the international crisis he and his boys have just ignited.

21

After witnessing the all-night bombing of Saint-Lô, it would be a couple of days before Edward and his squad could enter the town and safely address any UXOs. Even from the ridgetop, and alongside chattering cicadas and birdsongs, they could hear heavy fighting continuing as the sun rose. Artillery, machine guns, rifle shots, a cacophony emanating from all points of the compass had each of them thinking the same thing.

"Hope to hell this place is worth it!" Pete Ronzini said, vocalizing their inner thoughts as they rolled up their sleeping bags and prepared for whatever the day might bring.

"Ask Mr. Hitler if any of this shit is worth it," Hank threw in.

Morty Schwartz thumped the Star of David dangling from the chain around his neck. "Ask any of my people if they think the crazy son of a bitch putting them in ghettoes and work camps is worth it."

The men had slept little yet were up at first light, about to attack their K rations. A quick radio check-in led to delaying breakfast and immediately getting to work.

"Sorry, guys. Gotta go. Eat on the way!" Edward informed them, breaking out his maps. But he had one more directive for them. "New policy. HQ says we gotta wear the protective suits from now on."

There were groans all around. The outfits did offer a bit more protection but were terribly uncomfortable, especially in the heat. Back in Britain, they had only worn them a time or two, enough to experience their bulkiness and discomfort. The men vowed then they would never use them in the real war.

"I'd bet you a dollar to a doughnut nobody at HQ has tried out those things," Carl said. "And that field ops had no say in this."

"We'll follow orders and wear it," Edward told him. "I don't like them either, but as you know, I don't believe in disobeying orders. I choose my battles and usually pick the ones I think I can win."

"Sir, it's gonna slow us down," Pete persisted.

"Yeah. It's gonna cramp my style, sir," Carl said with a laugh.

"'Requiring' and 'wearing' aren't necessarily the same thing, Captain," Hank said with a wink.

"Take that up with Command when the war's over, Hank. Now, let's go save somebody from having an especially bad day."

The spot they were headed was not far from the outskirts of the smoldering town, behind a line of American troops noisily pushing their way through tough fighting, isolated skirmishes, and brutal hand-to-hand fighting. Casualties were heavy. So many injured that the 51st Field Hospital had to be hastily set up beneath a stand of oaks alongside the main road. Business was brisk, often more than the medical teams could handle.

In the middle of the cluster of tents, Edward and his squad—each red-faced and sweating profusely in the bulky protective suits—were soon curiously studying a German SC-50 fifty-kilo bomb, a device often used for anti-personnel purposes on the battlefield but not a factor in these parts since D-Day. There was practically no Luftwaffe presence over Normandy by then. But somehow, a rogue German fighter/bomber had snuck through overnight and dropped this fifty-kilo bomb, assumedly as an attempt at payback for all the recent Allied pounding of German troops at Saint-Lô. It had landed smack dab among the surgical tents. The guard detail reported it to HQ, but the UXB had not slowed traffic at all. Stretcher bearers now rushed past the BD squad, carrying gruesomely wounded men. Medics, a few female nurses, and doctors hurried from tent to tent.

Carl wiped his face with a dirty rag. "Jesus, this is one busy place."

The Kaboom Boys 237

"What'd you expect at a field hospital in the middle of a battle, Hollywood?" Morty asked.

"Room service...and a cold beer," Pete quipped.

"Why are you so damn immature sometimes, Pete?" Morty asked, irritated with his fellow New Yorker.

"I dunno," Pete answered. "Maybe it's like my ma says, it's 'cause I was born on Leap Day."

"Holy shit!" Carl said. "I ain't never known anybody born on February 29th!"

"Yeah, that makes me really only five years old in leap years," Pete proudly claimed.

"Wow! It all makes sense now!" Morty said with a sneer. "Lucky you don't shit your pants and eat with your hands like any other five-year-old."

"You're about as funny as hemorrhoids, Morty," Pete shot back, frowning. He was growing more and more tired of Schwartz and his constant needling. Nerves were becoming ragged, mostly due to one Nazi flag stowed away in Pete's gear bag.

"I can't believe I'm surrounded by such jagoffs!" Gene Wozinski offered. "That's what we call idiots back in 'The Chi.'"

"Surely the Krauts thought these were troop tents," Hank interrupted, redirecting the exchange before the heat, fatigue, and tension pushed the conversation farther toward the edge. Morty and Pete had come close to blows a couple of times already.

"Why?" Gene asked.

"I'd hate to imagine any human being could ignore the big red crosses on the tops of the tents and drop a bomb on purpose into the middle of wounded soldiers in a field hospital. It's even against the Geneva Convention."

"Bombs sometimes miss their targets," Gene noted.

"And it was dark," added Pete.

"Probably just some straggler bombing anything that moved or showed a light," Edward said. He was on his hands and knees, taking a closer look at the UXB. Sweat dripped from the end of his nose. "I'm wondering why this one didn't detonate."

The device was resting upright, almost four feet tall but buried halfway in hard-packed, dry ground. That left its tail, the fins shorn off, about two feet above the dirt. A busy surgical tent filled with maimed and crying soldiers was only about thirty feet away.

Hank began shooting photos. Morty and Carl headed back to the truck to get picks and shovels. Gene and Pete went off to scout for a place to dig a demolition hole.

Edward suddenly stood, cupped his hands to his mouth, and used his command voice to shout to anyone and everyone in the vicinity: "*Attention! Army ordnance here! Everyone must evacuate! Now!*"

The captain may as well have been ordering the bomb to defuse itself. Nobody paid him any mind. He wiped his face with the back of his hand and trudged awkwardly toward the opening of the tent, looking for someone with rank who might be able to order an immediate evacuation.

As he shuffled along in his new blast suit, he spotted a beguiling nurse who was stepping out of the tent. Edward was already sidetracked even before she pulled down her face mask and quickly lit a cigarette. She was disheveled, had sweat stains on her surgical cap, was obviously exhausted, but she was beautiful, with emerald-green eyes, dark brown hair mostly tucked under her blood-spattered cap, and a sultry air about her that rivaled the morning's weather. She was easily the most beautiful woman Edward Hume had ever seen.

He knew he probably should not talk to her. That might distract them from the unpleasant tasks both of them faced. He nodded, dipped his helmet out of respect for her, her tough job, and her bravery, parted the tent flap, and stepped inside. An overpowering, nose-tingling smell shoved him right back outside.

"Ho-lee shit! Chloroform!" he said, gagging.

"It's ether," the nurse told him matter-of-factly. "Not chloroform."

Edward sneezed. "How do you ever get used to that smell?"

"We don't."

"Okay. Maybe you can tell me where I could find—"

"If you're looking for the chief surgeon, Captain, he's busy at the moment, removing some kid's spleen before he bleeds out."

Edward could tell now that the nurse was young, likely no more than a year or two out of nursing school. And though she had on no makeup—or

The Kaboom Boys 239

needed any—she had gone to the trouble to put on some coral-red lipstick. He watched her take a long draw on the cigarette and blow a smoke ring. From inside the tent, a wounded soldier screamed in agony.

"Do you ever get used to that...not just the smell...you know, the...?"

"No. No, we don't. Not all the men screaming and crying and begging for their mothers." She looked at his protective suit, and there was finally a sparkle in her green eyes. "Do you ever get used to that zoot suit you're wearing?"

"Today's the first time we've used them since England, so I can't say," he answered. "But I'd bet not. Not even if they issue us matching ties and pocket squares." He stuck out his hand to her. She took it. "I'm Captain Edward Hume, Sixth Ordnance Bomb Disposal Squad, here to remove that ornament over there on your front lawn."

"I'm Lieutenant Virginia Brown, head nurse here at the butcher shop." She stuck the cigarette between her lips, then reached around behind her back and took something off her belt. Edward tried not to stare at her as the scrubs tightened over her striking figure. "Here. Use this. It'll help."

It was a gas mask. Edward had trouble getting the straps untangled, so she helped him, standing close to do so. He removed his helmet, pulled the mask over his head, but left it resting on his forehead. He had just decided he was not quite finished talking with Lieutenant Brown, and the mask might get in the way of conversation.

"You have quite the setup here, Virginia," was about the cleverest banter he could come up with on the spot.

"Built it in three hours, and the way things are going, and if your bomb doesn't explode, we'll be here at 'Hotel 51' for a week or more. No lack of guests for certain." She sucked in more smoke from her cigarette and slowly exhaled. "You could say my dance card is full of the dead and dying. But you know, we save a lot of them. So, we try to save them all if they still have a pulse. 'What the horrors of war are, no one can imagine.' Florence Nightingale said that. She knew. She saw a lot, too."

Two soldiers ran past them, carrying a stretcher into the tent with a badly mangled soldier aboard. The open flap emitted another caustic cloud of ether along with moans and shouts and pleas to God.

"Isn't it dangerous, you smoking around all that ether?" he asked.

She looked him squarely in the eyes. Edward suddenly felt weak, but not from the heat or the chemical burn in his nose or the abundance of blood in the vicinity.

God, she was beautiful. Such beauty in the midst of all this death, destruction, and ugliness. How could it be?

"Everything's dangerous here, Edward," she answered, her voice husky, sad, and, to him, incredibly sexy. "And damn final. I'd think a bomb squad man would know that better than any of us."

"You see it all day, every day, Virginia," Edward responded. "For us BD boys, we do our jobs right, we save lives. Nobody dies. We don't do it right, we don't live to see how anything else turns out. All or nothing. You, the other docs and nurses, you can't save them all. That's gotta be draining, frustrating."

She contemplated the logic of his answer for a long moment. Then she looked even harder at him with those deep, green eyes. Her lower lip trembled ever so slightly. He thought she might be about to cry and hoped he had not upset her. He was about to pull the gas mask down over his face and go inside before saying something else dumb or wrong. But then, she suddenly dropped her cigarette butt in the dust, crushed it with the heel of her combat boot, stepped closer, grabbed him by both arms, and kissed him, hard and relentlessly slow, as if overcome by passion.

"Thank you, Virginia," was all Edward could breathlessly tell her when she finally backed away. She looked mournfully at him, her cheeks flushed. There was true desire in those green eyes.

"No, thank you, Captain Edward Hume," she said. "You never know when it could be our last kiss. And, if that's the case, I damn sure enjoyed it."

"So did I." Then he stared back at her and smiled. "But I am hoping it isn't. Our last kiss, that is."

She smiled again, then pulled her surgical mask up from around her neck, parted the tent flaps, and motioned for Edward to pull down his gas mask and follow her into another world. Her world.

♠

The Kaboom Boys 241

It took a moment for Edward's eyes to adjust to the darkness inside the tent. But there were painfully harsh lights aligned over three operating tables. Squinting, he could see stretchers that held badly wounded soldiers, just off the operating tables or awaiting their turn under the knife. There was blood everywhere. The doctors, assisting medics, and nurses were covered with it. Buckets on the floor held amputated limbs and other body parts.

Oddly, it was Grossman's Butcher Shop back in Mahanoy City that popped into Edward's mind. Mom sometimes asked him to stop by on his way home from Doc's and pick up pork chops or ground beef or a pork roast. Chauncy Grossman, his apron bloody and specked with bits of meat and bone, always threw an extra bone or tad of gristly brisket into the bag for his beloved Sarge.

"That's Captain Richardson there," Virginia said, interrupting his memories, nodding toward one of the tables where a patient was just being carted away. A patient who had not survived, a bloody cloth now draped over his face. "Go talk to him. Now!"

The surgeon pulled off his head covering revealing a thick tussle of dark hair. Edward was impressed that this man could not have yet reached thirty years of age but oversaw this field hospital. Edward clumsily pulled up his gas mask and smiled at Richardson. But the doctor had a condescending air about him from the moment he yanked off his own gloves and mask, tossed them aside, and glared back at this intruder into his gory domain. The God Complex personified. In spades.

"Take ten, Crowson," he told the assisting medic. "Let me talk with this guy here."

Edward tried not to breathe in too much of the acrid air. "Good morning, Doctor. I'm Captain Edward Hume and—"

"Bomb disposal, I assume, judging from that fancy tuxedo you're wearing. And I suspect you have a bomb close by to defuze, too."

"That's correct, Captain. I do. And I need for you to order an evacuation—"

Richardson interrupted him again. "Not gonna happen. I suggest you get about your business posthaste."

"My business, sir, is for you and everyone here to evacuate beyond five hundred yards for the next hour," Hume replied.

The surgeon snorted and said, even louder and more defiantly, "Not gonna happen."

Edward drew in a breath and tried not to gag. It was not only the ether. The place reeked of rot and death.

"Let me be clear, Captain," Edward informed the surgeon, standing toe-to-toe with him. This guy had the medical diploma, but Edward had endured the school of hard knocks. "There's an armed SC-50 bomb...no, let me translate that to fifty kilos...no, more to the point, that's a hundred and twenty pounds of pure mayhem, and it's in the middle of your hospital. It could explode at any second. Everyone here could well die."

"'Could'? That's the operative word. Look around you. If we shut down surgery, plenty more boys will die, not 'could' die. There's no time for such vague possibilities. End of discussion."

Two medics dropped a stretcher down on the now available operating table between Richardson and Edward. The soldier on the stretcher was gurgling, struggling to breathe, his intestines visible through a gaping tear in his lower abdomen, his right leg missing from the knee down, the dressing wrapped around the stump soaked with blood.

"You've got a job to do, and I've got a job to do," the surgeon said as he pulled on a fresh face mask and allowed Virginia Brown—now back on duty—to help him put on a new set of gloves. "I suggest we both get back to work...Captain."

"Perhaps I did not make myself clear...Captain," Edward shot back. The voice of Colonel Kane was in his ear. "Our first order of business is to secure the area. Prevent collateral damage and injuries!"

The medic handed Richardson a scalpel as the surgeon nodded toward two military policemen standing at the other side of the tent. "This is as secure as it gets," he said, then made a bold incision across the wounded man's stomach. "MPs, we got a situation over here!" Richardson called out as he began stuffing the kid's guts back inside, using both hands.

The MPs started making their way toward Edward.

"I don't think you understand what it's like to dismantle a live bomb, Doc. Not with all these patients around. And doctors. And nurses." He

The Kaboom Boys 243

glanced at Virginia Brown, who had been intently listening as she helped the surgeon corral the rest of the young soldier's intestines.

Richardson looked over his surgical mask at Edward. "Half the patients...maybe more...are dying anyway. In the time I've wasted with you, I might've saved three." The MPs now stood ominously next to Edward. "Look, Captain. Is this the hill you want to die on? Your bomb hasn't gone off yet. It's probably a dud."

"It's delayed action. It will go off. Does your team get a vote here?" Edward could not help glancing at Virginia.

This time, the chief surgeon did not even look up. "They are fully aware of the risks, just like this kid here was when he enlisted in the Army and learned to tote a rifle. Just like you were when you volunteered for bomb demolition. Captain, as I've said already, this discussion is over." The MPs each put a hand on one of Edward's shoulders just as a spurt of blood erupted from a previously unnoticed wound somewhere on the young soldier's chest. Richardson stuck a thumb on the spot, a finger in the dike. "Another pint of O-positive over here. Stat!"

"Captain, for the record, you have been officially informed that you, your staff, and your patients are at high risk," Edward told him.

"Got that!" Richardson snorted again as he sutured the newly found wound among the young soldier's many, many more. Without looking up, the surgeon said, "Lieutenant Brown, for the record and to make the captain feel better, notate 'at high risk.'"

Virginia pulled out a small notebook and pencil from her gown pocket and did as the surgeon ordered. Then she looked at Edward, widened her eyes in warning, and shook her head. He should back off, she was telling him. Dr. Richardson was not going to relent.

With a defiant look on his face, though now visible to no one from behind the bulky gas mask he had just jerked downward, Edward did exactly what Virginia Brown had wordlessly suggested. He shook off the MPs, turned, and left the tent.

He found the squad still gathered around the bomb, still in their stiff, thick protective suits, still red-faced and sweating copiously, still grousing about the damnable outfits.

"Build a blast wall around the device!" Edward commanded. He fought to not allow his frustration to show in his voice. The squad needed to know he was cool and collected. "And help me dig out so I can access the detonator."

"Sir, we don't dig close until after the evacuation, right?" Hank asked.

Hume did not respond. He was already busy gathering tools and arranging them in precise order near the UXB. The squad looked at each other and then began to dig gingerly next to the bomb casing, piling up the extracted dirt around the perimeter of the hole to offer some meager protection to the tents should it go off.

A few minutes later, Pete could tolerate it no longer. "Captain, permission to take off this damn gear."

"Right, Captain," Gene chimed in. "It's hotter'n Hades. We could work faster and be a lot more precise without these things on. Besides, this thing goes up, this suit won't make a damn bit of difference. You can't get deader'n dead."

Edward sighed deeply and glanced up at the brutally hot sun, already burning a hole in a cloudless sky.

"Well, it's as good a day as any to break every damn rule we got!" sniped Edward. Then he unzipped his own thick canvas suit, stripped it off, and kicked it out of the way. Next, he unbuttoned and removed his sweat-soaked shirt and undershirt and stood there amid the hospital tents wearing only his farmer's tan, helmet, fatigue pants, and boots. There was now a breeze, slight as it was, that he had not detected before. It felt good on his body, once scrawny but now muscular after months of training and BD work. The other squad members promptly followed their captain's example, tossed the suits aside, shed their shirts, then got back to work, happily showing off their own honed physiques.

As they dug, Carl looked up and noticed they had an audience. A couple of cute nurses, wearing steel helmets, stood in the shade of one of the tents, smoking and watching them dig. Carl, his movie-star good looks on full display now that the hazard suit had been jettisoned, made eye contact with one of them. She grinned, winked at him, blushed, then giggled.

"Somehow and improbably so, this day just got a hell of a lot better," Kostas said.

The Kaboom Boys   245

Morty Schwartz paused long enough to wipe perspiration from his face, then grinned and joked, "Just remember these Army nurses know twelve ways to amputate your pecker before you even know it's missing."

Holding a rod with an attached mirror, Pete helped Morty lower the awkward device into the hole while Gene examined the reflection in the mirror.

"Pay dirt! I see the nose!" shouted Gene. "To the left there!"

Carl and Pete were digging the last bit, making sure the space between the bomb and the blast wall was a full twenty-four inches, just enough for one body at a time to maneuver inside.

"Guys, that should be good enough," the captain said.

"Sir, it's deep enough, but there's not much room in there for the both of us," Hank told him.

"It'll be enough, skinny as we are. Hell, there's not enough extra meat on me to make a sandwich. You neither. We'll fit." Edward did not want to take risks, but he did want to get along with this problematic job.

The captain lowered himself into the cramped space and put his stethoscope to the bomb's belly.

"It's twins," he shouted to the men. Everyone laughed, glad to see their captain was in a better mood. He had seemed especially tense after coming back from the medical tent. "Okay. No ticking. As I figured, delayed action."

"Thank you, Adolf," Hank grunted as he slid down into the narrow hole next to Edward.

As he ran his hands along the smooth casing of the bomb, Edward noticed a message scratched into the steel just above the access door: *Ein extra Havana fur Churchill*. He read it aloud in perfect German. "An extra Havana cigar for Churchill."

"Who knew the Nazis had a sense of humor?" Hank asked with a chuckle.

Then there was the metallic snap of Hank's camera as he documented the inscription. The unexpected sound of the shutter caused an abrupt uptick in Edward's pulse rate. Sudden clicks were not what he wanted to hear. He was now using his flat-head screwdriver to scratch out *4-U-Pops* into the bomb's skin, right next to the German scrawl.

"You know, Hank, from that message I'd say this bomb wasn't meant for us. It's for our RAF pals."

"Then I suggest we get out of this ditch and leave the thing right here for the Brits to handle," Hank replied with a grin.

"If I didn't know you better, I'd think you were serious," the captain responded, thankful Hank finally seemed in a better frame of mind. Then he turned his full attention to defuzing the bomb. Defuze it without blowing up half the battlefield hospital, his men, and himself. And Virginia Brown, his new incentive to survive another day. Defuze it without acknowledging just how much more pressure and dangerous distraction the decision of the chief surgeon was dropping on him and his team.

Defuze it because making this ugly device benign might save just a little of what had once been beautiful Saint-Lô.

The other members of the squad were a quarter mile away with all the discarded protective gear in tow, digging yet another hole. But the train of medics carrying stretchers into and out of the tents continued unabated. So did the screams and cries of the injured.

Two hours later, Edward finally had the bomb neutered and ready to be removed. The detonator assembly was inside a canvas bag and set to go into the newly dug hole. As Edward and Hank were climbing out of the excavation, two shadows fell across them.

Captain Richardson and Virginia Brown stood there, watching them. Richardson leaned over and offered each man a hand to help him out of the dig. Edward was wary. Why was the surgeon now suddenly being so damn cordial?

"Captain Hume, if you have the time, there's something else I need to show you," Richardson said. The expression on the nurse's face was one of distress, her full lips arced in a frown.

Edward's initial thought was to give Richardson a bit of the doc's own arrogance, but the tone of the man's voice and the look on Virginia's face led him another way. "We haven't checked in with HQ yet, and they haven't sent us a messenger, so I guess I have a few minutes."

Edward gave Hank the okay to clear the site and take the bomb remains to the blast hole. Richardson and Brown led him down a narrow alley between the tents and toward a nearby orchard, swarming with bees.

The Kaboom Boys 247

"You know, you're a lot like me, Hume," the surgeon said as they walked. He held up both hands before him. "I suspect BD work's a lot like surgery. We both have to be careful and use our hands the way we know how. If we don't do it right, somebody likely dies."

Edward glanced at Virginia. Their eyes met. They had had a very similar conversation a few hours earlier.

"Yes, I suspect you are correct," Edward responded, but still expecting the other boot to drop. "But if you make a mistake, only the guy on the table is gone. If I do, everybody within the radius of the blast dies or gets hurt. Including me. My corporal. Maybe others in my squad."

"Not quite true," Richardson said, and stopped alongside the hedgerow to explain. "Not for surgeons near a battlefield when bullets are flying. Injured men come in hot all the time. Medics in the field clear them as best they can, but when I cut into a guy's gut, I never know if I'll find a live round in there. Or a grenade still on his belt. There are random unexploded munitions on just about every soldier I see. And we only have time to carry it outside and dump it...in places like you see right here."

Richardson pointed just beyond the hedge. There was a small stock pond there. But it was filled with and surrounded by mounds of discarded munitions. Rusty, bloody, dented and damaged ordnance.

"God!" Edward exclaimed. "This, right here, is far more dangerous than that bomb we just defuzed! If this pile goes up..."

"We clear bodies, too, out there. Ours, theirs. They don't have time to detonate all the mines they dig up. We have to do something with the ammo and other bad stuff. Look, I've complained, Hume. Nobody listens. Some tell me not to worry, that it's not likely to blow up. I don't know. I'm a sawbones. You tell me, Captain. You're the BD guy. I've complained all the way up the chain."

"Not high enough or loud enough."

"So how dangerous is it?" Richardson asked.

"Dangerous as hell! Believe me, I've seen what a dump not nearly as big as this one can do if it goes up. I lost a good man that way a few days ago." Edward was already diagnosing the pile, figuring how to make it safe. "For this, we absolutely have to evacuate most of the tents, Doc. I'll go all the way to Eisenhower to see that happens before we touch one bullet or shell over there."

"We're in a lull right now. Maybe it'll last. It'll take us two hours to evacuate. That fit your plans, Hume?"

"We'll make it fit."

"Thanks. And just for the record, I would never want your job."

Edward smiled. "Nor do I want yours. I get woozy at the blood from a mosquito bite." As a kid, Edward had dreamed of becoming a physician. That was no longer the case.

The surgeon snapped off a sincere salute, turned, and hurried away to get things moving. Virginia was no longer frowning.

"I appreciate what you've done here, Edward," she told him as soon as Richardson was out of earshot. "Doc's not a bad guy. An excellent surgeon. He saves most. But he doesn't suffer fools. You handled him well. He respects you." She glanced over at the ugly ammo dump. "We've all worried about this mess since we set up here and saw it keep growing. More than we've worried about the Germans coming back."

"For good reason," he told her, a quick image of Ace Taft's face coming to mind.

She stepped closer and handed him something. A slip of folded paper from her bloody notebook. "I hope we see each other again sometime. If you're ever in Miami Beach..."

This time, the kiss was nothing more than a quick peck on his dirty, stubbled cheek. Then she was gone, following her boss to assist with the evacuation. When she caught up with Richardson, she turned and threw Edward a wave. A simple, girlish wave that snatched Edward's breath away and almost swiped his legs from beneath him.

He unfolded the paper. There was a telephone number written on it in clean, precise script: *JE2-8976*. And beneath it, an imprint of her lips in coral red.

He looked up again, but she was gone. The only thing that remained of her was the note with the phone number, the imprint of those lips, and what now and forevermore would be the enticing fragrance of ether.

Later, he would slip the note between the pages of his calendar as he marked off his eighth week of BD.

Marshmallow-white clouds fill a brilliant azure sky. The gold statue of Archangel Michael glistens beautifully atop the spire, as if reaching for the heavens, beseeching God for peace over the land he surveys. Just below, a scattering of villagers from the island and a few visitors from nearby towns quietly pray in the ancient, austere abbey. At the base of Mont-Saint-Michel, long considered "The Gateway to Brittany," there is a bustling town made up of hotels, shops, restaurants, and vendors carrying on commerce from beneath brightly colored umbrellas. There have most recently been German soldiers and Nazi officers there as well. But no more. A pair of German troops usually stood guard at the village's medieval entranceway, but it is now open to all. No one challenges identification papers.

A lone elderly priest, wearing a traditional white collar and black vestments, wearily makes the steep climb up the series of steps and walkways toward the abbey to prepare for evening prayers. The trek has become much more challenging for him, partly from age but also by the lack of attendees. Most have been forbidden by the German occupiers from attending services. Those who had not been conscripted for labor elsewhere were required to work instead of wasting their time with church and worship. With a furrowed brow, the priest greets a small group of elderly villagers just as he has been doing for decades, providing some inspiration and hope for them, regardless of the trials they have seen. They fall in behind him for the rest of the climb, hands clasped in prayer.

At the lowest levels of the island, on the rocks adjacent to the waters of the bay, fishermen continue to repair their nets near beached boats. They have been limited by the Germans in how often they may fish, and then because of land mines and obstacles—"Rommel's asparagus," for example—placed in the water by the occupation troops to deflect any possible Allied invasion here.

The scene now is bucolic, like a different world, one far from the war that has so much of the continent in flames. To the east are the battlefields of Normandy, where the heavier fighting and casualties have been taking place. Sheep—though far fewer than before the war—graze peacefully in the pastures that stretch right down to the water.

Inside the abbey, women dutifully scrub the stone floors, altar, statues, and pews of Mont-Saint-Michel Abbey, just as they have for the past four years, since German soldiers first showed up. These women are the wives of the abbey's prewar caretakers. They have necessarily taken over the duties of their husbands, who were forced by the Germans to become unwilling laborers at POW camps, some in France, others in Germany. The women have been supervised by their Nazi occupiers until D-Day changed everything. In honor of their missing husbands, and in subtle defiance of the Germans, as they worked, they sang an a capella rendition of an ancient Gregorian chant titled Days of Wrath. *They continue to do so even though the occupiers have now fled Mont-Saint-Michel ahead of the Allies. The chant's sentiments remain.*

"That day is a day of wrath, Earth in ashes," they sing, accurately describing much of their country, but thankfully not their village on the rocks. It remains mostly unscathed. The words also promise that on the day of final judgment, there will be eternal flames for those evil men who now cause the world to "tremor." But the Nazi overseers never did understand the chant, and so long as the women scrubbed and mopped and spoke little, the Germans left them to their chores. And their singing.

In truth, the Germans were more interested in what happened when off duty, frequenting the bars and restaurants and fraternizing with the very few local girls who, though scorned by their families and friends, willingly mingled with them for safety, for money, for some small bit of joy in a somber world. After all, there was no reason to believe the Germans would ever leave France, even if Great Britain and Russia never fell to Hitler.

For more than four years, most of those who traditionally made a pilgrimage or took holiday at Mont-Saint-Michel have not come. The few who walk to the island at low tide, crossing the mudflats that make up the bottom of the bay, are locals within the coastal zone and blessed with the proper papers. Scarcely a thousand French have been able to visit during that time, mostly to pray and meditate in the abbey atop the rockpile that forms the seventeen-acre island. A pilgrimage that has meant so much to so many for hundreds of years has been abruptly halted by the Nazis. The only visitors and money coming to the island have been from the Germans.

Indeed, more than a third of a million of them have come, but not to find inspiration or prayerful peace. It has been to use the island as a regional military headquarters. And for rest and relaxation. A spot for the German forces—primarily high-ranking officers and non-military officials of the Reich—to spend down time recuperating from the tensions of overseeing the occupation of France and preparing for the anticipated Allied assault. And do so by eating, drinking, and dancing away their off-duty time.

Now, though, the Germans are gone. The Allies have stormed the beaches of Normandy, not the Bay of Mont-Saint-Michel. Fighting still rages nearby. Bombers frequently fly overhead, but now mostly Allied planes, their pilots fascinated by the picturesque island, the bay, the statue atop the abbey. It appears the war has left this holy place.

All is not back to normal, though. The outcome of the Allied invasion is in doubt. The Germans might yet return. The many men conscripted from the island and its environs are still gone, their fate unknown in this new phase of the war.

But the fishermen—mostly elderly and set in their ways—have decided their nets are all repaired now, that their boats are seaworthy, and it is once again time for them to go back to work. But they are still unwilling to ride the tide back out to the sea and to net the bounty of fish they are confident awaits them.

The twelve bombs are still there.

The bombs set loose and allowed to plunge into their bay by the Americans. The superstitious fishermen are convinced the weapons, easily seen lying neatly lined up in a row in the quicksand after the tide races out, have chased away every fish from the bay. And if the fishing boats try to venture out farther, even into the English Channel, those bombs might explode as they attempt to hurry past them.

So it is that the fishermen of Mont-Saint-Michel refuse to go to sea.

There are no fish to sell. Meat and produce are no longer coming their way, either, because of the brutal fighting and explosive disruption inland. The occupiers made certain to slaughter and devour many of the sheep raised nearby, the ones famed for their amazingly delicious lamb, hogget, and mutton after having grazed on the salt grass. Now, with the Germans gone and no longer bringing stores in by the truckload, the people of the island are hurting.

Word of the plight of the fishermen—as well as the other inhabitants—of Mont-Saint-Michel quickly reaches the leader of Free France, General Charles de Gaulle. With all else that is going on in the war, he realizes this situation could have international ramifications. And that there is only one solution.

An urgent discussion with the highest-level Allied commanders made it clear this would be a far bigger operation than merely clearing "friendly" bombs from a body of water.

That, in effect, makes this mission more a major diplomatic effort than a typical BD job. It is one in which the squad assigned to the task must quickly and diplomatically deactivate highly explosive and unstable UXBs in the middle of a harbor characterized by dangerous quicksand and rapid tides, spiky Rommel's asparagus, maritime mines, and rusty barbed wire. And, of course, without causing damage to an internationally known holy shrine.

This will be far from just another day's work for the BD boys who draw this assignment.

22

Having just finished the ammo dump job at the field hospital and gobbling down a quick lunch, the Kaboom Boys were once again on the move. This time it was in response to a rather odd piece of correspondence directly from General Arnold's staff. Inside the top-secret envelope labeled *ONE*, Edward was instructed to drop everything as quickly as the squad could safely do so. They were to head south to the town of Avranches. Once there, Edward was to be permitted to open a second envelope for further instructions.

"Sure hope those generals take the time to figure out we've got a serious problem cropping up everywhere with these ammo pits, sir," Hank noted as he drove. He was trying to keep his mind off what that second envelope might contain.

"Yeah. It's a big problem," muttered Edward. His attention was on the map, calculating how long it would take them to reach Avranches, given the road conditions, checkpoints, and congestion. Curiosity about that second envelope was driving him nuts, too, a hot coal burning into his left thigh where he had it tucked away in his pants pocket.

In his daily reports, Edward had continued to strongly complain that the hazardous remains of discarded munitions were being mishandled and dumped into pits without regard for the possible dangers. Edward figured that ammo dumping grounds all over Normandy were second only to unexploded bombs as lethal hazards. And he knew that whatever was not cleared could remain volatile for hundreds of years to come, a legacy of war for future generations. The captain had said as much in his many communiqués and implored his superiors to act. There had been no acknowledgment from HQ yet.

Finally approaching Avranches—maybe a mile or two away—they found themselves on a particularly bumpy stretch of potholed roadway. Edward could now see on the map just how close they were to Mont-Saint-Michel. He felt a pounding in his chest as he touched the dot on the map representing the island. Was it possible the United States Army might be sending him and his squad there? Not likely, he decided. Nor was he apt to have the time or opportunity to divert to there for even a short visit.

As usual, theirs was a two-vehicle parade, the jeep and, not far behind, the truck, now equipped with a brand-new trailer. The caravan was moving along as fast as it could over the battle-damaged macadam. They met friendly convoys, troops on the move, and occasional lines of POWs being herded to Port de Cherbourg for the trip across the Channel. On both sides of the roadway, there was also a steady stream of displaced French citizens. Some carried only a suitcase. Others pushed carts loaded with clothing and maybe a piece or two of cherished furniture. Most were women, teens, children, and babies. Occasionally, an elderly man walked along, always with head down and subdued. Some appeared to have been injured. A few were fortunate enough to have an ox or horse pulling a large wagon filled with whatever the family felt the need to try to save.

"Where you suppose they're all headed?" Hank asked Edward.

"I'd say they're trying to get as far away from the fighting as they can," the captain answered.

"They'll have to do some swimming, then," Hank responded. "All the way to the US, Canada, or South America. Rest of the world seems to be on fire."

Anderson's assessment was not far from fact. Edward had reminded the squad to keep their weapons ready, with someone in the truck always alert and on guard. They had heard stories of snipers or the sudden appearances

The Kaboom Boys   255

of enemy patrols when things seemed to be most peaceful. Hume had his own sidearm loaded and in his lap in case he needed it quickly.

"Watch those damn potholes, Corporal," Edward said. "Wouldn't want this pistol to go off and make me a soprano."

Hank chuckled. It was good to see the corporal smiling again, Edward thought. Short-lived as such a display was lately.

The Germans were fighting furiously, assured that if Normandy fell, Paris would not be far away for the massive, sweeping Allied invasion forces. Word was the Führer had told his commanders to relay to their troops that they were to fight to the last man, that the Third Reich depended on them to stop the incursion right there in Normandy. Then to push the Allies back into the English Channel and reclaim the lost territory. And to brutally quash the French Resistance, now fighting openly for their homeland, alongside the Allies.

France must not fall! was the Führer's irrational demand.

Earlier that day, the squad had detonated the last of the UXOs at the field hospital and given the all-clear for patients and medical personnel to move back into their tents. They had just settled in the shade of a huge tree to rest and eat when a messenger came over to them, inquiring about where to find Captain Edward Hume.

That was when Edward got a look at the papers inside the first envelope.

"Captain Hume: You are to immediately cease all other operations and proceed directly to Avranches, where you will then—and only then—open, read, and follow the orders in the second envelope."

The moment they were fully within the confines of Avranches, Edward ordered Hank to pull over. When they were parked, he ripped open the second envelope. The orders stated that they must head directly onto Route D-275 and proceed to the town of Mont-Saint-Michel.

"Holy shit. I don't believe it, but..."

Hank knew exactly what Edward meant. "We're going to Mont-Saint-Michel, right?"

"Damn right!" Edward was stunned. Mont-Saint-Michel. That Holy Grail that represented the adventurous, out-of-the-ordinary life he so wanted to experience. He reread the orders and then waved at the men in the truck to join him and Hank at the front of the jeep for a quick brief.

"Men, we got orders to Mont-Saint-Michel."

Tired as they were, the men seemed happy—even enthusiastic—about the assignment. All except Hank.

"Well, sir, looks like you got your fondest wish after all," he said, a sour look on his face.

"Captain, I guess that means you're gonna win your wager with Captain Bennett," Gene noted.

"We all win, Gene," Edward said, perusing the orders yet again. "We'll share that carton of smokes. Frosting on the cake!" He glanced over at Hank, who now held Ace Taft's Camden Fire Department patch. "Look, I assure you all that I don't feel like a winner. I know what we're all thinking, and I agree. I wish Ace were here with us, too."

"Yeah, but he's not." Hank walked away, ambling toward the nearby town hall.

"Let him have a moment, guys. Gene, go keep an eye on him. I'll catch him up on the ride over to Mont-Saint-Michel."

Edward had been wondering how much more of Hank's attitude he could tolerate before it became a real detriment to the squad. He would have to weigh the value of Hank's innate knowledge with his immaturity and moodiness. And that determination would need to come sooner than later.

Edward quickly told Morty, Pete, and Carl where they were headed, emphasizing it was as much a diplomatic mission as a bomb demolition job. And that the orders came from the highest level of Army command.

As the captain talked, first Gene and then Hank came back to stand nearby and listen. Hank was also stowing in his satchel what appeared to be a paperback book. Edward talked louder so they could hear him.

"First, we find the town mayor and assure him we're there to resolve everything to his satisfaction," Edward told them. "When the mayor is satisfied with us as a team, we'll then need to fully assess the situation, decide how we'll do the job, and clear the problem."

Edward could tell that Hank had now become much more interested but that he was trying to appear aloof. It was not like him to hang back, to not ask questions or offer suggestions. And doing so was almost more than the corporal could handle.

"Now, before Hank can ask, I know that's backwards from how we usually do things," Edward explained. "But from the tone of the orders, let's just say we have no option but to fix the problem, somehow, some way. And we will need to convince the local authorities we will be able to do that before we even inspect the first device. Got that?"

The men all nodded—except Hank Anderson—but they still had questioning looks on their faces.

At no time had Edward ever had a reason to suspect he might make it to Mont-Saint-Michel. Or even close. Now, miraculously, it was happening. That is, so long as they did not run over a land mine or get shot by a sniper. Or, maybe worse in Edward's view, get pulled off this "crucial assignment" to go do something even more crucial somewhere else.

However, as he considered the expressions on the faces of his men, he also knew he needed to assure them his obsession with this iconic spot was not going to jeopardize their lives or the successful outcome of this mission. At least no more than the usual bomb demolition task would. He would make certain to do that when he shared details of the mission once they were there.

As they got back underway, the air around them began to feel and smell noticeably different, moist and salty. The flowers had more color. Gulls swooped low, as if dive-bombing the pair of vehicles. The scenery changed, and not so subtly, transitioning from woods and bocage to flat fields, streams, marshes, and grassy-green pastureland.

Suddenly, out of a low-clinging fog of vapor and battlefield smoke, Hank spotted it through the windshield of the jeep. It was the majestic Mont, rising skyward on the far horizon, as if floating on a cloud, the bottom half lost in mist. A jut of rock improbably poking its imposing head high above the flat coastline.

Under his breath, Hank said with a gasp, "Surreal!"

Next to him, the captain was intently studying one of his magazines. There was an image of Mont-Saint-Michel on its cover. Hank decided not to inform his captain that if he only looked up, he could see the real thing directly ahead of them. He still blamed Hume for what happened to Ace Taft. This minor sleight was a bit of retribution.

He'll see the island in due time, Hank told himself. *Damned if I help him, though.*

Entranced by the island, Hank seemed to be hitting every pothole head-on. That caused Edward to look up from the magazine and over at the corporal.

"Jeez! You aiming for those tank traps?" he asked, then went back to tracing with his finger the route on the magazine page from Saint-Lô to his dream destination.

It was a shout from someone in the truck that alerted Edward to the sight in the hazy distance.

"Look, Captain! Look over there! There she is! Big as life!" Gene yelled.

Edward looked up, out the bug-spattered windshield. But what he saw directly ahead of them was the lead truck in a long convoy barreling down on them, furiously blinking its headlights and now blowing the horn but not slowing down. Hank steered and braked for all he was worth, finally coming to a stop straddling the crest of a ditch at the side of the narrow roadway. The truck skidded to a halt behind them, too.

"Jesus. We'll never make ten weeks if we get killed by a convoy," Hank growled.

The procession passed mere inches away from them. The drivers of the vehicles, as was often the case in these much-too-common near-collisions, seemed fascinated by the red fenders on the BD jeep and truck.

"Hey, hey, red fenders!" they shouted, laughing. "Wish I had me a truck with red fenders!" Or, "Hitler can see you bastards coming from a hundred miles away!"

But one of the drivers pointed at a wide-eyed Edward, then at Mont-Saint-Michel, and yelled, "Guys! Ya gotta go see that place over there! It's crazy!" As they rolled past, the driver looked directly at Edward and shouted, "Better than Hershey Park!"

"Hershey Park? What's that?" Hank asked.

"Gotta be a Pennsylvania boy," Edward answered with a big grin.

Edward had been going to Hershey Park since he was a kid. Opened in 1906 as a park mostly for employees at the Hershey Chocolate Company, it had come to be known as "A Park for Workers." Pops and Mom had taken Eddie and Tommy there many times, and especially for a picnic every Memorial Day. "Honoring the dead from the Great War with ham 'n' butter sandwiches, sweet pickles, and root beer," Pops, the World War I vet, had once joked, but without a smile. Admission to the place was free, making it possible for the Humes to visit.

"Nothing's better than Hershey Park," mumbled Edward, but with a puzzled look on his face. What made the guy call out the name of the place here, on a roadway in a war zone in France, so very far from Pennsylvania?

But the quick reference immediately put Hume into an odd mood. Half thrilled. Half sad.

He looked straight ahead as the last of the loud, smoky convoy rolled by. Then he saw it. The magnificent and awe-inspiring Mont-Saint-Michel, across the fields and marshland, just like the pictures in the books and magazines.

"Jesus Christ, would you look at that!" The captain stood up and held onto the windshield for a better view. Even the mist was obliged to help with his first in-person look. It swirled out of the way, like a curtain being pulled apart. Now, with binoculars in hand, he focused on the structures clinging to the rock, on the golden glow of Archangel Michael at the very top. "I cannot believe it." He turned and waved excitedly to the men in the truck, alerting them to look ahead to see their destination, just as he had for Tommy the first time they approached Hershey Park.

Hank shifted into neutral, set the brake, and jumped out of the jeep to begin snapping pictures.

"Never seen the captain so excited about anything like this before," Gene said.

"Other than some big-ass bomb," Pete added.

"Or that nurse back at the battlefield hospital," Carl threw out.

"It kinda looks like Holy Name Cathedral back in Chicago," Gene noted. "Gothic, ya know."

Edward heard Gene's description. "Medieval, actually. Seventh century. Guys, I've studied this place for years...gosh...since before the war started. I'm not all that religious, but I do believe fate brought us here."

Hank started to say, *No, it was obsession. That's what brought you here*, but he stopped himself. "It's further than it looks," he said instead. "We best get back on the way. Right, Captain?"

"That's right. We've got a dozen bombs out there in the bay somewhere." He held up the now-opened second envelope, waved it, then looked at his watch. "And they sure as hell ain't gonna disarm themselves. Kaboom Boys, we better giddyup!" he shouted with a grin.

Giddyup. That was one of Hedley Bennett's favorite expressions.

Back on the road, the island seemed to hover on the skyline without getting any closer, no matter their haste to get there. It had been over a thousand years earlier, in 708 AD, that Saint Aubert, the Bishop of Avranches, had founded Mont-Saint-Michel after having seen the Archangel Saint Michael three times in three dreams on three different nights, each time ordering him to build a church at the summit of the island. Now, although they were tantalizingly close, it still seemed to Edward that they would never get there.

As he steered the truck, Gene pulled out his Saint Michael medal and gave it a kiss. "This feels way different than any of the other jobs we've done so far," he said, mostly to himself. This mission appeared to the young corporal more like a sacred calling, an act of destiny. Maybe even a holy pilgrimage.

Wozinski had no way of knowing his captain, now standing braced against the jeep's windshield, straining to get a better view, was having those very same feelings at that very same moment.

♠

"Hey, Hollywood!" Morty reached back. He had rolled up the canvas side cover of the truck so they could look out at Mont-Saint-Michel. But there was no response from a soundly sleeping Kostas. He was atop a sleeping bag on the floor of the truck, not nearly as enthralled by Mont-Saint-Michel as the rest of the squad was. "Sleepyhead. Wake up. You're missing the million-buck scenic route, dumbass!"

"Leave me the hell alone before I shoot you right between your running lights. Hell, my ancestors built the damn Parthenon, so what's the big deal with this place? Wake me when we get there."

"No, man. You gotta see this," Morty yelled.

Gene downshifted with a grinding of gears, moving slowly around another cluster of burdened-down refugees who were coming their way, pulling their belongings in an oxcart. But with no ox. The BD boys could hear the flocks of sheep, bleating.

"Shit. They really do go 'baaaa,' don't they?" Gene said with an amazed grin. "Just like in the cartoons."

"What'd you expect them to do, city boy? Stand on their hind legs and sing 'I've Got a Gal in Kalamazoo'?" Pete quipped.

"Look, I'm from the South Side of Chicago. I've never met any sheep in person," laughed Gene. "Except at the butcher shop. Lamb chops, maybe."

"I'm damned surprised the Nazis left any of them so we could hear them go 'baaaa,'" Pete added. "Nice of 'em, right?"

"Not a damn thing nice about Nazis," Gene shot back.

According to a bullet-riddled sign, the roadway they were traveling on became D-275.

Breathing in deeply, Edward said with a sigh, "Sea air. It's supposed to be medicinal, right, Hank?"

"They say the salt air can..." Anderson started, but then stopped. It seemed they were leaving behind all the death and destruction they had seen in the past few days. Everything was cleaner, brighter, more vibrant. Like that scene in the movie *The Wizard of Oz* in which Dorothy opens a door, leaving behind a black-and-white world for a Technicolor one. But damned if Hank was going to let Sergeant Taft's death go so easily.

Edward hardly noticed Hank's aborted answer. He was occupied with his map, checking to see just how far they were from their destination.

Operation Cobra had been aimed specifically at smashing the German defensive line in southeastern Normandy, enabling an Allied breakout and a significant victory on the way to liberating France. The squad had spent most of their time in France just behind the front lines and with some significant and hairy jobs, along with many small ones. Edward and his Kaboom Boys were much nearer exhaustion than they were willing to admit. Ready for something different, for a change of pace, no matter what that might be.

Now, there it was, on the horizon, a massive, welcoming talisman.

"Let's pull off up here, Hank," Edward said. "We'll get some grub and see what we'll be up against before we get to the gate. Maybe I can convince that mayor that we know what the hell we're doing, whether we do or not."

Hank cracked an unlikely smile as he eased the jeep off the roadway near a pasture filled with even more grazing sheep. From habit, he looked upward into an empty sky before he shut off the engine. There was no place to hide if an errant German plane were to suddenly appear to shoot anything on the ground that looked military. No place but beneath their vehicles. But at least they could see in the flat-land distance any approaching troops or vehicles.

After yelling back to the men in the truck to take fifteen, Edward pulled some publications from his leather bag. Hank took out a thick English/French guidebook from where he had stowed it beneath the seat. It was the book he had snatched from the town hall in Avranches.

"Jesus. Fifty feet," he said to himself as he studied a page.

"Say what, Corporal?" asked Edward.

"Nothing, sir."

Edward looked hard at Anderson. "Corporal, I expect you to speak up if you have something important to offer. Got that?"

"Oh, I will sir," was the answer, but Hank said no more as he scanned the guidebook. Edward gritted his teeth. Hank clearly had no idea of how his attitude was putting the team at risk, muddling the chemistry. Or how much the captain counted on him.

Hank had a habit from his early days in the service of swiping booklets, pamphlets, newspapers, magazines, and about any other reading material he came across. That included thefts from fellow enlisted men's bunks or items stowed in the latrine as well as from the desks of high-ranking officers when they were away or distracted. He had read every book in his duffel bag. And some of them twice. The corporal, who had not finished the tenth grade, had an insatiable thirst for knowledge, probably as a counter to his lack of formal education.

The tidal charts in the guidebook, with graphs, times, numbers, and sea levels, were easy enough for Hank to decipher, even if they were in French. Now, the corporal's incessant need to share all that acquired learning might even overcome the issues he had with his captain if Edward pushed him.

The Kaboom Boys   263

"Knowing all we can about this place would help us do the job right," Hume pointedly told him. "Improvisation is fine on most of our jobs, but in this case, we're dealing with tides and quicksand. I'm flying blind here. A naval demolition expert I'm not. And I'm happy to admit it. Just not to the town officials over there and all the way to the top of the French government-in-exile. They're pissed off at us already for dropping those UXBs in their front yard. They're calling it an 'international crisis.' Somehow General Arnold got the impression we were the best choice for fixing this mess. If the French get the impression the US Army has sent a squad of dunces to fix it..."

Hank took the bait. He spoke up.

"Sir, it says here that the tidal waters that surround Mont-Saint-Michel rise as high as fifty feet a couple of times a day. That makes them comparable to the Bay of Fundy in Canada. Pretty treacherous." Now it was Hank's turn to look hard at his captain. "Might be some swimming involved." Hank was aware Edward could not swim.

"Can I see what you're reading there?" Edward asked, holding out his hand for the guidebook.

"Sure thing." Hank handed it over.

"This book certainly isn't US government issue. Where'd you get this, Corporal?"

"Sir, let's just say I found it," he said. "I thought it might come in handy out here, and it's a far sight better than what the Army gave us."

"Well, it does look helpful," Edward admitted, letting the corporal off the hook for the theft as he perused the pages. Then, "I'm starving. Let's eat so we can get back on our way."

Their next stop was at the shore end of a long causeway. At the other end, Mont-Saint-Michel rose from the water, still shrouded in fog at the base, like a castle suspended in the air, impossibly hovering. They could not see the tidal flats they had been reading about. And certainly no collection of unexploded bombs. The tide was coming in.

"Magnificent!" Edward shouted, his eyes moist. "It's amazing. Like it's floating!"

"Like one of those hot-air balloons at the World's Fair," Morty added.

The others were awestruck as well. Gene was not quite as poetic as his captain and squad mate, though.

"Ho-lee shit!" was all he could say.

According to Hank's purloined guidebook, the ancient buildings on the rock island had never been occupied by invaders. Not at any time in its long history. At least not until 1940, when the Germans arrived. A massive seawall surrounded and fortified the village, but Hitler's finest troops simply walked in through the main entrance gate and made themselves at home. Thankfully, they left the place undamaged when they fled after D-Day.

There were signs along the causeway warning drivers that if they parked their cars anywhere between the mainland and the front gate, the high tide could wash them into the bay.

In addition to Carl, neither Pete nor Morty had been impressed by all the chatter about their destination. The New Yorkers had seen big buildings, tall cathedrals, and islands in a harbor before. But as they sat there, engines idling, looking out at Mont-Saint-Michel, Pete's mouth was open in awe and Morty could only stare.

"This place is incredible! Dangerous, ya know, but incredible."

Morty added, "It's kind of like...how do ya say?...mystical."

Carl now had his own point-of-reference comparison. "Place looks like a motion picture set they'd build for a Cecil B. DeMille film. You boys sure that thing's real over there?"

After a few minutes at the edge of the causeway, they gathered around while Hank snapped photos of the squad with Mont-Saint-Michel in the background. Then they prevailed on a passerby to take another picture, this time with Hank in the shot. The soldiers may just as well have been a group of eager tourists or road-weary pilgrims. But they noticed the man who took the snapshot—and appeared to be a fisherman—did not seem very friendly toward the liberators, especially when he handed back the camera without a word, scowled at them, and hurried off.

It was Morty who brought them back to reality. "I can't believe it was Americans who dropped bombs here. What kind of idiots would mess up a place like this?"

"They were just being safe, dumping them instead of landing back at base with the things armed," Hank pointed out. Then he came to a sudden realization. "Oh, wow! Yeah! Hey, Captain, looks like somebody up the chain read our reports. And your recommendation after that job on the runway."

"So, this is our fault somehow," Morty said.

"No, the captain's fault," Pete offered with a grin. "For writing that memo."

"Six fighter pilots let loose twelve bombs smack dab in the middle of those shallows out there northeast of the island," Edward explained, ignoring Pete's comment. "With the tide in, they didn't appear so shallow from their angle and altitude. No matter why, we still got to go out there and fix 'em or we'll rank right up there with the Krauts in the eyes of the people here."

"How we gonna do that, Captain?" Gene asked.

"We're gonna walk across—"

"You mean like Jesus?" Pete called out.

"No. At low tide." Edward grinned, then briefly explained the mission and how one of the primary difficulties, in addition to the speed and force of the tides, was quicksand.

"You mean like in the *Tarzan* movies?" Carl asked. "I met Maureen O'Sullivan on a movie set once. She was Jane. I'd wallow around in quicksand with her anytime."

"Sir, I'm no Johnny Weissmuller. Not too sure about working in quicksand," said Gene.

"Me neither," Edward said with a smile. "Nothing to worry about, though. At low tide, my number two, Hank here, and I will just stroll across to the UXBs and disarm them." Edward did not want the men worrying too much about a job he remained hazy about. He would have to see the bombs up close before he had a solid plan. But he did not want to come across as too cavalier about it either. "We'll wait until the next low tide to take the guts of the detonators out into the bay and detonate them. Like a walk in the park."

"And if you can't defuze 'em?" Ronzini asked.

"We'll have to blow them up in place," Edward replied. "But pray we can neutralize and defuze. That's what the French government has demanded we do."

Hank could hold back no longer. "If we don't get back to the island before the tide comes back in, maybe you could become Moses, instead of Jesus, and part the damn sea."

Morty had a grip on his Star of David. "Yeah, I'd go with Moses on this one."

Gene also held his neck chain and was rubbing his Saint Michael medallion for all he was worth.

"How much time do we have between tides, sir?" asked Carl.

"Not exactly sure," Edward replied. "It varies, depending on the season and the moon. A couple of hours, maybe. We'll find out from the mayor. Duval is his name. Mayor Albert Duval."

"The fishermen could probably give us some tips," Hank said, "if they aren't too pissed off to talk to us."

"No. We only deal with the mayor, according to our orders. Nobody else," Edward told them.

Indeed, the orders had been specific on that point. They were to work only and directly with the man who had been mayor of Mont-Saint-Michel for the past thirty years. Now they only needed to find him.

They hopped back into their vehicles and started out along the causeway, going slowly through heavy pedestrian traffic. The sun bounced off the wavetops like bright strands of beads. People were already gathering along the roadway, anxious for the tide to recede so they could search for clams for dinner.

Hank, eyes straight ahead as he drove, asked, "Okay, Captain, between you and me, how tough do you really think this job is gonna be?"

Edward thought for a moment as he watched all the people milling about, returning for peace and prayer and to forget for a few minutes that the still-undecided war raged all about them. He, too, stared straight ahead as he answered.

"Until I talk to that mayor, and until I get a look at those bombs at low tide, the truth is—and between you and me—it could well be impossible."

23

"Tell me again about the tides, Corporal," Edward told Hank.

They were sweltering, stalled in traffic on the causeway, the only land route to the Mont, stuck immediately behind an ancient, rusty truck partly filled with scrawny vegetables. The wheezing vehicle discharged clouds of blue smoke. Pedestrians were blocking their progress. Despite the war not that far away, there was pent-up demand from visitors to come back to Mont-Saint-Michel.

Edward could see three American soldiers in a guard shack up ahead, inspecting all vehicles for anything suspicious. Every delay was eating up precious time. They were to start the job upon arrival and get it done before sunset, as per their orders. The gist of the negotiations between the French government, Mayor Duval, and General Arnold was the mission would be accomplished by the end of this day so life could return to normal overnight. All parties anticipated that the fishermen would resume fishing then. Edward needed to find Mayor Duval as quickly as possible, learn all he could, and cogitate on a plan that would end with twelve bombs neutralized, one way or the other.

"Well, sir, the way I'm reading this chart here, there is a super-high tide tonight. The moon is full, and the waters here rise vertically fifty feet," Hank reported. "And they come and go about as fast and deep as they do over there in Canada at the Bay of Fundy between New Brunswick and Nova Scotia. Those are the most dramatic on the planet, but this place is a close second. We're talking about a fifty-foot range from dead low to maximum. That happens twice a day. It's a challenge, Captain."

Edward thumbed through Anderson's pilfered guidebook, studying some of the tidal charts, then looked out at the real thing, at the rapidly rising bay water that was now chasing some walkers off the flats and toward the causeway.

"Somehow, this is not exactly the way I pictured my visit to Mont-Saint-Michel. Certainly not with you guys instead of with some tall, stacked French gal."

"Aren't you the romantic? I look at this like it's just another workday," Hank said with the slightest of smiles. "And a chance to get some free smokes if we can just make it a couple of hundred feet farther down this road and beat your buddy Bennett here."

"Wouldn't surprise me one bit if the SOB met us over there, waiting for us at the top, his hand out for his carton of Luckies. Fact is, we sure could use his help right about now." Hume set the guidebook aside. "Only God and the US Army know where those squirrelly Bomb Merchants are and what they're doing."

"What we could really use is some luck, too. You sticking with your usual plan, Captain?"

"Blow 'em up nice 'n' neat at low tide and then skedaddle so we can help win the war somewhere else, yeah. Once we sprinkle in a little diplomacy and make the mayor and a bunch of fishermen happy, we'll be on our way," Edward answered, working to remain on an even keel. Understanding how to best lead men was still a challenge for the captain. Even more than how to defuze bombs. His self-assurance was shaken when Ace died. Still, Edward knew he must never show any hesitation or lack of confidence in his decision-making. That could negatively affect his squad and maybe even prove deadly. He had been far more open with Hank than with anyone else, but now he was not sure if that was working.

"Uh-oh." Hank spotted a sign on the right side of the roadway with large letters in English: *OFF-LIMITS TO TROOPS*. "That's a problem," the corporal noted. "Since we're troops."

The Kaboom Boys 269

"Good thing we got an engraved invitation," Edward said, nodding toward the orders in his bag.

They drove past the soldiers at the guard post with a wave and a smile. No challenge. Then, as they pulled to a stop next to the main gate into the village, they spotted an elderly, plump man waddling toward them, waving a cane, an angry expression on his ruddy face. A crowd of villagers, including a flock of kids, followed close behind.

But it was not this welcoming party that caused Edward Hume to abruptly jump from the jeep, to drop down on both knees on the hard-packed sand. Not what put a huge smile on his face, his arms open in a warm greeting.

It was the dog that ran alongside the approaching herd. A large, muscular, brown-black-and-white male boxer playfully loping along beside some of the youngsters. And the pup was making straight for Edward as if he recognized the captain as a long-lost friend.

It was Sarge. No doubt about it. Those markings. That silly grin. Tongue hanging out the side of his mouth. Running straight toward Edward. And the dog seemed as happy to see his master as Edward was to see Sarge.

"Sarge? C'mon, boy!"

For that moment, it was just a boy and his dog, all alone. Emotions of all kinds took hold of him. Home. Mom and Pops. Tommy. Doc. The mine. The quarry. Fritz. The shirt factory. Even Rachel Levine. All those things he had missed horribly but had shoved aside to concentrate instead on his men and BD.

But the dog, nose high, galloped past Edward as if he were not even there, on his knees, waiting to grab him and embrace him. No, he went right on by to greet two young boys who were coming up behind them, from across the causeway.

Edward's heart tumbled, and he was surprised that he had to fight back tears.

Of course, it could not have been Sarge. Not here. Not on the northern coast of Normandy, France, south of the Channel Islands and the English Channel, at the gate to Mont-Saint-Michel, in the thick of the swirling horror of a world war, 3,553 miles away from Mahanoy City, Pennsylvania. But the dog was a dead ringer.

Embarrassed, Edward stood, dusted the sand off the knees of his fatigues, wiped his eyes with his sleeve, and struggled to remain erect when his legs threatened to buckle. He braced himself against the red fender of his jeep. His squad members stood beside the vehicles, looking oddly at him.

What the hell was that all about?

"That mutt looked a lot like my dog back home." Edward felt the need to explain to his men. He went on jokingly, "Good way to start. Establish rapport with the local pets and kiddoes, right?"

Nobody said anything.

When Edward turned back, the rotund man with the cane was standing ten feet away, angrily eyeing him, using his walking stick to steady himself as he caught his breath. He wore a long-out-of-style dark-blue blazer with big gold buttons and a tattered, white-collared dress shirt. His rumpled appearance and unkempt flowing white hair gave the impression he had just crawled out of bed. It did not at all diminish his superior attitude. He looked askance at the jeep's red fenders, stepped over and tapped his cane hard against the front bumper. The squad stood resolutely behind their captain, even if Edward had appeared to have lost his ever-loving mind over that pooch a moment before.

"*Capitaine*? I am Mayor Duval. Albert Duval," the mayor said in heavily accented English. "You are looking for me, are you not?"

Edward again called on high school French but relied mostly on English.

"Mayor Duval, *je suis Capitaine* Edward Hume, Sixth Ordnance BD Squad, Ninth US Army Air Forces. I am here on behalf of the Army to fix the issue of the bombs that were dropped into the bay. It was a mistake to do so, and we are here to make it right." It was impossible to tell from the man's blank face if the mayor had heard or understood a word. Then, an exaggerated scowl confirmed without a doubt that he was one very pissed-off public servant. Or at least acting like one to impress the throng of citizens behind him.

"I speak the *Engleesh, Capitaine*," the mayor finally said, tapping his cane in time to the speech he seemed bound to deliver. "My village, we receive many visitors who do not bother to learn our language. Americans,

Germans, especially. I am required to be a man of the world and learn their tongues. Now, regardless of the vocabulary in which we engage, you must understand our anger and...how you say?...*les frustrations*. *Pas de péché. Aucun moyen de subsistance.* No fish. No fishing. No livelihood. You see, it was the Americans who dropped those bombs so adjacent our historic island. The bay is part of our home! My people, my fishermen, the Mons— the people of Mont-Saint-Michel—they always look to me to solve the issues. I handle the occupation by the Germans as best I can, but for the bombs, I can do nothing, of course, but inform and...what you say?...file the complaint with the leaders of the Free French." Edward had never seen a man sputter before. Mayor Duval was sputtering. "General de Gaulle, he is able to make your commanders understand the problems these weaponry they have caused on us. The Nazis, they come, they stay four years, they allow no visitors, they steal precious artifacts and tapestries, but they leave no damage, do not threaten our fisher industry. Never once did the Germans do anything of this nature to harm Mont-Saint-Michel. They never dropped one *bombe* here. No, it is the Americans and *des bombes*, *douze*, twelve, the dozen bombs, placing a pox on what God has blessed us with. *Comprenez vous?*"

The crowd behind Mayor Duval cheered him on. Though most did not understand his English words, they got the essence by his demeanor. Several appeared to be fishermen. Most were women and children. Even the dog—the one that looked like Sarge—barked, showing support for the mayor and his speech.

"*Je comprends*," Edward answered, now modeling the demeanor he had observed being used by Doc Fenton when he spoke with upset constituents. "I pledge to you my squad and I will take care of the problem as quickly and safely as possible." Hume put his hand to his heart. "Fully. To the bitter end."

The squad stood nearby, bewildered. They hoped whatever their captain was promising would put them past this puffed-up politician and on to the job at hand.

"You understand, *Capitaine*, that the poet and writer Victor Hugo once described our tides as being as swift as a galloping horse, *oui*?" There was silence as the sea breeze carried away the mayor's words.

"*Oui*, your honor, we are aware of the tides," Edward replied. Now was not the time to challenge the mayor's comparison of the four-year German occupation of the island to the dropping of American bombs a mile away in the bay, but he could not resist. "But the obstacles placed in your bay by the German soldiers. They have surely caused you and your fishermen considerable problems."

The mayor did not seem appeased or at all interested in that bit of recent history. "Now you will submit to the checkpoint at the gate, and we will meet at my residence to further discuss steps and the urgency. My assistant will guide you and your men up. I suggest you avoid contact with Mons. Especially the fishermen. I cannot accept responsibility, *oui*?"

"Mons, ah, *oui*," was all Edward could say about the locals as the mayor turned around and marched back through the main gate, his entourage in tow. Edward stepped into the shade of the jeep and truck, feeling like a reprimanded schoolboy just out of the principal's office.

"He's pissed," he told the squad, wiping his brow with the back of his hand. "He must be up for reelection or something, and he has everybody in town up his ass about the bombs. As our orders say, the fishermen are pissed off because they can't fish, and the villagers are just generally pissed off. They're all voters, too. The French government from de Gaulle on down are all over Eisenhower and Arnold about this while they're still trying to manage the biggest war in history. Thousands of UXBs from all armies ticking away all over Europe, and we happened to draw the dozen that's giving everybody the red ass here on this island."

"Guess that means we can't meet up with some nice ladies in there, then," Carl told Pete.

"Bet they'd be glad to see such a handsome bunch as us," Pete replied, "and with no sauerkraut breath or swastikas on our uniforms."

"I reckon not," Edward said. "Once we get past the guard shack, we'll be on our best behavior. Smile from a distance. At every-damn-body, not just the females. Tip your hats. No missteps. Be diplomatic." If the limited details in their orders were correct, they had 144 hours total from the moment the bombs were released before they exploded. "We've already lost valuable time."

The men looked at each other. Not exactly what they signed up for. Defuzing those bombs might be the best part of this mission after all.

"Some of the girls in there probably got Kraut cooties all over 'em, anyway," Pete noted.

"I volunteer to do a thorough inspection," Carl said with a grin, well past ready to fraternize.

A US Army military policeman waited for them at the guard shack adjacent to the entrance gate to the island fortress. He quickly reviewed Edward's paperwork, then handed it back with another set of papers, including more details of the impending job and additional warnings to be happily accommodating.

"Good luck to you and your men, Captain," the MP offered. "But I got to tell you. Between the angry folks, what's left of obstacles in the water, and that insane tide out there, sir, you got your job cut out for you." He looked around to be sure nobody could overhear. "If you don't mind me saying so, this place, the island, the buildings, the bay and tide, it's all kinda spooky. Eerie. It's almost like there's a curse on the place or something."

"Well, let's hope that curse only applies to those who plan on disrespecting or harming the place," Edward responded. "We're here to fix it, you know."

"So, you say...but you'll have to go out there to do it, right?" He nodded over his shoulder, toward the bay. The water had already risen to the stone walls of the village, a mere thirty feet from where they all now stood. "They say around here 'the tides roll in like a galloping horse.'"

"Yeah, we've heard something like that."

"Some writer, poet, or something," the guard added. "I've been here. I've watched it. I mentioned going swimming, and you'd've thought I was proposing suicide or something crazy like that. Nobody goes out there 'cause of all that shit left by the Germans. And them bombs now, too. Be damn careful, Captain Red Fenders. Damn careful."

"Got that," Edward said with a smile, signing a paper the guard had put before him.

"That mayor fella, he's pretty hopped up, too," the guard went on. "Like we say back in Alabama, that peckerwood's got his dauber up for anything American. I served under Patton, and Patton had a temper, but this guy's something else. Good luck, Captain. You're gonna need a croaker sack full of it."

Edward asked the guard to keep a close eye on their vehicles. The guard slapped the jeep's red fender and waved them into a parking spot. They then met an impatient member of the mayor's staff who led them up a series of steep steps toward his honor's official residence.

As they climbed, Edward considered all that they now knew and pondered what he suspected they did not. With every passing moment, the laws of nature were aligning against the Kaboom Boys. The tidal waters were bound to recede but would rush back in, whether the BD squad had completed their work or not. Nature did not care. The laws of physics were also at work, as the detonator on each bomb could still be advancing, shaving off the time he and his men had to defuse them and make them dormant. Edward was determined these twelve angry bombs would soon be gone. His preference would have been—and his orders were—to quickly form a plan and start work as the next tide rushed out toward the Channel, exposing the bay's bare bottom, the muck, the quicksand, the ugly German obstacles, and whatever else there might be to contend with.

However, they were now also required to do the dance of international cooperation. Edward did not want to contemplate the consequences of failure.

"Dammit, Ace," Edward mumbled to himself in frustration as they climbed. "You would have loved the complications of this job."

"What's that, sir?" Gene asked.

"Aw, nothin', Corporal. Just talking to myself."

As they walked up the cobblestone path that led to the staircase to the abbey, a disgruntled fishmonger stood in front of an empty bin, hands on hips, staring at them. And as they passed by, he stuck out his tongue at the squad members. All along the way, angry people eyed them, some even spitting rude, angry words in French as they passed.

Pete stuck his own tongue out at the fishmonger.

"Pete, cut it out!" Morty told him under his breath. "We're behind enemy lines up here."

"We'll win them over, guys," Edward reminded them as they climbed on. "Imagine how we'd feel if Canada left a dozen UXBs under Mount

The Kaboom Boys   275

Rushmore or the Golden Gate Bridge or in the harbor next to the Statue of
Liberty."

But it was still difficult for them to ignore the harsh looks of the
villagers, people for whom the squad was about to risk their lives.

Over the centuries, a variety of vendors had maintained shops along Le
Grand Rue, the main cobblestone street—more a footpath—that led to the
Grand Degré, the series of steep steps that climbed to the defensive tower
of the abbey. Resourceful merchants manned restaurants, shops, bars, and
hotels positioned on prime real estate, catering to the steady stream of
pilgrims and visitors. There had been tough times. The place had been
used as a prison during the French Revolution. The Great War and Great
Depression had made it difficult for the merchants to survive. Then the
Germans had stopped allowing most visitors, only those with coastal zone
passes, practically ending all commerce on the island. Businesses catered
only to the occupiers.

But even in the most trying times, the fishermen continued to fish. The
Germans on the rock wanted fresh fish and made certain the boats went
out most days. That stopped immediately when the American fight-
er/bombers jettisoned their unused ordnance into the bay.

The squad was followed up the path by an assortment of people, a
growing crowd, some in an almost festive mood in anticipation of having
the bombs removed. Others remained sullen and angry. Mons and fishermen mingled with the Americans as children raced up and back down
the steep stairwell, happily dancing around the BD squad. Along the way,
the dog—the Sarge doppelgänger—pranced happily ahead, as if leading a
parade.

One thing was clear to the Americans. Things here looked unscathed
compared to most other villages they had seen throughout Normandy.
The Germans made certain that commerce in the village met their needs.
Shops, hotels, and restaurants lined each side of the central street. Many
displayed trinkets and Saint Michael medallions. Sparse but brightly
colored vegetables were neatly displayed in bins. Fresh meat hung in
shop windows. Baguettes and loaves of bread were arrayed in baskets
alongside fruit pastries and croissants. Fragrant flowers were displayed in
ceramic jugs along the way. The smells were fresh and clean. Absent were

the obvious ravages of war that overshadowed everything beyond these walls.

But those dozen bombs were still out there in the tranquil bay. And as he climbed, Edward was thinking hard about how he might win the mayor over, get his help in completing this increasingly complicated mission, and do it right damn now.

♠

Mayor Duval was preaching again, repeating the same mantra he had not so subtly shouted into the telephone the previous morning. That came after fishermen alerted him to the twelve bombs lined up at the bottom of Mont-Saint-Michel Bay. The mayor had unloaded on a US Army liaison, a sergeant, who immediately alerted his superior, who promptly spoke directly with General Hap Arnold. He and other local officials had also reached General de Gaulle, who promised a solution. The Americans were already dealing delicately with French indignation over the handling of the devastation and carnage at Saint-Lô. They could not afford another mismanaged, self-induced catastrophe. And definitely not one occurring at such a beloved French religious site.

Now, Duval and Hume were seated at a large, cognac-brown oak table on the porch of the mayor's residence. From there, they overlooked the rooftops of buildings and courtyards below and had a view above them of the iconic abbey and Saint Michael the Archangel statue. Up close, this place was even more impressive and beautiful than Edward had imagined, yet he had not been able to enjoy it. Even so, he knew he must keep his mind on the work at hand.

Many of the townspeople and fishermen had gathered in an open area just below the mayor's residence, as they often did to eavesdrop on official town business. The rest of the squad rested on a wall in the shade of a nearby rose trellis, far enough away so their comments to each other could not be heard by the mayor or, hopefully, any of the Mons.

A couple of fishermen seemed to be placing wagers on something. Hank watched with interest, trying to figure out the stakes, but without luck.

The mayor sipped freshly brewed French-roast coffee from an ornate cup. Edward could smell its wonderful aroma, but Duval had not bothered to offer the captain anything. He would have to be satisfied with warm water from his canteen as they talked. To further establish his authority, Duval was now wearing across his chest the official Mont-Saint-Michel sash. It bore the colors of the French flag with a gold rampart at the top, two white fish against green and blue water at its center, and ornamental red-berry ivy on either side.

Hume was already tired of being lectured by this self-important politician. Edward thought the man's flamboyance and constant chattering might be due to his not having an attentive audience since the Germans arrived four years before. And from being so humiliatingly humbled in front of his constituency for so long. Now he had someone who had to sit there and take it. But Edward needed information, and he wanted to get it from the mayor as soon as he could.

"Not to put too fine a point on it, Mayor Duval, but the Germans did put mines and barbed wire and the vertical poles out there in the bay, which I assume hindered your fishermen far more than those bombs. And I do believe they conscripted many of your people. The caretakers of the abbey..."

"Yes. Unspeakable tragedy. But you compare *des pommes aux oranges*... how you say, 'apples to oranges.' Understand, our fishermen, they learn how to get past the obstacles, the underwater mines, the what-you-call 'barbed wire,' and they could fish. That is until the American airplanes dropped the bombs into our bay. Then, no more fishing. Too dangerous!"

Pete kept a straight face as he whispered to Morty, "In their eyes, we're worse than the Germans. What a blowhard!"

Morty and Gene both shushed him.

The mayor was eyeing Edward suspiciously over the rim of his coffee cup. "You are but a young boy, *Capitaine*. Are you sure you are mature and properly trained for such important duty as this?"

Once more, Hume managed to swallow what little pride this pretentious man had left him. "Sir, we are ready and able to go out there and do this dangerous duty and return things to the way they were. Before the bombs came. But we must get to work now so we can finish before it gets too dark and it's again high tide." Now, on the open-air front porch, Edward was trying to get the mayor to focus on the details he and his squad needed to plan and complete the job they were sent here to do. "Mayor Duval, let me be clear. I appreciate the challenges those bombs have caused. Now, my squad and I are here and—"

"Are you hungry?" the mayor interrupted, smiling. It was as if someone had thrown a switch. Duval's demeanor changed from belligerent to accommodating. So did the mood there on the porch.

"I would say so," Edward answered.

"Very well. We will go up to one of the best restaurants on the island of Mont-Saint-Michel," the mayor told him, and then stood, pointing to a set of steps near where the squad waited. "And from there, as you eat, you will be able to evaluate the challenges while enjoying a truly fine meal."

Now that, Edward thought, *sounds like a damn fine plan.*

24

The BD squad was not quite prepared for what they found at the restaurant the mayor had so highly recommended. From the street, La Mère Poulard Café—circa 1888—was not all that impressive with its faded red awning and four small tables out front. But that changed once inside, where they could see all the way through to the rear, onto a much larger courtyard, and to a panoramic view of the bay. The tide was beginning to recede now. As they followed the mayor in, the men saw a chef grab one of the many copper kettles hanging from the walls. He would use it, the mayor noted, to make one of the restaurant's famous omelets. The wonderful aroma from the kitchen was intoxicating. An attractive waitress in her late twenties cleared tables. Attractive but with a sad, weary look that suggested years of hard work and the suffering of war had worn her down.

"*Eau! Eau*, Adeline! Water! Water for my American *invités*, Adeline," the mayor commanded, his tone distinctly different from only twenty minutes before.

The waitress nodded and disappeared into the kitchen while Duval stood there, smiling proudly. Several older men—obviously, from their dress and demeanor, important town elders—followed the squad inside. One of them, a silver-haired man wearing a bright red ascot, handed the mayor an official-looking piece of paper. Duval opened it, quickly read it, then nodded to the man before turning back to Edward.

"You tell your American friends that this is where you come for the best *omelette* in all of Normandy," the mayor bragged. "No, in all of France!"

"Ah, then, sir, it must be the best omelet in the world," Edward said with a grin. He was getting the hang of this diplomat bullshit.

"*Oui*. You are correct, Captain Hume," the mayor responded. "Now, my simple offer to you and your men: today, you enjoy our freshest cider and a sandwich *au fromage*. No fish, I regret to inform, and as you well know. Tomorrow, after you take care of the *bombes* with success, you try the *omelette*, compliments of La Mère Poulard, the Mons, and their grateful mayor." Duval bent gracefully at the waist in a bow of respect.

"Tomorrow?" Edward responded. "Sir, our orders were to handle the twelve bombs tonight. That was your wish."

"Your superior will understand," the mayor said with a nod. "Who is he...General Arnold...*oui*? Perhaps you inform him that you are being held captive by the Mayor of Mont-Saint-Michel! You tell him that from *moi*." Mayor Duval beamed, quite pleased with his executive decision, then confirmed it with a nod to the elders standing nearby.

However, Edward and the Kaboom Boys were very confused.

"Sir, I cannot do that," responded Edward, remaining tactful. "I must reach out to headquarters to get approval for any change to my directives, and then we—"

"*Non!*" The mayor interrupted, holding out to the captain the official-looking piece of paper. "They know, and you have their permission."

Edward took the paper and quickly scanned it. It came from Army headquarters and, indeed, appeared to be official.

"Due to the unusual situation you have encountered, you are hereby authorized to take one more day to complete your mission as detailed in your previous orders." It was signed by the same attaché to General Arnold who had issued the previous unusual mission directive. Edward reread the document and did the math in his head, still not sure if waiting a day was the best thing to do.

"Sir, I know you should receive credit for this change. Thank you for speaking to my superiors on behalf of myself and my squad. So generously allowing us this extra time will greatly assist in the successful completion of this mission and a return to normal for your town."

The mayor smiled broadly and puffed out his chest with pride. Edward was satisfied he had achieved some kind of breakthrough with Duval.

The BD boys perked up, too, first at the suggestion of a couple of free meals that happened to not be K rations or mess-tent leftovers, and then upon learning they would not have to deal with the dozen devices in the dark while facing a returning tide.

Duval led them through the cramped café, past tables covered with white tablecloths and candles at their centers, and out into the expansive rear courtyard. There were more dining tables, mounds of ivy draped down stone masonry, and hanging baskets filled with fleur-de-lis. At an ancient stone wall overlooking Mont-Saint-Michel Bay, the mayor stopped. Hume and his squad noticed that a legion of people had followed them single file through the restaurant and were now gathered around them, intent on hearing what the mayor and the American Army captain would next discuss.

Edward glanced over his shoulder, in the direction of the bay. While all this was going on, there were a dozen bombs out there, growing more and more menacing with each tick.

The waitress, Adeline, reappeared then with glasses and pitchers filled with *cidre de Normandie*, a drink made from fermented apples and pears. Other servers brought in icebox- chilled spring water. While the squad drank thirstily—the day's heat had left them dehydrated—the mayor angled for a spot near the wall and next to a small herb garden where a chef selected leaves for a diner's meal order. The chef took his time, though, curious as well to see what was about to be discussed.

Facing northeast, toward the Cotentin Peninsula and, eventually, the English Channel, Duval pointed downward, toward the tidal waters. Edward could clearly see the difference from when they had crossed the causeway and arrived at Mont.

"Low tide coming?" he asked.

"Now, just past a full moon, it is what is called a 'spring tide,'" the mayor explained. "The most maximum difference between the low and the high points. Dangerous. She is very dangerous."

"And the quicksand?"

"Always the hazard." The mayor singled out an elderly fisherman in the crowd. At least old enough to not be of interest to the Germans for labor. "Denis. Denis. *Montrez exactement où se trouvent les bombes.* Show the demolition men exactly where the bombs are located."

The fisherman pointed northeast, the same direction as the mayor had. The same direction Archangel Michael pointed from his perch.

For more than twelve hundred years, pilgrims journeyed at low tide to pay a visit to the island and abbey. Some lost their lives from the hazards, especially before the causeway was in place. Those who could afford to hired a guide, but those who could fill that role were now in German work camps elsewhere.

"You are certain there are twelve bombs, sir?" Edward asked in French. He knew a dozen had been dropped, but some may have exploded already.

"*Oui,*" the sad-faced fisherman confirmed, nodding. "*Douze.*"

Mayor Duval grabbed Denis by the shoulder. "*Exactement?* Exactly?"

"*Oui.*" Then the fisherman added more that Edward did not quite catch.

"He says the bombs, they are one mile out," Mayor Duval translated. "*Capitaine*, you will require a guide. The US Army will be expected to pay the fee."

Edward listened attentively, going along for the moment with what the mayor was saying. He wondered, though, if there was about to be more negotiating.

"The most important question, how much time will we have to work?" he asked. Hank, Gene, Morty, Pete, and Carl leaned in. They needed to hear this.

"This part I do not understand," the mayor said, ignoring Edward's question. "The *bombes*, they could explode at any time. How do you work on such a challenge? Without getting blown up? Without...dying? It is such a risk you are taking." The mayor pulled a large handkerchief from his back pocket and wiped perspiration from his forehead. So, Duval did know the danger the Americans faced, that the men with whom he was talking could possibly die because of his demands about the bombs.

"Sir, this is what we do. The bombs are delayed action. Twelve of 'em. Armed while in flight. This is what we have been told. What the pilots told headquarters. We also know this because they would have exploded on impact had they not been set to blow up later," Edward explained. "Headquarters told me we have up to a hundred and forty-four hours from the moment the bombs were armed in flight. Six days. We've already lost one day and several hours. We also need to complete this mission because we have many other jobs to do, lives to save."

"Jobs bigger than this one?" the mayor asked, apparently taken aback.

"Perhaps." Edward looked directly at the mayor. "So, to be extra cautious here, are there any witnesses who can tell me exactly what time those bombs dropped? My orders do not say the precise time."

Duval scratched his chin. "Well..."

The fisherman shook his head. No one in the crowd seemed to know the answer to the crucial question. Or if they did, they did not want to take the responsibility to say.

"Okay, so, depending on some other factors, like the weather, we need to make some decisions. Tomorrow, before it's low tide again and we can even begin, we need exact times of the tides."

Hank handed Edward the tidal chart. Edward held it up and announced, "This does not tell me about tomorrow." The mayor took the chart from Edward and placed it on the stone wall, then looked out to the water. Edward continued, "The next low tide comes at four thirty-one today, and it will not be low again until later tonight. I need to know about all the tides between now and then. Who can tell me what that exact hour will be? That way we can figure exactly when low tide hits in the morning."

The mayor tapped his jawbone with a thick finger. The fishermen only shook their heads. No one seemed willing to answer the crucial question. Edward was puzzled. Did they not know, or did they not want to say and thus somehow be indirectly responsible for the fate of the mission or the lives of these young men? Nobody wanted the blame should any of these Americans die here.

"Sir, I do not want to belabor the point, and I am asking as politely as I can. I really need to know the timing of the tides and details about the quicksand. Is the man who first saw the bombs here? I really need to know what he saw," Edward pleaded, now running short on diplomatic patience.

Meanwhile, the waitress returned with a large tray piled high with warm cheese sandwiches and apple slices. The soldiers started to grab at them, but Edward held them back.

"Wait for the mayor."

Duval lifted his hand and gestured for the squad to sit and eat. Each man politely took a sandwich and a glass of cider.

Hank tapped Edward's shoulder and whispered a suggestion. "Captain, we can take out some of those small rowboats while the water's still high but receding. There's a bunch of them tied up down there." He pointed down to where the small, colorful boats were lined up, beached along the rampart. "We row out there on the tide, then as the water level drops, the boats float to the bottom, we ride them down, and they stay in place in the mud while we walk the rest of the way and do our work. We'll be better able to take all our gear out there, too. That would give us more time to do whatever we have to do."

The captain smiled. He had hoped Hank would do what he usually did: think creatively based on his acquired knowledge.

"I say that sounds like a good plan, Corporal. What could go wrong?" Edward replied, patted Hank on the shoulder, then turned toward the mayor again. "Sir? Because of all the uncertainty, we have an alternative plan. We need to borrow three rowboats. And we would like for you to provide one person to guide us to the bombs."

Several fishermen moved in closer. They seemed to understand what Edward was suggesting, and things were getting interesting. But they had doubts. Several of them spoke at once, more to their mayor than to the American captain. Rowing would be very arduous, even for someone accustomed to crossing the bay that way. The tide could sweep them past the bombs and out to sea. No fisherman would be willing to become a guide and then take the blame if something went wrong and the Americans died. And the fishermen were still convinced that the bombs would explode if anyone so much as touched one of the beasts. They were reluctant to give information because they wanted no part of a potential disaster, whether their fears were based on reality or superstition.

The mayor shook his head. "It is impossible."

Edward tried to come up with his next move, but for the moment, he was stuck. No precise information on the tides. No permission to take the three boats. He sat down at a table, calmly drinking the cool water, staring out across the tranquil bay. He ignored the sandwich Adeline had placed in front of him. Meanwhile, the squad ate quietly, but their minds were churning with what-ifs.

The initial orders they had received indicated the bombs were not equipped with anti-handling devices. That was good. But they were almost certainly armed and had been ticking for a while. Bad. The fact was, though, that he really needed to see the beasts for himself. Only then could he decide whether to attempt to deactivate them or detonate them in place. That judgment call was always left to the BD captain in charge. That was what Colonel Kane had taught and what RAF Captain Duncan Smythe and others had instilled in him. Orders were one thing, reality was another. He assumed the fishermen were objecting to the mayor about the dozen big blasts and their effects on fishing. But in Edward's mind, that solution might ultimately be necessary.

"Mr. Mayor, we need a place to spend the night, to get a good night's sleep, whether we visit the bombs tonight or with the first low tide tomorrow. But sir, we can pitch our tents down near the vehicles if that is better."

"*Non*, no. We have fine rooms for you and your men so they will be well rested and at no cost to you or the Army," the mayor said. "Your great American author and journalist, Mr. Ernest Hemingway, he stayed there until a few days ago. Some of the war correspondents only left two days ago, just before the bombs were dropped. Had they still been on Mont-Saint-Michel, they would have filed breathless stories as respected journalists do, and the whole world would now know of this travesty. But so far it remains a top secret, which I believe is best for diplomacy." One of the fishermen approached the mayor and whispered something in his ear. "Oh, and I am pleased to report that we have someone we will recommend as a guide and to direct your efforts with the bombs. *Capitaine* Sébastien Chantrelle. He just returned from fighting, and as an officer, he is very good at overseeing men. He spent time with the British. Though he is now a baker with his wife here in our village—they prepared the bread for your sandwiches—he was once a fisherman and a guide before the war. He knows the safest routes around the bay. He is an expert."

Well, now we're getting somewhere, Edward thought, temporarily ignoring the "directing" and "overseeing" references. But he said, "We appreciate the help, sir."

Duval leaned in, whispering, "Sir, I must say, though, that even though he has seen the worst of war, there is some reluctance on his part. He, too, is afraid to go near the bombs. His wife objects. He is a young father. Two children he has hardly seen since their birth. He has recently returned home after four years."

The mayor nodded in the direction of two young boys playing with the "Sarge" boxer at the far side of the restaurant courtyard.

"It's not necessary to have a guide with us, then, sir. I just need information," Edward told him. Now, the "overseeing" thing was raising red flags in Hume's mind. It would be problematic to have a non–US Army, non-BD person along, whether he had seen battle or not, much less have a Frenchman supervising a very precarious US operation.

"But I will order him that he go with you," Mayor Duval proclaimed. "It is his duty as a Frenchman, an army captain, and a Mons. France must... will...play its role."

A reluctant French captain leading what was a BD squad's mission, under Edward's command? *No way that's happening*, Edward thought.

"No. No, sir. There is no need," Edward said firmly but calmly. "He has already done his part for his country. Maybe Captain Chantrelle would tell us more details of what we need to know, however. That would be most valuable." Edward turned and gestured toward his men. "We can take it from there. But let's get this settled. We must borrow three rowboats." Edward knew none of the boats were being used. Not with everyone spooked by those silvery weapons resting out there in the bay. "I must impress upon you that the boats are key to our success."

The fishermen gasped. Their boats, their means of earning a living, could be lost, sunk, or blown up.

"*Non. Non.* You walk the flats then," the mayor proclaimed. "No rowboats."

"Walk the flats?" inquired Edward. "At dead low tide, the entire way out and back?"

Hank could hold his tongue no longer. "Captain, it would take at least

The Kaboom Boys   287

an hour and a half to walk across the flats to the devices. And that doesn't take into account the quicksand and obstacles out there."

Edward held up a finger, telling Anderson to hold off. "No, sir. This is not negotiable. We need the boats. The plan will not work any other way. It will save invaluable time and allow us to transport our equipment and tools."

"Even so, you cannot go alone. Too dangerous. You must use our guide, a Mons, a Frenchman, *Capitaine* Sébastien Chantrelle," the mayor stated emphatically, poking the stone floor with his cane.

So, they were back to being political. Edward wondered why he had to always be butting heads with somebody. They wanted a French fisherman to lead them on a mission. Edward sipped his water and considered the options, none of which included giving anyone else command over his BD job.

"Sir, one last time, please tell me precisely about the timing of the tides," he finally said. "And details of the quicksand."

The mayor settled down at the table across from Edward, unwrapped a loaf of bread that filled a basket, pulled off a piece, and chucked it into his mouth.

"*Faire bouillir*," he finally said as he chewed vigorously.

"Boiled? I don't understand."

"*Oui.*" Duval used his stubby fingers to indicate a boiling motion. "Boiling."

"Oh. You mean we are to look for air bubbles in the sand? Avoid that area?"

"*Oui. Oui.* The fishermen, they will tell you it is very dangerous. You can become caught up. Very difficult to become free."

"And the tides?"

"They depend on so many factors. It is difficult to know for certain." The mayor now seemed genuinely apologetic that he could not be more specific. "I...I do not know what to tell you."

That confirmed the mayor was being honest. He did not know jack-shit about the tides.

Just then, a younger man stepped forward. He wore a baker's apron, and there were flecks of flour in his dark hair and smudged across his face. He shoved aside the basket of bread and placed a large nautical chart on the table between the mayor and Edward. A gust of wind threatened to blow it away.

Morty, Pete, and Carl hustled to grab rocks and put them on each corner to hold down the map. They seemed happy to finally be able to do something besides stand by, nod, eat cheese sandwiches, and chug cider. Hank had already been busy taking notes and shooting pictures of the gathering, the restaurant, the fishing boats, the view of the bay. And using his camera lens and binoculars to see what he could see in the waters surrounding the island.

So, Sébastien Chantrelle had been there in the crowd the whole time, listening. And that crowd had only grown larger. It was as if Edward and the mayor had an audience, watching their performances. Hume ignored them to take in what Chantrelle might share.

"Ah, Sébastien will explain," Duval said, still chewing.

As the fisherman/guide/captain/baker began indicating points on the map—including a rough location for the bombs themselves—he explained what they were seeing on the chart. Edward was not certain he was getting it all. He finally sat back and interrupted the man.

"Captain, we first need to know how much time we have between tides," Edward told Chantrelle. "If low tide lasts long enough, each man can easily rig two bombs each." The squad all looked up, surprised by what they had just heard. The math should have been the tip-off. The timing and number of bombs naturally required the work of six men. Against regulations, but necessary in this situation. The men looked at each other. They understood. Edward went on, "I just need to get out there and see what we're really dealing with. We're losing too much time. I'll show my men exactly what to do on the first bomb, then they'll work on the others."

Chantrelle looked skeptical. Mayor Duval chewed bread and sipped cider.

Edward stood, ignored Chantrelle, the mayor, and the townspeople as he walked over to the stone wall, then waved his squad closer. "Okay, change in plans. For some reason, we're not getting much help from these guys. I have to get a close look-and-listen to the bombs, and with low tide approaching, now's the time to do that. Right damn now. Once we know

The Kaboom Boys   289

what we're dealing with, we can either go to work and do the job today or we hustle on back, convinced the job can wait a few more hours, and then hit low tide in the morning to finish up."

The Kaboom Boys looked at each other. Then, to a man, they grinned, eager to do something other than jawbone.

"May as well," Hank said. "I don't have any plans for the next couple of hours."

"And my date stood me up already," Carl said with a grin. "Once she realized I ain't had a shower in more than a week." The men laughed, the tension effectively broken.

"Look, guys, I just need to see the detonators on the devices and where they're located in relation to the muck. God forbid some or all of them got their noses and detonators planted too deep in mud." Edward turned to tell the mayor that due to lack of details, they would simply head on out and learn what they could on their own. But Duval was involved in animated discussion with two other men, likely advisors. "Hell, let's go," the captain ordered. "Thanks for lunch, Mayor Duval."

The mayor did not seem to hear or notice Edward and his men heading down a back stairway that led away from the restaurant courtyard.

As they descended, Gene asked, "You mean we might have to roll 'em over to get access to the detonators?"

"Nope. Dig 'em out. Youse guys know a thing or two about digging out UXBs, right?" Edward answered with a broad grin.

"You ever dug on a wet beach before?" Pete asked. "I have. Coney Island. Sand's heavy and wants to slide right back down into the hole."

"I buried a girl up to her neck at Malibu once," Carl told them. "You're right. Hard digging."

"I betcha it was hard," Morty growled, and everyone laughed at his unintended joke.

"Sir, none of us has ever actually defuzed or detonated a bomb, you know," Gene said. "APG or RAF protocol or whatever, we've never actually touched a live bomb. Except for Hank with the RAF guys. Rest of us, we're ditch diggers, pretty much. We make damn good mud pies."

"You know more than you think. You've learned through osmosis. If you pay close attention, once we're out there, I'll show you all you need to know once I get a plan for how we'll do things," Edward assured them, but he was also reassuring himself. "God knows you've all seen it done plenty of times already."

They walked down the steps and onto the main street without talking, everyone deep in his own thoughts. Then Hank chimed in.

"See, I told you guys formal APG training was way overrated. And once we do this job, I'm sure our boss here will give us all a field promotion to captain. Right?"

Edward snorted. "Do it right or we'll all be busted to buck private and assigned to latrine duty. And if we really screw one up, that duty could be in Hades."

They all laughed at the usual dark humor. They were now at the level of the steps that led to a path where the rowboats were tied up. Edward pointed over his shoulder with a thumb, back toward the main gate where they had left the truck and jeep.

"Go grab the usual shit," the captain ordered. "Hank and I are gonna appropriate us some boats for a leisurely row out into beautiful Mont-Saint-Michel Bay."

"Yeah, I'll bring my bathing trunks, too," Pete shouted back. "I could use a swim!"

"God willing, you won't need 'em," Edward yelled back, hoping he sounded confident. But he was wondering, too, if this might be the day he learned to swim.

When the others were gone, while shielding his face from a sudden rush of gusting wind, Hank quietly asked the captain, "You're really intending to blow those suckers up today, aren't you?"

"Hell, I don't know, Corporal," Edward replied. "We just don't know enough. We get out there and those things are ticking, and if we can fairly easily locate, isolate, and reach all twelve detonators, we charge 'em up and let 'em blow. Right then and right there. All this fuckin' talkin' is what's gonna get us all killed."

"The fishermen would swear we scared off all the fish."

Edward snorted. "First fisherman who dares to come out and then returns with full nets will dissuade them of that notion, I suspect."

"And if the UXBs are not on the verge of going boom? Or we can't easily

The Kaboom Boys 291

get to even one of the detonators?"

"We'll punt the ball and row our happy asses back here on the incoming tide and tell that damn mayor to pound salt. We sleep tonight where Hemingway slept and then do the job with the first of the ebb tide tomorrow morning." Edward looked over at Hank, glad the corporal was once again asking all the right questions. "I just need to see 'em, Hank. Touch the casings. And smell their stinkin' breath."

Hélène LeRiche had hoped the crowds would be smaller when she and her friend Pierre Devereaux next visited Mont-Saint-Michel. Twice since the German soldiers left, they have ridden their bicycles from Pontorson, but both times the numbers of visitors prevented them from fully enjoying the day. Still, it was worth it, escaping the constant convoys of the Allies through the lovely streets of her new home, the long lines of German prisoners being marched toward the port at Cherbourg, and the roar of airplanes from the Allied airdrome nearby.

Upon their arrival, though, there is some kind of turmoil outside the main gate. A disturbance involving a rotund, red-faced man with long, white hair. Pierre says he is the town's mayor, Monsieur Albert Duval. He is having quite a noisy confrontation with some soldiers. Americans, they hear someone say. But their vehicles do not look like other American military ones they have seen. They have odd, red fenders, like the ears of some exotic animal. A large crowd has gathered to watch and listen, partially blocking the way. Hélène and Pierre have to carefully steer their bicycles through the mob to avoid being separated.

Then, as the two young people enter the main gate—thankfully with no demand to show their papers or submit to the ogles and veiled threats of the crude Nazis—they must wait for enough space to squeeze into the mass of people along the main street leading upward.

"I know a back way," Pierre says as they park their bicycles beside the post office. Of course he does! Pierre knows far more than any teenaged boy should.

Hélène watches the action below as the American soldiers drive their vehicles in through the gate and the commotion grows.

"We should wait until tomorrow," Hélène suggests. "Things are too hectic. We need time to pray and reflect and to enjoy our picnic. My mother helped me make a tarte aux mirabelles. Your favorite." She pats the basket covered with a blue-

and-white serviette napkin that contains the cherry plum tart. "We do not need all this to ruin our day."

Pierre is flattered that she made the pastry for him. But he prefers that they carry out their plans for the picnic.

"No need," he tells her. "With my back way, we will be at the top soon."

Hélène glances skyward. "I'm afraid it will rain, though."

"If it does, we can move inside the abbey and picnic there," Pierre Devereaux tells her.

She agrees to follow him. As they climb, they hear—and sometimes see—the crowd, accompanying the Americans, sometimes shouting rudely at them. She does not understand why the Mons are so unhappy with the soldiers. They are their liberators, after all.

Finally, they are in the large courtyard, adjacent to the main entrance to the abbey.

"Pierre, have I told you how much I appreciate you bringing me to this place?" Her large, gray-green eyes are expressively sincere. As she hoped, the crowd was not quite so daunting this time of day, and they quickly make it to the top of the island. Everyone also seems preoccupied with the Americans and the mayor's dealings with them.

"Only a hundred times," he answers with a laugh. It is still early for their meal, so they step into the cool, quiet abbey, where they can sit quietly, reflect, and pray. They lose track of time there, but that is one of their goals. Hélène even takes time to carve her initials in a slate on the floor near a wall, using a butter knife from the picnic basket.

"God will not mind," she tells Pierre. "And the world will know I was here, even if they never know who I am." He so wants to make fun of her, but nothing clever enough comes to mind.

They wander through the many rooms and gardens around the abbey, the areas once occupied by nuns and monks. The rooms where supplies were brought up on big lifts using foot power provided by monks, walking like hamsters in a cage in the interiors of large wheels attached to a series of ropes to drag crates and barrels up to the top.

Finally, much later than they intended, hunger overcomes them. They retrieve the basket, and Pierre helps Hélène spread the blue-and-white linen blanket and food atop a wall with a view of the bay. The food is every bit as good

The Kaboom Boys 293

as they expected. So is the scenery from the courtyard, despite the clouds and occasional raindrops.

As they finish their leisurely picnic, a noise from below distracts them. An excited noise. They walk over to see what is happening. A crowd is spreading out onto the level ground along the top of the ramparts. The people seem fascinated by some activity going on out in the bay.

"The Americans are here to remove the bombs," Pierre explains. "It has become a show for the Mons to watch."

"Bombs? But I see no damage."

"My father told me a little about it. There are bombs out there somewhere under the water. They have not yet exploded but reveal themselves at each low tide. Wait for the tide, and we should be able to see them from here, I suppose. The Americans will either neutralize or blow them up before they blow up on their own and hurt someone." Pierre looks sideways at Hélène. Her lovely face has become stormy.

"Well, all this noise is ruining the day for us, Pierre." She looks up to the abbey, its spire pointing toward shadowy clouds. "I thought with the Germans gone, our problems were over."

As her mood sours, Pierre looks for a way to distract her. He climbs up onto the wall.

Just then, a brisk gust of wind almost turns the picnic blanket into a sail and threatens to scatter what remains of their food all over the small nook where they have chosen to eat. Hélène runs over and sets an almost empty jug of cider on one corner, the basket once filled with croissants, apples, and cheese on another to try to hold it in place.

Pierre Devereaux is no help. He is now up and trotting fearlessly along the top of the wall, using his outspread arms for balance, as if he is navigating a tightrope.

She knows he is trying to impress her with his dangerous antics. Foolish boy! A fall from there would be fatal. She would be far more impressed if he would come help save their lunch from the blustery winds.

"Get down this minute!" she orders. "If something happens to you, your parents will never forgive me. It is not a good day for flying."

She knows he will not obey her. He is totally and completely smitten by her. He is trying to impress her. But he is so young. She is a much older woman. Pierre,

sweet and doting as he is, has seen so little, experienced so few things. He is a boy.
She is a woman.

She has been a victim of war. A refugee, twice. He is a child who lives farther
away from the worst of the war. A youngster who likes to balance dangerously on
the abbey wall, hoping to catch her eye.

He suddenly stops, looks out across the bay, and points at something, even as
bigger drops of rain begin to pepper down.

"Not a good day to go boating either," he tells her.

She looks where he points. Three rowboats, red, yellow, and blue, are just
launching far below where the two young people have chosen to picnic. The men
in the boats seem determined to ride the ebb tide out toward the much broader
part of the bay.

"Who is that?" Hélène shouts, standing, then joining him on the wall to better
see. "The fishermen are not..."

"They are not fishermen," Pierre tells her. No, the men in the boats are shirtless and wearing US soldier helmets.

"The Americans!" she says. Yes, she can see the young Americans, awkwardly
splashing their oars in the water. The men they had seen outside the gate earlier
being scorned by the crowd and berated by the mayor. Then further scorned by
the locals once they were inside the walls of the town.

"They must be going out to remove the bombs," Pierre says. He is a bit miffed
that Hélène is taking such interest in the young warriors and not his antics atop
the wall. "But there will be a storm. See? They are fools for being out there."

Sure enough, black clouds continue to roll in. There is the rumble of distant
thunder. Even as accustomed as they are to artillery fire and exploding bombs, the
noise of the deteriorating weather is disturbing.

"We must find a dry place now," Hélène tells him. "But a place where we can
still watch those men and what they do."

They quickly fold up the blanket as more raindrops fall. They find a spot just
inside one of the anterooms near the abbey. One with a broad, open window
facing toward the bay but with an overhang that keeps them dry. From there,
they can still just make out the Americans, oars flailing, more in the air than in the
water as they try to keep the rowboats aimed toward their destination.

Hélène abruptly kneels and prays for what she always prays for, a quick end
to the war, but this time she adds a plea for safety for the American soldiers.

Pierre makes a quick sign of the cross but has a jealous frown on his young face. Hélène remains transfixed on the Americans out there in their small boats on rough water. Even when they are soon so far away and almost erased by the wind-driven rain.

Ultimately, Pierre can no longer hold back his question.

"So, tell me, Hélène. Why is it so important for you to watch whatever it is that the Americans are doing instead of talking with me? Could it be you find them more daring and handsome than you do me?"

She watches the rainstorm for a long moment. "Oh, Pierre. I have seen so much of the darkness of war. These men, though they are soldiers, they still represent a small touch of goodness. They try to prevent the explosions, not make them happen. They remove the danger, not create it. And they are so brave. So very brave to do so."

"The Mons are angry with them," he says. "And Mayor Duval. They certainly would not agree there was any goodness going on. You saw and heard how they feel about these men."

"The people will think differently once the American soldiers remove the threat," she tells him with a smile. A beautiful smile.

Just then, there is a sharp crack and an immediate boom of impossibly raucous thunder. The two young people are startled. Hélène drops her cup of cider and holds both hands over her ears, her eyes shut tightly, her face screwed up with fear. The thunderclap is so much like the sound of bombs.

"It cannot happen here! Not at Mont. Not here," she says.

"It is only thunder," Pierre tells her, but his face has gone unnaturally pale, too. He slides over, embraces her, genuinely, not in a forced way. She is happy to be held. He can feel her racing heartbeat. It almost matches his own. "Lightning, you see. Lightning strikes the spire and the statue above us scores of times a year. It is only God's lightning and thunder."

"But the Americans, they are in danger." Hélène pulls away slowly from his arms, but she still bites her lip, has tears on her cheeks, her eyes still closed. Then she opens them and looks grimly at her companion.

"Pierre, you have seen much of the war, but I have seen more. For me, for so many others, it will never be merely lightning and thunder again. It will be the crack of a rifle shot or the roar of the bombs and artillery with every thunderstorm. It will not be the shouts of men playing football or youngsters in the street

but instead the yells of soldiers arresting and marching away the Jews just for being Jews. Or of the Nazis conscripting our brothers and fathers to go work for the Reich in the labor camps. And it will be that way for us for the rest of our lives."

"I know, sweet Hélène," he tells her, and covers her hand with his. "I know. That is why I brought you to this place. So you could forget all that for just a bit. I am so sorry this is happening here and now."

When she turns back to the window to try to find the Americans out on the bay in the red, yellow, and blue boats, she sees only a curtain of rain, swirling in the blustering wind.

The brave bomb squad members—that lone example to her of goodness amid so much evil—can no longer be seen.

25

Several older fishermen—locally known as "the wisemen of the bay"—
were gathered, smoking and talking, near where a dozen or so of their
small rowboats were beached and tied to rocks. Another boat was bobbing
in the water with two men aboard, readying nets, hoping they would soon
be able to fish once the Americans removed the bombs. Each vessel was
brightly painted in primary colors. It could easily have been a scene from
one of Edward's magazine covers had it not been for the barbed wire
fencing and timber obstructions all around. But the captain paused only a
moment to take in the view before sorting things out.

"I'll talk with these guys and tell 'em we're borrowing their boats. I hope
we don't have to get forceful. Gene and Carl can take that red boat. Pete and
Morty, the blue boat. Hank, you'll be stuck riding shotgun in that lovely
yellow one. Since they don't appear to have anything in white..."

"I get it. Red, white, and blue. Like our flag," Pete said.

"And the French flag, too, you know," Hank added. Edward winked at
him. Hank was reverting more and more to his old self.

Now that they were near the water, they could tell that it dropped
noticeably lower where it lapped up against the rock walls of the ramparts.
And they could feel a few cooling gusts of wind from the direction of some

new and dark thunderheads that were building in the broad sky not that far off to the southwest.

"Captain, with all that posturing up there, did we ever really find out exactly how long low tide lasts?" Hank asked.

"Not really. I'd guess the fishermen do their jobs mostly by intuition, the way they have for hundreds of years, not by graphs or guides. And they can't feel it if they aren't out there in a boat," Edward answered, hazarding a guess. "We'll rely as best we can on the published charts. Says here it's just over six hours from high tide to low tide. That means we have about three hours before the racehorse shows up again. We need to be close to finished with the job by then to give us time to hike back to the boats and ride the pony into the barn again."

"Giddyup!" Hank said with a laugh.

In the distance, there was a low rumble of thunder, but it appeared the storm was moving parallel to them, toward the island of Jersey, not in their direction.

"I hope to hell that thundercloud heads to England and not to France," Edward said, a worried look on his face. "Our bigger problem now might be the rain, wind, and rough seas once we're coming back after taking care of the bombs. And we can't have our fuse lines or fuzes get wet if we decide to detonate."

"Looks like it might blow north," Hank guessed, but he was not convinced. The guidebook had noted how unpredictable the weather could be here.

"I don't mind getting wet if you and the guys don't," the captain said calmly, hoping this would not be the day he would have to sink or learn to swim, spur of the moment. But in his head, he ran over the details. They needed perfect conditions. No wind, no rain, dead low tide, and plenty of light. He said a silent prayer, asking for just those things. The sun would set about 9:23 p.m., and that was not that far off. And he still knew far too little about the quicksand.

As he approached the assembled fishermen, they warily stepped back, eyes growing wide, as if Edward and Hank were specters, walking ghosts. Edward began speaking in broken French and using gestures, indicating what they intended to do and that they needed three of the boats. The sun-weathered men watched and listened in silence. Some nodded in agreement, listening quietly, but none offered any help. Edward thought they understood what he was trying to get across, but he could not be certain.

Finally, one of the younger men stepped forward and told them as best he could and by gesturing to his watch that absolute low tide would be at 2:30 p.m. That was only an hour and a half away. Then the waters would turn and start to rush back into the bay in the form of a fierce "bore tidal wave." Hank nodded his understanding. That was in the guidebook, too.

"The strongest tides take place thirty-six to forty-eight hours after full and new moons," he said. "Tonight is a full moon, so we might have to ride it back in. It would be like an avalanche in the Rockies I saw once, but..." Edward looked oddly at Hank. Both men craved adventure, the rush of adrenaline. This one, though, could be downright deadly.

Behind them, the squad had arrived and were stacking up their gear, ready to load it into rowboats. That caused more consternation among the fishermen.

There was no sign of Captain Sébastien Chantrelle.

Guess the madame put her foot down, Edward thought. But he was, in a way, relieved. Just as at the field hospital at Saint-Lô when he butted heads with the chief surgeon, he needed to be in charge of his site when he was dealing with deadly ordnance. He would be damned if he would ever allow anyone clueless about how BD worked to oversee his job.

"The tide is still headed out. Gene! Start the stopwatch now," Edward ordered.

"Yessir! Time started," Wozinski confirmed.

Edward waved the men to their respective boats while the fishermen looked on, making no move to stop them. "Okay, once we're on the way, I want you to shout the time every quarter hour. Got that?"

"Yessir!" Wozinski shouted.

"From what I recall, all of you can swim. As most of you know by now, I cannot. But don't worry about that. Thanks to Hank's smart thinking, we've got boats now, and that'll make up for that." Edward looked at the faces of his men. He wanted to reassure them as much as he was also reassuring himself. They seemed ready to be on the way, to get this chore done.

"Captain, you act like we ain't never been in a rowboat before!" Morty Schwartz said.

"Have you?"

The squad looked at each other. "Well, no," Morty confessed. "It's just a mile out there, right? How hard can it be?"

"I suppose we're about to find out." Edward grinned, pleased with his men's enthusiasm and hoping he looked more confident than he felt.

"Sir! I've rowed before." It was Carl. "I used to go catfishing on the Coosa River with my pa back in Alabama all the time. There was a pretty swift current in places."

"Give us a quick lesson, then."

Carl proudly stood just a bit taller as he shared this bit of helpful knowledge with his squad mates. "So, one man rows, facing backward, while the other sits in the stern facing forward and navigates. For the rower, it's gonna take you some time to coordinate. Both oars go in the water at the same time and then come out at the same time. Keep both oars in the oar lock, and don't dig too deep or you'll actually move slower and get tired quicker. Pull hard on both oars at the same time. You're gonna screw it up, but stay calm, go slow, get a rhythm. Switch off when the rower gets tired."

It did take some time for them to get the hang of using the oars. Then, when they looked back toward the ramparts, they saw they had quite an audience watching them.

Mons and fishermen, hundreds of them along stairways, in courtyards, from windows, and lined up several deep along stone walls, all anxiously observing. Many appeared to be praying. Others openly admired the bravery of Hume and his squad, acknowledging with cheers and applause, whistles and enthusiastic waves. They did, after all, have their own stake in how this job turned out.

And at the lowest level, a group of hardened fishermen openly made more wagers, gambling on whether or not the Americans would be able to neuter the bombs and get back alive.

"None of these boats have life preservers, Captain," Hank noted with a worried look on his face. "Maybe we ought to scare up some."

"No time," Edward told him.

"Well, *some* of us can't swim, remember?"

The Kaboom Boys 301

"We go now and do what we gotta, we won't have to," Hume said.

Once the three boats were away from the island and able to maintain somewhat of a tempo in their efforts, the rowing became surprisingly easy. They were riding on the current of the tide and the gusts of wind from the distant storm, and that gave them a boost. But then, when the time came, it was considerably more strenuous as they began to angle their boats more toward the spot where the bombs lay in wait instead of riding the outgoing flow.

Hank, doing the rowing in the yellow lead boat with Edward, was the first to have his oars strike sand.

"I found bottom," he announced. In only a minute or so more, the boat had stopped, settling onto sand. As they gathered tools and composition C-3 explosives, most of the water was gone. No more rowing for now. They would have to hike the rest of the way, a few hundred yards. The soft sand and piled-up obstacles would make it seem much farther, though.

The other two boats were about a hundred feet behind them. They, too, had settled onto the bottom of the bay. Behind them and from this angle, the island was even more striking.

In the blue boat, Pete told Morty, "Last stop on the A-train!" Both knew that stop well. Rockaway Beach, Queens, New York City's most distant strips of sand and sea still within the city limits.

"Wish I had me one of them Eye-talian ices right about now. Ralph's Famous, remember?" Morty yelled back to Pete, the first civil words he had spoken to Ronzini since the Nazi flag incident back at the château. But the deliberate mispronunciation of "Italian" rubbed Pete the wrong way. The two men still had a score to settle.

"Why don't you learn the right way to..." Pete started, but Morty was up, standing on the side of the boat, ready to step out onto the wet sand. He was pointing at something. He could see their destination, the neatly arranged row of bombs.

"There they are. Twelve beached whales like a flock of them fat Lower East Side broads on summer break coming out to Rockaway. I'd rather see them Brooklyn girls, all lookin' fine in their one-pieces..."

"Shut the fuck up, Schwartz!" Pete shouted.

Morty turned angrily, ready to punch Ronzini.

The captain, unaware of the sudden flare-up in the blue boat, was waving for them to hustle and follow him and Hank to the bombs.

"Men, use your shovel handles to test the sand in front of you at each step," Edward called out. "Don't get in a hurry. Look for air bubbles, too. If you step into quicksand, stay calm. Don't struggle. Your foot will float to the top if you stay calm and keep your weight on more solid sand. Got that?"

Edward gave the thunderstorm a worried glance. Had it moved closer, or was it just an illusion? Regardless, they were stuck and would have to wait for the returning tide to lift their boats once more. There was no way they could walk all the way back to the island from way out here. He could see bright sun glinting off the metal hulls of the bombs. He would have liked to have gotten the boats even closer, but this would have to do.

What was it one of the fishermen had said to Edward as he walked away from them? "May Archangel Michael, the Protector of all Warriors, look over you."

Okay, Mike the Angel, Hume said to himself. *Do what you do!*

And with that, Edward stepped over the side of the boat and onto soft, squishy sand. At first, he thought he was going to sink in above the tops of his boots. But the sand supported him, even loaded down with all his gear. As he had instructed the men to do, he used a shovel handle to poke the sand ahead, looking for solid footing and "boiling" air bubbles. There were seagulls everywhere, taking advantage of the buffet the receding water had left behind.

They could also see long runs of rusty barbed wire and wooden poles sticking up at odd angles. And naval mines. Round, spiky mines, tethered by chains to the bottom and designed to float to just below the surface at high tide.

"Glad we don't have to screw around with those ugly things," Hank said.

"Hush, Hank," the captain responded. "That mayor might demand that de Gaulle makes us fix those, too. They'll be clearing this place for the next hundred years. But not us, and not today. Ocean mines are attracted magnetically to ships, so I doubt we are magnetic enough to arm and detonate one of those old things. Unless you're carrying a few tons of iron in your pockets."

The going was still maddeningly slow. For Edward, it was like wading through snow back in Pennsylvania while helping deliver kegs of beer for Pops. He could hear the squad complaining—mostly good-naturedly—behind him. But they were keeping up.

The men in the blue boat had not exchanged blows, though it was close. The captain's call had likely prevented a fistfight between the two New Yorkers. But then, Pete pulled out a couple of tools from his bag and something heavy dropped out, tumbling into the sand.

The Nazi flag. The damn Nazi flag from the noblewoman's château.

"I told you to get rid of that damn flag," Morty erupted. And then, even louder, he screamed at Pete, "What the hell is that thing doing here?"

"I didn't know it was in there—"

"It's bad luck!" shouted Morty, then smacked Pete hard on the back of the neck.

Edward heard the shouts and looked back to see Schwartz hit Ronzini. "Not here, guys!" he called out. Jesus! He thought those two had worked out their simmering issues. Clearly not. And now was not the time or place for them to boil over.

The two privates now stood next to their boat on the sand flats, glaring at each other.

"You know damn well that flag is nothing but bad luck, and you brought it out here? When we need all the good luck we can get!" Morty told Pete.

Ronzini stood there, frowning. Then he yelled, "Okay! Okay! I'll burn it!"

No way to know if he meant what he promised. "I'll take your word for it, then. But listen, if anything bad happens out here, it's on you and that damned flag."

Morty turned and trudged ahead, toward where Edward and the rest of the men were standing, watching the confrontation between the two. Meanwhile, Pete pulled the flag out of the sand and draped it across a run of barbed wire that had been attached by the Germans to timbers. For a moment, the brisk wind caught it, lifted it, unfurled it. It momentarily waved in the breeze but then suddenly ripped and was torn from the wire and dropped unceremoniously into a deeper pool of water.

Morty looked back and smiled. Though he had not burned it, Pete had made good on his promise to destroy the cursed Nazi flag.

"Shit!" It was Gene. He had stepped into a pocket of quicksand and was struggling to get out.

Carl moved quickly to Gene's side. Main thing was to keep his buddy calm as he gently pulled on his leg, slowly maneuvering and then extracting Gene out of the sucking hole. After a few minutes of distress, Wozinski was free. He fell to the ground, trying to find his breath.

"This shit gets a hold on a fellow! It felt like my leg was being ripped from my hip," he said, laughing shakily. "Jeez! Carl, I owe you. I'll give you a big kiss when this is all over."

Carl had no comeback but smiled ever so slightly. He offered Gene a hand to help him up. They had to keep moving forward. There was no time to waste.

Now, as they slowly, awkwardly, made their way across the flats to the bombs, Edward Hume came to a realization. All his earthly concerns this day up until this moment—politics, pecking order, rowing, tides, quicksand, distant storm, a squabble between two of his men, and even possible death—were nothing compared to the problems they were slowly approaching. Twelve armed bombs. Devices that could quickly send him and his men to where Ace Taft, Fritz Schneider, and Tommy already were.

Firing pins. Locking balls. Primers. Detonators. And the entire job depended on the condition of the fuzes near the noses of the devices. Edward's mind would have to be clear, focused. What position was each of them in? Could the men even get to them with picks and shovels? Were they still working properly? Reduction gears in the vane assemblies functioning? What was the status of the vane nuts? Were they still secured by safety cotter pins? Or were they now unthreaded from each respective plunger? After eighteen to twenty-one vane revolutions, had the whizzing earthbound projectiles been able to arm the stems? Or had the bombers been flying too low to allow time for them to arm? Could they possibly be lucky enough this day to be working with unarmed UXBs?

Only until he had answers to those questions would he know for certain what they could do.

It was still a zigzag course from the boats to the bombs, dodging deeper pockets of standing water and rivulets—the pools filled with trapped, flopping fish—and bogs of bubbling quicksand. But they were getting there. Only another fifty feet, if one of the damn things did not decide to detonate.

Then, they were there, mere steps from the first UXB. Edward and Hank stopped, considering the weapons and the task ahead, as the other four men slogged up to stand next to them. Each device was six feet long and just over two feet in diameter at the middle. Luckily, the detonators were easily visible on nine of them. Two more would require a bit of digging. And the last one rested atop one of Field Marshal Rommel's "asparagus" poles. It would require considerable effort.

"Didn't lie. Five-hundred-pounders," the captain said. "And I do, indeed, count a dozen of the bastards. I'll take this one. And thank you, Army Air Forces."

"Captain, I see bubbles and a big patch of quicksand between two and three," Pete added.

"Good eye, Pete. Now, I need everyone to come closer for lesson one on setting charges. We'll go step-by-step."

A welcome gust of wind off the storm offered a cool respite from the blistering afternoon sun, but it also blew drying sand and an assortment of flying bugs into their faces. Still, it was welcome relief until they noticed an especially dark cumulonimbus cloud had now billowed up and was smudging a much broader expanse of sky. No one said anything about the threatening weather. They had been conditioned to work in all elements.

"Men, we can do this. Each bomb will take less than ten minutes," Edward told them, almost shouting to be heard above the gathering wind. His face was steely with determination.

Hank worried that Edward's time calculations would work only if everyone doing the job was a BD expert. Since APG and RAF protocols only allowed the squad captain to do the actual task of disarming a bomb, none of the other boys had gotten any practical hands-on BD experience. And while Hank had done the deed on quite a few devices back in England and taken photos of even more, he still had minimal dealings with anything as hefty and complicated as these.

"Sir? Are we for sure doing this here and now?" Hank asked.

Deep in thought, Edward did not answer. He was learning what they were up against, figuring he was about to toss protocols out the window. Once again violating all the rules. Each man would soon be put in the position of being responsible for setting charges on two very large bombs. He was coming to terms with the fact that as captain, he simply could not handle all twelve bombs before a rising tide would consume everyone and everything.

It was getting hotter. The wind and drifting clouds helped a little, but they could feel the sun dehydrating their bodies and blistering exposed skin. Rain might even be welcomed. Just enough to cool them off as they worked but not enough to affect the lighting and burning of fuses.

"We can do this, men!" Edward shouted optimistically as he stood over the first bomb. "Now that we got out here, it'll be a cinch."

Gene peeked at his stopwatch. "Sir, it's been fifteen minutes since we left the boats."

The detonator on the first UXB was visible where it rested. Edward ran his hand along the rough metal exterior of the bomb's casing and then inspected the fuze at the nose. Finally, he got down on his knees and placed his stethoscope to the steel shell.

Even with the calls of the gulls and the distant rumble of thunder, he could clearly hear an ominous, relentless sound.

"Delayed action. Every one of these should be armed and counting down just like this one is. Check for the sound first on each device." Edward quickly moved to listen to his own second bomb.

It was armed and counting, too.

The men moved in closer and mimicked what they had seen their captain do. Each one moved to his assigned bombs. They had no stethoscopes, so they had to put their ears to the bombs. To a man, they raised their hands and offered a thumbs-up over each device.

Every bomb was in detonation mode. Every bomb was armed and could —and likely would—blow up sometime soon.

"Captain, question?" It was Hank again.

"Go ahead, Corporal, but make it snappy."

"If they're all armed and ticking, and if they're going to blow up soon on

The Kaboom Boys   307

their own, and since they're way out here in the bay away from everything and everybody…"

"You're asking why we even need to take the risk to stay here and detonate them?" Edward interrupted.

"Yessir." Several of the other squad members nodded as they gathered back around their captain.

"So, let me beat this dead horse some more for you guys. First, we don't know one hundred percent that they will blow on their own," the captain said, talking quickly. "That would mean we would have to come back out here and work on devices that would by then be even more unstable. They will have dug themselves more deeply into the sand with each incoming and outgoing tide. More risk, more time lost when we could be doing other crucial jobs. But primarily, our orders say we are to render safe or destroy all twelve devices as quickly and efficiently as possible and bring an end to this situation, whether we agree or not. They'd rather we blow 'em up. Tonight. Those are our orders. We will obey them. Got that?"

"Got it…sir," Hank answered.

That settled it. They would deal with all twelve bombs. And they would do it right now, before the tide began rushing back toward the Mont.

"Okay, so let's stop socializing and go make everybody happy," the captain called out. "Let's go blow these sons of bitches to hell!"

Edward waved the men forward.

26

As he was taking C-3 explosives from his bag, Edward was distracted by a sudden near-darkness, like a total eclipse of the sun. It was that same menacing cloud, but much larger now. It was an "angel cloud." What the French called *le nuage d'ange*. And it did seem to take the form of an angel, but a very dark and threatening one. This particular "angel" also appeared to be looking over Edward's shoulder with a disapproving air.

"All right! Quick consult!" Edward shouted to his squad, all shirtless and sweating from the heat and hard rowing and getting ready. Each man carried a long stick he had found in the bottom of his boat.

They were aware their lives were on the line, and what he was about to tell them offered marginally better odds for survival. Heavy rain had blown across the sand flats toward the Mont and had begun to bombard the crowds that had gathered up and down the island to watch the demolition job from a distance. But the thunder seemed willing to hold off long enough for Edward to give final instructions to his squad.

"First chore is evacuate. We're a mile away from the island, so we're good there. Then we evaluate and decide: defuze or detonate? We now know they're armed, ticking, and unstable, so we'll detonate." Edward spoke sternly, decisively, with no hesitation. He was in his element, the part of the job he knew well. "We may not be doing exactly what Hap Arnold and Charles de Gaulle and that mayor wants, but it's our best bet." Edward urged his men closer, gathering over the belly of the first bomb. "Your BD 101 Fuze Detonator class is about to begin."

"Got it!" several of the men shouted, ready to go.

"Don't think about the weather. Or the tide. That's nothing we can control. We work in any conditions. Thankfully, this is chemical-based, delayed action, and there's no anti-handling device to keep us from doing what we need to do. However, the delayed-action switch was flipped by the pilots, set to detonate a hundred and forty-four hours later. But our real pressure is the tide. Dead low tide came at 1430 hours when our row boats hit bottom. The next high tide comes at 1900. It's a fifty-foot tidal range. Once water covers the devices, we are out of time. It'll come in fast and catch us still out here at the bombs if we're not careful. Gene, you also have the job of keeping an eye on the time."

"It's been twenty-seven minutes, sir."

Now friendlier since the Nazi flag had been discarded, Morty leaned into Pete and whispered, "Yeah, like them galloping horses they keep yapping about!"

"Used to bet on the ponies at Aqueduct...lied about my age," Pete said. He, too, felt better that they were back on speaking terms.

Edward ignored the chatter and went on. "We have one other time constraint. That storm. If it steers clear, we're fine. And we'll be okay if it only hits us with a little bit of rain. We can work in the rain. But if it's like what we're seeing back at the Mont, it's torrential. Fuse lines can get a little wet and work fine. But not if they're soaked. We have to work fast."

"No pressure at all, sir," Carl shouted. The men laughed nervously.

"The M-112's fuze includes a firing pin, locking balls, primer, and detonator," Edward started, then had a second thought and stopped. He could see the confused faces on some of his men. Too many new terms, like learning a foreign language. Doc Fenton had once stopped Edward in the middle of over-explaining something by saying, "I ask what time it is, don't tell me how to build the clock, Eddie."

Edward decided he had best change tactics. "You guys don't really need to know all those finer details, but you do need to know this." He pointed to the nose of the bomb as he gingerly unscrewed the cover plate. "First thing you do, find the detonator and take the cover plate off. Here, at the pointy end. Now watch me set the C-3 on this one." Edward began pressing the yellow C-3 putty all around the detonator as the men watched. "You'll do your two the same exact way. Remember, don't touch the C-3 with your bare hands. Use your gloves. It's highly irritating to skin. If you do get some on you, scrub it off quick as you can with sand and then rinse it away with seawater from one of those pools out there. Then get the hell back to work. Got that?"

Nods all around as the men leaned in even closer, watching the captain as he applied more putty to the detonator, talking the men point-by-point through what he was doing.

"Any questions?" There were none. Seemed simple enough, but they knew, in the volatile world of BD, things rarely were.

Hank looked at the storm cloud. It also caught Edward's attention. The angel and her wings now covered the western and northwestern sky and carried an even blacker frown.

Edward suddenly felt an overwhelming craving for help. Help like the day at the quarry, at the mine disaster, times when the job was crushingly daunting, people's lives at stake. A need for help from somebody or some thing, but, just as it was then, he had no idea who or what or from where that assistance might come. Meanwhile, it was all on him.

Then, he realized he had better heed his own words. Concentrate on what he could control. Don't allow the stuff he couldn't control to distract him. That included the black cloud hovering over them.

"Okay, each of you. Look. Get in here close and see how much I shoved into the compartment. An ample amount of C-3 has to touch the detonator or we risk it not triggering. Do it like this," Edward instructed, holding up an unused packet of the yellow, claylike substance, then placing it directly on the nose of the bomb. "Some armies are now using C-4 'cause it stays flexible at low temperatures and doesn't get tacky in hot weather. But we still use C-3 'cause our RAF brothers do. It's gonna be sticky in this heat, but it's damn sure better than C-2. Remember, don't get it on bare skin. Make sure this—see it here—the blasting cap gets fully covered, and the plastique is built up snug all around the detonator." Next, Edward pulled out of his bag a coiled spool of fuse line, holding the end in his left hand and the

The Kaboom Boys   311

spool in his right. He extended his arms as far out from his sides as he could, approximating six feet. "Unspool and do this twice—like this—then cut it. That'll give you about twelve feet. Next, drape it across the length of the bomb. Use bits of clay to hold it in place." He showed how to use the clay as adhesive to stick the fuse line to the bomb's slick metal surface. "Twelve feet should be a long enough line to give us ample time to get far enough away from these bastards to be okay. Account for the fact that we can't run in this mud, that we'll be mucking our way through quick-sand, barbed wire, Rommel's asparagus, dead fish, and all kinds of shit. Twelve feet should give us enough time, and just hope it doesn't start pouring rain."

"I'm gonna do mine for eighteen feet," whispered Pete to Morty.

"Just hope none of these dumbasses makes his too short by mistake," Morty whispered back. "Only takes one of these things blowing up too soon to maybe set off all of 'em before we get out of range."

Edward was now inserting the fuse line and blasting cap into the explosive compound. "You've all seen this plenty of times, but watch anyway. This is crucial. Attach the tip of the line to the blasting cap and wrap it up in the C-3, inserting it plenty deep. Just be sure the fuse line doesn't get detached from the cap. Then drape the line high up onto the top of the bomb casing so it has less chance of getting wet. If any part of it gets wet, throw it away, blasting cap 'n' all, and start over." Edward strung the line like it was Christmas tree lights. A sudden gust of wind almost shoved him off-balance. "And, just like that, we don't want the wind to blow it loose. That's what this modeling clay is for. Like I said, use bits of it to hold the line in place. As long as the heavy rain holds off, we won't have to abort the mission. Okay, I'll come around and check your work. Got that?"

Though nervous, the men were obviously enthusiastic and ready to take on their first bomb. "Ready to go, boss!" Morty sang out as he headed to his first device.

"Whoa! Wait, wait, wait," Edward said, standing up, ignoring a few big raindrops on his face. He had forgotten one of the most important points. They would need to coordinate lighting the fuses and scrambling away. "When we're all finished and the charges are set, wait for my signal. Then we all strike matches in unison, light 'em up, and get the hell outta here.

Just like you did with the cherry bombs or globe salutes or whatever kind of fireworks you used on Fourth of July when you were a kid." The men were now eager, excited, finally doing something positive. Not just digging a ditch or listening to some self-important politician blowing off steam or enduring a surly-ass fisherman sticking his tongue out at them. "Look, use those sticks to feel for quicksand. And while we're at it, we might not be able to make it back to the boats before the bombs blow, so at first boom, go facedown in the sand. Make sure your hard hats cover your head. Probably a good idea to put your shirts back on before we light up, too. There'll be shit flying every which way, and some of it could do some damage. The shirt might help protect you. You got that?"

"Yessir!"

"Okay, bomb one is now set," shouted Edward as he finished up. "I'm gonna do my second device, then I'll come help anyone who needs it. Go!"

They split up, and each man trudged over to his first bomb, quickly opening it up, applying C-3 to detonators, and attaching fuse line as Captain instructed. Simple as it was, it was still slow work, especially making the explosive compound stick to the wet bomb hull and detonator —they used a glove to wipe a dry spot on the metal—and being certain the fuse wire and cap were inserted deeply enough and the line tacked to the bomb's hull.

No matter how brave they were, this was nerve-racking as hell.

Again, Edward eyed the storm cloud, dark, thick, and billowing skyward thousands of feet. Taller than the gold Saint Michael statue. Inspiration came to him. Maybe he could get that help he needed. He began to speak to the angel cloud in a quiet voice, as if it were Ace Taft, keeping watch over Edward and his former squad members. Maybe his sergeant had helped already, prompting him to escape from Mayor Duval. Inspiring Hank to come up with the idea of commandeering the rowboats. Developing the plan for all six of them to work on the bombs. Getting them out there to the UXBs without incident. Keeping the rain and lightning away from them. So far.

"Don't jinx yourself, Hume," the captain muttered, looking up at the roiling cloud. "But if it's you, Ace, thanks."

But as he talked to Ace and worked on his second bomb, Edward heard

The Kaboom Boys

a shout from Gene, who was working on the next set of bombs adjacent to the captain's. The corporal had again gotten himself caught in a patch of quicksand. Edward stood and started toward him, but Morty and Pete were already there.

"Sir! Let us handle it." It was Pete. "We're short on time."

He was right, of course. Edward waved his stick and shouted to Gene, "Don't fight it, Gene. Use your stick!"

"Shit! We're short on time!" Gene yelled. "It's been an hour now."

With a little help from Morty and his shovel handle and some serious tugging from Pete, Gene was able to get free, though his leg had been thigh-deep in the muck by that time.

"See, even this nasty bay bottom didn't want a taste of you, Woz. It got a nibble and spit you right back out," Morty proclaimed.

Edward began to speak to Ace Taft again. And to the angel cloud, grasping for any bit of karma he could find.

"We need your help about now, Ace. Whatever you got. Keep that rain and wind off us just a little while longer if you can, Sergeant."

There was a not-so-far-off clap of thunder. An answer?

Hank looked up. Was the captain talking to himself again?

Back toward the island, heavy rain was falling. They could hardly see the village and abbey. And a brilliant bolt of lightning struck the Saint Michael statue. Happened all the time, they had been told. But the BD boys tried not to see it as an omen.

A much closer, much louder thunder boom sent them all diving into the mud face-first, hands gripping helmets tightly onto their heads. Then they sheepishly stood back up once they realized that it was not one of the bombs deciding to explode.

Edward stood there for a moment, heart still racing, looking up. "I know you're pissed off, Ace. So am I. I wish you were here to help us. Maybe you are. But you're about to see what these boys are made of." And boys they were. Not a one over twenty-three.

"Who's the captain talking to?" Gene asked no one in particular as he moved to his second bomb, limping a bit.

"Maybe he's praying to that angel," Hank replied.

"What angel?" Gene asked.

"The one in that cloud. They call it an angel cloud here in France."

"We call it a goose-drowner in Chicago," Gene responded.

When Gene got to his second bomb, he saw at once he had serious problems. It had landed precariously amid a considerable number of German obstacles, timbers and barbed wire, and was propped up against an "asparagus" pole. Some of the junk was in the way of the device's nose and detonator.

"Captain! I need help!"

Edward had just finished up and was double-checking his second bomb. On his way over to help Gene, he glanced at Hank's work. "Good going!" And it was. He expected no less.

Then, at Wozinski's bomb, Edward immediately spotted the issue. To get into position, Gene had tried to squeeze in between some timbers and rusty barbed wire hung thick with seaweed. It was going to be difficult to reach the area where the C-3 needed to be applied. Even tougher for Gene since he was nursing a sore leg after his two encounters with quicksand. He was now using his hands to scoop trapped sand away from the nose of the bomb. Edward found a position in the muck next to him.

"Lucky you, Woz! You drew one of the problem ones. I guess all that wire and shit shifted the bomb and snagged even more junk when the tide came and went."

Once they had clear access to the nose, Edward helped Gene apply several extra layers of C-3. "Okay now, run the line up and over. It should work. I'll go check on Carl."

Edward trudged a few minutes north to the next bomb, one of the ones that belonged to Carl Kostas. It, however, was the one they already knew would be the biggest challenge. The one that was resting at an awkward angle, tail stuck straight up in the air, supported by debris, its snout plunged deeply into sand.

"Shit! Where's the damn detonator?" Edward asked.

"I've been digging since I got my first one done, and it's slow going," Carl told him. "The sand just shifts right back into the hole as I dig." There was no room for shovels. They would have to move all that silt by hand.

Edward fell to his knees and started to dig with both hands beneath where the front tip of the bomb would be. Carl kept on scooping, too,

The Kaboom Boys   315

working with every muscle to get the nose of the device cleared so they could apply the explosive clay. They tried to shove the sand far enough away so it would not fall right back into their excavation. The stuff seemed to have a mind of its own, though, determined to keep its hold on the intruder it had greedily claimed when it fell from the sky. Bits of debris sliced into their hands as they worked, but they ignored the pain and blood.

"Men, if you've finished both your bombs, get over here now!" Edward called out. "We need help!" All four of them rushed over and went face-down in the sand, pulling heavy, wet sea bottom away from the bomb.

Even so, that process ate up at least ten valuable minutes before Carl, now practically standing on his head, called out, "There it is!"

"I see it. I see it. Another foot and we'll have good access," Edward confirmed. "Let's just hope this fat son of a bitch doesn't tumble over on top of us before we get it ready."

"You think we can make it work, Captain?"

"We have to. Everything works. No option but success. It just needs to be finessed. We'll lay it on thick, put some extra stuff in here." Edward felt around with one arm underneath him as the squad held their breath and watched. From there, he faced Mont-Saint-Michel. The island was still being doused by heavy rain. "Just pray that storm stays way the hell over there or all this is for nothing."

"But it'll still explode on its own, right? It'll be just as gone either way," Carl reasoned.

"Maybe. Maybe not. We can't be sure. Our job is to kill it now. So, that's what we do."

Hank stood over them then, asking if he could help. "My two are ready to light off," Hank said.

"As a matter of fact, Hank, give me all the C-3 you got left. We need some more down in here to be sure we get the detonator," Edward told him, grunting, grimacing as he worked at such a difficult, awkward angle.

Carl took the explosive from Hank and handed it down to Edward. "Here you go, sir. Sorry I can't be more help."

"We would've never gotten this thing dug out without your help." Edward placed the C-3 all over and around the part of the detonator they had revealed, applying several layers. "And it had to be dug out. There's no other way to assure we detonate one of these things, other than waiting for it to blow up itself, which is, as I have tried to explain, not an option. Carl, give me your blasting cap and fuse line." Carl already had the wire in his hand and passed it carefully down to the captain.

Soon, Hume was out of the hole they had dug and catching his breath, sitting there on the sandy bottom of Mont-Saint-Michel Bay, relishing the breeze. Then he shook his head, stood, and made his way over to where Morty and Pete were still working on their bombs. As he walked, he noticed that there was now an inch of water underfoot. Like a leak in the basement. It was ankle-deep in low spots and noticeably rising.

The tide was coming back in.

"Fuses gotta stay dry!" Morty yelled to Pete, who seemed to be having a tough time with the second of his two devices. One of his fuse lines was dangling from the spine of the bomb and onto newly wet sand. "That one's wet. You'll have to redo it."

Pete took a look, then cursed before quickly digging into his bag and measuring out a new line. Morty helped him string it along the length of the bomb.

Just then, a blinding streak of lightning unzipped the sky directly above them. Thunder was immediate and bone-shaking.

"Holy shit!" Gene shouted as he hit the ground with a splash, right in the middle of a tidal pool. Edward and the rest of the men stopped, closed their eyes, but then realized it was only lightning and thunder and not one of the dozen bombs that had made the flash and boom.

"Captain, can lightning set this stuff off?" Pete asked.

"Sure as shit, if it struck something that could cause a spark or activate the cap," he answered bluntly. "But we're the highest objects out here on the flats, so it's more likely to strike one of us."

The men looked at each other. The thought made them work more quickly. But they also tended to stoop over, making themselves at least a little bit shorter and less of a target for lightning.

Just ahead of schedule, Morty signaled that he had completed the fuse on his second bomb. All twelve were now packed and wired, ready to detonate.

As if to mock them, the wind picked up dramatically, whipping up bits

The Kaboom Boys 317

of muck and debris and salt spray, stinging the men's faces and causing noticeable whitecaps on the distant deeper water. All they could think about was if the fuse lines would remain dry.

Edward had already given a quick check of each man's work. All appeared acceptable. He then checked his own fuse lines one more time. It would be embarrassing if everyone else's devices exploded and he was the dunce whose work was the dud that caused them to have to come back out there.

Then, with a dramatic flourish, he pulled out a box of matches from his supply bag, raised them into the wind, and shouted, "Okay, boys! Light 'em up and run like hell! Fire in the hole!"

It was not lost on Edward Hume that "Fire in the hole!" was an old coal-mining expression, indicating a fuse tied to dynamite was about to be lit.

"Fire in the hole!" the men each shouted as their fuse lines caught and sparked and began burning toward the waiting C-3. Amazingly, all of them were flickering. "Fire in the hole!"

And then, to a man, they did as they had been commanded. They ran like hell back toward their red, yellow, and blue rowboats.

27

The Kaboom Boys were unaware of the audience they had. Mons—including the mayor—along with fishermen, Free French officials, and a huge crowd of visitors from nearby villages had assembled along the island's east side, watching the frenzied event taking place a mile away in the bay. Most had sought shelter from the rainstorm in porticos and beneath overhangs while others looked out windows of shops, cafés, and apartments. Still more stood mostly unprotected, lined up from the abbey courtyard down to the ramparts, causeway, and beach.

They watched the six men scattering, escaping from the lineup of bombs. Six men, shrouded in the deluge, canopied by the black angel cloud that swirled above them while occasionally anointing the scene with forked lightning. Whatever sent the Americans scrambling at full gallop back toward their grounded boats also appeared to overrule any caution about sucking quicksand or half-buried obstacles.

"They have lit the fuses on the detonation charges," Sébastien Chantrelle explained, offering a play-by-play just loud enough for the mayor to hear. "The fuse lines cannot be allowed to get wet or they will not spark. They have very little time before they explode. The men must run or die."

"My God," was the only thing the politician had to say. Was the mayor

The Kaboom Boys   319

now remorseful that he failed to convince the men to wait for another tidal cycle?

Likely not, Chantrelle decided.

The few villagers who had binoculars could see in the stormy darkness that the fuse lines were spitting and sparking, defying the humidity. Seagulls that had been perched on the bombs scattered. The men were running, splashing through shin-deep tidewater as they approached the rowboats, which were already rising, rocking, ready to float back toward the island on the building tide.

A hundred feet from the boats, Edward ventured a quick look back at the UXBs. He could see sparks from one of the fuses a few inches from the C-3 wad.

"On your bellies!" he screamed. The blustering wind stole his warning, so he yelled even louder. As loud as he had once called out for Tommy in the hell of the collapsed, smoking coal mine. "Facedown! Facedown! Cover your heads! They're gonna—"

KABOOM! KABOOM! KABOOM!

Those three blasts were infinitely louder than the thunder that simultaneously ruptured the sky above them. Each man landed face-first in the water and sand, hands clamped to helmets, trying to hold them in place and to root deeper into the mud and eddying tidewater that was refilling shallows just as it had twice a day for millions of years. The squad members were pelted by jagged bomb fragments, rubble, seashells, shattered rock, sand, muck, and dead and dying fish.

Then again and again, eight more times, as they tried to find protection from more far-flung debris.

Each boom bounced the men an inch or two off the bay bottom. Every combustion compacted the air and momentarily silenced all other sounds. Birds all around the bay scattered, uncertain which way to go.

Adeline, the waitress, was serving an omelet in the café when she glanced out a window, trying to catch a glimpse of the action that had the attention of the whole village. There was a sudden vibration, like an earthquake, and the window slammed shut and shattered from the impact of the blasts a mile away. Air whooshed throughout the streets and alleyways of Mont-Saint-Michel, animating banners and quickening pulses. Adeline screamed as everyone inside the restaurant scrambled for cover.

It was all happening in a blur. That made it difficult to count the number of blasts, but when a half minute passed with no detonation, the squad began getting up. They were unsteady. They wiped stinging salt water and sand from their eyes, inspecting bleeding cuts and gashes on their hands and arms, faces and necks, pulling fragments of debris the explosions had angrily showered upon them from the skin of their backs and butts.

"Everybody okay?" Edward shouted.

"Nothing fatal," Gene called out, helping some of the others.

"Feel like I been shot at and missed but shit at and hit," Carl answered. The others reported themselves battered and bleeding but otherwise all right, still breathing and no missing parts.

"This helmet saved my life," crowed Morty as he cradled the damaged hat. "Gawd! Look at this damn dent."

"I can't hear for shit!" moaned Pete. He wriggled fingers in each ear, trying to clear the ringing.

"Then let's get our asses in the boats before they float off all the way to the sheep pastures," Edward yelled, grinning, relieved his men were okay. Strangely, he now felt as alive as he had ever been. But he needed to keep everyone that way. "We don't wanna have to swim."

"But Captain, you can't swim," Gene reminded him. "Remember?"

"Seems I recall something along those lines..."

On the ramparts, some fishermen quietly exchanged cash, gamblers with more skin in the game than just fish. Losers grudgingly paying winners. The curse had been removed, the Americans had accomplished their mission and were alive.

"Captain, better take a look." Hank was pointing through the raindrops to the spot where the bombs had been lined up so neatly.

"Jesus Christ, we can't catch a break, can we?" Edward shouted. He hoped he had miscounted during the series of blasts, but he could now see that was not the case. There had been only eleven explosions. One bomb, the one that had been the most difficult to work on, was still there, its tail in the air like a middle finger raised in defiance. And to make matters worse,

The Kaboom Boys   321

the detonator was now under several feet of seawater. Then, in yet another insult, the bottom dropped out of the sky just then, unleashing a drowning downpour on the men. Edward looked up. "Hell, Ace, whose side you on, anyway?"

Hank gave his captain a long, sorrowful look. The man had lost it for certain. So it was the late Sergeant Alistair "Ace" Taft he had been talking to off and on for the past hour.

"Captain, that one'll blow on its own eventually," Hank reminded him. "Don't worry. We can still get out ahead of this tide if we go. Now!" The other men stood nearby, listening, wondering what their commanding officer was about to do. Or ask them to do. Hank blinked hard and pressed on. "Sir, let's get outta here! It'll blow!"

"Point taken, Corporal, but the job's not done yet," Edward replied. He frowned as he looked back at the stubborn bomb. It still leaned nose-down against the accumulation of poles and barbed wire, seemingly unmovable, its detonator compartment now unreachable beneath the water.

As Edward stood there, rain in his face, he saw something very odd. A swirl of mist and debris from an approaching gust of mighty wind. The men turned their backs and braced themselves, but Edward could not turn away. He watched as the squall struck the problem UXB broadside. Then, as if by miracle, the bomb slowly inverted within its nest of debris, as if turned over by a huge hand.

"Jesus!" Edward shouted. That caused the others to turn and see what he was seeing. And to all immediately dive into the sand and water again, certain the movement would cause it to detonate.

But no. The thing had slowly shifted when shoved by the gust of wind. Instead of hitting hard, it flipped backward on its axis, settling almost gently back down atop the rolls of barbed wire and nest of "asparagus" poles. The bomb's tail fins were now in the water and its nose poked upward, the tip with the detonator beautifully accessible.

Luck is what happens when preparation meets opportunity, Edward thought. *And thank you again, Seneca.* And Mrs. Crocker, his high school history teacher, who often mixed in a bit of philosophy.

He looked back at his men, all sprawled in the shin-deep water. "You guys can get off your asses and back to the boats before it decides to go off after all."

"Okay, but you're coming, too?" Hank asked. "Right?"

"Job's not done," Edward shouted, already trudging back toward the bomb. "Hank, soon as our boat clears bottom, row closer but stay back a hundred yards. I'll re-rig the charge. But if I wave you off, ride the tide and row like hell back toward the island. That's an order, Corporal." Over his shoulder, he added, "The rest of you, get to your boats and ride the tide back to the island. That's an order, too!"

The men were shocked by what they were witnessing. Was this a repeat suicide mission like the one with Ace at the overflowing munitions pile?

Edward stopped, turned, and yelled, "The bastard bomb just survived eleven blasts close by. With all that C-3 still attached to it, it's more dangerous than ever. No need to put you boys at risk. The captain always does the defuzing, anyway. Got that?"

"Sir, you don't have time," Hank said. "The tide. It's going to rise at a rate of—you're gonna die!"

"Go! That's an order! Obey it, goddammit!"

The thunder, lightning, wind, and rain had only grown worse. As Edward lifted his gear bag to his shoulder, he checked to be sure he had enough fuse line, caps, and C-3. Wading through the thigh-deep water, he again beseeched the skies for help.

"C'mon, Ace. You know I can't swim. Gimme a break here if you have any pull up there at all."

Maybe there was no connection to Ace or the heavens, but the moment Edward reached the bomb, an eerie tranquility fell over the scene, the rain shut off as if a faucet had been cranked closed. A lull in the storm like the calm eye of a hurricane. Edward wiped the sand and water off his watch.

"Captain, we got less than half an hour before the bomb'll be underwater," Hank yelled from two hundred feet away. He was just audible.

And, Edward knew, at that point he would no longer be able to touch bottom.

His orders were explicit, not open to debate. Edward looked up at a surprisingly brighter sky. A rainbow arced over the peninsula.

A few lingering raindrops moistened his dry lips and washed away some of the sand and muck from his cheeks and eyes. Seagulls, excited by the return of the tide, played and squawked. Or maybe they were warning him this was a fool's errand, all to appease his superiors, the mayor, the irate fishermen, de Gaulle, and the Free French government. They all should be happy that thousands of Americans had died already in the effort to liberate their country.

"Nobody else can do this," he shouted at the birds as he kneeled next to the bomb. They did not seem impressed by his logic or his determination.

Sure enough, the fuse line he and Carl had set had fizzled out and stopped a yard from the charge. He snipped the line and dropped it into the water to prevent any chance of an errant spark reigniting it. Edward pulled from his satchel two bars of C-3—more than enough for this job, especially since a hefty charge was already in place from their earlier work—and he slathered the yellow clay inside the detonator box. Unreeling a long fuse line and without measuring it, he snipped off what he thought felt about right, inserted one end into the blasting cap, and pushed it into the explosive compound.

Edward decided he would have to use another law of BD: improvisation. Instead of draping it down the side of the bomb, he encircled the nose like a coil, using pinches of putty to hold the fuse line in place. He calculated that would give him six to eight minutes before it blew. Hopefully before the tide or more rain quenched the spitting spark.

The rain had held off so far, but the wind across the flats was still fierce. He pulled out one of the few remaining matches from the plastic container specifically designed to keep them dry. But had it done so?

Cupping his hand to shield the flame from the wind, he rubbed the head of the match across the sandpaper attached to the bottom of the container. It failed to strike. On the second swipe, the head broke off and dropped into the waist-deep water.

"For Chrissake!" He pulled out another match and tried again. Nothing. Then another. They all appeared to be okay—still dry—but they would not strike. The striking surface must be damp. There were only two matches left, and the clock was ticking.

"Why don't I have my windproof Zippo?" he asked, but nobody answered.

Pops. When Pops lit up a cigarette or one of his cheap, smelly cigars, he never struck a match on the box. He used a thumbnail and, with a flick, set it brightly ablaze. Every time. Same when he lit the furnace at home with a kitchen match. Flick! Fire every time. The trick had always fascinated young Eddie.

Edward replicated the method, and the match flared brilliantly the first time. He quickly placed it to the end of the line. It caught immediately, scattering about a beautiful eruption of bright sparks.

"Thanks, Ace, if you had anything to do with that...and Pops, I owe you one," he said with a grin. "Line set. Time to go."

Then, satisfied it was all working, he spun around and started to run, muttering, "Fire in the hole!" But his running was more a plod through chest-high water.

Looking back toward the island, he could see the red and blue boats bobbing in the distance, his men looking back at him. Hank, his back to Edward and facing Mont-Saint-Michel, was fighting the tide with every ounce of his being, rowing the small yellow boat, trying to stay close enough to rescue his captain.

Edward tried to make his way toward the boat, the tide thrusting him forward toward the iconic rock, then the waves pushing him back again. The water was now almost up to his neck. No longer worried about quicksand or wires or mines or any of the other junk in the bay, he concentrated only on reaching the boat before he would have to try to swim. And on the lit fuse inching toward the charge behind him.

He stepped into an unexpectedly deep depression on the sandy bottom and slipped under before he could catch a breath. After a few seconds, he resurfaced, desperately flailing, sputtering, gasping, clawing to escape the hole and find air.

On tiptoe, his face was just out of the water.

It was one of those nightmares. The ones in which he was trying to run but not getting anywhere. Running in mud or quicksand or swamp water or molasses. Being smothered by foliage, smoke, or deep water.

Frustration. That was Doc Fenton's diagnosis when Edward mentioned the disturbing dreams to his boss. It was the way a sleeping brain countered vexing frustrations that Edward probably did not even know he harbored.

Running on fumes and desperation, Edward knew his last bit of energy reserves were his only hope for survival. He tried to recall how long the fuse line was, how much time it would take for it to reach the new blasting cap and C-3. How much time had passed. But he had no idea. He had uncoiled more than the usual length of line but had not taken the time to measure or even estimate.

That rapscallion bomb could go off any second.

Hank was rowing as best he could, fighting the current, his boat's keel and his oars bumping sand and junk on the bottom and then floating high to where he had little control. He just had to rescue his captain. Maddeningly, he was making no progress against the swift waters of the tide and the continually blustering wind.

The men in the other two boats were three hundred yards farther away and having their own issues with the wind and racing tide. They were waving, shouting, begging for Hank to row harder, for him to hurry, for the captain to not give up. They could just make out the sparks, relentlessly spitting and almost to the detonator. And only occasionally see their captain's helmet pop up.

Instinctively, they crouched down to avoid the flying debris. The bomb was about to blow.

Still recovering from the tumble into the tidal pool, the captain looked back over his shoulder at that lone, stubborn, deadly bomb, still giving him what Pete Ronzini had dubbed "the Bronx salute." Had water gotten to the fuse by now?

The swift tide was just beneath Edward's chin most of the time now. Remarkably, he could still see that the lengthy, serpentine cord still spat, crackled, and sizzled like the longest Fourth of July firecracker fuse he had ever seen. The sparks were inches from the double mound of C-3, but he was more occupied trying to grab water and swim.

The flickering flame did precisely what it was designed to do. It ignited the blasting cap, which made the explosive clay erupt, and that immediately caused the hundreds of pounds of chemicals inside the metal shell of the five-hundred-pound weapon to explode with a stunning discharge.

Edward was brutally concussed, shoved forward hard by a wave-blast. The flash and kaboom were simultaneous. Water crashed down from everywhere in a chaotic downpour. Bites and stings of thousands of bits of sand, gravel, steel, and more pecked at his face, the only part of him above water. Once more, before he even had a chance to suck in a breath of air, he was rudely shoved under. He unintentionally breathed in a bit of nasty seawater.

The extra C-3 he had stuck onto the bomb's nose made the power of the blast greater than any of the previous eleven bombs. And he was much closer to this one when it blew, too.

Struggling to reach the surface and find air, Edward could not tell if his face was in or out of the water, could not tell up from down, forward from backward. The eruption of mud and seawater was raining down, pelting him. The thunderstorm had kicked up again and now covered the rising tide with a curtain of falling water.

Edward knew he was drowning.

Through nothing more than desperate determination, he got his head above the surface again, using his hands like scoops to claw his way up, and kicking his tired, aching legs the way he had seen frogs do in the quarry back home.

In the distance, he caught a glimpse of the Archangel Michael atop the abbey's spire, highlighted by a sudden shaft of sunlight, appearing like a beacon. But Edward was quickly underwater once more, eyes closed, holding his breath, but still possessed by a will to survive.

This time he could not find the surface again. The current seemed determined to hold him under, to wash his lifeless body all the way to the ramparts of his long-sought Mont-Saint-Michel, his symbol of a richer life. His lungs were aching, craving air. Where was up? How could he somehow scratch his way to breathable air?

Had he come all this way, forsaken his 4-F and a way out, been thrown into the midst of brutal war, taken on all these dangerous missions, only to drown in the tide in Mont-Saint-Michel Bay within sight of the island, its namesake archangel, and all the people he was supposed to be helping? Was he being punished for not keeping that long-ago promise to learn to swim?

Then he heard the voice—one with a hint of a German accent—as clearly as if the speaker were there in the water with him.

The Kaboom Boys

"Don't panic! Doggie-paddle, dumbass! Swim like dogs do! Like Sarge!"

Fritz? Fritz Schneider. From that day back home at the quarry when the two kids from the neighboring town jumped in and died.

Doggie-paddle!

Edward did what the voice commanded, pulling his way to the surface long enough to inhale a few huge gulps of air. Long enough to see the yellow boat and Hank, furiously rowing against the inrushing tide, trying to get to him but still about the same distance away.

Beyond, Saint Michael was still there, though, his gold countenance glowing vibrantly, hopefully.

Back beneath the surface, Edward felt his foot hit sand. He tried to stand, to push off and propel himself upward. He willed himself not to panic or give up. But he was suddenly very weak. Not sure how much longer he could fight, doggie-paddle, defy the inevitability of the tide.

"If you give up, it's lost. Long as you fight like hell, you still got a chance, Captain."

Ace. Ace Taft. The voice echoed inside Edward's head. He was there.

And then, still dog-paddling, the captain's hand struck something hard, solid, slippery, maybe something floating past him on the surface. With all his might, he clenched fistfuls of water and tried to pull himself upward so he could grab hold of whatever it was.

A ten-foot-long wooden post. Field Marshal Rommel's asparagus. Covered with slime, difficult to hold onto. But somehow Edward managed to hook an arm around the thing and cling to it with all his might and what little strength he had left. That got his face out of the water. Got him to where he could take in another lungful of rain-cooled air between gasps and sputters.

Exhausted, he knew he would not be able to hang on for long. The length of timber was barely floating before he added his weight to it. And the "galloping horse" threatened to rip away from him his best chance for survival.

"You can drown in six inches of water," Fritz had told him once, urging him to overcome his most primal fear and learn to swim. Now, though, there was more than ten feet of bay water beneath him. His arm and shoulder had grown numb from clinging so tightly to the slippery wood.

He dared not try to switch arms. If he lost his grasp, he was too tired to doggie-paddle anymore.

Then, he was aware of an ominous darkness falling over him. The storm? Was it worsening? Had his oxygen level finally hit bottom? Was he blacking out? Was it finally about to be over?

Edward Hume had always been a realist. That was enough to keep him from panicking. But he also knew Hank would never be able to row that boat against the tide all by himself and get back to him. If he lost his hug on this fortunate piece of timber—ironically placed here by his enemy, the Germans—he would be too weak to swim anymore.

Saint Michael could do nothing for him now. Neither could Fritz or Ace.

Worst of all, as the shadow above him grew even darker, he knew he no longer had any fight left in him.

None at all.

28

Captain Sébastien Chantrelle had continued watching through his binoculars as the whole scene played out, keeping the mayor updated on what was happening. Then he went silent, at a loss for words to describe what was happening. He saw the six American soldiers dive to the ground to avoid the blasts from the bombs. Saw all of them get back up—amazingly uninjured—and make it to their boats. Then one of the men—likely the captain—abruptly turned and hurried back to a still-unexploded member of the deadly dozen.

"But why?" Sébastien wondered out loud. "If one of them could not be exploded, simply leave it there and attend to it at the next low tide."

"What? No!" Mayor Duval sputtered, his tune changing once again on how he wanted the mission accomplished. "I have required, General de Gaulle has required. The situation must be concluded in one trip to remove this curse. The Mons, and especially the fishermen, they insist. It must be completed now. One trip. That is the agreement. That is the order, and Captain Hume must do it as ordered."

Chantrelle, a disapproving frown on his face, glanced at the mayor. The captain was a military man. He knew orders were sometimes difficult, sometimes impossible—sometimes deadly ridiculous—but a soldier was still bound to carry them out. Without complaint. Without question. But a brave warrior should not necessarily have to die because of a sense of duty imposed on him by others who may not understand risk versus reward.

Chantrelle handed the binoculars to Mayor Duval.

"I must go help," the captain said, then kissed his two boys on their foreheads, turned, and headed down, running hard. His own sense of duty had taken over.

"Captain, where are you going," Mayor Duval called out. "Stop!"

Chantrelle was a hero to his people. Nothing must happen to him. But the captain ignored his mayor as well as the earlier promise to his wife to not be involved.

Once at the beach at the entrance side of the ramparts, Sébastien commandeered the first two-man rowboat he came to. Despite the protestations of this boat's owner, Sébastien untied the lines, jumped in, and began furiously rowing against the incoming tide.

Kaboom! The twelfth bomb detonated.

Unlike Hank and the others, Sébastien knew how to row, how deep to place his oars with each pull. As a younger man, he had rowed against the tide many times in search of fish to feed his family. And his recent military training had left him strong and able.

But it was still not easy. Not even for the young French officer, now dressed as a baker and with flour in his dark hair and beard. As he rowed, he looked back toward the island, to maintain his bearings and in hopes of seeing his wife and boys. She would have to understand his need to do this, no matter its danger. The boys, he knew, would consider their father a hero. They already did.

He turned to see the red and blue boats, their occupants paddling as best they could but losing the fight against the wind, rain, and racing tide.

"I will help your captain!" he yelled as he rowed past them, waving them toward the island.

"Captain's in trouble!" one of them called back while furiously bailing water from his boat with his helmet. "We thought he was coming with us..."

Then Chantrelle was out of earshot. The boats were riding the bore tide, being carried toward the rocks at the base of the island walls. Sébastien could only hope they did not get tossed there, upended and

The Kaboom Boys

331

injured, and that they did not die in the waves as so many had before them. Surely the other fishermen there would help the brave Americans.

Then the French captain realized he was growing tired. And that the lone American soldier in the yellow boat was losing his own battle with the rough water of the bay, too.

Sébastien Chantrelle called upon a discipline he had acquired as a soldier, fighting for his country. He focused only on what he knew he had to do if he was to save the two men. He had to stay within the moment. Ignore the storm, the swirling waterspout that had suddenly danced out from beneath the black cloud like a snake's tongue. It was near nighttime, and the falling darkness left little time for Sébastien to rescue them.

Hank saw the captain approaching and shouted, "Save the captain!"

"Where is he?" Sébastien yelled back.

"He is holding onto a timber, but..." Hank pointed east, to where he had last seen Edward.

"Can he not swim?"

"No! No, he can't."

"*Mon Dieu!*"

Both soldiers knew they would have to work together. Sébastien used all his strength and skill to maneuver his boat near enough that Hank could get a grip on Chantrelle's boat's stern gunwale and slide out of his own boat. Then the Frenchman helped him climb in. Sébastien rowed furiously to regain the distance they had lost during the transfer while Hank tried to spot his captain in the waves.

"There he is!" Hank shouted. But it was only the wooden pole. And the captain's fingers, knuckles white, holding on in a death grip. Edward was under, lost in the dark shadows of the rowboat and Hank hanging over the side, trying to grab him.

"Give me your other hand!" Hank shouted to Edward as Sébastien furiously maneuvered the oars to try to hold the boat in place. He let go of an oar long enough to grab a cork-filled life ring from the bottom of his boat and tossed it to Hank.

"Throw him this!"

Hank grabbed the life preserver, stretched his body, and leaned over the side as far as he dared. "Captain! Grab this!"

No sign of Edward beyond the hand gripping the timber. Hank reached even farther out, touched the hand on the wood pole with the life preserver, and shouted, "Come on! You can do it, sir!"

Still no response. Then a sudden surge of tidal water shifted the boat away. Hank could see Edward lose his grip on the slippery timber and slide deeper as the wave lifted them all. Then his captain's face, whiter than white against the dark blue water. Impossible to tell if he was alive or dead.

Hank fought for balance, took out his knife, cut the laces of his boots and kicked them off. Then, without hesitation, he dived into the water.

"*Mon Dieu!*" Sébastien again shouted. No way could he save two drowning men. It was taking all the strength he had to hold the boat in place. The tide, wind, and rain were unrelenting.

Hank swam the breaststroke, keeping his eyes on the timber where he had last seen Edward's hand. Nothing but bubbles. Those had to be from the captain, showing Hank the way. He sucked in a breath, held it, and dived as far down as his lungs would allow. The water was now more than fifteen feet deep. It was murky, his spectacles were obscured by seawater, and his eyes stung from sand and salt. He shut them tightly, feeling the grit under his eyelids and resorted to searching by touch for the captain.

There was no sign of him.

Resurfacing for another gulp of air, Hank caught a brief glimpse of disbelief on the French captain's face. He went back under. There was no other way. He could not allow another man in his squad—a friend—to die. Not again. Not like Ace.

He had to find Edward Hume.

He immediately bumped into something solid. The seemingly lifeless floating body of the captain. He grabbed an arm and with his other hand started scooping water, pulling both of them upward. Boy Scout Lifesaving Merit Badge back in Denver. It all came back to him.

Somehow, from somewhere, an unexpected reservoir of strength enabled Hank to drag an unconscious Edward to the surface. It seemed as though Hank was being helped by someone else. Maybe Ace was pulling Edward out of the water, too. Hank gasped for air and struggled to keep Edward's face above the surface.

Whether the captain was dead or alive, he could not tell.

The Kaboom Boys 333

Now it was Sébastien who was helping. He had rowed over and braced himself against the gunwale, placed his hands under Edward's armpits, and dragged the captain's dead weight into the boat. Hank caught a glimpse of the French officer's Saint Michael medal on a chain around his neck. Maybe Sébastien was getting some supernatural help as well.

Hank managed to get himself out of the water on his own and back onboard. Facedown at the bottom of the bobbing boat, Edward did not look good. He was not breathing or moving. Hank turned him over. The captain's eyes were half-open and glassy.

"You row! Man the oars!" Sébastien shouted. "Do not let us go sideways to the current or we might overturn. Let us float toward the island. *Faites confiance à la nature.* Trust nature."

"But what about Captain Hume?"

"I will do what I can," the Frenchman said, but without much confidence as he kneeled over Edward.

In the cramped space of the boat, Sébastien rolled Edward over and stuck his fingers into the stricken man's mouth and down his throat to check for obstructions. Then he clamped his mouth over Edward's and blew a big gust of air into the captain's lungs before beginning to vigorously pump his chest with both hands, massaging the captain's lifeless heart. It did not seem to help.

"You wanna let me try?" Hank called out, grappling with the oars.

Sébastien did not answer. He just continued his chest compressions.

Then, a booming clap of thunder stunned and almost deafened Sébastien and Hank. But it appeared to awaken Edward. He abruptly choked and spat out a surprising amount of water and bits of seaweed. He gasped, began to shake, and vomited profusely, then sat up so quickly he almost knocked Sébastien backward.

With his eyes wide, gulping for air, Hume called out, "Ace? Fritz?"

Sébastien eased him back down. Edward had a nasty gash on his left forearm, likely from barbed wire wrapped around the wooden timber he had used for an unlikely life raft. He was bleeding badly.

"Sir! You will be all right!" the French captain told him. He stripped off his shirt. "Let me wrap this around that wound. You try to breathe. Clear your lungs."

Hank looked on, amazed his captain had come back to life. "Jesus! We've gotta get you out of here. This damn storm just won't let up."

Edward lifted his good arm and weakly pointed toward where the waterspout was receding into the clouds, as if being reeled in by a giant hand. "It'll be okay, Hank."

A bright ray of sunshine unexpectedly illuminated a big patch of emerald-green water between them and Mont-Saint-Michel as the tide obligingly carried them and their little boat back toward the ramparts.

"Corporal, for the day's report?" Edward started, then paused long enough to cough up more seawater.

"Yessir."

Edward lay back on the boat bottom, took in clean air, and continued in a weak, strained voice. "All devices successfully defuzed and volatile remains disposed of. Mission satisfactorily accomplished in all respects."

29

The calm after the storm allowed for a brilliant sunset, the suddenly tranquil sky filled with vivid blues, vibrant pinks, and fiery oranges. Now, the very same fishermen who had been so reluctant to help several hours earlier were willingly assisting Gene, Pete, Morty, and Carl out of their rowboats, hailing them as heroes. As Sébastien's boat arrived, the captain waved and called for other fishermen to help them. Sébastien helped lift Edward out into the waiting arms of three men who carried him to a level patch of grass. Then Sébastien gave Hank a hand to help him from the boat, but the young corporal was still too exhausted to move. A local doctor was rushing down the hill to help whoever might have been injured.

Hank finally caught his breath, regained his composure and some of his strength, and accepted Sébastien's outstretched hand.

"*Merci*," whispered Hank with a proper salute to Sébastien.

The fishermen now enthusiastically offered praise and thanks.

"*Merci beaucoup!*" "*Bon travail!*" "*Courageux!*"

These fearless American soldiers had removed the curse from their bay, and they were truly grateful. But still disgusted with the American pilots who put the bombs here in this sacred site in the first place.

Edward tried to keep their gratitude in mind as he coughed and wheezed and acknowledged their thanks. Every word of praise made him stronger. Now, though, all he really wanted was to breathe and find a quiet place to lie down for a bit. The whole episode out there in the flats and with the returning tide had drained him. It was about all he could take for one interminable day. But he did make the effort to shake hands with and thank Sébastien Chantrelle. The French captain's help had come late but had saved Edward's life. Likely Hank's, too.

The squad was shown the way to the Hotel de la Mère Poulard, where writer Ernest Hemingway and other well-known journalists and film-makers had recently stayed. Edward knew he would use that information as part of the lively tales about this day that he would eventually share with Hed Bennett and Duncan Smythe, and, someday, folks back home.

The mayor had promised the Kaboom Boys a chance to clean up. Then an aide led them back to the restaurant for the omelets pledged to them once their job was done. Delightful dishes prepared over an open flame by Madame Poulard herself. In a pleasantly different way, the meal was as surreal as their day out on the flats had been.

In the open-air courtyard, the spire towered above them in a starry sky as they enjoyed fluffy omelets, buttery croissants from the bakery next door —the one run by Sébastien Chantrelle and his wife—regional cheeses, and fresh, salty, steamed asparagus. It was all washed down with abundant red wine and Normandy hard cider, topped off with shots of the quintessential local brandy, Calvados, made from apples and pears.

"Far sight better than K rations," Hank observed.

"Breakfast for dinner. I could do this every day," Edward said with a laugh that ended with a cough. Still, he smiled. "I just wish we could stay longer."

Mayor Duval, seated next to Edward and now in his warmest welcoming mode, chimed in. "Oh, Captain, you must stay here tonight. Go back to your duties tomorrow morning." He put his arm around Edward's shoulder, now old friends. "Each man will have his own room. Good enough for the SS, more than good enough for you who have risked your lives for Mons."

"Thank you, Mr. Mayor, but we should get back and see what is next for us," Edward responded, ignoring the crestfallen faces of his Kaboom Boys.

"But it is already dark. You and your men can enjoy the luxuries of a

The Kaboom Boys 337

proper bed, a private toilet, excellent food, and drink. It is dangerous to drive in the pitch dark, yes? Germans are still here, *oui*? Go tomorrow. Tell your superiors you were held captive by Mayor Duval!"

Everyone laughed, including Edward. It was true that their orders had been updated, allowing them to return late the next day, assuming they could possibly be tied up in a two-day mission there at Mont-Saint-Michel.

Edward grinned, raised his wineglass, and shouted, "*D'accord!* All right!"

Later, carrying lanterns, and now fully feeling the effects of the day, the rich food, and the drinks, they slowly hiked all the way to the top, to the entrance to the abbey. They were followed by the mayor, townspeople, and fishermen, now in a much better mood. There, they were greeted by a group of older women, the caretakers, who handed each member of the squad a gold necklace with a Mont-Saint-Michel medallion.

"Nobody sticking their tongues out at us now," Morty quietly noted.

"Maybe we stay a few days, we find out how much some of these ladies appreciate what we did," Carl added.

"Come, over here! Look," Mayor Duval called to them. "A full moon, and you can watch the sea cut us off from the continent once more. It is a beautiful sight to behold, *oui*?"

Indeed, it was. But in the far distance, they could also see what appeared to be heat lightning. The squad knew better. It was the flashes and occasional thunder of artillery and bombs. The sights and sounds of more work to come for the Kaboom Boys.

In this ancient holy place, it would have been easy to forget they were literally in the middle of a brutal world war. However, the flickering and rumble of distant death and destruction were powerful reminders of the horrors that still lay ahead, and who knew for how much longer.

The entourage climbed the Escalier de Dentelle—the "lace staircase"— that led them to the top of the rock. As they entered the eleventh-century abbey, they were greeted by the lone, elderly priest.

"You are all most welcome here," he said, shaking each man's hand. "I am *Père* Louis, Father Louis. May God bless you after the ordeal of this day."

"*Merci, Père,*" Edward told him. "It has been quite the day, Father. But God did bless us and saw us through it all."

"Are you Catholic, Captain?"

"No, Lutheran," Edward answered.

"I am. Sometimes," Pete said, smiling. "I mean, you know, Christmas, Easter. All the big holidays. I haven't been to confession in a while."

Gene stepped forward. "I'm Catholic, Father. South side of Chicago. Polish church. Went to Catholic school, too."

Father Louis smiled and motioned for the squad to follow him as he slowly made his way inside to the altar.

"Gentlemen, a special low mass is offered for all faiths in the main sanctuary. It is especially for you and what you have done for us, if you would like to attend." The priest waved a welcoming hand, and they followed him to sit on benches that served as pews. "Please join me in prayer," Father Louis said.

Everyone—including Morty, who had only been inside a synagogue as a place of worship—clasped hands.

"Saint Michael the Archangel, defend us in battle," the priest said, using English and beginning a prayer that had been said on this very site for hundreds of years. "Be our defense against the wickedness and snares of the devil. May God rebuke him, we humbly pray, and do thou, O Prince of the heavenly hosts, by the power of God, thrust into hell Satan and all the evil spirits who prowl about the world seeking the ruin of souls. Amen."

After the service, the squad exited, thanking the priest and caretakers on the way. They relied on the light of the lanterns as they tiredly made their way down the 350 steps toward the hotel. No one spoke, feeling the atmosphere of this ancient place as well as the enormity of what they had done this day.

Edward nudged Hank to stay back, to walk alongside him.

"Look, Hank, I just wanted to thank you for what you did today."

"Mostly it was that French captain," Hank humbly replied. "But you would have jumped in for me, sir."

"Yeah, but I just want you to know how much I appreciate it," Edward said. "And I need to tell you something else. Don't think I'm crazy, but I'm convinced that Ace was out there for us today. His spirit."

"Oh, yessir, I felt it, too. When I was down there looking for you, I felt something or somebody give me a shove and help me."

The Kaboom Boys   339

"Then you don't mind if Ace shares a little bit of the credit for me still being here?"

Hank looked over at the captain, a tear in his eye. "Aw, I guess I could let the crazy bastard have a bit of the glory. Look, sir, I'm just glad it all turned out okay. And know that I recognize that you have to make some tough decisions we may or may not understand or agree with. Letting that dump linger while we cleared the château. Doing this job in one trip. You have to follow orders, too, even if you do have leeway sometimes. But I understand you use your best judgment, sir. And it isn't fair for me to judge one way or the other."

Now Edward had a tear in his eye. "Thank you, Hank. And that's another reason you'll make a fine BD captain before this war is over."

The two men stopped, shook hands, then merged awkwardly into a full man-hug. The rest of the squad noticed, but, for once, nobody felt the need to throw out a snide comment. They just kept walking on down to the first good night's sleep they had enjoyed in months.

♠

Somebody—a group of somebodies—was singing "Yankee Doodle" noisily off-key and at the tops of their lungs.

Edward rolled over in the comfortable bed, unsure for a moment where he was. Then he remembered. A nice hotel on the island of Mont-Saint-Michel in Normandy, France. It wasn't a dream after all. He was here.

But who was caterwauling at...what? Seven o'clock in the morning?

He stepped out onto the balcony that overlooked the courtyard. He could not believe his eyes.

"Least you could do is put on a pair of trousers, Captain Hume," Hedley Bennett yelled up to Edward, who was still in his olive drab boxer shorts. The rest of Bennett's Bomb Merchants just kept singing, segueing into "The Star-Spangled Banner." It was Bennett's thing to encourage his men to sing while they worked.

"What in the hell are you doing here?" Edward shouted back.

"Command thought you might need some help with the bombs in the bay so the French brass would quit squawking about it," Bennett replied, taking a bite from the fresh baguette he held in his hand. "So, they sent the best BD squad in the US Army to bail your ass out. The guard down below tells me you got the job done already and the locals would name you king of France if you'd just put on some pants." Bennett then held up a carton of cigarettes. "Guess the Army heard we owed you something, and that's the real reason they sent us."

"Further evidence the Bomb Merchants are second best," Edward shot back, then disappeared into the room before their high-volume kibitzing woke up the rest of the island.

Shortly after, the two squads gathered in a small restaurant for breakfast and to share tall tales. There were plenty of both. Bennett also brought a set of orders for Edward, who took a quick glance. They had a new place for the squad to work from. Half a dozen miles up the road in Pontorson. But there was an odd addendum in a separate envelope stamped *TOP SECRET*.

Hume opened it and quickly read its contents. He was to be prepared to immediately go to Paris the moment the city was liberated. A secret assignment, not even to be shared with his men. And when he was summoned, he was to go alone except for one member of his squad to serve as his driver.

What the hell? was his only thought. But he guessed he would find out when the time came.

"They're basing you out of Pontorson is what I hear, Eddie ole pal," Hedley told him, then drained the last bit of cider from his glass. "But I doubt you'll get much chance to come back over and visit here at this fine island. I know it's been your life's ambition. Word is you bribed those pilots to drop those bombs out there. Right? So, since things are busy and everybody's on the move and there's enough UXO now to keep a thousand BD squads busy, you better enjoy the view and the fancy vittles while you can."

"Where you and your guys headed?" Edward asked. He was taking the last bite of his cheese and mushroom omelet and sipping *un café noir*. "Surely you'll be in the vicinity if there's that much business for us."

"Germany."

"No, really."

"Really. Germany. Hitler won't let his commanders withdraw and regroup, so we're picking them off and rounding them up as best we can.

The Kaboom Boys   341

My squad's supposed to be up front all the way to Paris, disarming and defuzing all the livelong day, and then be in Germany—at least the other side of the Rhine—by the end of the year." Hedley took a big swig of his own black coffee and grinned crookedly. "Somebody's thinking positively. Paris will fall in a month or two. I believe that. But Adolf ain't gonna let us cross the Rhine as long as he has a tank or a Messerschmitt or a Hitler Youth with a rifle and some shells. Hope Eisenhower and Patton and them ain't writing checks we can't cash, but I don't think they'd ever put us in a position where we can't succeed. Not now. Not with this momentum. We're in it to win it." Bennett drained his coffee cup. "Besides, the Bomb Merchants are well past our ten weeks by now, so they must be assuming we're immortal."

"Paris, huh?" A smile played on Edward's lips. He sometimes wondered if Bennett might one day become a diplomat in Washington. "Couldn't interest you in another bet, could I? The Kaboom Boys are into our ninth week, you know, so maybe a wager would give us an incentive to bust right on through ten."

Hedley was immediately intrigued. "What you got in mind, Captain Hume?"

"First one of us..." Edward struggled to remain deadpan, to not give away that his secret orders would send him to Paris. "Not necessarily the whole squad...first one, you or me, to reach the Eiffel Tower wins."

Bennett looked at Edward sideways. "You not trying to snooker me, are you? You know me and my compadres are headed to Paris as quick as we can wade through all the SS between here and there. Word is that General Patton is taking the Third Army to Paris, and you know he's not gonna wait around for nothin' or nobody. They'll need us to sweep a bunch of build-ings in Paris, assuming those bastards will booby-trap 'em all. Probably museums and galleries and monuments, too. The sons of bitches. Mean-while, you're back here, drinking wine and picking daisies and playing hide-the-sausage with the grateful gals of Normandy."

"Bet or not, Hed? For a bottle of Jägermeister."

Bennett's eyes grew large. "Never figured you for a connoisseur of fine liquor, there, Hume."

"Well, back in high school, my best friend was from Germany. Fritz

Schneider. His father was the real expert, and he had a special bottle. So, on graduation day, he let me and Fritz taste the stuff. Only once. Man, oh, man! I never got that first sip out of my head." Edward leaned back, remembering the moment. "Yeah, my boss, Doc Fenton, he used to say that stuff was strong enough to be medicinal, but he was a teetotaler and never tasted it. Thirty-five percent alcohol by volume. Made out of fermented nuts. I'd love to try it again. I heard they're finding warehouses full of the stuff the Germans brought to Paris to remind 'em of home. Along with all the French wine and champagne they stole 'n' stored for those special occasions, like, every day. And, shit, ole Adolf is a teetotaler, too."

"Sounds like that stuff would grow hair on your balls, all right," Bennett said as he finished off another buttered croissant, covered with more butter and jam as the Americans always did it. Then he pounded Edward hard on the shoulder. Hume winced. His arm was heavily bandaged from the previous day's laceration.

"Oops, sorry, buddy," Hedley said. "Forgot you had a rough day out there on the pond. Fermented nuts, huh? Sounds like the next nickname for your squad, Eddie, when you get tired of 'Kaboom Boys.' But, yeah, I'm good on the bet. Considering me and my guys are headed to Paree in a minute, no way you guys are gonna beat us there. And I may even give you a sip of that...what do you call it? Jägermeister. If you say, 'calf rope,' that is, when you and your guys come straggling in, late to the party."

"Say what?"

"Oh, calf rope's what the cowboys say for, 'I give up.'" And he motioned for Edward to pass him the cheese platter.

Edward only grinned.

After the meal and a ceremonial delivery of the carton of Lucky Strikes to settle the original wager, both groups gathered for photographs with the mayor and other town officials and residents.

"Better get going before the tide comes in," Edward advised.

"You would know, Captain," Hedley Bennett acknowledged.

Edward bowed slightly as he shook Mayor Duval's hand. "Sir, it has been my honor. On behalf of my squad, thank you for your hospitality."

"*Oui*, but it has been my pleasure. Captain Edward Hume, you should

The Kaboom Boys

one day receive *la Légion d'honneur*—the Legion of Honor. I will investigate it for you."

Edward knew little of the Legion of Honor, the highest French decoration and one of the most famous in the world. For two centuries, it had been presented on behalf of the French head of state to reward the most deserving, an award extended to French soldiers and others, including Americans.

Everyone shook hands and piled into their various red-fendered vehicles. As Bennett and his squad pulled away, Edward paused to look back once more at the mysterious, magical, and historic Mont-Saint-Michel. At the spire jutting high into a cloudless sky and Saint Michael surveying the bay and the sheep-salted countryside beyond. It was still difficult for him to believe he had actually come to this place of his dreams. Now, he was reluctant to leave.

However, if this dream had miraculously come true, what else might he one day see or do? Truth was, he now had a new Holy Grail, another symbol of a life that was everything his little coal-mining town and his future in that place were not.

Paris. The City of Lights.

Reality pulled him back in. His squad was already loaded up, ready to drive off to the next job. And soon, their tenth week in BD.

A quick thought of Tommy flashed through his head. Edward and his squad were on the verge of making it, of beating the odds. It was Tommy who had not made it, though. Tommy and Ace. Life and death, twists and turns. Edward wondered why he felt no survivor's guilt. Maybe he simply had not yet had time for such emotions. Maybe it was about to hit him in the face like a misdiagnosed bit of bad ordnance.

He shook his head and slowly—still sore from the previous day—climbed into his seat on the passenger side of the jeep as Hank cranked her up.

"Ready to go neuter some ugly bombs, sir?" Hank asked.

"Might as well," Edward answered. "Can't dance."

Then he reached and straightened the sign in the jeep windshield. The one that proclaimed them to be "The Kaboom Boys."

Hank paused long enough to snap several more photographs of Mont-

Saint-Michel. Then he pulled the jeep into gear and scooted away, followed closely by the rest of the guys in the truck. Hordes of people stood along both sides of the causeway that took them back toward the mainland and the European continent. They all waved happily at the squad and shouted their appreciation. Likely not just for the bomb defuzing but for coming to liberate their country from the Germans.

There, on the side of the roadway, two people stood out from the crowd. A beautiful young woman and a teenaged boy, leaning on their bicycles. The girl waved vigorously, motioning for them to slow down and pull nearer. Hank Anderson obliged, but Edward kept his hand on his pistol grip.

"My name is Hélène," the girl told him in accented English. "This is my friend Pierre. We watched from up there"—she nodded toward the spire—"as you worked. We just wanted to say thank you. We are forever grateful." The boy nodded enthusiastically.

"*Mademoiselle*, we only did our jobs," Hume told her.

"*Non*," she said, and Edward had to lean in to hear her words. "You did so much more. You returned a bit of order amid the chaos of war to this holy place where so many of us come to seek peace and beauty, Mr. American soldier. I do not believe you realize how much good you and your men have done here. All we can do is say *merci!*"

Big tears streaked down her cheeks as she blew him a kiss. God, she was beautiful!

Edward nodded. The wide-eyed sincerity on her lovely face and in her simple gesture of appreciation almost overpowered him. What had this young woman been through? How had her life and dreams been changed by all that had happened around her during the past few years? What beauty had she seen reduced to such stark ugliness?

He had not considered just how much of a symbol the removal of those bombs had been for the people of this island and the pilgrims who longed to return here in search of serenity and hope and the breathtaking majesty of the place. Something beautiful saved from the fate of so many other sites left in mounds of ugly rubble. Could it be that everyone from Eisenhower to de Gaulle to Mayor Duval knew all along what this mission represented? Why it was so important for those bombs to be removed?

Hume smiled, his steel-blue eyes filling with tears. He blew the lovely, smiling woman his own kiss in return and tossed her younger companion a sharp salute. The teenaged boy stood at full attention and returned the gesture, lower lip trembling with emotion. Hélène was smiling, even as she cried big tears.

Then, only a few yards farther down the causeway, Edward saw Captain Sébastien Chantrelle's two boys, also waving at the BD squad from the appreciative throng. And their dog, lying at their feet, maybe asleep. The pooch that looked so much like Sarge. The boys were offering their own goodbyes, happily jumping up and down, shouting, *"Merci! Merci! Au revoir, soldats Américains!"*

When Edward waved back and smiled at the youngsters, the boxer suddenly awoke, sat up, and excitedly began barking his own enthusiastic farewell.

A strange feeling washed over Hume.

He could have sworn the dog was grinning back at him, just the way Sarge always had in another time, in another place, in another life.

The Blacksmith of Dachau
A Call to War Book 2

A powerful chronicle of moral courage, human resilience, and the haunting choices made during history's darkest days.

As World War II reaches its final, desperate throes, Captain Edward Hume and his battle-hardened squad of bomb disposal experts—the Kaboom Boys—move methodically through the shattered remnants of Europe. While working to maintain steady hands and unwavering focus, they neutralize the silent killers left in war's wake, each defused bomb a small victory against chaos.

As the Allies liberate France, Hume finds an unexpected connection in a field hospital—a sharp-witted, dedicated Army nurse named Virginia who sees the man beneath the uniform. Their paths cross again in newly freed Paris, where war momentarily fades into something resembling a future.

But war does not wait for love.

Duty calls the Kaboom Boys back to the front, and deeper into Nazi Germany, where the devastation left in the war's wake is impossible to ignore. Their journey brings them to Dachau as they are tasked with aiding in the camp's liberation. The team quickly realizes that the terror and reality of the place are beyond anything they have seen or known before. And there, among the survivors and remnants of suffering, The Kaboom Boys meet a man whose inner strength defies the very war meant to break him: The Blacksmith of Dachau.

Get your copy today at
severnriverbooks.com

30% Off your next paperback.

Thank you for reading. For exclusive offers on your next paperback:

- **Visit SevernRiverBooks.com** and enter code **PRINTBOOKS30** at checkout.
- Or scan the QR code.

Offer valid for future paperback purchases only. The discount applies solely to the book price (excluding shipping, taxes, and fees) and is limited to one use per customer. Offer available to US customers only. Additional terms and conditions apply.

ACKNOWLEDGMENTS

From Elaine:
Without your help, Lauren Peake Murphy, this project would never have been possible. Don Keith, I absolutely could not have done this without you. To my husband Christopher and sons Colin and Wyatt Peake, you were my backbone. And, in loving memory of Michelle Perotte Desrues, who brought my father back to life with your stories of your time together in Normandy during the summer of 1944.

From Don:
First, my appreciation to Elaine, who insisted I be a hitchhiker on this amazing ride. And, for yet another time—but not nearly enough—I acknowledge the faith, encouragement, and understanding of my wife, Charlene.

ABOUT ELAINE HUME PEAKE

Elaine Hume Peake was born on Aberdeen Proving Ground in Aberdeen, Maryland, the site of the first United States Army Bomb Disposal testing and training base. Here her father, Captain Edward Hume learned the fundamentals of BD and became part of the first American army ordnance squads of World War II, setting the stage for the origins of the historical drama series, "The Kaboom Boys".

Elaine studied journalism/mass communications at Towson State University leading her to a multi-year career in television news. She received multiple journalism awards including Emmys and the George Foster Peabody Award for her 9/11 coverage.

Elaine lives in Leiper's Fork, Tennessee with her husband Christopher where she writes and has been enjoying life with their precious golden retriever Lucia.

Sign up for the reader list at
severnriverbooks.com

ABOUT DON KEITH

Don Keith is a native Alabamian and attended the University of Alabama where he received his degree in broadcast and film. He has received awards from the Associated Press and United Press International for newswriting and reporting. He is also the only person to be named Billboard Magazine "Radio Personality of the Year" in two formats, country and contemporary. Keith was a broadcast personality for over twenty years, owned his own consultancy, co-owned a Mobile, Alabama, radio station, and hosted and produced several nationally syndicated radio shows.

His first novel, "The Forever Season." received the Alabama Library Association's "Fiction of the Year" award. Keith has written extensively on historical subjects including World War II, submarine warfare, and fiction, biographies, and non-fiction works on a variety of subjects. He has published more than forty books, two of which—HUNTER KILLER and COLORS OF CHARACTER—have been adapted for the screen.

Mr. Keith lives with his wife, Charlene, in Indian Springs Village, Alabama.

Sign up for the reader list at
severnriverbooks.com